ULTIMATE LESBIAN EROTICA 2005

ULTIMATE LESBIAN EROTICA 2005

edited by
NICOLE FOSTER

alyson books
los angeles

© 2004 BY ALYSON PUBLICATIONS. AUTHORS RETAIN THE RIGHTS TO THEIR INDIVIDUAL
PIECES OF WORK. ALL RIGHTS RESERVED.

MANUFACTURED IN THE UNITED STATES OF AMERICA.

THIS TRADE PAPERBACK ORIGINAL IS PUBLISHED BY ALYSON PUBLICATIONS,
P.O. BOX 4371, LOS ANGELES, CALIFORNIA 90078-4371.
DISTRIBUTION IN THE UNITED KINGDOM BY TURNAROUND PUBLISHER SERVICES LTD.,
UNIT 3, OLYMPIA TRADING ESTATE, COBURG ROAD, WOOD GREEN,
LONDON N22 6TZ ENGLAND.

FIRST EDITION: DECEMBER 2004

04 05 06 07 08 **a** 10 9 8 7 6 5 4 3 2 1

ISBN 1-55583-896-0

CREDITS
COVER PHOTOGRAPHY BY DUANE RIEDER/STONE COLLECTION/GETTY IMAGES.
COVER DESIGN BY MATT SAMS.

FOR ALL THE LADIES WHO CAME THROUGH FOR ME
(AND ALL THE LADIES WHO CAME FOR ME)

CONTENTS

INTRODUCTION

There's erotica, and then there's *erotica*. And then there's *Ultimate Lesbian Erotica*. And I know of which I speak.

This hot and heavy book you're holding in your hands simply *explodes* with stories of ladies licking, fucking, worshipping, and most of all, *desiring* other ladies. You'll see what I mean: The word *want* appears in this collection, in some form, 348 times. In fact, it appears in two of the story titles: Marilyn Jaye Lewis's affecting, bittersweet "Wanted" and Isabelle Lazar's steamy, fantastic "Want Ad." Stefka goes so far as to name it "Need"; her compelling story is one of must-have muff.

If you're reading this, you probably agree that getting off is an absolute necessity. And you probably also know that, under the right circumstances, just a *look* from a certain sister is all it takes to get you moist. A lot of these stories are about that kind of control, about the extraordinarily hot dynamic that occurs with someone who knows how to push all your buttons—especially when they take for-freaking-*ever* to get around to pushing them, like the pirate/Daddy in Amie Evans's "Virtue" or the sequined lover on ship for Ronica Black's "Voyage Aboard the Queen" or the strip-searched, strapped-on frequent flier in Kai Bayley's "Next Flight Out." Especially when there are orders to be followed: River Light's Master achieves "Deliverance" with the obeisance of her charge; Jess Davis's protagonist, whose body is a "Canvas," responds to demands with, "Please, amuse yourself with me"; and Rachel Esplanade's "Slut" is willing to suffer a little degradation for "a good, strong fuck."

The babes in this book are sure to blow your mind. You will meet, in no particular order, an eight-months-pregnant goddess (and her cousin) in Elizabeth Wray's exquisite "Afternoon at Lovejoy's," a literally "little" lady in M. Christian's feisty

"Amazon," a hearing-impaired hottie in Alex Beal's inspired "A Sign," a gorgeous ghost in Beth Greenwood's lovely "Passing Fancy," a knife-collecting thief in Lori Selke's evocative "The Robber Girl," a down-to-earth dominatrix in Spring Opara's decadent "Sex and Chocolate," an adorable elf (and her sexy Santa) in Heather Towne's creative "Merry Fucking Christmas," a heroic cop in Sacchi Green's poignant "Healing," and the title characters of both Barbara Pizio's heated "Hey, Sailor!" and Rakelle Valencia's babe-a-licious "Biker Barbie." There are many more bad girls I could mention—none of whom I'd turn away should they show up, 2 in the morning, dripping wet on my doorstep.

And I haven't even begun to talk about the things we'll do for love. Some of the stories in this collection do just that, so beautifully…like Lynn Cole's surprising "Minding the Gap" and Judith Laura's brutally honest "In the Swim." "The Butch Doesn't Eat Strange Fruit" by Urszula Dawkins deserves special mention for its sublime, heart-wrenching attempt to portray the poetics of the butch-femme dynamic. Caelin Taylor, in her very romantic "Over and Again," manages to express both the fear and fulfillment of the first time and the precious promise of the next. The two more-experienced ladies in Rachel Kramer Bussel's "Fire and Ice" meet at a party and use an ice cube and a candle to get straight to the heart of each other. In "At Liberty," Toby Rider writes of a couple dealing with the aftereffects of a war—and coming away from it undefeated. Karin Kallmaker's couple in "Steam" can't resist adding some high-altitude hanky-panky to their hike. And Erica Morgan's no-nonsense "Monkey Business," Lisa E. Davis's hilarious "Virility Plus," and Kristina Wright's dirty "In the Pink" make us laugh over their heroines' misadventures in love.

Ultimate Lesbian Erotica starts with Kate Dominic's elegant "Zhenya's Dance" and ends with tatiana de la tierra's torrential "El Baile"—proof that the dance of lesbian lust is never up. As we all know, it takes two to tango—or sometimes three (see Tanya Turner's hot "Rock")—and now and again even four (witness the wily protagonist of Aurora Spark's "A Little Help From My

Friends"). Or if you prefer '80s metal, there's a chick in Bianca James's "Paradise City" with a mullet so fierce she'll have you banging your head against a certain something very soon, if you know what I mean.

Whatever moves you like to make, I guarantee one of the amazing writers in this book will inspire you. So grab a partner (or two or three) and get your groove on!

—Nicole Foster

ZHENYA'S DANCE
KATE DOMINIC

As always, Zhenya's dancing made me wet. She twirled around the room, her finger cymbals ringing as her veils shimmered in a blur of silken blue. She was enticement in motion, her breasts high and full and firm beneath the sparkling translucent band. Her hips undulated in her filmy, billowing pants, the creamy flesh of her slightly rounded, muscular belly swaying to the sinuous rhythms of the music. Even in the noisy room, the rows upon rows of tiny bells and beads adorning her jingled sensuously, reflecting the soft, almost torch-like glow of the dimmed coffee-house lamps. An enormous, burning-blue crystal flashed in her belly button. I doubted anyone thought the sapphire was real.

It was. I'd given it to her the night I'd claimed her as my own. Zhenya wore it, she said, to remind her each time she danced for a room full of amorous men that there was a woman there who would keep her safe. A woman who truly knew how to appreciate her body, a woman who would be taking her home that night.

Zhenya told me she had learned the dance in Cairo. I'd never asked where she was originally from. She was tall and slender, with a wide, Slavic face and bright blue eyes framed by long, wavy blond hair. She sometimes spoke Russian in her sleep, and she laughed in all the right places at movies from a number of European countries, even when she wasn't looking at the subtitles. Her English was flawless, though. The papers I'd paid a month's salary for said she'd been born in Milwaukee.

Wherever Zhenya was from, she had mastered the dance in Cairo. I watched her work the room, swaying to the hand claps of the men who eyed her so raptly. Several women also watched her, though not so obviously. Each time Zhenya's veils lifted, in that flash of movement, her flesh seemed to swell against the silken confinement of her sparkling top and flow like music within her low-riding, full-legged harem pants. She liked to play games, teasing the men and enticing them with her movement. Not that she was any more interested than I was in coming within 50 feet of a real-life sultan. She wanted me to be her sultan.

I was more than happy to oblige her. I was butch enough to pass for a younger man, short and slender, with expertly styled light brown hair, hand-tailored clothing, and exquisitely understated diamonds on my watch—a man whose obvious wealth entitled him to one of the choicest seats in the house, alongside the other preferred male customers. If anyone there had eventually thought to question me, my generous patronage had caused them to turn a blind eye to my perhaps overly smooth face. I watched comfortably with my companions, smelling their unrequited arousal, sipping my tea, and smiling quietly to myself. No matter how they lusted after her, it was the wet slit between my legs my Zhenya would be satisfying tonight.

As she once more swirled past, I stretched my legs out under the table and ran my hand down my crotch. I was packing a cyberflesh cock tonight, the one Zhenya liked so well when I teased the skin-soft, heavy shaft over her face.

She could swallow it whole. She knew just how to press and move so that the base rubbed against my clit. I came so hard I shook with it. More than once she'd colored the shaft with row upon row of cherry-red lipstick rings. Then she'd lick the rings off, her laughter daring me to move as she serviced me—those were her words, she was "servicing" me—taking me into her throat and rubbing the dildo into my clit until I threw her on her back and buried my face in the honey juice of her cunt. I couldn't get enough of her. I loved that I couldn't get enough.

The faintest scent of her arousal wafted from her skin as she danced past—sweat and musk and the echoes of the desperate desire of men who watched, but couldn't have her.

Tonight her perfume was even more of an opiate. Tonight my Zhenya was going to let me fuck her. She never had. She'd never let anyone fuck her. I'd been stunned when she told me. I'd assumed she'd made her way to Egypt working as a prostitute, the way so many other young women from the former Eastern Block had. But Zhenya had learned to use her mouth so well that even the owners of the brothels where she'd first worked had used her exclusively for that talent. And when she'd mastered belly dancing, as a nonnative in ruthlessly competitive Cairo, she'd bought her freedom from the dicks of men. She teased, she enticed, she kept them coming back, night after night, hungering for what they couldn't have as they filled the coffers of her employers.

There was ballet—somehow I saw ballet in the way she glided across the room, her arms and legs weaving sinuous, sensuous stories. There was even a hint of European folk dancing in the way she tossed her head, sending her hair swirling as she smiled wickedly. And always, there was Cairo. Zhenya's breasts and belly and hips undulated to the beat of the tambour, the blood pulse of desire and passion, the universal mating song that was purely Cairo.

Together, her motion and the music vibrated through my skin, flooding my heart and groin with molten desire. Not just mine. The men in the room eyed her with pure, naked lust. I licked my lips, caressing my cock through the rough linen of my pants, imagining how my Zhenya's satiny nipples would feel on my tongue tonight when I once again suckled her to tears. From across the room, her eyes flashed as they caught the movement of my tongue. She blushed, her hips undulating until the men beside me were panting.

Hours later, after the patrons were gone, we dutifully joined the owner for baklava and hot Turkish coffee in a secluded corner. As always, we had waited until the last dancer had finished and was safely on her way home in a cab. It was repayment, Zhenya once told me quietly, of a debt to someone who was now far beyond the need of human protections. I thanked the owner for his hospitality. As he rose to speak with a departing dishwasher, I wrapped my hand firmly around Zhenya's wrist.

"We're going now," I said softly, in a tone that let her know the decision had already been made. She smiled, stretching nervously as she slipped her feet into her boots and gathered her bag. I eased her coat over her shoulders, letting my hand linger on her neck as I lifted her hair from her shoulders. From the corner of my eye I saw the owner grinning at me, an envious, possessive, thoroughly male smile of appreciation that made my cunt wet. I waited while my lady twisted her scarf around her head. Then I opened the door for her, took her hand, and led her out into the cold night air.

It was snowing again, our feet muffled crunches in the otherwise silent night, the air so clear and clean and crisp it almost hurt to breathe.

"I'm going to lick your pussy," I said quietly, feeling her jolt as we walked under a street light. The snow swirled like millions of crystalline stars as we walked through the halo of light and back into the darkness. "I'm going to tongue your slit until you scream."

Zhenya didn't answer, just gripped my hand more tightly and kept holding on. A single car drove slowly past, the sound of the engine muffled by the snow as the tires squeaked. Snow sparkled on her eyelashes and in her hair, around the edge of her scarf. I stopped and turned her toward me, brushing the snow sparkles from the hair above her forehead, then trailing my leather glove down the side of her face.

"Does it bother you when I tell you what I'm going to do to

you?" I asked quietly, gently rubbing a finger over her lips. They were still deep red from her dancing makeup. I wondered vaguely if her lipstick would stain the leather, as it did some of my dicks. For a moment she just looked at me, then she smiled against my fingertip.

"It embarrasses me," she said softly. "But I think I like that." Her blush was beautiful. I stifled a moan as she sucked the tip of my glove. Through the thick black leather, I felt only pressure. No heat. No moisture. But the sight of her pink tongue on my glove made my cunt ache. I slid my other hand under her scarf, stroking the yellow strands that slid beneath the dark leather of my glove, running my finger over her ear until she trembled.

"I'm going to tongue your clit until you're shaking." I pulled her head to mine and kissed her. "I'm going to bathe your pussy lips until they're wet and hungry. Then I'm going to slide my finger into you." Her mouth was cool under mine, our breath rising in one cloud as I sucked her lower lip. She was shivering hard now, not only from desire. I needed to get her home.

"I'm going to tease inside your pussy until you're so turned on you can hardly breathe, Zhenya," I whispered, straight into her mouth. "I'm going to eat you until you beg me to fuck you, then I'm going to fuck you until you come."

She shuddered, and I kissed her hard. Then I took her hand again. We didn't speak until we'd climbed the steps to our apartment and I'd put the key in the door. Zhenya hurried past me, tossing her coat on the hook by the door, then kicking her boots off and tossing her hat and mittens on top of the dryer. She rubbed her hands together, like she was warming them. As I threw the deadbolts and unbuttoned my overcoat, she gave me a quick kiss.

"Sit on the cushion on the living room rug, Beth. I want to dance for you first." She said it quickly, then she turned hurried down the hall to the bedroom. "Make yourself some tea!"

Zhenya had made some changes to the living room since I'd left for work that morning. The Persian rug from under the dining room table had been moved to the middle of the floor. I had no idea how in hell she'd managed to do that by herself. As I got closer, I realized it was a different rug, complementary, but new, with intricate designs woven in the deep, rich colors. All the furniture except for my favorite armchair had been pushed back to the walls. Cushions covered one end of the rug. The fireplace mantle and the coffee table—in fact, every flat, solid surface I could see—were covered with candles, everything from the votives from our bedside tables to the tealights we used in our camping lanterns. I grinned and threw my suit jacket over the back of the couch. Tea and glasses and sugar were all laid out. All I had to do was heat the water. When it was ready, I kicked off my shoes, lit the candles, and settled into my chair.

The music started softly, a pulsing that flowed into my skin as the sound crescendoed. Zhenya had danced for me often, though never in such elaborate settings in our own home. But my breath caught when she glided into the room. She was wearing her veils again, but this time, only her veils. My eyes caught flashes of sparkle. The sapphire shimmered in her navel, and thin golden chains with dangling crystals hung from her nipples and between the shaved lips of her pussy. I choked on my tea.

"They're clamps—play piercings," Zhenya blushed, inhaling sharply as she swirled her veils and the jewels swung. "They pinch, but the hurt feels nice." She laughed shakily, shivering as she grinned at me and twirled again.

My crotch thrummed as I watched the golden chains and their sparkling weights move against her naked skin. Her nipples were hard. If she'd come near me, I would have grabbed her. But she didn't. She undulated her hips, murmuring softly as she swayed just out of arm's reach. Her kohl-lined eyes glowed in the candlelight as she lifted her arms, letting the veil fall free from her breasts as she flexed and reached. Her nipples swayed on their own, her exquisitely toned muscles causing the jewels to dance beneath them. Her face was flushed, her head back as her hips softly rocked to the haunting beat of the drums.

"Come here," I said gruffly, leaning back in the chair and holding out my hand. Zhenya glided over to me, her arms still over her head, her breasts still moving. Her nipples pointed slightly downward from the weight of the clamps. I held my hand up, close enough for the jewels beneath her breasts to bump against my hand. Zhenya inhaled sharply, quivering as I left my hand there, bumping again and again. I caught a swaying jewel in my hand and tugged it gently toward me. She moaned, biting her lip as she leaned forward.

"Lean over me," I said quietly. "Put one hand on the back of my chair and the other on my shoulder, so you can keep dancing."

Zhenya stepped to the side of my chair and bent toward me, rocking slowly from side to side. She gasped as the motion put a new pressure on her nipples. I looked into her eyes and tugged softly on a jewel.

"It will hurt when I take it off," I said quietly, tugging harder. The clamp was tighter than I'd expected. Tight enough to let me know how painful it was, and to keep me aware of the depth of the gift she was giving me. She whimpered as I drew her closer.

"Keep dancing. I'm going to suckle you."

Her nipple was a deep red against the gold. I pulled until her breast was even with my mouth, the nipple stretching out long and thin as she swayed. I tongued around the clamp, still tugging as I licked her straining flesh. Zhenya leaned over me, her moans growing louder, her breasts and her hips undulating until the jewelry seemed to dance on its own. With no warning, I released the clamp and sucked her nipple into my mouth.

Zhenya's cry vibrated through her chest. Her nipple was cool to my tongue as I sucked heat and circulation and what was obviously exquisitely painful sensation back into her well-used flesh. The clamp had left indentations in her skin. I worried them with my tongue, sliding my hands around her waist to hold her to me as she trembled and sobbed. I sucked her until she was shaking. Then I looked up into her tear-filled eyes, watching them widen as I pulled her wet, glistening nipple all the way out and clipped the golden clamp back on. Zhenya threw her head back, a long, thin cry leaving her lips as I set the jewel to swaying again. Then I tugged on the second chain. She trembled, a single tear falling down onto my lips as I waited. When she nodded, I released the second clamp and took her other nipple into my mouth.

Zhenya shook as I sucked the warmth and sensation back into that nipple as well. She trembled when I dried her skin with my breath and then clipped the jewel back on.

"Dance for me," I growled, easing her upright and getting to my feet. Tears sparkled in her eyes, her blue veils swirling and her jewels glittering in the candlelight. I took my time disrobing, my hands resting halfway down the buttons of my shirt as Zhenya spread her legs and rocked her hips, gasping as she set the clit jewel rocking in a flash of fire. When I was naked, I checked the straps on my harness.

The cyberflesh cock jutted out, velvety stiff as it warmed to my touch. Even though Zhenya was a virgin to penetration, I'd worn a realistic-size cock, five inches long and well over an inch wide. Zhenya wanted to be fucked, and I wanted to fuck her. We weren't going to play around with it. She was getting my dick in her cunt.

Zhenya had sucked that particular dick many times. But tonight her eyes widened, like she was really realizing its size. I stroked up and down my shaft and tugged on the tight, silicon balls resting against the harness. Then I lay down on the pillows on the rug, still stroking my dick as I held out my other hand to her and said, "Kneel over my face, so I can play with your clit jewel."

Nodding tremulously, Zhenya straddled me, her veils falling like shadows around me as she lifted her hips. I leaned up, catching the swaying stone between my lips. She gasped, leaning toward me, crying out. I laid back and, using just my tongue, slowly took the chain into my mouth. The smooth lips of her labia brushed against me, slick and glistening with her juices as her painfully pinched, tender clit quivered against my lips. I tongued her until she was trembling. Then I reached up and touched my fingers to the clamp.

"Look at me," I said quietly.

Zhenya shook as she lifted her shimmering eyes to mine. I tugged, and a single tear leaked from each brimming eye. Then, with my eyes locked on hers, I released the clamp. She bucked forward, throwing her head back as she yelled. I grabbed her hips and pulled her down hard onto my mouth, holding her tightly as my tongue flayed her clit and her soft screams echoed in my ears. Her body stiffened and her chest flushed. This time, when I released the nipple clamps, she shook through an orgasm that had her juices running down my face. I slipped my finger into her, into the tight heat of her cunt, feeling the ridges wrap tightly around me as I slid past the thin film of membrane. Zhenya gasped, her body stilling as her eyes flew open. Her juice was sweet and light on my tongue, mingling with my saliva as I sucked her clit and wiggled my finger, gently stretching her.

I sucked her until she was trembling again, her cunt walls contracting around me as I pressed toward her belly button. I had originally thought to have her sit on my shaft, so she would be less frightened. But Zhenya had told me so often how she liked my weight on her, liked the feeling of possession and safety. I set my hands to her hips again, tipping her onto the rug as I rolled to my knees. When I went to ease her onto her back, though, she shook her head.

"Take me as a man takes his woman," she choked out, getting up onto her hands and knees instead. She lowered her head, a single blue veil still caught in her hand as she lifted her ass into the air. Her slit was deep, swollen pink, her pussy lips glistening with our mingled juices as I ran my fingers over her, rubbing her clit and teasing my finger into her until she was frantically waving her backside at me. I slathered lube on my dick, then poured more onto my hand, massaging the slick oil deep into her smooth, tight cunt. I rubbed until she was shaking, my pussy humming from the pressure and friction.

I touched the head of my dick to her vulva lips, to the edge of her cunt hole. Zhenya froze, her body stiffening as her breathing stopped.

"Let me in," I whispered, rubbing the head over her clit, then back to her hole. Zhenya whimpered as the tip of the head slid in. The pressure echoed up into my clit. "It will hurt for a moment, love," I said. "I'm sorry about that. But after that, I swear, I'll never hurt you again." I rocked against her, feeling the way give a bit more as she gasped. My shaft slid deeper, the base rubbing exquisitely against my clit as Zhenya stiffened. My cock was in her now, each slow, shallow fuck letting me further in. "I'll always be here for you, beloved. Always."

Her hips relaxed the tiniest bit, and this time when my cock slid forward, I thrust hard. Zhenya screamed softly as my dick slid deep. She lay beneath me, panting, shaking and shaking and shaking. I felt each vibration echo into me, felt her tremors on my clit, felt the slow roll of an orgasm flow over me as my body realized, all the way to its core, that my Zhenya had let me into her body.

As she slowly relaxed and her frantic breathing slowed, I started to move. Zhenya groaned, still shaking as I held her hips and thrust slowly—deep, tender, loving strokes. I fought off the sudden, almost primal need to thrust into her, to claim her hard and fast as my own, as mine, damn it! I fought the urges until I was shaking with them, until she was slowly, awkwardly arching her hips back to meet me, until finally she braced her knees and thrust up to meet me, fucking me back.

"I love you, Zhenya," I panted, not trying to hide the desperation in my voice as my thrusting sped up almost imperceptibly. "God, I love fucking you. My dick looks so hot sliding in and out of your pussy lips." There was blood on my cock. Not much, but it glistened with the lube and her pussy juice. Part of me hated doing that to her. And part of me burned almost to orgasm with the smell of her blood and the knowledge that she had let me, only me, into her body. I thrust in again, grinding softly against her, praying it wasn't too soon, but so desperate for the feel of the cock inside her pressing back against its root on my clit. "You are mine, Zhenya. Mine!"

The climax was so sudden and so strong, I couldn't control it. I couldn't even tone it down as I thrust frantically through the waves of orgasm. Still shaking, I grabbed her hips, forcing myself to hold still.

"Am I being too rough?" I choked out, rocking slightly against her in spite of myself, wanting to thrust again, and again. Zhenya laughed softly, and to my total surprise she lifted her hips to me, pressing back as I shook again.

"I like feeling you do that," she laughed throatily. "Fuck me harder. *Da!*" Her voice thickened as I thrust. "Oh, yes. More. Please!" An accent I'd only heard in her sleep was creeping into Zhenya's speech as she thrust back up against me. "*Pazhahlstah!*" she groaned. "Harder, please, please!"

She got up onto her hands and started to move her hips, move them in the slow, gentle, seductive sway that she danced. I couldn't stop. I thrust into her, harder and faster, meeting her as she bucked up, juice squirting from me in streams as I came. Then my Zhenya was coming with me, yelling and grinding up against me, her clear, slippery juices running down her leg. She shook against me, crying and rocking as her body rolled with the tremors flowing through her, flowing between us.

When she finally fell forward onto the rug, tears filled my eyes at the loss of the connection between us. My cock glistened with our juices, shining clear and slick and flecked red with her virgin's blood. I lay down and took her in my arms. We lay there laughing and crying like a couple of lovesick fools while I stroked her and told her how beautiful she was and how much I loved her and how I would always be hers.

A long while later, I'd taken off the harness and we lay on the cushions, covered with her veils and my shirt and jacket and the afghan from the couch. The candles had guttered, though the snow still swirled madly outside the windows, with only the glow of the distant streetlight. I twirled one of Zhenya's silky curls beneath my fingers.

"So, that's how a sultan fucks his woman in Cairo?" I smiled, kissing her softly. Her giggle surprised me as she shook her head.

"I wouldn't know about Cairo." Her face glowed in the moonlight. "But it is how a man takes his woman in Petropavlovsk." I threw back my head, laughing out loud as she grinned wickedly and purred, "I believe that's a suburb of Milwaukee."

THE BUTCH DOESN'T EAT STRANGE FRUIT
URSZULA DAWKINS

1.

Waiting for her drink, she runs a broad hand over her scalp; leans over to hide her breasts. Thighs heavy inside rubber pants, big and tactile. Oblivious to me—but how could she be? Because I've done it before, walked past her, with the look of acknowledgment that doubles as a careful look away. She stands defiant, silent, vulnerable, proud. Doesn't see the compromise in my posture, the way my decadent body leans toward her from across a room. I smell the femaleness inside her clothes. Beneath her lowered voice. Behind the body language. Inside her hands, driving their sensitivity. She knows the gaping need of a woman for her penetration.

Leaning against my car with our groins together, heaving. I reach round the back of her waist to feel its thickness. Fleshy and womanly even in its hardness and strength. The base of the spine, the small of her back. Want to feel her weight on me. So good to feel her grind herself against me—just as rubbing sticks together produces fire, it's as if rubbing her cunt against me will produce a cock between us. And at the same time her breasts: I draw myself close enough to feel their heat.

She runs her hand down the front of my neck and keeps it against my throat. I know she is feeling her power, and my response to her. For the flesh of the throat is full of sensors. It knows the danger and eroticism of that touch, the hand of another in that vulnerable place. It is the body releasing a memory of life and death when the butch places her hand against my throat.

An orphaned eagle chick is placed into the nest of a falcon. Riveted by her image, it imprints itself to her and believes itself her fledgling. It is sometimes the first sane face we see, or the face we see as sexual ecstasy takes us, that we bond to and believe in.

I'm waiting: feel it all swimming round me, feel the mosquitoes rise up out of their dirty pools and bite, feel the sun casting rays through a thundercloud.

Smooth skin of her shoulders. Can't reach her jeans or belt. She kneels on the floor and spreads my legs with her torso. Pushes my shoulders down before she buries her face in me. I collapse backward at some unnatural angle; a sapling pulled back and tethered to the ground. It is right that I should feel this, the bark ready to split. And the rope and the peg. She holds me.

I remember her whole hand in me and my whole body shouting to release her. For more of her. I wanted her in there but could never come that way. It was stretching my world to have her in there. I could never find means to grasp it, only that it meant way more than fucking. The treetops outside the window, the sleeping dog outside the bedroom door. Blankets strewn, clothes strewn, some kind of drunkenness still in our bloodstreams.

She fucks me till the storm is finished, then takes me further. She takes my body into ruin, spreading her fingers more and more around my cunt, her tongue doing things that became unholy after coming. It is indecent, the pushing of my body beyond where it wants to go—and I'm ready to spray, with the excruciating pregnancy of urine held in the tip of my urethra.

She won't let me fuck her. I want her to let me. I don't care about her bleeding; I have a glove. She's so wet she's embarrassed. Then I fuck her. And for a long time, slowly. She almost comes, and I think I've lost her. But she keeps moving, and I keep my fingers there. She comes back to me. I know I will have her, don't know how but slowly, slowly...until finally it is my mouth against her clit that slams her against the wall; she bursts like something ripe flung there and I feel her shudder against me.

In the butch's containment lies great safety and assurance for the femme—a respite from hysteria. She receives a huge, quiet love from this woman who is not a woman. And though the butch is repelled by the abyss, there is an enigmatic *order* in the femme's fearlessness in the face of passion, her grasp of it with manicured fingers. Butch-bitch is magnetic: intense attraction and equal repulsion. The femme draws closer to death-by-reason.

It germinates in the gloom of nightclubs, bars, and parties. There are soupy stains on walls and grimy music in the atmosphere. These rituals belong in the darkness, in the Dionysian belly of the city: They are hidden and visceral behind the neat facades, the controlled exteriors; black bitumen and disinfected streetlight.

Her mouth is a scar; unyielding. My heart pounds in my chest knowing my involvement, however slight, with that *animosity*. She doesn't just protect: She sends out hardness. Her body says "Don't fuck with me," and adds "or I will fuck with you right back." There is an aggression, a lassitude; a sublimated violence. And having seen her vulnerability, her desire, her characteristic manners, I am drawn toward that shell of elaborate retreat.

Words unravel me: You undress me with questions, use thoughts to caress me, then slide your hand between my thighs. You're above me, kneeling; my legs are parted. I'm ready, but all you do is talk. And not about sex. You pose the question and then work for the answer. Slowly, lots of pauses. You prepare me. I'm sharpened on the whet of your intentions. You uncover me letter by letter, go to places that are not so run-of-the-mill, and when finally you take me to your bed—it was at your direction, for you had subtly required my passivity—I am seduced, before the fact. It is a seduction that ignores the dripping cunt. You set out to read me, and I have opened a few pages for you to run your fingers down. I feel myself smudged slightly by your probing. It is enough to open my legs just that little more carelessly to you.

In the shallowest part of the night, when the hours have small denominations and skim the surface of the city, we breathe what we can of the thin air and taste the space that exists between those times; the soundless times when everything is sleeping. Our small noises are amplified by that street-side calm. We begin, and you take me emphatically.

The skin of my breasts warm from the skin of your breasts. The nipples hardening against one another. The raw explosion of your groin against me. And the cracks in the curtains let in splintered sun—but how can I sleep when turning my back brings your hands around to my stomach; when my closed eyes draw you into conversation?

My arm across your body was not enough; you drew my leg up to rest between yours, as if you already knew me well. As I curled close to you to sleep, my body's memory flexed to bend that leg into you, and retreated. But you pulled it close, as if you too wanted to remember that feeling.

Do I tremble sitting at your table? Or at the sight of you with your knuckles in the chicken, stuffing it with garlic? Or sliding buttery fingers between skin and breast? When I am eating the meal you prepare for me: the shape of my mouth against the spoon, conscious of the thickness of my lips and your tastes on my tongue. Your food makes me crave my mouth on the nipple. I regress, eyes hungrily on the plate.

The day I saw your freckles when we went to the beach my hide softened up against you. You let me put my hands on your belly. I saw your face above me and behind it a kestrel hovered on bright white wings, its keeled belly holding it steady, black tips splayed and a fierce eye upon us. You curled your toes up on the clutch pedal— your bare toes—and I said, "Raptor feet." Your eyes are doe but your feet take me in their grip like a hawk's. Your hands hold mine against the sheets, and I feel my half-removed top tying my fingers in knots. Your eye forbids me when I move to discard it. I let the black lace stay wound around my wrists. The dog whimpers outside the room, and I sympathize. You have this power over both of us, to make us whimper for more, for you; for more you.

You call me bitch. I wrap my cunt around your hand. I stick my arse up in the air. I fuck you with the reluctant smile wiped right off your face. I love every minute of your nakedness, of my vulnerability. I anoint you with my bitch fluid and you drown in it, and you're flat on your back too you bitch. Your femininity only turns me on more.

The wooden boats on the bay remind me of last summer. I remember my tears in the darkened cabin of a sailboat, floating off San Francisco. My wings were frayed badly then, and I cradled my hopes and buried them in the rocking canvas hammock and my piss held tight in my bladder and my tears washed over the side. Now the sun shines. No love here, but sunshine. And my hand on the back of your neck.

The butch quakes in her boots at the first touch of a woman's hand. A femme has her power, and knows almost certainly that the butch will find a way to thwart it. Perhaps before the courtship is sealed, but maybe not. For years she may engage in the dance with her butch lover and be embraced, cooked for, cared for, like never before. But caught up in the seduction of desire and difference, the butch struggles to evade her clutches: The beautiful chthonic must be kept at bay. The femme can never allay that fear. For there is indeed everything to lose in the erratic mire of the woman.

You're on top of me, and we're playing. And you provoke: "Do you always get what you want?"

My breath thickens in my chest. I close my eyes. And I tell you, "No, I don't."

Last night I wanted to imagine I loved you. More accurately, I wanted to see what was behind the sheet of glass that separates us. I knew it was between us, all night; I noticed you put the light out when we went to bed. But I said, "Switch it on," and looked up at your face and your eyes and the curve of your lashes, and it was a shocking moment, because we were together. We were both there. I wanted to see who I was fucking, not close my eyes and do it in darkness. I wanted my heart to be as real as the fuck. So I looked at you, and you saw the glass flex, ready to shatter.

The room and the night were swollen with contradictions. I knew that you were leaving me, at exactly the moment that I was letting you in. We slept tight-wound with the salt-dried grains of your tears against my back. You curled so tight against me, all night, *clung* to me—and I could not help but be swayed further by that gesture, played out in your sleep.

When you spoke to me in daylight and said you couldn't do it, I steeled myself. I held you, and held back, until I felt your kiss, and even then held back. And finally you let go and we kissed with the connection of lovers. And you let me touch you, and it blew my mind how easily—and then it just blew my mind.

What mechanism is it by which I become wetter than anything when you roll into my arms and let your tears flow? Why did my undoing lie in this? It was not your hands that tore out my desire—it was the progression in the course of every night from stiff formality to absolute spacelessness, skin to skin and thoughts pressed mercilessly into the cleavage between breaths.

2.

The butch doesn't eat strange fruit. I hold out the softening fig and she is faintly, perhaps fervently repelled; takes a precarious bite, under sufferance. I do not press her—and now I am become that flesh-filled fruit that she refuses, seeds pushed down into damp clay and the nutrient flesh long decayed. She has riven me gently in two like the halves of it to try me; she has rent me gently from top to bottom to see the crazed pattern of myriad spores within. I am her mysterious food, staining her fingers, sending her away to lick at them cautiously.

In the shower I lost my balance for a split second and felt my weight's possibility leaning toward the glass screen. I regained consciousness, and the soap slipped from my hands. I picked it up and continued, scrubbed my feet and saw my nails needed trimming. I shaved my pussy because life goes on, with or without the butch.

Is this how it is, with love trying desperately to get in the door while both our feet stamp at it, to keep it clear of the jamb? I am flung, flung hard. Against the jamb, the wall, the glass divider. This room, where finally we hug and her hands are drifting down my shoulder blades. Still she wants to kiss me.

Even now we are playing the game of desire and resistance. But I tell her not to mess with me. I lean back like a kangaroo about to box, put my palm on her chest and tell her, don't play games with me.

I loved the stretch marks on her breasts. The brown skin was the skin on warm milk. I felt the nourishing liquid beneath it, felt its strange binding to my lips.

I drove through mustard-colored rain like it was viscous, yellow blood. It was the liquefaction of sun and storm, and the drains ran thick and muddy between cobblestones. I could smell the earth; the wetness crept under my arms and into my crotch. I dreamt sex that night: a strap-on, harness, and wrist restraints. Dreamt everything and received nothing. The thought of her makes my blood rise up yellow and profound. She knew she could have me. She knew something more than my body.

When you fuck someone, and fuck them more than once, there are hazards in the dark, in the hands and fingers that ply your arse and cunt. There is a lot more in the room than candlelight and sex toys. The lube is lubricating the passages while something far slipperier arouses the surface of the heart—two hands rubbing that raw meat for dear life, feeling its beating, its warmth, in the wetness of the membrane.

We choose our methods of protection. I make myself beautiful, unapproachable: seductress in my artificial finery and short skirts. She goes skinhead, scares away the gaze. But I dared look at her. I shook my tail at her, raised my bum up to where she could see it: the fine detail, the tilted vagina, the reddened exterior, the swollen lips. I put it where the scent could travel. She stroked the skin of her head and followed me to my car. She humped me like a dog against the fender. We were skanky hyenas rutting under the streetlight. Two baboons in the cages of the city.

And then to the safety of her room, where silty water starts to rise. The flood that carries away roofs, leaving lower levels underwater. Sandbags, small dinghies floating down unmarked roads. The way is deluged, the passage of fluids renders the city streetless. The edges are all gone; it is night and the boats float listlessly.

There is the car; always that first journey, when for long minutes the dog's dick and the cat's raised tail retract into their rightful, decorous places. She put her glasses on and the streetlight slid off the bonnet, reducing everything to slick grays. No multicolored ape-bum, no smell except nice new vinyl. My hands lay nicely in my lap. She drove carefully, put the radio on. Verbal silence, the animals held in their pens.

Here in the big room, her opposing thumbs working to get my boots off, a tawny hand reaching up beneath foundering skirts. And the waters so high I hardly know where home is. The plains drift out east and west and the creatures are in high branches, stark wet trunks of trees in the outskirts, and then the washed-out desert. Forever deluged as her tongue found the crevice of my cunt, plunging to taste metal, moisture, and skin all at once. She came up thick with the muddy breath of me; not only had she licked me clean, she had smoothed out a hollow in the cage for us both. We curled into the nest and took that space together.

We talked about the lions. How they fuck for a week, the winning male does all the work, all that humping and biting—and he does not eat for that seven days. I said to her, "It's natural selection—the male doesn't survive unless he's really strong and together." "Strong and together," she smiled. "You don't think you're projecting a bit, do you?"

When I feel her eyes upon me and know that I play havoc, it is the delicate triumph of intersecting gazes. I know she sees my power. So if I long to be known as myself—for my power to be read—it is she who satisfies this longing. She recognizes my *force* but does not expect me to protect her. There is not a price on her desire.

And when the butch has laid me bare, and I am shaking in her arms, and she is trembling with the power of my undoing, there is no such thing as yearning. Ironically in that moment—for yearning in some ways is greater then than it ever will be—I am exactly who I wish to be, and there is no difference between interior and exterior, no distinction between my desire and my reality. The yearning dissolves in a seamless integration of power, beauty, and absolute openness.

I lean close to feel her nipple in my mouth, hardening, and I enjoy its hugeness, and I feel her body shift while I caress her, without looking at her face. When a butch is closed to me, what makes me think she will change her mind? She touches herself, and I move upward to her shoulder; the clavicle and immense curve of her neck. The energy of my desire feeds her. If she cannot come freely to me, why should I imagine it will ever be easy? Breathing close against her head, the temples, the ear. And feeling her breathing, hard against my belly. As I hold her close to my chest she trembles, and I know in this last moment that I still have that hold.

I have never asked her what she feels for me. I have let her be contained, as she needed to. Reason does not want a lover like this, but I have sensed more than she gives me. I have loved like this before.

Flat on my back and her fingers inside me. The grain gripping like wrong velvets: locking, not smooth. Difference. My head is turned away from her, toward the pillow, but I can't evade her gaze. She is triumphant—for there is nothing more powerful than her fingers as my cunt contracts around them, so that she feels the clean, lined ridges of the front of my vagina. It's all anatomical: the juices and lube and her persistent fingers. Cliff falls away, different surfaces exposed. So you can see it. The friction, the coexistence, the bed of dreams, the layers. Then the subtle shift. I feel those shocking ridges and know how she watches as those jellyfish places harden into reefs.

She fucks me, doesn't make a sound, just grinds her teeth until I know it's coming.

The orgasm pulled right out of my gut.

She's got me, holds on tight, and her breath deepens against the soft part of my face.

What the fuck.
Still writing to me, plying me with intimate questions.
But won't see me.
I want her.
She is tickling me.
Don't fuck with me.
Stop messing with me.
Just grab me

AFTERNOON AT LOVEJOY'S
ELIZABETH WRAY

I insist on dramatic settings, and you indulge me. Today it is driz-
zling and we are at Lovejoy's Tea Room, a miniature establish-
ment next door to a book shop. After tea perhaps we'll go next
door and read. We're lounging now, spread out on a Victorian settee, floral mismatched crockery and heavy pots of tea set before
us on a chipped marble table. The scone-complexioned waiter
has a thick Upland accent. I've been reading Emily Brontë and
am ripe for this place. You are beautiful in your eighth month with
child, Rubenesque on the red settee. My arm hangs in its sling,
broken during a stupid act of bravado in the country some weeks
ago. Emily would have cast me as your sharp-boned cousin.

You take my good hand and guide it to your belly. *She's kicking,* you say.

We sit for some minutes, me with my hand on your palpitat-
ing belly. I'm reminded that we're standing on the ledge of our
friendship, inching ever closer to the place where you let go of me
and head up the safe and steady path of new motherhood; I'm left
teetering, a girl on a ledge.

I sip the Turkish Gold (*Our strongest tea, miss*) for both of us.
I'm not hungry, and I watch you devour the sandwiches. I remind

myself that life goes on. We've both had babies before, and we know the girl on the ledge holds fast, waiting for the chance to scramble off on some naughty escapade. Besides, here you are on this afternoon of perfect drizzle, available to me, sipping peppermint tea.

Someday you'll call from New Zealand and say "I needed a change," you say. You romanticize me.

I wouldn't leave the kids, I say, and you smile a comma and leave it at that. Because I ran wild in my youth, you think me capable of rash acts. But we are both grown-up women, and *You're the one who's daring another child,* I say.

Would you ever be unfaithful to S? you ask.

I consider this; we both examine our partners in this new riotous light. We're just getting started on the anything's-possible-and-yet train when the door to the tea room opens and frames Adonis in blue jeans. Right on cue, Adonis is almost as tall as the door, with dark curls, a Roman nose, Mediterranean skin, and peach-ripe lips. We can't stop staring. A striking blond follows Adonis into the tea room; they're both in their 20s. They fold themselves into straight-backed chairs, arch and lean toward each other across the tiny table, their hair falling forward like a curtain of secrets.

I force myself to look away as you say, *He's the kind of man I used to hunger for.*

He's a she, I say.

Oh? you say, not quite convinced, but pleased that this Adonis is someone who might satisfy us both.

Out the trompe l'oeil window is an English heath stretching greenward to a distant horizon. My thoughts turn to Heathcliff and a storm, but this moor is washed in spring. Nearly all the patrons of the tea room have ducked back out into the San Francisco drizzle and supper plans to be met. The light is almost gone; in the distance a streetlight clicks on. Besides us, only Adonis and her friend remain. They argue and we watch as the blond leaves quickly, in tears. Adonis looks bewildered. She's no

Heathcliff, but it's clear to me that she's put here for our pleasure.

The waiter brings our crumpets and lemon curd. I rip the silk lining from my shoulder bag and retrieve a $500 bill, the price of a one-way ticket to Venice. I dunk the bill into my half-drunk tea and, speaking low, ask the waiter to bring me a clean cup.

It's closing time, I say. *We'll take care of the tea room while you and the staff wash up.*

Certainly, miss, he says, replacing my cup. *Shall I draw the curtain to the back?* We exchange polite smiles.

You spread lemon curd across your crumpet and watch me turn the sign to "Closed." I pull the shades. Adonis is sad and lost in her cup; she doesn't look up until I begin to unbutton her loose-fitting shirt with my good hand. She merely regards me quizzically. *As you can see,* I say, *my cousin and I are not capable of the usual pleasures.* I hear you giggle, a rather gaspy sound I'm quite sure I've never heard from you before.

You make the next move—a brilliant one. *Perhaps she would like some lemon curd,* you say. I dip the fingers of my good hand into the creamy sweet and offer Adonis my hand. She pauses only a moment before she lifts her chin to my smallest dangling finger and sucks every slippery bit of sweet. Adonis takes her time; her hands remain at her side. There's a slow precision to the pleasure as each finger loses its sweet to her lips.

I hold out my still-damp hand to you and pull you to her. You raise your blouse, and together we rub the slick curd on your belly. Adonis simply watches us, her shirt open to the waist, her palms upward on her thighs. Her tongue flicks your belly just once and you say, *I don't think I can stand up for this.* I lead you back to the settee; Adonis drops to her knees and savors you. I hold on to the back of a chair until it's over.

I push the chair toward her. She stands up, watching you straighten your blouse. I pour three cups of tea, still warm from the thick brown pot. She sits. As you and Adonis drink, I cut the last crumpet into thirds and spread the remaining curd across each spongy piece, making sure yours is spread thickest. After all, you're eating for two. When she's done, Adonis crosses the room and opens the door; for a moment she lingers at the doorstep, then without looking back she plunges into the night.

The cold air cuts a sharp path through the steamy room. Your cheeks are flushed, as if you have run all the way across the sunny heath to meet me here, in the drizzle, among the disheveled crockery. A bit of lemon curd sticks to your upper lip. I remove it with my index finger and bring it to my lips, this sweet bit of our lavish friendship.

PARADISE CITY
BIANCA JAMES

I left Karla when her bad taste in music and worse fashion sense reached a breaking point in my life. I was embarrassed to be seen in public with a mullet dyke in an Iron Maiden T-shirt; I refused to be finger-fucked to Mötley Crüe's "Shout at the Devil." I still miss her though. It's been six months since we broke up and I still think about her all the time. Sometimes I wonder if I made a mistake by breaking up with her, though really it was Karla who dumped me in the end. Perhaps I should have overlooked Karla's lack of college education and her unique predilection for having me wear Payless hooker pumps when we fucked. I should have overlooked these things because Karla was not only the best fuck of my life, she was also the best cook I've ever dated. And what's more important in life than food and sex?

My short-lived tryst with Janet had been starved of both things. At the point I met Karla, it had been three months since I'd stopped calling Janet, four since we'd had sex, thanks to premature lesbian bed death. Janet had seemed like a good catch when I first spied her at the Thursday Night Lesbian Support Group. She was a 22-year-old with a shaved head, lean and tan with tufts of brown hair peeping out of the edges of her braless tie-dyed tank tops. I fantasized about being the older femme who would teach Janet the finer points of dyke sex, the sort of lover that she would have fond memories of as years went by. But I was wrong. Very wrong.

Janet insisted on dental dams and finger cots for every tryst, the plastic trappings of lesbian safer sex that seemed as useless a safety measure to me as confiscating nail clippers from carry-on luggage in airports. Moreover, Janet refused to be penetrated by my dildos or more than one finger; she wouldn't kiss me if I'd bathed with any kind of scented soap or eaten meat, and she wouldn't do any of the things I needed to get off. Janet's cunt seemed like an impenetrable fortress: I'd eat her plastic-wrapped pussy until my jaw was sore, and she still hadn't come. She'd roll off of me without returning the favor, then cook me vegan tofu stir-fry for dinner. Janet refused to eat at my house, knowing that dirty animal flesh had once touched the pots in my kitchen. Her cunt looked like hairy meat under the slick latex square, and I'd fantasize that I was eating steak instead of her hirsute cleft.

The road to hell is paved with good intentions, and Janet was living proof. The proverbial mercy fuck from hell wound up being my masochistic punishment for picking up women at self-help groups. I promised myself I would never go back to the Dakini Center any night of the week—from now on, it would be strictly bars.

Months of involuntary celibacy finally wore me down, though, and I was so desperate to be fucked that I was willing to endure hours of whining if need be. Luck was with me. I stumbled into a woman's 12-step meeting by accident and decided to stay. Narcotics Anonymous beat the crap out of the regular lesbian support groups: tales of blow jobs for heroin, cocaine binges, marriages torn asunder by perversity. The scruffy and dejected women of NA exuded a raw, predatory sexuality I found oddly appealing. Karla was the token butch in the group, clad in parachute pants, combat boots, and a camouflage crop-top muscle shirt that exposed a tasty pair of brown biceps. She had a shaggy black rock star mullet that hung down over searing blue eyes and a hard, mannish face. I got wet listening to tales of dishonorable discharge from the military for lesbian sex and methamphetamine possession, stories recounted in a voice like a rusty razor blade. She had been clean and sober for two years now, and she drove a forklift in the receiving department of Home Depot. Karla wasn't anything like the other girls I'd dated, but I knew I wanted her from the moment I saw her. It took me three meetings to work up the courage to ask her to be my sponsor.

I went to Karla's apartment the next night. I wore my white trash finest in the hopes of a tawdry hookup: mounds of cleavage courtesy of a push-up bra, gaudy crucifix jewelry bobbing on aforementioned cleavage, and fishnet tights under a little black dress. Karla served me dinner from Burger King. The savory animal grease wiped the taste of Janet's latex-covered cunt clean from my memory. Karla insisted we listen to a Metallica tape while we talked about our recovery: I'd fabricated a story about being a divorcee three months clean from a Valium addiction. Once we had exorcised our personal demons, Karla had slipped off my fuck-me pumps and tied me to her bed with my own fishnet stockings. She was very particular that I leave my dress on while we fucked but removed my panties and pushed my bra down to expose my nipples. I suppressed a giggle as Karla began squirting K-Y jelly all over a huge strap-on cock she'd been hiding under her baggy pants. The whole scene seemed unbearably absurd, but I stopped laughing once she eased the slippery dildo deep into my cunt and proceeded to fuck me. I moaned and growled as I felt months of sexual frustration released every time Karla's thick cock pushed against my G spot. I slammed my hips against hers, starved for dyke cock, my wrists straining against their fishnet bonds as Karla rubbed her wet thumb on my clit while pinching and twisting my nipples above their dainty little bra-shelves. The sensation was so intense that I came within a few minutes—I couldn't control it, the orgasm that ripped through my body left me feeling completely drained. Karla wasn't content to finish so quickly, though—she fucked me deep and slow for an hour straight until my pussy was swollen and sore. She had positioned her cock so it bumped against her clit with every thrust, and I felt her come against me time and time again as she fucked me.

This sort of behavior is known colloquially amongst friends of Bill W. as "The 13th Step," as in "Step 13: Fuck Another 12-Stepper." Karla pulled her drenched cock out of my cunt, untied my wrists, and gave me a quick kiss before reaching for her cigarettes. I had collapsed on the bed, feeling utterly ravaged and good. We didn't talk, Karla just laid beside me smoking cigarettes and absentmindedly flexing her abs, finally drifting into a deep sleep punctuated by loud snoring. I rested my head on Karla's buffed arm and pulled the covers over us before falling asleep.

I felt utterly, perfectly content in the company of this intimate stranger, despite a sense of inexplicable danger. I had crossed the line with Karla in more respects that I could count: She wasn't my type, for starters. I had lied about my past, violated the trust of the 12-step group in the wettest possible way with an ex-junkie Army girl. But after 40 hours a week of my bullshit office job, drowning my sexual frustration in late-night trips to the gym and sci-fi novels, Karla was the unpredictable variable I had been craving. I not only wanted to spend the night at her place, but maybe the next day too.

The next morning Karla cooked me a greasy Southern break-fast with two fried eggs, a tangle of crispy bacon, hash browns, toast, and black coffee. She played a Jackyl tape while she cooked, caterwauling along to "She Loves My Cock." Her house smelled like cigarette smoke and dog, even though she didn't have a dog. When I left for work, she grabbed my face with her strong hand and tongue-fucked my mouth, burrowing two fingers into my panties to feel my cunt juicing from the kiss. She smacked my butt when I walked out the door and said, "I'll see you at the meeting." I was utterly infatuated and couldn't stop looking forward to seeing her again.

I think one of the reasons I liked Karla was because she reminded me of my high school boyfriend, Dave Randell. Dave wore a leather jacket (that he let me borrow when it got cold, his muscled arms prickling with goose bumps) and carried a switchblade knife (for protection, natch). He smoked hash out of a Coke bottle and called me "baby doll" and "angel face" without any sense of irony. My mom always hated him and forced me to break up with him when she caught him going down on me on our couch on a day that we'd ditched school to get stoned and fool around. Dave was admittedly a loser; he made out with other girls at parties, flunked all of his classes, didn't bathe often enough, and showed up to school with a black eye on a semi-regular basis, but I was completely in love with him. He had the sort of body that comes from skateboarding and hopping fences, and he kissed better than any boy I've met since. He insisted on going down on me every time we had sex, and he would offer to beat up anyone who messed with me, including teachers. He was dumb as a post, but beautiful and vital, appealingly dangerous and insane. Karla was the kind of girlfriend I'd been secretly waiting for all these years—a sober, older, dyke version of Dave Randell.

We met up at the meeting the next night, and Karla sat next to me and held my hand the whole time. I felt vaguely uncomfortable when I saw some of the housewife types staring and whispering, but the hetero biker chick posse winked and gave me thumbs up. After the meeting, we got ice cream at Baskin-Robbins and saw a late-night movie. The movie was Karla's suggestion—my cunt was so wet, all I could think about was going back to her place and fucking again. It was clear that what I had intended to be a one-night stand was taking an entirely different direction, and I didn't mind. I was completely smitten.

We saw some inane Hollywood crapfest at the two dollar theater, the floor sticky like a porn house. The film was some action blockbuster that Karla loved. I ignored the movie for the most part, concentrating instead on Karla's hand. Her fingers played circles on my knee, my thigh, creeping ever closer to my panties, then shying away. I squirmed in my seat, frustrated, trying to arch my hips to meet her hand. She wouldn't give me what I wanted. I reached over into her lap. I was curious to see if she was packing. I suspected she was. She grabbed my hand, like a teenager caught shoplifting, and pushed it deeper into her crotch, so I could feel the throbbing length of her dick, the heat rising from her pussy.

Karla leaned over and breathed on my ear just a little, so the fine hairs on the back of my neck stood up and sent an electric current from my spine to my pussy. I was hoping she'd say something along the lines of "Let's blow this pop stand and fuck at my place," but instead:

"I want you to suck me."

I was taken aback. It wasn't so much that I was averse to sucking dyke cock, but the thought of kneeling on the greasy floor of a two dollar theater with *Armageddon* showing in the background to deep-throat a rubber dick seemed sort of ridiculous and unsexy. And yet, it was totally like Karla.

Karla unzipped her pants and pulled her dick out, stroking it gently, making me hold it in my hand. "If you want to get fucked later, you got to suck now," she growled in her cigarette voice, rolling a cheap, unlubed rubber over her cock. I leaned over the theater seat for a tentative lick. Karla grabbed a handful of my hair, easing my head down, and I felt her shudder. She seemed more in touch with her dick than some men I'd known. When I felt her thick cock hit the back of my throat, my eyes watered, and I felt my pussy flood. *She'd better make good on her promise,*

I thought to myself. Karla gradually eased me out of my seat so I knelt before her, the length of her dick buried deep in my throat, my nose to her pubes. She came when I sucked her—really came, tensing her buffed thighs beneath my palms, which impressed the fuck out of me. She was positively glowing when we left the theater, me feeling vaguely sheepish yet horny as she gripped my hand tightly.

Walking home, she pulled me into an alley and pinned me to the wall. I squirmed beneath her. "Come on, Karla, we're just a few blocks from your house. It's not safe here."

She kissed me hard, pinching and twisting my nipples through my dress. "Don't worry, baby," she said. "I've got a knife and I know how to use it." She really was the dyke incarnation of Dave Randell.

I gave up control. Karla told me to face the wall, with my dress pulled down over my tits and up over my ass. My palms flat against brick, legs spread, ass out, she pulled aside my panties, and her cock entered me like a knife into butter. I was so fucking wet, my panties chafed against my labia while she fucked me. Karla squeezed my tits from behind, her sharp teeth buried into my shoulder as she stroked inside me. I had purple bruises on my neck the next day. I was so spaced out at work, too distracted by the afterglow of fucking to pay attention to my various menial tasks. I'd be standing at the copy machine, imagining Karla had me bent over it, pulling my hair and fucking me up the ass, and my hands would start shaking. During my lunch break I wasn't hungry, so I smoked an entire package of cigarettes instead of eating, Karla's brand, trying to recapture her sex smell, ruled by my desire, wondering when I'd get to see her again.

I was laid off my job a week later, with no severance (turned out my boss had been reading the e-mails where I called him a "micromanaging cocksucker"). I had no savings, I didn't know how I was going to pay my $800 rent. I went to the NA meeting and cried for the entire fucking hour, hysterical and spastic while sitting on Karla's lap. I felt like an asshole, taking up everyone's time when I wasn't even an addict in recovery.

After that night Karla and I became inexplicably entwined. I was so fucking vulnerable after losing my job and my apartment, and Karla was incredibly generous with me. I moved into her place, vacuumed and burned incense so it didn't smell like dog anymore. Karla went to her forklift job every morning, and I stayed at home, half-heartedly looking for work and writing my novel on my laptop computer, which looked very expensive and out of place on Karla's kitchen table. Karla would come home and cook dinner, we'd eat, go to a meeting, come home, fuck, sleep, and start over again. It was a strangely stable, tremendously comfortable existence.

One of the best parts of living with Karla was eating the dinners she cooked for me, shaking the pan with one muscled arm while a cigarette dangled from her lip. Karla's excellent Southern cooking lingers as a shimmering grease spot on my memory: oily waffles with melted butter and brown sugar syrup, delicately crispy fried chicken and beer-battered prawns smothered in tartar sauce, pork chops with caramel baked apples, biscuits and mashed potatoes drowning in sausage gravy. I quickly forgot about Janet's dry humping and vegan guilt trips. Dinner at Karla's was orgasmic bliss, the surfacing of all my repressed food fantasies.

Karla had kicked meth and heroin but refused to give up cigarettes, black coffee, and saturated fat. She could bench press her own body weight and had arms like a sailor, so it didn't matter that she ate 6,000 calories every day. I preferred to spend my days reading books and writing on the computer and consequently gained 30 pounds in a short six months. The extra pounds went straight to my ass, thighs, and tits, and Karla would grab a handful of my puffy flesh, delighting in my new curves. When I bitched about my clothes being too small to fit anymore, Karla took me to Stormy Leather and blew her meager paycheck on a form-fitting leather dress, size "Extra Lusty." I begged her to return it but wound up getting it sweaty while having doggy-style sex on Karla's couch to "Paradise City," my bobbing tits hanging out of the low-cut top.

(How you can tell a loved one was raised on redneck liquor store porn: They prefer strategically placed bits of naughty flesh peeping out of trampy clothes to actual nudity. Karla liked it when I didn't wear panties, but she liked it better when I wore skimpy thongs that she could hold to one side while she fucked me.)

Life with Karla was good. But there was only one problem: the meetings. I only cruised self-help meetings for sex, never love or emotional support. Self-helpers, despite many well-intentioned hours of processing and sharing, tend to be completely emotionally unstable as a result of wallowing in their neurosis on a regular basis. There are those 12-step junkies you see at every meeting, so addicted to the drama that fills the hole that drugs or booze left behind. These people are alternately clingy and cold and are terrible at relationships. Karla was a rare exception. The program actually seemed to make her stronger. But it drove me insane. I told her after I moved in that I thought we should start going to separate meetings, and that I needed a sponsor I wasn't sleeping with. She agreed. To tell the truth, I would have been happy if I never had to attend another meeting ever, but I had to maintain the facade for her sake. I told her I attended a fictional Thursday night meeting in a neighboring city and that I had a sponsor named Janet. After becoming so deeply involved with Karla so quickly, I liked having time alone, time I didn't have to account for.

I began to look forward to Thursday nights. After dinner I'd kiss Karla goodbye and promise to be home by 9. I spent all week plotting how I'd spend those stolen few hours. I did all the things that Karla wouldn't have been interested in: foreign films at the art house movie theater, poetry slams at the local cultural center, live jazz, cocktails with friends at trendy bars (I always carried mouthwash and cologne to mask the scent of booze so Karla wouldn't be suspicious). I even went to the vegetarian restaurant I'd gone to with Janet once, almost daring myself to bump into her. As much as I loved Karla, part of me missed being able to talk art and politics with other people with college educations, people who listened to public radio instead of Black Sabbath.

Hoping to scratch my itch for increased intellectual stimulation, I got a job at a womyn's bookstore in town. It didn't pay much, but it was a step toward reclaiming my independence. Even though Karla barely made enough to support both of us with her forklift job, she became jealous when she found out I'd be going to work again. She demanded I change my outfit on my first day of work—a plain skirt and a low-cut top.

"Handsome bulldaggers go into that store all the time," Karla had hissed. "How do I know one of them isn't going to steal you away from me? I may not read a lot of books, but I'm in love with you, and if anything were to happen…"

Karla's possessiveness irritated me. I started dressing sluttier on purpose, flirting with customers every chance I got. Sometimes I even went out with customers on Thursday nights, but I never slept with any of them—I owed at least that much to Karla.

I thought I had it all figured out, but my water-tight plan got busted. Karla found out that I'd been slacking on my sobriety. She'd shown up at the Thursday night meeting to surprise me on our six-month anniversary, only to discover me missing in action. Not only was there an actual Thursday night meeting, Janet attended it, and when Karla asked about me, Janet had told her everything. I hadn't known that Janet was a 12-stepper, but it made sense. She'd use any opportunity to whine and process and obsess she could get her fucking hands on. Part of me resented her for contributing to my breakup with Karla, but in a weird way I was relieved.

Karla had come home that night and caught me drinking a

beer. I still had the occasional drink when Karla wasn't around—after all, I wasn't the one with the problem. Karla was so pissed at me that she screamed and threatened to kick me out, saying she couldn't trust me. I couldn't bring myself to tell her the truth, so instead I apologized. Finally, she burst into tears and forgave me. We didn't have sex that night, but she fell asleep with her entire body so tightly wrapped around mine that I could barely breathe. I wanted to squirm free. The next day I started looking for a new job and an apartment of my own.

Karla had gone from being my lifeline to a guilty pleasure, a dozen Krispy Kremes with a use-by date stamped on the side of the box. I was addicted to the home-cooked meals and scorching sex, but I couldn't deal with any other aspect of our peculiar relationship. I knew it was time to call it quits when I kept getting yeast infections from her cheap dildos and the polyester lingerie she liked me to wear, refrains from Bon Jovi songs were constantly stuck in my head, and I couldn't see my feet from all the fried food I'd enjoyed. Something had to break.

The incident with the beer had given me a way out of the relationship. I took up drinking and was sloppy about it, leaving vodka bottles for her to find in the trash. I even considered leaving some syringes and burnt pieces of tin foil lying around the bathroom but decided that was too cruel. So I drank instead. I took up drinking not because I wanted to become an alcoholic, but because I knew Karla would so abhor my rejection of sobriety that she wouldn't be able to take it. Karla attempted to drag me back on the wagon, kicking and screaming, but I refused. So she dumped me and kicked me out of her place, and I moved into the apartment I had signed the lease on a week earlier. I couldn't help that my feelings for her had died. We had irreconcilable differences in class and morality. I hated that I had to hurt her feelings, but I didn't know any other way out.

I respect Karla's integrity. She gave 100% in our relationship, and I treated her like crap. I know I was the bastard in this situation, but I had to get out. I know she's probably at a meeting right now, bitching about her dysfunctional ex-girlfriend.

But she changed my life, and I can't stop thinking about her. I think about her when I drink Pabst Blue Ribbons to unwind after work. I think of her every time "You Give Love a Bad Name" comes on the radio. I think about her when I eat bland salads for lunch instead of bacon cheeseburgers, trying to lose the weight I gained from her cooking. But most of all, I think of her when I'm jerking off to issues of *Hustler* purchased from the gas station down the street, trying to resist calling her up for one last booty call at 1 A.M.

CANVAS
JESS DAVIS

I'm not what I look like.

None of us is, I suppose. But I'm really not. Most people think I'm a man. Not only that, they think I'm a Nice Young Man. You can hear the capital letters, can't you? At least once a day I have the urge to show them what's under my clothes; let loose my tie, unbutton my shirt, and watch to see which hits them first: the swirl of color and texture that landscapes my muscle and fat, or the breasts that don't match the Man category in most people's gender codex. Either way, it's usually a shock. And I love it.

Sometimes it scares people. Not the ink, but the scars—the fat white lines of pain emended and highlighted with silvery filaments of remembered intimacy, crawling down across my shoulders and upper back like a mantle, blending into the designs of my tattoos; the tracks of my tears, as they say, immortalized.

I like wearing my marks. It hasn't been an easy life, in this body, this time, and I like the idea that it tells on my skin, that there's a visible sign of what I have lived through on my body. The scars on my skin echo the ones on my heart, invisible and inelastic. Did you know that?

They didn't scare Her. You can hear that capital letter too, eh? Herself. That's how I think of her, now, how I probably always will. That kind of girl, the kind who—when she enters a room—makes you think for sure you hear the bones of a fanfare in the not-too-distance. Who makes you want to lay down over puddles—fuck your coat. The kind of girl who always smells good enough to draw every girl-oriented person for miles, dragging them over with the fingers of her scent by their noses like a pie in a cartoon. But she shook her head at me when I tried to protest her hands on my buttons and then popped them off in a parody of savagery, and when she saw the dark ink of my skin in the ink-dark of her room, she dragged her palms warm down to my belt and murmured in my ear:

"Perfect."

And then, after a moment's consideration:

"The only thing better would be if I could lick you clean and start all over for myself."

I shuddered. I wondered if she might like to try anyway. I thought I might even let her.

That first searing night, I struggled, wanting to give her everything she wanted, but my repertoire was sadly limited by my past experiences: I'd lay down with femmes who lolled and sighed while I wrung every increment of pleasure I could out of their bodies until they were wet from head to toe with sweat, and come, and tears. I'd stood up and taken it from butches who wanted to watch me shake like my walls were coming down while they fucked me. And after every grand night of communion I had handed these women of whatever flavor a fresh blade and bid them or begged them to please leave some outward sign of what I had given, and taken.

She had a different idea. Something I have become very used to in the years since. But that was the first time, and I remember parts of it like it was yesterday.

She looked down, I remember, and then back up at me

through her eyelashes, in a way that might have been demure if her gaze wasn't so frank, so predatory. She reached out her hand and stroked my cheek with heart-melting tenderness and then wrapped that pretty hand around my throat and shoved me back onto the bed, on top of me in an instant, not big but strong, and with her compelling hand around my windpipe I felt disinclined to either resist or complain. She came to rest on my chest, skirt hiked up around her thighs so high I could see her stocking tops, could feel the velvet of her inner thighs against my gussets. She held my hands down, over my head. I groaned. She said:

"If there's anything you need to tell me, you'd better say it now, boy. Before your mouth is full."

I looked up at her, hair haloed by the neon from a bar on the corner, eyes and teeth glittering. I marshaled my composure, tried to organize my thoughts enough to give my brief but comprehensive list: bad shoulder, no ass play, not too rough with the hood ring, it's still healing. I opened my mouth, and what came out was:

"Please, amuse yourself with me."

A surprised, avid smile was my reward. She kissed each of my cheeks, so gently I could have cried, and reached past me, buckling my hands into soft leather restraints while her breasts fell in my face and I nuzzled against them, brushing my lips over her hard nipples, pressing my nose into her skin. She made a noise, low and feral in her throat, and…got up. She left me there, naked to the waist, so wet I could feel the come already starting to run down the crack of my ass. I heard rustling, a snap, the crinkle of cellophane. Nothing telltale. The sum of the noises did not prepare me for her return: Suddenly her knee was next to my ear. Then the other one was next to my other ear, and she was straddling me, her cunt unfurling itself for me, smelling richer than wine and settling itself into my mouth like—I know, but I can't help it—manna from the gods. Her breasts grazed mine, and I slid my tongue out of my mouth and into her with a groan of pure lust.

She started giving me instructions: "Put your tongue in me. That's right, boy, lap it up." I did, growling my happiness from between her thighs, stilled under her sweet weight on my body and her voice in my ear, "Good boy" walking so warm out of her mouth I couldn't help but believe it.

I dimly noticed that she was unbuckling my belt, hauling on the waistband of my jeans. I wasn't exactly used to taking my pants off with a girl around, but I was focused on the delicious cunt in my mouth, making my tongue rigid as I could and opening wide to slide it in as far as I could manage while she pushed my jeans to my knees.

And then I felt the sharp point of something, still against my skin. I heard her voice, musical even for being so muffled:

"I forgot to ask—is this a reward, or a punishment?"

I said "Reward" as clearly as I could with a mouthful of her, and I assume only the distinction between two syllables and three made me intelligible, but she understood and shifted herself above me slightly, giving me better access to her clit, saying, "Lick that, boy—suck it until I come," and scraped the flat of some blade I couldn't see from my throat to my navel in a generous sweep of promise.

I licked. I licked until my cheeks ached, until my eyes stung, until my neck burned; sucking her clit into my mouth, fucking the juice out of her hole with my tongue, tapping the very tip of her clit as fast as I could. And her? She started decorating me, slowly flicking open half-inch lines of perfect pain in my skin from hipbone to knee, down one thigh and up the other, marching like tire tracks across me, patting her palms in my blood and drawing on the abundant surface of my belly with it. I imagined her drawing patterns with it. I wondered if she were licking it off her fingers. I wanted her to. I wanted to, when I was done licking her cunt. I wanted to lick her clean too. I suddenly understood the urge.

Too soon she was coming over me, letting all of her weight onto me and shuddering and growling and sweeping the knife across the fronts of both thighs, laying down a thin, electric, stinging line of pain and saying, "Oh, fuck, yes, suck me, you son-of-a-bitch, yes, goddamn you, oh, you did it, oh, you, you…"

She trailed off, slumping onto my body as though I were a sofa. I licked a bit more, tentatively, and got my fresh cuts slapped for my pains. I arranged my legs to support her, took deep breaths, waited for her to come back to herself, release me.

When she finally sat up and turned to me, fuzzy around the edges and so sweet, murmuring about how handsome I was, and how good, and what a good boy I had been, she reached her hands—marked with my blood—up to release my wrists. When I thanked her, nuzzling her neck with my tired, grateful lips, she pulled back and said, "You deserve it."

And still holding my eyes, raised one bloodstained finger and deliberately, insolently, put it into her mouth.

She has given me another thousand cuts since that day and watched as each one disappeared or resolved into the lattice on my skin. Sometimes I wish she could lick me clean and start all over too. But reading the road map of my desire written on my body led her to me, and that makes each mark precious, precious as she is to me.

FIRE AND ICE
RACHEL KRAMER BUSSEL

The party's host has her hair in pigtails, short ones that look beyond adorable. On an older girl this wouldn't work, but at 22 they strike just the right balance between cuteness and flirtation. She looks just young enough that I get a slight chill, wondering if the six years between us signal my (or her) utter corruption, but she is an adult, after all. As she sits surveying the party crowd, cigarette in hand, she looks like she doesn't really care if people are having a good time, is waiting for it to be over so she can crawl into bed with her smoke and her stare. While she's waiting I check her out surreptitiously. I know she's mature enough to do justice to my fantasies, the ones she clearly wants to provoke with her short black denim skirt, patterned fishnets, and skimpy V-neck white T-shirt with black bra peeking out underneath, perfectly trashy. Her intense stare darts out from the mess of disheveled hair she constantly pushes from her face, the better to hide from the world with, though really she is the type of girl who desperately wants to be seen; you don't dress like that to be ignored.

We've met before but you'd hardly know it; I know just enough details to intrigue me, to find her the most fascinating girl in the room, a bundle of contradictions I'm dying to unravel. Otherwise, this party doesn't have much going for it; what had seemed like a fun night out has devolved into a crowd full of strangers, tired drinks, canned music, fun-by-numbers—but it's still better than watching the same old videos at home for the umpteenth time. And her; she makes it worth every idle minute of sipping my drink and trying to look lost in thought or at least casually busy. I stick around, knowing she's exactly the kind of girl who likes to be kept waiting, even if she doesn't know it yet.

Her skirt falls to mid-thigh and immediately makes me want to get under it, hiding and showing just enough of her leg, tempting and teasing me with the promise of what lies beneath. She's looking around with that calm, icy assurance that belies her years, but it's not that typical New York swagger, that do-I-have-somewhere-else-to-be/is-there-anyone-important-here-for-me-to-talk-to look. I can sense the hesitancy as she takes each drag, fingers shaking infinitesimally, not wanting to admit to anything but her self-imposed bravado. As I watch her, that is what I long to crack as in my head I press my hand up against her eager cunt, make her buckle underneath me, claw at the wall, drop her cigarette and her facade as she succumbs to what she truly wants.

Looking at her all cool and calm, a vision comes to me—her, naked, on her hands and knees on a bed, her clit sparkling with the silver sparkling hoop surely dangling from its hood, her wetness so palpable I can feel it before I even touch it. Me, ready to fuck her, my hands tingling with arousal, my pussy jumping like it's been touched by a violet wand. I squirm as I fight off the urge to touch myself, to do anything to offset the almost agonizing arousal that has overtaken me with this fantasy, and with that surge I know that I'll have to overcome any lingering nerves and go up to her. Just as I stride toward her, I see her walking toward me, and I fix my gaze on her, not smiling, not frowning, not giving anything away.

She halts right in front of me, so close we are almost touching, and holds her cigarette up to my lips for a puff. Normally, I'm not a smoker and can't stand the smell, but from her the tobacco is somehow erotically charged, and I inhale and then slowly let it out, plucking the cigarette from her fingers and stubbing it out before pulling her head in for a kiss. Her lips are soft and hot and moist, and I slowly, sensually devour her mouth. I could spend all day like this, and instead of the frantic groping I'd anticipated, I move slowly, my tongue gently parting her lips and deliberately crawling along her mouth, teasing and tickling, coating her teeth and then moving back to her tongue and luscious lips. Being so close to her mouth is making my pussy spasm again, hurrying me along when I would prefer to take my time, wanting both to savor and devour her. Her skin is hot, almost burning up, and I know that her pussy will be too. I tease her, toying with her tongue, sliding it between my teeth, biting her lips, small, sharp nibbles that leave her wanting more. I want her to pant for me, beg for me, lose all sense of control as she squirms in her stockings, no longer giving a damn what any of the overgrown hipsters here think about her.

Memories of her surface, in that magically convenient way they do, coaxed forth not with the deepest of thought but the logic of the unconscious. I recall other parties, restaurants, where I've seen her idly playing with the candles, her finger darting into the flame, flirting with the heat to get to the wax, which she swirls around her finger, poking it into the wet, warm morass and then coating her hands with its flaky whiteness. I've observed the casual way she poked at the wax, utter concentration as she went about her solitary task, unflinching. I myself have never even been able to draw my finger through the palest part of the flame, the heat scaring me off even though I know it will not actually burn me if I move quickly enough. Just the hint of that danger, though, excites me, and I know exactly what I will do to her once I get her alone.

I excuse myself and head for the kitchen, the tension between us suddenly too much for me. It's a welcome break, one I know she's not used to—once she has you in her clutches you're usually trapped, but she doesn't really want the upper hand, just gets it by default most of the time and doesn't know how to get rid of it. This time she won't have a choice. I feel the same familiar energy coursing through my blood, the kind that tells me I am about to do something that will change my life profoundly. It's not so much arousal as intense excitement, and I'm not all that surprised when she follows me into the kitchen, standing there silently as I pour myself another soda. When I turn around she's surveying me intently with those dark, smoky eyes, rimmed in black but shining brightly at me, seeking something that I hope I can deliver. They are issuing a challenge and I put down my cup, knowing that I have no choice but to take her up on it. I walk closer to her, also silent; the first one to talk will clearly lose this game, and I need to have the upper hand. I reach behind me and fish an ice cube out of my drink, bringing it to her lips, letting the icy droplets fall onto her neck and chest, drip down into her luscious cleavage. She opens her mouth and I slide it in, hearing it crack with the sharpness of her teeth.

While she bites, I do what I've been wanting to do all night: bring my hand up under that skirt and press against the fire I find there. I push against her wetness, palpable even through the thin layer of clothing, my arm tilted so the edge of my wrist presses against her, not caring who might walk in; fucking the party host has its privileges. I move away slightly and then bring my hand back, nudging her, tapping against her, forcing her to react. She bites down again, splintering the ice, grinding her teeth as I'm now grinding into her. I bring one of her hands up above her head and the other quickly follows, and when I look in her eyes they tell me all I need to know. She is mine, wholly, completely, just like that, and that look melts me. I have to catch myself, force myself to stand up straight rather than sinking down to the ground, pulling her with me. Instead, I push my body flush with hers, biting her chilled bottom lip, licking along its plumpness. I bring my knee between her legs, feeling her sink down against me, needing as much contact as she can get, her pussy aching. I nudge her with my knee then shove it hard against her, and she whimpers, her nails digging into the wall, and then just when she's dying for it, I pull my knee away. I turn her around with my hands so she is facing the wall, her gorgeously beckoning ass sticking out, the skirt sending the most heated of siren calls. I leave it in place for now and bring my hand back, spanking first one cheek and then the other. The impact is dulled by the layers of clothing but is meant only as a tease. In between smacks I bring my hand back between her legs and push hard against her cunt, practically pushing the fabric up into her, and I can hear her breath hissing out. I pinch her pussy lips lightly, then her clit, wanting just as much as she does to tear off her tights and touch her for real, but I go back to her spanking, and she leans her head against the wall, no longer certain what she wants or needs, too overcome to do anything but stick her ass out and let me decide.

When it's too much for either of us to take, we make our way into the bedroom, a cloying, writhing mass. Candles dot the room, some in modest little glass holders, some big and bold enough to stand on their own. I push her down onto the bed and dim the lights, and we are surrounded by darkness, with only the flickering flames to guide us. She moans quietly, catlike, and raises her arms above her head, making it easy for me to lift her skimpy shirt and push her skirt down around her ankles. I tear at the tights, the rip of the fabric ringing through the air, leaving her naked lips exposed. Of course she's the kind of girl who doesn't wear panties, but I have a hunch nobody's ever exposed her in quite such a way. I pull them off her and lean forward to bind her wrists with the webbed rags, and as I do she thrashes and moans louder, clearly in a new kind of heaven than the one she'd imagined. Every stroke of my fingers along her skin, whether a light, easy fingertip over her bicep or the pinch of a hardened nipple, makes her pant even more. She is struggling, frantic, needy, combative, but with me rather than against me.

I couldn't walk away now if I wanted to—the force of her lust would surely overpower me in a second. Her struggle is only with herself, with her need to strain and stretch, to feel the shivers that wrack her body as the fabric presses against that thinnest of skin on her wrists, as it sends tickles up through her arms, as I complement those gentle skin taunts with bites along her arm, her stomach, her thighs. I'm scraping, biting, stroking everywhere except her famished cunt, which she pushes at me, begging me to finally, finally fuck her like I've promised to all night. But it's too much fun to watch her squirm, to watch her try to get a word out—even a short one like "yes" or "please" simply becomes a ragged rush of air, a sigh, a moan, a clench. I stroke the backs of my fingers along her slit, so wet I almost slide inside against my will. Her feet try to kick off the skirt, but I tsk at her and she stops. She knows she won't get what she wants until I do and keeps it in place, moving within the limited confines the fabric allows, her legs only allowed slight room to part.

Maintaining the silence, I keep my eyes on her as I walk across the room, picking up a small white candle whose flame arches into the air. I walk back, my hand cupped in front of it to further the fire. She stills now, slightly uncertain, not sure if she truly wants this particular fantasy to come true anymore, but damned if she does, damned if she doesn't, because the need is so clear in her eyes it could burn me hotter than this candle. I tilt it slightly, letting a few drips spatter her belly, and she jerks but keeps those cool dark eyes on me. I continue along, splashing droplets of wax here and there along her torso, darting along the path between her sumptuous breasts, rubbing the wax into her once it has fallen. She is so still now, her body on high alert for danger, for pleasure, for anything that will ease the fire between her legs. I hold the candle still in my right hand and shove two fingers deep into her pussy, with no warning, and now she lets out a cry, a scream of arousal and frustration, of pent-up need, of everything she has contained for far longer than the length of this party. I push farther, then pull out and enter her again, her body easily navigable. I have to fight to control myself, to not throw the candle on the ground and myself on top of her.

There will be time for that later, but for now I go slowly, slower than either of us wants, but I know we will be grateful for it later. Delayed gratification is highly underrated, and I want to show her exactly how so, keep her on edge until she is ready to explode into a million pieces, a million tiny bursts of pleasure that leap from her body, coursing out in an orgasm worthy of a fireworks explosion, all bright light and loud boom, obliterating everything else in sight. I keep my touch light, stroking, teasing, feeling, rather than ramming them in the way I might do another time. I get to know her every curve, every lingering stroke telling me something new, feel each simple shudder, each reaction, a slow fizz that will build and build. I pour more wax, watch the way it melts within the holder, the hot liquid swimming and sloshing. I watch it harden on her, and touch the residue, her skin slowly cooling beneath it. She looks up at me with glossy, wet eyes, filled with unshed tears of need and joy and fulfillment, eyes that have probably not cried in front of someone else in longer than she can remember. I pull my fingers out, paint their wetness along her leg and move up to kiss her. I kiss her hard now, strong and furious, wanting to push the tears back in, strike them from the record, give them to someone else. She is so fragile inside and I don't need words to tell me that this is more than a simple fuck to her, more than a one-night stand with some older woman she'll later brag about to her friends.

"I'll be right back," I tell her, needing a moment away. In the hallway I feel like I need my own cigarette, but instead I rush to the kitchen, not wanting to leave her for more than a few moments. I hurriedly fill a cup with ice, keeping it behind my back as I enter the room. Those eyes watch me so fiercely I almost want to blush; if I didn't know better, I'd say they see right through me, a sexual sci-fi heroine whose power lies

squarely in her pussy. "Close your eyes," I tell her, and her obe-
dience is more powerful than a blindfold, a tacit trust placed
solely in me. Power can't exist in a vacuum, it feeds off the need
for others to respect it, and each time she does I feel it surge
through my body, keeping me safe and alive, needed and needy.
I again hold a candle over her, moving lower down her stomach,
letting it drip near but not onto her cunt, teasing her with the
heat's potential to sear as well as soothe. While the candle is
hovering, so close she can feel the heat without the actual wax,
I fish out an ice cube and trace it along her tender slit and smile
softly to myself as she arches her back and lets out a squeak.
Her hand moves to sneak down toward me but can't, and I
watch as the reality of her immobility passes through her brain.
She wants to protest even though she likes it, the body's instinc-
tive urge to push away anything that might be threatening. But
even if her hands hadn't been tied, I think she would have
inched forward then lay still as she does now, her teeth gritted,
eyes slammed shut as she arches against the dripping ice while
I keep rubbing it along her sweet skin before shoving it inside
her, watching as the icy water dribbles out of her. As I shove the
frozen cube inside, I let a drop of wax fall on her lower stomach.
The combination of fire and ice prove too much for her, and
while I work the cube into her deepest hiding places, she
comes, clenching my fingers, pushing the cube out of her, letting out a roaring scream that has been building for who knows
how long. She shivers from the chill, from the orgasm, from all
the intensity I wrung from her, and I watch as she comes back
down to earth, her face momentarily slack, at peace, no longer
any facade to maintain. I hold her down by her bound wrists for
a moment, letting her feel my weight, my power, letting her
know that I want to be in charge of her again but will let her go
for now.

I untie the knot and let her wriggle free, then blow out the
candle and place it on the ground, allowing her to relax in her
postclimax haze. I trail my icy fingers along her arm, teasing

her with the lingering cold. She shivers and I pull her close, wrap her up in my arms. We huddle there, candles blazing around us, our bodies hot where our skin meets, cool where the breeze hits. She's still an enigma to me, but I've gotten a little closer to her core, and even if that's the closest I ever get, it will be enough.

AMAZON
M. CHRISTIAN

It was the middle of the night, after Fala Lalafaluza's opening pink feathers act, but before Amazonia's whip-cracking to "These Boots Are Made for Walkin'," and Valerie VaVoom's closing bare bush special. They were all up there, the three headliners of the Black Cat Club and a few assorted girls digging for their own 20-minute sets in the spotlight. The Parade is what they called it, and sometimes it was fun—seven or so girls bouncing their tits or swinging their asses, boas sweeping the stage in slow motion, glitter scratching underfoot, trying to work out some kind of chorus line to a current top 10 tune.

It was halfway through the 15-minute set, eight girls kicking up their legs, shaking their tits, when it happened. "Sorry, shorty," Claire—Amazonia—said in a thunderous stage whisper after her muscular thigh smacked hard into Vivian's face, sending the dwarf tumbling to the stage. Fala quickly bent down and helped Vivian back to her feet. This got Fala a smoldering look from Claire, who cracked her whip, sending the girls on either side of her skittering away.

When "Sugar, Sugar" finally ended, Vivian knelt down and

retrieved her boa. From the opposite side, Fala watched her for a few seconds—until Claire, a scowl on her thin face, looped her whip around Fala's neck and violently pulled her toward the dressing rooms.

When the lights finally went down, the last person on the stage was little Vivian, until she stepped quickly off into the wings.

✳

"Fucking bitch," Claire said. She was standing by the door, which was closed, whip still in her hands—the cheap leather creaking as she flexed it. "She's disgusting. She's just here to laugh at—but they're laughing at us too."

"Oh, yes, Claire…I know." Fala was wearing only a silk dressing gown, and her full figure swayed beneath the thin fabric. She stood, leaning back against her backup table, with the same sensual grace she brought to the boards, the same almost-innocent poise she used when she took off her clothes to a hall full room of heavy-breathing men.

In a hall of cheap feathers and glitter, Claire was cheap leather, buckles, and fishnet. While the other girls stripped down or slipped on comfortable, sensible underwear as soon as their acts were over, Claire kept her leather, buckles, and fishnet on until it was time to step out into the early morning—and then sometimes she'd simply throw a heavy raincoat on over it all and walk out, not changing till she got back to their apartment, if then.

Claire still had her whip, still stretched tight in her hands, but as she eyed Fala, the twisted leather sagged, just a bit. "Yeah, Fal, you know," she replied. The handle end dropped, then the thin end, until the whip was a sloppy coil on the floor.

"Tasty," Claire's voice was low and gruff as she reached out and slowly, carefully opened Fala's gown, revealing by fractions the swell of her breasts, the pushy swell of her belly, the few brown strokes of down between her legs, and then—as the silk slid over her shoulders and to the floor—the twin pink knots of her tightening nipples.

"Very tasty, indeed." Claire said, gazing down at Fala's full, rich body. "Yeah." She reached down and pushed her fingers between Fala's thighs—until Fala took the hint and, with a sigh walked her feet apart, opening herself up.

"You understand, don't you, doll? She's a fucking joke, right? She's a freak, they laugh at her—so when we walk out there they laugh at me too." Claire's fingers pushed, hard, up and into Fala's cunt.

Fala started with "Claire…" in a firm tone, but then didn't say the next word, or the next—instead substituting "Whatever you say, Claire."

Never taking her hand out, Claire slowly eased herself down into a squat in front of Fala's tangle of pubic hair. "So sweet," she said, as if she were speaking to Fala's cunt and not the cunt's owner. Her hand started to move, slowly at first but then faster and faster, until her clutch of fingers were blurring in and out of Fala's cunt.

As she fucked Fala, Claire mumbled: "Sweet fucking cupcake sweet fucking slit sweet fucking slut sweet cup sweet cake…." It took a little clumsy effort, but eventually Claire got her own fingers into her own cunt, pushing her right index deep inside, thumb pressing and circling her own throbbing clit.

Above, staring out into space, Fala grunted—each thumping out of her chest to Claire's rough thrusts, hips moving back and forth in sync with the deep sound. She noticed a bit of feather on the top of her right breast and, without breaking the rhythm of her hip-sways, reached up and carefully plucked it off.

Below, lost in the actions of fingers in Fala's cunt, fingers in her own cunt, Claire reached boiling point. Her face and body were covered in a thin layer of salt and feverish excitement. Her eyes flickered from one tiny sexual detail to another—the way Fala's mons was thick and padded, the way her slit open/closed with each thrust of Claire's fingers, the gentle swell of her belly, the shadows of her big breasts cast by the overhead lights—until, with a single, very hard press, she pushed herself up and over into a shuddering, gasping come.

Breathing quick and sharp, Claire lost her balance, tumbling backward away from Fala's cunt. With a less-than-dignified impact, Claire's ass hit the floor—where she sat for a moment, then two moments, gasping in ragged breath.

"Cupcake," she finally managed to gasp, smiling deliriously—staring up with wide eyes at Fala.

"Yes, Claire…cupcake," Fala said with a furtive smile. Then she closed her robe and extended a hand to help her lover back to her feet.

✳

"—so the wife says, 'Honey, this one's eating my popcorn.'"

Their laughter was hard, deep, fast, and true, and Fala felt a quick smile flicker across her lips even though she'd only heard the punch line and not the setup.

As Fala pushed through the curtain, she saw one, two, three of the girls—Bunny, Doris, and that skinny little girl who also worked the front cash register. They were all sprawled out, eyes sparkling, as little Vivian held court backstage: shoulders back, purple boa tossed over one shoulder—somehow stately in miniature garters, fishnet hose, black panties, black satin bra.

"Now go on, my pretties!" Vivian cackled with theatrical glee, "Go out into that dull, dull world and shine with your delightful brilliance: Go on, beat it, ya bums!"

Laughing, the girls floated away, every one of them tossing a "Good night, Vi" or a "Sweet dreams, Vi" or even a "Love ya, Vivian" as they walked past.

"What a great bunch o' gals," Vivian said, laughing lightly, one leg up on one of the crates, a miniature Blue Angel. She adjusted her boa, stretching it out as if inspecting it for missing feathers. "Something I can do you for?" she said, her eyes penetrating Fala.

"I just wanted to…well, I'm sorry. For Claire. She can just be really…difficult sometimes." She found it hard to look the dwarf in the eyes.

Vivian laughed, quick and short, hopping off the box and strutting toward her. "No big deal anyway—besides, for all that leather and shit I bet our Miss 'Amazonia' is a real pussycat, right? Bet she even has some kinda silly pet name for you, right. Lemme guess, something cute and frilly, right? Something like…Kitty? Princess? Sweetie? Cookie? Cupcake—"

Fala twitched, blinked, took a short breath—and the dwarf was beaming: Vivian's face lit up as if caught in one of the spots.

"Knew it—oh, man, that's rich. But, you know, that's also a little sad—'cause you're not sweet." Vivian's eyes narrowed as she stepped even closer to the stripper. "Nah, you're nasty—aren't you, girl?"

Vivian's hand, somehow, was on Fala's meaty hip—and somehow, Fala didn't mind. Her face felt uncomfortably warm, like a bourbon blush on her cheeks, and she found her legs aching, just a bit, as if she had either run a mile, or was just about to.

"Nah, you're not sweet—there's nothing innocent, nothing precious about you." Conveniently close to Vivian was one of the crates, and Vivian nimbly hopped up on it—putting her face close to Fala's. "No, Fala, I know what you really are. You radiate it, you reek of it. You're a slut."

Vivian was maybe four feet high, and that was being generous. Her legs were stumpy, her feet like plump miniatures. Her arms were the same, bulbous in some places, like adult muscles on a child's frame. But Fala's nipples were aching, her lips were slightly parted and—distantly, as if it were happening to someone else—she was aware of her cunt's steady pulse.

All kinds of words were trapped in Fala's throat. Too many of them, with diverse meanings, everything from "No!" to "More!" So her body was left to respond on its own: She nodded her head.

"I knew it—knew it straight off: a true blue, all-the-way-to-the-core slut." Her voice dropped down low, so Fala had to bend down slightly to hear each word: "And there's nothing better than a slut."

The kiss was sudden, hard, and good. One minute Fala was stretching her ears to make out each word and the next their lips were together.

Pain made Fala break the kiss—a sudden, sharp shock. Looking down, she saw that Vivian had deftly parted her robe and was expertly pinching her left nipple. It was right, perfect: not enough to make her pull away, but hard enough to bring tears to her eyes.

Fala felt her legs grow weak, and she collapsed back against another of the crates. The world had shrunk down to her cunt—aching—and her nipple—aching—and Vivian's voice: "You live for your cunt, don't you? You have nice eyes, Fala; real nice tits, real good lips, a wonderful laugh, damned fine legs, but your cunt—ah, your cunt is a marvel, a treasure, a prize."

With no hesitation but also no hurry—slowly, savoring every inch—Fala swung her legs apart, exposing her downy hair, her plump, swollen lips.

"That's why you get out on that stage—to show that pretty, pretty cunt to the world. But showing it just ain't enough, is it? No, because a real slut can't just show off her cunt."

With a quick hop, Vivian was back on the boards, standing between Fala's spread legs. Looking down, focusing from her pulsing lust, Fala saw the little woman staring up at her with pure malicious intent. It was something she'd never seen before: control, power, will—all in a package dressed in feathers and frills and no more than four feet tall.

Vivian's hands were small, but not childlike. Even though she couldn't exactly see what she was doing, Fala instantly became an admirer of her skill. It was as if a brilliant conductor was playing her cunt: fingers tracing her slick, plump lips, dipping in just enough to break the seal and allow her juices to flow, a tap—then several taps—on Fala's heart-beating clit. Soon Fala was hissing, then she was moaning, then she was panting, then she was doing it all together at once, as Vivian spread Fala's moisture all over her cunt with her deft touch.

"But you are a special slut, aren't you, Fala—because you don't want to just be filled, right?" Vivian's words were growls, deep thunder, and Fala could do nothing but nod in response—but then there was pain, a blinding burst of light behind her eyes.

Reflexively, Fala glanced down to see Vivian's hand on her left nipple, savagely twisting the sensitive brown tip. "Say it, slut—be proud of what you are!"

From somewhere down deep, Fala knew what she wanted, more than anything. Proudly, in a voice that shocked her with its volume and determination: "Yes! I'm a slut: Fuck me!"

"Anything you want, slut," Vivian said, her rough voice dripping with playful sarcasm.

Her hands were small, but they were absolutely, positively perfect for fucking—which is what Vivian did to Fala. It was a hard-driving fuck that thrilled Fala from her outer lips to the deep insides of her cunt. It was a fuck made her ass scoot back and forth on the crate, made her nipples ache, a fuck that made her moan, sigh, pant—all of that and much, much more.

Then she came, with a crash and a cunt spasm that locked onto Vivian's hand like a handshake. Smiling broadly, Vivian remained between her legs, hand firmly up inside Fala till the bigger woman's contractions and moans boiled down and down and down to just a blissed-out smile on her sweat-shimmering face.

"Th-th-thank you," Fala managed to say as she slipped down, collapsing into a frills and feathers pietà.

Vivian walked around the crate and, bending down, kissed her: a sweet, innocent, rewarding meeting of lips on lips. Then, in a simple, honest voice, she said, "Anytime, slut. Anytime at all."

✳

"Hey, Fal, get out here. They're closing up—get your fat ass out here!" Claire said, standing at the top of the aisle, hand on the door to the lobby. She was dressed to leave, heavy topcoat over her patent leather, whip coiled like a belt around her waist.

"She'll be right out," Vivian said, sprightly jumping down off the stage. She also was dressed for the outside world: tight blue jeans, white T-shirt, leather vest, and biker boots.

Claire didn't respond with words, but her face tightened into a stone mask of displeasure. It was like she wanted to say something but couldn't.

Then Fala came out from the dressing rooms. She looked at Claire—a quick glance—and then at Vivian, smiled, and gently dropped her eyes.

"Hey, you coming or not?" Claire said, voice trying to be strong—but instead coming out strident.

"No, bitch, she's not," Vivian said, her words thundering in the hall. Then, softer, to Fala: "Come along, slut."

Fala smiled, wide and true, and took the tiny woman's arm. They pushed open the side door and stepped outside, Fala's "Yes, Master" echoing as the door swung shut behind them.

OVER AND AGAIN
CAELIN TAYLOR

She didn't know what she was doing walking through the massive wooden doors of the downtown hotel, across the elaborate marble floor of its lobby toward the large, dimly lit lounge. Rainwater was still rolling off her coat, running down her sleeves as she stood there, one hand on the brass rail of the bar, the other pushing wet hair out of her face. All but vacant on a weekday, the hotel lounge was still unusually dark, and she wasn't sure she would be able to find her. Instead of looking around, instead of peering in the dark corners or the bathroom, she ordered a rum and Coke and put a cigarette between her lips. With hands shaking, she held a small brass lighter to the cigarette and took a drag. She coughed as the smoke stung her throat and lungs and instead of crushing out the cigarette, she took another drag. This is where it had started.

A month ago, sitting at the bar with Mattie, drinking martinis and reading a local magazine, it all seemed so innocent, so fun. Mattie was reading the alternative personals aloud, in between bites of fries and sips of beer, the two of them snickering occasionally at some of the ads. Mattie's voice changed as she read a long column of ads written by married people, people searching for discreet afternoon trysts with any interested party. Lighting a Nat Sherman, after offering one to Eren out of habit, Mattie laughed.

"Can you imagine what that would be like instead of the buffet line at the Wallace Grill during our lunch break?"

"That's insane," Eren said, wanting a cigarette but having quit almost a year ago. "I barely have time enough to eat, let alone…well, you know. Besides, some of us are married, remember?" She elbowed her friend.

"That's the point, Eren. So are these people," and Mattie, wiping her mouth with a folded napkin added, "No one would ever have to know, right?"

Later that day, at home, reading Mattie's magazine in the bathtub, Eren flipped to the personals section and began to read. About halfway down the third column, there she was, summed up in six lines.

```
ARE YOU WONDERING WHAT ELSE THERE IS?
I am. 29, GF, new to town seeks F,
18-45, for discreet lunch meetings.
Will try anything for right woman.
You: be comfortable in your own skin,
but needing more. RESPOND: # 891595
```

Over and again, she read the lines, her mind digesting the idea, like a theory of happiness that might be hers. She sat in her office, the folded paper held beneath her desk, and read the ad, silently mouthing the words. For the fifth day in a row, it was raining outside and a blanket of gray cast a somber darkness over the city. She punched in the phone number on her cell phone and waited. Eren stood up at her desk, folding the paper and putting it under her arm. On her tiptoes, she looked over the top of her cubicle, carefully watching her supervisor as she collected mail and disappeared into her office. Sitting back down, Eren entered the mailbox number

891595 and waited for the message. There was a quiet click.

"*Buon giorno.* I want to thank you for responding to my ad. My name is Rochelle. Because you took the time to call, and are paying for every minute, I'll be brief. I will return your call. Just leave me your name and a number where you can be reached." Eren was not prepared for the succinctness of the message, was not prepared for the smooth accent of the woman's voice, was not prepared when she heard the tone signaling her to begin. She spun her chair to the window and caught her breath.

"Um, hi. My name is Eren," she hit her forehead, mad she forgot to use a fake name like Mattie suggested. "I saw your ad in the paper and, well, I really enjoyed it. I want to," she paused, watching a woman, three stories down, trying to cross a busy street. No umbrella, no coat, the rain running through the material of her clothing, dampening her hair. "I would like to talk to you, and maybe meet for lunch." She left the number to her cell phone and said goodbye. She sat for a moment, watching the woman as she climbed into a taxi, waiting for the remorse to set in, for the feeling of doubt to climb into her. But it never did, not even when she received Rochelle's first, or second, or fifth phone call. As she woke up just that very morning and spent two hours dressing and undressing, not once did it occur to her to change her mind and cancel their meeting.

"Eren?" a voice questioned behind her, a hand on her shoulder. Eren turned around quickly, splashing excess rum and Coke over the top of the glass. She felt her cheeks flush. She had come, like she said she would.

"Rochelle," she smiled, as the woman took the glass Eren held and placed it on the bar. There was a moment, as Rochelle's hand slid over hers, as they looked at one another, that Eren felt a blush of excitement. Eren straightened her blouse, looking down at her feet. Rochelle was a tall woman, with black hair that fell around her chin. Her eyes were green, Eren knew, but in the dimness of the bar they were dense, colorless pools. She was beautiful.

Rochelle held out her arm and, gesturing toward a table, lightly touched the small of Eren's back. Through the wet fabric, through the blouse she wore underneath, Eren could only imagine she felt the woman's hand, like a subtle suggestion, motioning her toward a candlelit booth in the corner away from the bar, away from eyes.

Rochelle helped Eren as she wiggled free of her wet coat, flicking it once, briskly, before hanging it on a brass coat hook behind their booth. As Eren sat down on the bench, Rochelle continued to stand, a small smile pulling the corners of her mouth as Eren grabbed and pulled at her skirt while she scooted over. Rochelle's heart was thrashing against the confines of her chest, but she continued in her silence, determined to make an impression. The brief hesitation she thought she heard in Eren's voice, calling earlier that day from a cell phone on the West Side, necessitated this display of calm surehandedness.

"Would you like something else to drink?" Rochelle asked, tucking a strand of hair behind her right ear. Her left hand was charmingly slunk in the back pocket of her silver pin-striped black pants. Eren looked up at her, her stomach tight, feeling warm.

"That sounds good," Eren said softly, her fingers rolling the small brass lighter over and again.

"OK, be right back," Rochelle smiled and quickly tapped the table before turning and heading toward the bar. She moved gracefully, her round ass swaying smoothly as she walked away. As soon as she was gone, Eren, with a hand on her forehead, sighed.

"What the hell am I doing?" she said quietly, pulling out her cigarettes and lighting one quickly. She bent forward to see where Rochelle was, one thought passing through her mind swiftly: Could she, should she, sneak out? Yes, before anyone saw her. Before she made a terrible mistake, one she could never correct. The urgency, the sweet sound of Rochelle's voice earlier that day, halted her. She sank back in the seat and closed her eyes, inhaling deeply. She wanted this. She knew that. She wanted this woman.

"Rum and Coke?" Rochelle slid into the booth, holding two glasses. Surprised, Eren removed the cigarette from her mouth and crushed it out in the ashtray.

"Thanks." Eren smiled, looking across the table at Rochelle.

"You can smoke, Eren. I don't mind."

"Oh, I don't smoke," she said, laughing, grabbing hold of the glass and taking a long swig.

"That's what I thought. I remember you said something about quitting." Rochelle leaned back in her seat, her long arms casually crossed in front of her. It was quiet for a moment while Eren cleared her throat, looking everywhere but at Rochelle, to whose mouth, neck, and dark eyes she found herself inexplicably drawn.

"I don't usually drink on my lunch breaks either," Eren said before again placing the glass to her lips and tilting it back. Rochelle reached out then, across the top of the table, and placed her hand on Eren's. When Eren flinched, Rochelle did not recoil.

"Just relax. I'm not going to attack you, Eren," Rochelle said quietly as she watched Eren looking over the rim of the glass. Her blouse was open at the neck, where a silver pendant dipped and hung against her pale flesh.

"I know that," Eren whispered. "It's just, I don't know." She looked around, pushing back her damp hair. "I guess I'm nervous. I feel like I've already done something, you know…wrong."

"Without anything naughty to show for it," Rochelle laughed, grabbing Eren's hand playfully. At this, Eren laughed too, feeling relieved. Rochelle's fingers were long and slender and they ran across Eren's hand softly, tracing her knuckles. "When do I have to get you back to work?"

"Well," Eren felt the warmth of Rochelle's hand, enjoying it, scared of it. She did not want to say she had taken the whole day off from work, did not want to say she was so nervous she hadn't slept the night prior. "I love your blouse," she said suddenly, moving her hand away from Rochelle's, grabbing the cuff of her shirt and feeling it between her fingers.

"Thank you, I got it in Italy last summer when I was home visiting my family." Rochelle pulled the pack of cigarettes close and tapped out a cigarette. Placing it between her full red lips, she lit it and offered it to Eren, who took the cigarette quickly with her other hand, not letting go of Rochelle's shirt. As she took a drag, looking at Rochelle, she knew if she left that lounge, if she left Rochelle, she would never find her way back again. She knew there would never be another woman, there would never be another chance. She wouldn't allow herself this situation again. She would never know. Her fingers gently caressed Rochelle's wrist, feeling the vibration of the veins running below the skin.

"Rochelle," she began, finally letting the woman take her hand, their fingers intertwining. "I was scared about today. I didn't know what to expect. I didn't realize what this all meant, the phone calls, the notes. I didn't know what this was leading up to, you know?" She lied a little because the words wouldn't come out of her throat, the words that she wanted to say, needed to say. Rochelle nodded, feeling their knees touch under the table. She could smell Eren's perfume, could almost imagine the feel of her skin, the delicate planes of her body. She knew women like Eren, their moral hesitation. She knew women like Eren with their heads tossed back, pants down, calling her name, needing more. Her eyes followed the length of the silver chain around Eren's neck to where it formed a triangle above the pendant it suspended near her breasts.

"I thought you were pretty clear about what you expected, Eren." She paused, leaning forward. "I think you know exactly what you want." Under the table, Rochelle's left hand was on Eren's leg, barely beneath the edge of her skirt, feeling the lean muscle, the silken skin. "Come on," Rochelle was saying as she stood, holding Eren's hand, pulling her up, pulling her away. Rochelle's hair flowed around her face as she confidently strode toward the lobby, toward the door. Eren watched Rochelle as she walked, car keys in her hand already, the sureness of her movements, the way her charcoal-colored blouse hung across her back, the sway of her hips. Eren stopped walking, standing on the busy sidewalk, people rushing around them, but did not let go of Rochelle's hand. Her head was pounding. Was she really going to do this? Rochelle stopped, feeling Eren's hand pull away slightly, and turned to close the distance. As the rain drove down on them, she took Eren in her arms. With their faces close, Rochelle whispered, "Don't give up on me. Not yet."

Fired to life, Rochelle's old Volkswagen shook a little as they roared up the steep streets toward her East Side apartment. The car was cold, even with the canvas roof up, and Eren's body jerked involuntarily as brisk air rushed in through the window Rochelle had cracked while Eren smoked. Grabbing Eren's hand, she pulled it over to her leg and held it briefly before flipping on the heat. As she drove, she caught glimpses of Eren's bare legs, raindrops sailing slowly across her smooth skin, leaving tiny goose bumps in their wake. When Rochelle pulled the car down the long driveway to her apartment, Eren felt the pounding of her heart all over her body. In a wonderful mixture of fear and excitement, she tucked her hair behind her ear and squeezed Rochelle's leg. After Rochelle shut off the engine, the two of them sat silently for a while as a hard rain pelted the car. It was now or never, she supposed.

In the quiet, she took Rochelle's face in her hands, and with mouths slightly parted they looked at each other. Eren could not explain how much she wanted her, how much she had wanted her, wanted this for weeks. Instead, she drew Rochelle closer, her small hands holding onto the material of her blouse, and kissed her gently, delicately. Her head swam with the softness of Rochelle's lips. Her kiss hardened, became hungry, desirous. She felt Rochelle's tongue graze her own, felt Rochelle's teeth biting her bottom lip. She let her hands fall to Rochelle's small, firm breasts. Beneath her shirt,

Eren could feel no bra, only subtle curves and the suggestion of beautifully petite nipples. She put a hand on Rochelle's thigh, massaging the muscle, scared to get closer but wanting to feel her. Her hand went quickly, perhaps out of fear she would lose her nerve, and she cupped Rochelle's crotch, warm through her pants. Rochelle groaned, whispering something in Italian, her head rolled back against the car seat, her thighs tight. Her pussy was already throbbing, needing Eren to press into it, wanting to open up for her. Rochelle grabbed a fistful of hair at the nape of Eren's neck and pulled her close. She knew the want building in her and the need she felt in Eren would not be satiated with any number of kisses in the front seat of a car. Rochelle's blouse fell from Eren's hands as the two inched apart.

"What is it?" Eren said, breathing hard, her hands still hovering near Rochelle's breast, near Rochelle's crotch.

"Wait." Rochelle grinned. "Just wait." And she withdrew the keys from the ignition and ran around to Eren's door, opening it and extending a hand. Through the rain they jogged to the front door, and as Rochelle's long fingers fumbled with the keys, Eren stayed close, under Rochelle's arm, breathing her in.

Inside, Rochelle threw the keys on an entry table and took hold of Eren's wrists, wrapping them around her back, pulling her close. Water hung in their hair, covered their faces, rolled down their bodies, and glistened on exposed skin. Eren let her coat fall to the floor. Without hesitation, without words, Eren raised her arms and Rochelle lifted off the damp blouse she wore, before unfastening and removing her faintly pink bra. Eren's hands rose to Rochelle's neck, her fingers trembling as she quickly unbuttoned Rochelle's blouse, her eyes never leaving Rochelle's, never showing any doubt. Rochelle was much taller than Eren, with light olive skin that seemed rich and decadent, that tasted slightly of lavender.

In Rochelle's apartment there was only the blue light from an aquarium and the dim red lights of a stereo that was quietly pushing out music in the other room. Unpacked moving boxes rose to the ceiling against a far wall. Rochelle moved her away from the door, her arms wrapped around her tightly, toward a large bed set in the middle of the room. Slowly they kissed, their hands exploring warm, bare skin. Rochelle pushed Eren down onto the bed and stood over her at the foot. She swayed back and forth, hands on her hips, a smile pulling at her open mouth as she took in the sight of Eren's half naked, supple body. She bent down, with one knee on the bed between Eren's legs, and with an unhurried hand unbuttoned Eren's skirt. While her fingers worked the skirt's zipper, she watched the quick rise and fall of Eren's stomach, the widening of her eyes, the way her hair fell around her face. With her fingers hooked onto the top of Eren's underwear, she grabbed onto the skirt and pulled both down over Eren's hips and wet legs. She looked at Eren then, at her lush body, and began to unzip her slacks. Rochelle stood before her, naked, as her pants slid down her legs. She lowered herself onto the bed.

She lay next to Eren, curving her body against her, gently kissing her as she traced the line of Eren's breasts, the supple planes of Eren's stomach, the arch of Eren's hip. Her skin was tingling as Rochelle kissed her ear, her neck. With one motion, assured, confident, Rochelle moved her fingers down, feeling the fine downy texture of Eren's light brown hair.

"Do you want me?" Rochelle said, her voice low, coarse, her lips close to Eren's ear. Eren could not speak, could not reply save for the movement of her own hand clasping Rochelle's, pushing it down between her legs.

Rochelle moved her fingers slowly, delicately, in small circles around Eren's clit, pressing gently, then harder, before moving down to feel Eren's warmth and her wetness. Eren's breathing became sporadic, the beating of her heart changing its very rhythm to match Rochelle's movements. Rochelle rolled halfway on top of her, pressing her hip against Eren's clit, their sweat, their desire, their wetness combining, mixing together. Their breasts brushed against one another, already damp with sweat. Rochelle entered her deftly, using three fingers, pushing strongly with one motion into her aching pussy. Eren inhaled deeply, feeling as though she were going to come with every movement Rochelle made. She held Rochelle's shoulders, digging her fingers into the woman's flesh, pushing her down, holding her there with her. They stared at each other then, as if suspended alone together by a single thread. Eren's mouth was open, her lips barely parted, teeth bared. Rochelle moved faster, quickly in and out of Eren, deeper, pushing her hip against her hand, using her whole body against Eren's body. They moved together like an engine, breathing as one. And then, as if taken, swept away by some invisible force, Eren's gaze drifted over Rochelle's shoulder, and she felt such a wave of energy curve across her body, rippling every muscle. She came violently, her legs stiff, her fingers holding and grabbing at Rochelle's ass, her voice vulgar and uncontrolled, and her eyes wide.

They lay together. Rochelle still felt the inner convulsions of Eren's body pulsing around her fingers, soft and wet, warm like some kind of fire burning in a place that she couldn't quite reach. Her own body aching and sore, she did not want to move, to sever herself from Eren's body. Their breathing slowed in the quiet of the room, their bodies slick with sweat and saliva. Eren's eyes were closed tightly, her fingers loose on Rochelle's shoulders, her muscles twitching with the last impulses of electricity that ran through her body. Her damp hair stuck to her forehead and cheeks. Rochelle lay her head on Eren's chest, listening to the rhythm of her heart slow.

She looked up at Eren, wanting her again, still needing her, and began to move her hand once more, slowly. She was still so wet, so incredibly wet, the feeling of her arousing within Rochelle such want. Her fingers digging into Rochelle's sinewy back, Eren moaned in a muffled voice, her teeth clenched around Rochelle's shoulder. Rochelle slipped her fingers from Eren and grabbed her hips, moving her body between Eren's legs, their clits smooth against each other, their stomachs covered in sweat, so close that they could not tell their own body from the other.

Rochelle moved slowly for only a moment, enjoying the tension she immediately felt converge upon her, until the pulsing of her own body began to drive the motion of her hips, quicker and harder. She moved smoothly, then erratically, as she swayed her hips, pushing her pelvis against Eren's, pushing her body into Eren's, and sliding her clit against Eren's. Eren opened her eyes and looked at her, at Rochelle's small, perfect breasts as they jutted out. Her hair was drenched, falling around her face. The woman's mouth was closed. She was biting her bottom lip. Her eyes remained open, fixed on Eren. She was going to come. She wanted to hold on, to come with Rochelle, but the sight of her rising above her, using her body, needing her so completely was enough, too much. Eren felt the orgasm rise within her, from the depths of her burning womb, to her toes, to her scalp. At this, Rochelle felt her own body reach its plateau, burning, tense. Rochelle came, yelling in her faint Italian accent the same words over and again, "Eren, oh, God, oh, fuck!" Her body rigid, her eyes wide, taking in the beauty of Eren coming with her head rolled back against the bed, her back arched, her body wildly tense with every muscle rippling and locking.

Eren in the darkness of the apartment, naked, tangled in a single damp sheet. Someone was walking around upstairs, and there was the sound of a heated discussion down the hall but nothing else. Eren propped herself up on her elbow, pushing the hair out of her face. She saw Rochelle's silhouette as she crossed the room, the curves of her naked body dimly highlighted. It was late, but Eren could not read the hands of her watch or see a clock anywhere in the apartment. Rochelle was walking toward her in long, loose, and easy strides. She sat on the edge of the bed, an arm draped behind her, steadying herself. Eren reached for her, caressing her bare back, the curve of her hip, before pulling her down, playfully laughing. They lay together in silence for some time, looking at each other.

"Do you need to go?" Rochelle finally asked, touching the side of Eren's face, stroking her neck, her shoulder.

"I should," Eren whispered, and, smiling, added, "but I don't want to." Rochelle pulled her close, their bodies stretched out, balmy, against each other.

"So don't." Rochelle sighed into Eren's neck, kissing her below her ear, her arm slung low on Eren's hip. She tasted both sweet and salty. Rochelle lay on top of her then, pinning Eren's arms above her head, straddling Eren's hips. "Don't go," she said, over and again, kissing her way between Eren's heavy breasts, across her stomach. Eren twisted her fingers in Rochelle's thick hair, knowing she would not be able to leave even if she wanted, not with the sweet suggestion of what was to come, not with the need that grew and spread over her as Rochelle's lips, full and warm, grazed her stomach, her hip, her thigh. Rochelle looked up at her, her deep green eyes half open. "Just relax," she whispered, taking Eren's hands from her hair, kissing them.

For a moment Rochelle did nothing, nothing but breathe. Her breath was hot against Eren's skin, her arms stretched out loosely, her hands gliding over trembling skin. She watched Eren, the tension growing until she opened her mouth, her tongue soft and warm, and circled Eren's clit. Eren, with eyes closed, with fingers clenching the disheveled sheet beneath her, slung her right leg over Rochelle's shoulder. Rochelle ran her tongue around Eren's clit slowly, elaborately, before dipping down quickly and pushing her tongue into her pussy, tasting her. Eren's hips rose against Rochelle, her pelvis rolling forward as Rochelle flicked her tongue in and out of her. As she took her clit into her mouth, sucking, she found Eren's rhythm. She held Eren's ass, squeezing when Eren's muscles tightened, pulling her, wet, hot, toward her face. Moving slowly, taking her time, wanting only to give, to please, Rochelle watched her body respond.

Eren opened her eyes. The whole of her body seemed to

sing. Not just between her legs where Rochelle's open mouth nestled, not just where Rochelle's hands and fingers met her body. Everywhere. She felt Rochelle deep in her tissues, spreading out across her, consuming her. Her body pulsated, burned and craved Rochelle's touch, Rochelle's kiss. Their fingers entwined, they held onto each other as Rochelle's pace changed. As she circled her tongue quickly, fluidly, she knew Eren's body was ready, hungry for release. She felt high, her breathing shallow. Eren's head fell back against the bed as she let out a sigh, her back arching. Sweat rolled down cool against Rochelle's shoulders as she released Eren's hand and touched her fingers to Eren's warm, wet lips. She slipped her middle finger inside. As she took Eren's clit between her teeth and worked it with her tongue, she began to pump her hand forcibly. She moved easily in Eren's wetness, feeling Eren's muscles tighten as her finger began to slide away, out of her throbbing cunt, feeling Eren rock her hips as she slid her finger all the way back into her. They moved together, their thoughts, their doubts, their expectations lost. In the quiet room with only the sound of their breathing, Eren came, hard, her pelvis thrust against Rochelle's face, her hands covering her eyes, hot tears rolling down her cheeks.

For a moment they lay quietly, not moving. The both of them still breathing hard, Rochelle rolled onto her back beside Eren and took her hand.

An hour later as they sat parked outside Eren's office, the streetlights hummed overhead. It was no longer raining. A few bright stars began to shimmer in the crisp, clear sky.

"Lunch, tomorrow?" Rochelle asked, shyly smiling as she looked at the side of Eren's face. Eren turned to Rochelle, putting a hand on her thigh.

"I don't know if an hour is long enough." Eren's voice was quiet in its longing. She pushed on the door and walked around to Rochelle. "Tomorrow," she said, finally, nodding. With her hand on the door, through an open window, Eren said good night. And though their faces were only inches apart, Rochelle did not kiss Eren's tender lips. There was not time enough for that kind of kiss, for those things she wanted to do to her, over and again. She felt the sadness of knowing this and caught Eren's hand in her own as she turned to go.

"Tomorrow," Rochelle smiled. "I'll meet you tomorrow."

THE ROBBER GIRL
LORI SELKE

The robber girl owns 13 knives. Twelve, actually, for one is a straight razor. They all have names. "This one's Judith," she says, pulling the blade along the sharpening stone. "This one's Salome. Jezebel, Delilah, Shemamah the Desolate, Mara the Bitter," she recites, running her fingers along the edge of each blade. "They are my daughters; they are my coven."

"You can trust steel," she tells Gerda. "With steel, you know where you stand. It's glass that's treacherous, like water; it looks placid, but it bites. Steel is hot, glass is ice. But you already know all about that, don't you?"

"I could pierce your heart with steel the way she pierced Kay's heart with glass," she whispers to Gerda one night in bed. "I could turn you hard and hot, the way she turned him hard and cold. I could make you forget him. I could turn your heart."

"Yes, you could," Gerda replies, her breath coming in gasps. "Oh, oh, yes you could."

"I can feel the furnace inside you," the robber girl whispers. "I know how to stoke it."

"Yes," Gerda says and kisses her lover hard. Their conversation stops for the night.

By day the robber girl teaches Gerda how to ride a horse, how to pick a lock, how to keep a band of unruly men in line. She is the Robber Queen.

"They think you're pretty," the robber girl says. "That's because you are."

Gerda blushes.

"Your pretty face can be a liability, or it can be a tool," the robber girl says. "I myself am plain. I have learned to use other tools." Her hand strays to Gerda's waist. "Let the men admire you. Let them do you little favors. Do them favors in return. They will be loyal as dogs. But don't give them everything," she adds. "Leave them wanting more."

She leans in to whisper in Gerda's ear. "Right now, what they want is you. But I won't let them have what they want. You are my prize." Her hand pinches Gerda's rump. Gerda jumps. "But I will let them look. They will drink in your face like a draught from a well. They will know that you please me, and that will please them too."

"Do you ever let them touch you?" Gerda asks, ducking her head into the robber girl's pungent armpit after she speaks.

"Sometimes," the robber girls admits. She looks down at her blushing lover. "Did you ever let Kay?"

"Sometimes," Gerda admits.

"He wasn't really my brother."

The robber girl nods. Her mouth is full; she and Gerda are sharing a dinner bought with stolen coin.

"People thought we were brother and sister because we looked so much alike. It was probably our hair," Gerda says, fingering her smooth blond braid. "And our eyes." Her eyes are a guileless blue. "But we weren't related."

"He was your lover," the robber girl states.

"My first," Gerda says.

The robber girl nods and fills her mouth with roast chicken. Gravy spots her chin, her shirt.

"You're my second," Gerda says.

The robber girl grins. Gerda wipes the gravy from her chin with a kiss.

Gerda remembers the morning the robber girl found her.

She was wearing leather. Black leather, the crevices caked with dust from the road. Leather pants. Leather vest that left her arms bare. Her skin was dark, a deep brown, not the brown of a crust of fresh-baked bread, but the bronze of temple idols. Her hair was black and long; it hung free past her shoulders, tangled by the wind. Her eyes too were black.

Her smell was strong; it mingled with the scent of the horse she rides. It was a smell both pungent and clean.

"I could have killed you when we first found you," the robber girl says. "But you were too pretty. I could have let my men have their way with you, but I stopped them. We thought you were a princess. You were wearing a princess's clothes."

"They were a gift," Gerda says.

"From your lover?" the robber girl sneers.

Gerda laughs. "No. You know you are my first."

"Your first woman," the robber girl corrects.

"Yes," Gerda says soberly.

The robber girl's hands are on Gerda's breasts, her thighs, the cleft between her legs. They are restless, roaming. Like the robber girl, they cannot settle down.

"I cannot erase his traces from your body," the robber girl says.

"He took my virginity," Gerda confirms.

"I cannot erase his impression upon your heart."

"He broke it."

"I can never be first. I can never restore you." The robber girl rolls on her side, away from Gerda.

Gerda reaches out to touch her shoulder, then her buttock. "Do you love only broken things?" she says.

The robber girl turns and grins over her shoulder, then grabs

Gerda by the shoulders and kisses her until her lips bruise. "Yes," she replies. "I like broken things best of all. I have strong hands; they take to mending well."

"You cannot mend the break," Gerda replies, "but you can stitch the seam."

"I like girls with scars," the robber girl says, and bites Gerda's nipple. Gerda laughs and falls into her arms.

"If I find him, I will kill him," the robber girl says. "I will kill him for hurting you."

In bed one night she puts a knife against Gerda's throat. "This is Salome," she says. "Small but sharp. Say her name."

"Salome."

"Kiss her."

Gerda kisses the tip of the blade.

The robber girl draws the tip down Gerda's body, through the notch in her throat, along the breastbone. She stops at her heart. "Salome likes to slip between the ribs of her victims," the robber girl says. She pushes against Gerda's flesh until Gerda goes rigid. Then the robber girl pulls the knife down her abdomen, past her navel. Then she sheathes the blade.

She draws her razor. "My head was shaved once," she says, holding the edge near Gerda's ear. "As a punishment. They sought to make me ugly and ashamed. Ashamed of my wantonness, my free ways." The robber girl grins and bites Gerda's earlobe. Gerda squeaks. "But do you know what? I liked it. Would you like it? All your pretty golden locks shorn away? No more tangles in the morning. No more dubious looks from men." She wraps her hand in Gerda's hair and tugs. "No more convenient handhold. You could learn to be like me. I would teach you the names of my blades and the ways of my art. My art with men, and with women. The art of commanding a band of brigands. The art of robbing. The arts of love."

"If you did that," Gerda whispers, "I would no longer be your lover, but your daughter."

"Yes," the robber girl replies. "You would be sharp, like my blades."

"You like me soft," Gerda says. "You like me vulnerable."

"Yes," the robber girl says, and bites Gerda's neck. Gerda gasps and struggles to continue.

"I want to be your lover," she says. "Not your protégé."

"You will leave me," the robber girl says, and pushes Gerda's face into the blankets. She kicks Gerda's knees apart and works her hand inside. Her touch is rough.

Gerda persists. "Daughters leave too," she says. "Oh."

"I could make you a toy," the robber girl whispers fiercely in her ear, her hand working all of Gerda's tender parts. Gerda's moisture floods out of her and pools in the robber girl's palm. "A plaything. A possession. I could put a collar and a leash upon you, hitch you to my wagon like a pet. Use your tongue to please me, your dumb unspeaking tongue." The robber girl rocks her hips above Gerda's buttocks. "Then you would never leave me."

"But you would tire of me," Gerda says. Tears squeeze from the corners of her eyes. Her thighs clench around the robber girl's wrist.

The robber girl's wrist twists, finds the spot that makes Gerda cry in earnest now, in joy and in pain. Gerda howls her tormented pleasure into the dense night.

"You're right," the robber girl says as Gerda screams. "I would tire of a toy. I would break it. But I would never break you."

Later, after they have put the lamp out, the robber girl whispers into Gerda's ear. "You will leave me anyway, daughter or no. You will leave to find Kay."

Gerda says nothing. Her breathing is even and deep.

"I will give you a knife, to cut out his heart."

"To cut out the cold splinter, you mean," Gerda says. She rolls over and strokes her lover's cheek.

"As you choose," the robber girl says, and grasps her wrist.

She kisses it tenderly and lays back down again.

The night before they visit a metalsmith in town, the robber girl performs the ritual again. "This is Judith," she says, holding the blade to Gerda's lips. "Kiss it." Gerda obeys. "The real Judith cut off the head of a king," the robber girls says, her hand on Gerda's neck, pinning her to the sleeping pallet spread over the hard ground.

Gerda opens her mouth; the robber girl slips the blade inside. "Suck it," she says. Gerda obeys. The robber girls grinds her hips against Gerda's thigh; her mouth tears at Gerda's nipples, which are exposed to the cold air. Her mouth ravages Gerda's throat. Still Gerda sucks, eyes closed, her body held perfectly rigid and still. Finally, the robber girl withdraws the blade. Carefully, deliberately, she nicks Gerda's lower lip. Gerda flinches at the touch. The robber girl licks the blood away and smiles. She pricks herself, just above the notch of her collarbone, and presses Gerda's head against it so that Gerda may taste the salty flow as well. As Gerda licks and suckles like a puppy, the robber girl rummages between Gerda's thighs until she finds her wetness. Her touch is not gentle, but it causes Gerda to moan. "I would like to sheathe my blade in you," the robber girls whispers as she chews on Gerda's ear. "In your lovely wet hole, I would like to bury myself. Your slick scabbard. Would you take it for me? Would you sheathe my sharpness?"

"Yes," Gerda says with a gasp. The robber girl buries her hand in Gerda's moist space.

"If you are wet enough, soft enough, I cannot harm you," the robber girl breathes. "If you yield, I cannot conquer. You will melt away at my touch, I will leave you unscathed."

"No," Gerda says.

"You want me to scar you, to mar your pretty, soft flesh."

"Yes," Gerda says.

The robber girl points Judith at the spot below Gerda's navel, just above her mons. She pushes and pushes until the blood wells up around the tip of the blade.

"A sharp blade leaves a cut that heals," the robber girl says. "Only a dull blade marks." She removes the knife, smears the blood on her palm, and gives it to Gerda to lick clean. "I cannot mark you. I will pass through your life like a clean cut. It will sting; it will heal."

Gerda answers her by nuzzling the robber girl's breast, by allowing the girl to pull her hair, pinch her flesh, be as rough and as ruthless as she wishes with Gerda's body. She is left with bite marks, with scratches and bruises, with soreness and wetness. They are both left fulfilled.

In the morning the robber girl buys a knife for Gerda. It is a plain knife with a bone handle. The robber girl teaches her how to sharpen and care for it. Then she teaches Gerda how to fight with it. How to make a bold challenge and how to deftly slip it between someone's ribs. She spars with Gerda.

"Name the knife," the robber girl commands one day. "All knives have names."

"How do you know a knife's name?" Gerda says.

"Ask it."

Gerda thinks, *The blade is a tongue, it will speak to me.* But her knife is silent, though she asks every night.

She takes to whispering names to her knife in the darkness. "Athaliah, Zillah, Rahab, Tamar." The knife is still and cold in her hand.

When, one day, Gerda parries her strike and flips the knife out of the robber girl's hands, she laughs, grabs Gerda's wrist, and kisses it.

"You have bested me today," the robber girl says. "Now you must be on your way. Go. Find your lover Kay. Cut out his heart. Slit his queen's snowy throat. When you return to me, I will lick his blood from your hands. I will lick you clean."

Gerda sheaths her knife in her boot. "You will find another

broken thing to nurse to health, to mend," says Gerda sadly.

"No," says the robber girl. "I will wait for you to return. Not as my daughter, not as my toy, but as my equal. My fierce, wild lover. My vengeance-seeker. My murderess." She speaks the words as endearments. "I look forward to fearing your hands," she says. "As men fear mine."

"I don't fear your hands," says Gerda.

"And that is why you must go."

So she sets Gerda on the road, with a fierce kiss and a gift of gold, and a promise elicited to return. And it isn't until Gerda is well away from the camp that she realizes she never even learned the robber girl's name.

STEAM
KARIN KALLMAKER

Our breath clouds together in front of us. We reach our turn-around, a flat rock ideal for admiring the high country view. The rest of the world is far away. There's only the sound, above us, of trees moving in the cold wind. The air itself is like wine.

We catch our breath, then our kisses are like wine too. It's easy to feel intoxicated at this altitude. The look in your eyes leaves me dizzy. When you kiss my palm I don't try to hide the tremble that shoots up my arm.

You hear my gasp and your lips curve in a knowing smile. Your sparkling eyes gaze into mine, and I see your intent there. You aren't settling for kisses. You are going to have me, right here, because I love meeting your demands. Your ingenuity has always been sparked by my perpetual "Yes."

My jacket unzipped, you put your cold hands under my sweater. I protest, but you quickly move up, scooting closer. Your chilled fingers find my nipples, which respond to both the cold and your touch.

"Take that off, Beth," you say, your finger tweaking my bra strap.

Shivering with anticipation, I manage to wiggle out of the bra without taking off my sweater. You take the black lace from me. "Not exactly hiking gear."

"I wondered if you'd notice."

You shove the bra into your pocket. "I noticed that." Your fingertips close around my nipple, erect through the sweater. Your grasp is firm, and I moan when you twist, then let it slide between your fingers.

"Will you come for me?"

"Yes, Ellen, yes, darling," I answer. I feel the heat of you inside me already.

"When I give you permission."

My heart pounds louder. You're going to have me in this remote but exposed place. I feel my cunt swell at the thought of your touch, and I welcome surrender to your loving, always gentle control.

I gasp as you bare my breasts to the light of the sun and the cold of the air. My nipples are so hard I wish I could tease your clit with them. When your mouth covers them, I shudder. Your hand massaging between my legs feels so good too; many, many times I have come for you like this. A contraction begins in my cunt and I moan, spreading my legs.

"Don't come yet." Your teeth bite down, and I shake again. "Don't come, or I'll stop. You know you want more than one."

I tangle my hands in your hair, holding you against my breasts. Your teeth and tongue are biting, teasing, tugging, working them. I want to come against your hand.

"Please, let me...let me..."

"No." You raise your head. "Not yet."

My nipples quickly chill. They feel sore and raw and it makes my clit ache. Your hand is bumping against it, teasing me. I fight back a contraction. "Please...please. Anything, I'll do anything."

You reach out to tug the left one, hard. "Tell me."

Words spill out of me—all the things I know you love. I'm hoarse with panting. Every other word feels like *please*. Another tug. "Like...that dinner. Remember that night? I couldn't get enough of your pussy in my mouth? Like that, baby, please let me come for you, please—"

"Unzip your pants."

I unsnap the waist pack and fumble with my zipper, all the while trying not to give in to what your cold fingers on my hot nipples make me want to do. I push my jeans down; the rock is icy under my ass, making my cunt feel even hotter. I swear I see steam rising from between my legs.

You show me your chilled hand. "Are you hot enough?"

"Yes...please..."

Two fingers take me, then I can feel you add two more. I clench down against the cold inside me, then lift my ass to meet you. "Please....."

You lean in to kiss me, and I can tell how much you're enjoying my body. "Don't come yet. You feel so good to my hand, so good to fuck."

All of me seems wet now. "I can't hold it back, please."

Your other hand is still tormenting my nipples. I'm a frozen arc, steaming in the air, your fingers pumping into me. I hold myself there, moaning and whimpering. If I move or respond to what your fingers are doing to me I'll come without your permission, and you'll stop. I don't want you ever to stop being this way for me.

Waiting. Still. Time burns along every nerve.

"Beth? Look at me, darling."

You're there, swimming in my vision. You know every place to push inside me and what your fingers don't touch you stroke with your voice and your knowledge of me.

Your face is fierce with concentration. You take in every nuance of my body. I can't wait any longer. I can't hold it back. You say, just before the first big wave, "Come for me, come now."

My cry of release echoes off the trees, and my cunt tightens around your fingers. You anchor me to the rock and groan your pleasure at my frantic gyrations. I can't stop coming, gushing for you.

"I know you love this, just like this. Come when you want to, come when you have to, come for me again. Enjoy it all...come for me again. As hard as you can."

I am shaking in the cold air, driving myself onto you. I have more control now; I want to enjoy it for hours, the feel of you deep inside me. Then you say the one thing I can never resist from you.

"Please."

The pleasure surges up from the inside of my cunt to a burning fever at the top of my head, then ripples down my body in a wave of contractions that make you cry out as I do. Your grip on me is iron as I grind on your hand, groaning out my love for you.

I'm drained and dizzy. You've zipped my coat. I sit up, feeling parched, and gratefully drink from the water bottle. I realize my pants are soaked.

You open your backpack and hand me another pair of undies and jeans. I laugh as I take them. "Did you bring a pair for you?" My laughter fades as I put my hand between your legs. You are very hot and very wet. I can smell you.

You take my face in your hands and whisper, "They're in the car, baby. I want you to make me need them when we get there."

I hesitate before changing my clothes. "Maybe I should go behind a tree or something."

"If anyone's watching, they just saw me fuck you."

I blush hotly. "If we went into the trees, they wouldn't see you do it one more time."

Your hunger burns me as you reach out to open my jacket again.

A LITTLE HELP FROM MY FRIENDS

AURORA SPARK

There are some things I am perfectly capable of doing on my own, but there are other times when I need a little help from my friends. I was starting to realize that sex with my gorgeous girlfriend, Brooke, was one of the latter. Not that things weren't going well in the sack; in fact, they were going more than well. They were marvelous, with us contorting into all sorts of wonderful positions and bringing each other to incredible orgasms, but lately I was getting frustrated that I alone couldn't seem to do everything I wanted. I'd be leaning down on her, spreading her legs apart, pushing them down so her pussy strained toward me, then trying to press her vibrator against those gorgeous lips while keeping up the pressure and kissing her all over. I wanted to be everywhere at once, but being only human, I couldn't, and while she seemed perfectly happy with the screaming orgasms I'd provided her, I wanted more. I wanted to bring her to complete sensory overload, where she couldn't think or do anything but feel every sensation wafting through her gorgeous body. So I did what any self-respecting dyke would do—I recruited a committee, an experienced sex team to help me fuck my girlfriend in the best and brightest way I knew. They were all too willing, having secretly lusted after her since we all first met her at the local bar, where she was dancing away without a care in the world, to the beat of her own mind as much as that of the DJ. We met in secret to go over the details, and because I'd never even so much as hinted at the possibility of a threesome, I knew she'd be totally surprised.

So there we were, splayed across her luscious queen-size bed. I had her hold her legs in front of her while I teased her by stroking along her very wet opening; that's one of the best things about her, she's almost always wet, spurring me on to find new ways to fuck her senseless. I worked three fingers into her and could see her straining and stretching, wanting to make the most of this digital invasion. Then I reached for the dildo lying next to us, the big black one that was our favorite. I lubed it up and slowly worked it into her, and in practically no time it was all the way inside. "You do that so well, don't you? You dream about being on your back like this for me, spreading your legs, letting me fill your pussy with whatever I want? All for me, right, Brooke?"

"Yes," she moaned, "I love you." And then it was my turn to melt, to almost turn into putty, but I caught myself.

I leaned over her, looming over her body while continuing to fuck her, keeping up the dildo's in-out motion as if it were simply another day at the lesbian sex factory, even though we could both tell what every stroke was doing to her. "Well, my darling, I have a little surprise for you. Because I know how badly you need to get fucked and that you'll do anything to get there, I've invited some friends over to help me. You're just such a handful for me with all your twisting and teasing and struggling, and they were kind enough to offer their assistance to help me keep you in line. Isn't that sweet?" She looked surprised and confused and a little uncertain, and I smiled. I liked to keep her on her toes, so to speak. I fished out the velvety purple blindfold and fastened it around her head—we were both more relaxed when she couldn't see my every move. I tied her wrists above her head; her whole body looked elongated, perfectly, gracefully bound. I slid the toy out of her and replaced it with my thumb—the short digit teasing her with its only slight effectiveness—while I motioned for my friends to enter the room.

I'd known that Zoe and Felicia thought Brooke was hot, so I wasn't surprised when they jumped at the chance to find out exactly how hot she was. And Zoe was an even meaner top than I was, from what I'd seen at parties and overheard from her day-after bragging. She was just itching to get the chance to sink her claws into my girl. And secretly I was looking forward to getting a glimpse of her in action.

I'd already told them what they were expected to do; it was time to get down to business. I leaned forward and kissed Brooke deeply, and she practically melted into my body, offering up all of herself with her lips, wrapping her legs around me, drawing me into her delicious body. So delicious that I almost got caught up in her enough to send my friends away…but instead I pulled back and looked at my girl: totally, beautifully helpless, willing to do anything I said.

I got up and silently opened the door, beckoning Zoe and Felicia inside. When she saw Brooke all trussed up, Zoe got that cute little wicked grin she gets; she'd heard about some of our exploits but had never seen us in action. She grabbed Felicia's hand and darted across the room, eager to get to work on my girl. I sat back for a moment and watched as she traced her slightly elongated nails along Brooke's tender skin, waiting for the moment when Brooke would realize that it wasn't me touching her, but some unknown person. Brooke's mouth formed an "O" when those nails started to dig into her; mine were always bitten to the quick, and she knew it. Felicia used Brooke's open mouth to her advantage, leaning forward and swaying her voluptuous tits back and forth against her open orifice. Brooke stuck out her tongue to try to get at them, without even knowing whose nipples she was trying to feed from; I smiled proudly as

I watched my gorgeous slut of a girlfriend do what came naturally for her.

I let Zoe and Felicia play with her for a while, Zoe finding out just how wet Brooke can get when she's turned on. I reached my hand into my own panties, pressing urgently against my clit as I watched Zoe's fingers disappear into Brooke's pussy, watched as she fucked her in exactly the same way I had while Brooke's mouth was clamped firmly around Felicia's breast, suckling away like a baby.

I'd had enough fun on the sidelines and decided to reclaim my territory. I placed my hand on the back of Zoe's neck in a proprietary move that I knew would send darts of lust traipsing along her spine, an added bonus to our adventure. When she moaned, I pinched that sensitive spot, then tugged gently on it, beckoning her away from Brooke. I whispered in Zoe's ear—though Brooke was probably too far gone with her new toy of Felicia's breast to hear me anyway—"I need your expertise, madame," and Zoe, bitch goddess extraordinaire, known to shut down rooms with her steely stare, became putty in my hands, ready and willing to do exactly as I commanded. I also managed to grab Felicia away from Brooke's mouth, though that took a little bit more effort. I indicated where I wanted them—on either side of Brooke, to stretch her legs out just so by tugging on them. They each understood and went to work, putting just enough pressure on her legs so I could feel the tension in her thighs, perfectly taut. I pinched the sensitive skin there, and she arched her back. I stroked along her slit, loving that she was even wetter than she'd been before, then held open her clit's hood as Zoe and Felicia instinctively pressed down a little harder, leaving me with a lovely vision of Brooke's perfect cunt. It was wonderful having my very own human restraints to hold down my girl, who always tried to stay as still as possible but would involuntarily jerk away at the most important moment, nearly ruining everything. I loved that she got so excited, but I wanted to help her push past that urge to move away when things felt like they were about to get too overwhelming. And with Zoe and Felicia's help, I was doing just that as I held her clit open and tapped it with my fingers, causing her to let out a little cry. Then I pinched her clit as I slammed three fingers into her. They slid in perfectly, as if they were made to fit inside her pussy, that cunt that I knew so well it felt like a second home.

But this time, something about it was different, and I marveled at having both hands free to work her the best way I knew how. My friends were now moving in sync, making her do little stretches, pushing and then easing up just slightly and then pushing again so her legs were constantly tugging, pulling her pussy nice and tight; I could feel the muscles straining as I stroked her. It was the same gorgeous cunt I'd been fucking for a year, and yet suddenly it all felt different and wonderful, the same girl in a new body, and I knew she felt it too by the way she looked, flushed and alert and overwhelmed, ready to break my hand in half at any moment with the force of her arousal. I slithered along, sliding another finger into her while pinching the jiggly flesh of her stomach. Even now, with my friends' assistance, her body was still too vast an expanse of gorgeousness to take in, to devour all by myself. I wanted to lick every inch, to bite along her neck, her inner arm, her stomach and thighs, all those tender, pale spots that so often get overlooked for the more pulsing, bold ones, bodily wallflowers just waiting for someone to ask them to dance. I shoved my fingers into her and then dove for her clit, licking and sucking greedily, loving the light coating of stubble that abraded my lips. I lapped at her clit, its perfect combination of hard and soft, wet and seeming to melt underneath my tongue, yet firmly standing upright, demanding its due. Brooke's body was a constant whirl of arousal, a tempting amusement park ride for one very lucky customer. Or in this case, three.

I could tell that the sight of Brooke splayed out in all her erotic glory was doing a number on Zoe and Felicia, who were licking their lips and murmuring lightly under their breaths about what they'd do if they were in my position. I fumbled under the bed and produced Brooke's favorite vibrator, the one that can send her into convulsions with just its whirring noise. I smiled as I pulled it onto the bed, grateful for the mercy of the blindfold to hide my eagerness to finish her off. From the neck up, she could be a lady of the manor getting her beauty sleep, but from the neck down, all covered in sweat and bite marks, piercings and promise, she was clearly a wanton hussy.

I leaned forward and bit her outstretched lower lip, suckling it. "Are you ready, baby? I hope you're having fun; I hope you're going to show the others exactly how much of a slut you are." I still had one hand inside her and felt the jolt at her favorite "s" word. "You don't care who knows, do you, now? You wouldn't really care if I had a camera crew in here taping your every move, because it feels so good, isn't that right? Because you'll do whatever I want you to, right, baby?" She let out the smallest of whimpers, and I slammed my fingers into her hard. "What was that? You can talk to me, sweetie," I said, all sugar-voiced and gentle, at odds with the frantic fucking I was treating her to.

"Yes, Mel, yes, I want everything you want to do to me. I don't care, I love you, I need you, and you feel so fucking good—" I cut her off, her rushed, anguished words all I needed to hear. I kissed her on the cheek and then got back into position, slapping her firm thighs once each, making the paleness morph into a splotchy red, just because they looked so tempting. I pressed the head of the whirring toy down against her clit and simply held it there while my hand kept working her from inside, then teased the vibe back and forth over her slippery entrance. All three of us starting to move faster, and Felicia even began pinching her upper arm, along the inseam, that delicate, pain-prone spot, before simply moving her big hand all across Brooke's chest and neck, trying to find the most deserving area for her attentions. She landed on her breast, cupping it and then scraping her nails over it. When Brooke jerked around, twisting her whole body, Felicia zoomed in, twisting her nipple, pulling it toward her and then the other way around before slapping her breast, spanking it like it was the ass of the most naughty child ever. Brooke's body seemed to almost levitate at that, her hips rising and bringing my fingers with them.

It was time. I cranked up the vibrator to its highest level, catching her by surprise as it sped to life, the powerful surge tingling my hand as I pressed it into her clit. I could practically see the vibrations traveling through her body, and I know we all felt the heightened crackle of energy in the room, the power being pumped through her limbs and especially through her cunt. She started to shake, almost violently, like a rocket poised for takeoff. She had reached the critical moment I'd been waiting for, when she lost all control of herself and simply let her body take over. "That's a girl, you know what to do," I coaxed, and watched her squirm under the ropes, begging for something she couldn't articulate, her moans and screams pleading for me to stop and keep going all at once. Zoe and Felicia stretched her out even further, then brought her legs forward, pressing them toward her chest, pushing them together so they hugged the fast-moving toy. All four of us bore down, enervated by our common goal. Brooke squirmed mightily, each twist of her hips sending rockets of sensation everywhere, until she was thrashing so hard I wondered if we'd be able to contain her. She screamed, then bit her lip and scrunched up her face, and I knew it was time. I pushed the toy fully against her and slammed my fingers into her, feeling the vibrator's movements from within. It only took a few seconds before she screamed, louder than I'd ever heard her, her legs trembling, her pussy clenching around me. She took deep, noisy breaths, tears leaking from her eyes. Zoe and Felicia gradually lowered her legs, easing her down as I shut off the toy and slipped out of her before undoing her blindfold and bonds.

She reached for me, pulling me to her so tightly I almost

couldn't breathe. We stayed in that embrace for a long minute before she opened her arms further, welcoming Zoe and Felicia into our love circle. I'd gotten a lot of help from my friends and so had Brooke. My eyes twinkled as I pulled the girls close. Maybe someday soon I'd get to return the favor.

VIRTUE
AMIE M. EVANS

I wait. Patience is a virtue.

I wait because I have no choice but to wait. I'm tied with very white rope to this damn wooden-plank seesaw. Even if I wasn't bound, I'd probably wait anyway. My blood is too thick with lust for me to go anywhere, but that doesn't matter to me now. What matters is I'm bound by my hands and feet—not to mention the neat little trick she did on the rest of my body—to this seesaw contraption in her homemade dungeon, and I am alone. What matters isn't that I'd be here waiting if she hadn't bound me, but that she *did* and then she left me—almost upside-down—alone. I feel like Gulliver, only my Lilliputians used industrial-strength rope.

She did a wonderful job with the ropes—very intricate knots that are secured in a webbed pattern over most of my body. They are too tight for me to work my way out of, but not tight enough to inflict any circulation problems. And, yes, I tried to get out of the ropes. That's why I'm here—alone. I'm a bad bottom. Well, "bad bottom" are not the words she used. "Undisciplined, ungrateful, bratty bitch," I believe were the words she used. But that was *after* she tied me up.

She told me to lie on the seesaw. It was flat like a bed then, so I did. She attached my arms at the wrists to metal D rings on both sides by my hips. She then worked the ropes crisscrossing my body to my feet. There's a split in the middle of the board at the bottom so the ropes can be wound individually around each leg, and there is also a hole, so my butt is exposed. My legs are spread apart and she has access to me from the front or rear. Little D rings line either side of the leg boards like fishing-pole eyes to guide the ropes. She anchored the rope on either side of my feet in big D rings. She then took another rope and secured my upper body, creating a really cool web design in the middle of my stomach where the two ropes come together. I can't move—well, I can move my head from side to side and up a little, and I flap my hands and make little circles with my feet. It is a wonderful piece of bondage equipment. Sounds like a dream for a bondage nut like me. So far, so good.

We are in a relationship—not a modern open relationship or a traditional S/M relationship, but a love relationship. We have S/M sex, but we don't live by a relationship contract. Since we are in a monogamous relationship, all of the sex we have is with each other. We play all kinds of sex games—bondage, role playing, and plain old vanilla sex. Tonight I was to be her captive and she was to be the evil, nasty pirate to break in the new toy she made—the Plank.

So, what am I doing here alone, tied up?

She took out her knife and cut my shirt open. She slowly licked her fingers then pulled the left demicup of my red lace bra down to expose my nipple. She ran her wet fingertips over it, causing it to become erect; then she pinched the other nipple hard through the red lace. I was wet, wondering what the evil, nasty pirate would do to me. The options were mind-blowing.

Now, well, now I'm here by myself and I feel like part of the sick joke we heard over the weekend at the party. I cannot remember who told it, but I am sure it was a top. It had to have been a top, since no bottom in her right mind would have found it funny.

It goes like this: "A masochist is bound by the world's greatest sadist. The sadist started to leave and the masochist said, 'Hey, you didn't even touch me. I thought you were the world's greatest sadist.' The sadist says, 'And what do you want me to do to you more than anything in the world?' The masochist, excited by what the evening could hold said, 'To have you touch me and work your magic. It doesn't matter what you do, just touch me.' The sadist says, 'I am the world's greatest sadist' and left the room."

Laughter from all the tops.

After the evil pirate excited my nipples, she went directly to my wet cunt. She let just the tip of her finger probe into the opening, twirling it around my outer wall, just inside my vagina, then plunging it in deep, only to pull out to the very entrance and stroke again. Maddening. But still, at this point, I believed the possibilities were endless. What I wanted was a good old-fashioned fisting. I would have settled for a fucking, but I wanted a fisting. You know the kind where once she's inside, she fist-fucks you like your insides are part of a butter churn. Then she puts her mouth to your clit and you come before she even finishes the first lick.

The pirate slid her wet fingers out of me and pulled my clit-hood up while lightly teasing me. I moaned and tried to move my hips but couldn't. This is where everything imploded. Yep, this is where I made my first big mistake. I don't know who she's been having lunch with, she's never been such a touchy top before. All I said was, "Fist me," and I even said "please."

Instead of a groan and her fingers in my cunt, she stopped touching my clit and walked away. At first I thought she was getting lube. I should have known it would be close at hand on the toy table. She usually thinks ahead. I strained to see but couldn't. Then I felt the riding crop come down quickly on my thigh—*whack, whack*. It wasn't until she spoke that I realized I was really in trouble.

So the pirate called me an undisciplined, bratty, ungrateful bitch.

I cooed, "I just wanted to feel you inside me."

Whack, whack—again with the riding crop, which was all right by me but wasn't getting me fisted. That's when she went on her tirade about patience and virtue. She looked awfully cute yelling at me. Telling me what a spoiled-rotten bottom I was, telling me how I didn't know how good I had it. Yelling up a storm about how I didn't know my place, how demanding it was to top, and how selfish I was. I believe the word "insatiable" was used in a negative context. She was awfully cute, until she said she was going to teach me patience once and for all.

I felt the gears on the side of the seesaw plank click, and I was upside-down in a second. Then I saw her making her way to the door. It was that moment that I realized I was in trouble for real.

She turned toward me with her hand on the knob and said, "You'll stay there until I think you've learned patience." She was still yelling, but she wasn't cute anymore.

OK, so my second mistake was yelling after her through the closing door, "Does this mean you are *not* going to fist me?"

Yeah, definitely a mistake. Illustrating her point, and making her just that much more angry, probably increased my waiting time by an easy 15 minutes. But I couldn't help it. Of course I knew she wasn't going to fist me, but the words just tumbled out of my mouth.

Patience is not a virtue I care about at all. I've had time to think about this—being bound to a plank and left alone gives you time to think. I don't care if good things come to those who wait; I don't want to wait. I've always received good things, and it isn't because I waited. I believe if you don't ask you shan't receive. I believe life is too short—so why wait? While those aren't virtues, they are good mottoes to live by, and I've lived well by them—at least until now.

Virtue? If I had virtue, would I be here bound to her seesaw pirate plank in the first place?

According to the Bettie Page wall clock, she's been gone an hour and 20 minutes. I have not been able to come up with what the other virtues are. Could there be just this one virtue? Is it possible that only *one* virtue exists and I am unable to master it? I *was* able to come up with all seven of the deadly sins. And I now have to pee. I am no longer as angry as a wet cat, but I haven't been able to figure out how to turn the tables back to my advantage. Really, I don't understand what I did that made *her* so angry.

The doorknob turns and she enters the room. Finally, but I still don't have a plan for how to get myself out of this. She walks over to me, flips the switch, and cranks me upright. I decide I'll just be quiet and try to be humble. She looks into my eyes, and I look down, as if I am ashamed of my behavior and understand my sins. She walks over to the table and selects something that I cannot see and lubes it up. She steps back over near me and holds it in front of my face. It's a huge butt plug. She walks behind me and spreads my ass apart and jams it into my anus. I groan as the big balled-out part spreads my hole before it is swallowed. I try not to move or make too much noise. I can be good. I'll prove it. She pulls it out again with a pop, and I grunt as the mixture of pain and pleasure goes through me. She pushes it back inside me and turns it. I try to wiggle. It stings and feels too big. I'm used to something much smaller.

"Stop," she says, "Daddy is very mad." I obey her. Now that she is no longer the evil, nasty pirate, but Daddy, I might be able to get out of this after all. She strokes my face, then heads for the door.

"Wait. Please, Daddy," I say in my best little-girl voice.

"What?" her voice is still harsh.

"I have to pee." I whine.

I see a smile on her face, "Patience is a virtue. You will have to hold it."

My mouth drops open, but she walks back to me. There is still hope of getting out of this mess. Her hand touches my cunt, and she slips a finger inside me. She moves it, slowly tickling and stroking me.

"Don't pee while I am gone. Do you hear me?"

I nod.

"Oh," she walks to the table. "Drink this. You've been in here over an hour."

She holds the glass of water to my lips and makes me drink all 12 ounces of it; then she leaves.

Sadist. Rotten sadist. This time I don't yell any witty, sarcastic comments after her.

The butt plug pushes on my insides, making me feel I have to pee even worse. I no longer care if there are any other virtues besides patience. I no longer care why she is mad at me. All I can think about is peeing. My clit is hot and tingling. I want her to touch me. I make a vow that I'll never let her put me into bondage again—ever. I swear I'll never let her fist me again—ever. I set my mind to thinking up ways to torment this sadist of mine. I'll suggest we open our relationship up, but just to men. I don't want to have sex with men, but it'll make this jealous Scorpio crazy that I am suggesting it. I'll buy tickets to every women's folk music performance this year, and I'll make her take me. She hates women's folk music. I'll rearrange the dresser drawers on a weekly basis so she cannot find any of her clothing. She thinks I am a brat now—just wait.

It has been half an hour since she left for the second time when she returns again. I can barely hold my pee anymore. She walks around to the back of the plank and withdraws the butt plug. I can hear her strapping-on, then feel the head of the cock push against my asshole.

"Now don't piss while I am fucking you." She pushes into me deep with one firm stroke.

The pressure pushes against my full bladder, and the sensation of bursting scares and turns me on. Her cock slips in and out of me in even strokes. I struggle to hold my water in and not succumb to the painful pleasure she is giving me. After about 20 strokes she stops and withdraws her cock and reinserts a new, freshly lubed butt plug. This one is tiny, without the balled-out section.

"It feels like it is going to fall out, Daddy," I say as humbly as possible.

"Well," she pulls it out and works it in and out of my asshole. "It's pretty straight up and down, and I lubed it up good." She thrusts it in all the way. "Better hold on to it. If it falls out, you're in trouble."

I clinch my ass muscles to hold it. It still feels like it is not going to stay in place. But that's the point, isn't it?

She walks in front of me. Her body is long and lean and almost without curves. She has on a pair of tight black pants tucked into high black leather boots and a too-tight tank top with a barbed-wire design across her breasts. She has removed the white, blousy pirate shirt and head scarf. She must be mad, she loves pirates.

"Have we learned patience?" she asks as she runs her fingers down my face and neck, stopping on the nipple of my right breast.

What I really want to say is "Fuck you," but instead I say in a little voice, "Yes, Daddy."

I feel defiant. I think about pissing all over the floor. I don't, though. since she'll probably make me wait at least two hours for such an open act of insubordination. I concentrate on not peeing and holding the tiny butt plug in place instead of on smart-ass remarks and disrespectful actions.

"I don't think you have. I think you are a bratty bitch, but I know you are smart." She pinches my nipple. "I know you know exactly what I want to hear." She runs the fingers of her other hand down my face and neck to my left nipple. "I don't think you have learned anything." She pinches both nipples, then pulls my breasts together.

I moan and attempt to squirm as she licks the valley she has just created between my breasts. All I can think about is the strong sensation of having to pee, which is becoming increasingly more erotic, and the fear that the butt plug, which I can barely feel, is about to fall to the floor.

"Daddy, I…"

She pinches my nipples harder. When she releases them, it feels as if she has ripped them off.

"Did Daddy ask you anything?" She walks to the table, returning with a medium-size vibrating dildo in her hand.

"Now, Daddy has a bratty, selfish little girl." She slowly pulls the dildo in and out of my wet cunt. "Don't let that butt plug fall, or I'll *never* give my selfish girl another one to play with."

She strokes again. I can feel the strong sensations of pleasure, the urge to pee only increasing it. The need to keep everything clenched, to keep everything inside, is magnifying the intensity of the whole affair. She works the dildo in and out of my cunt while she kneels in front of me. She places her face against my leg and her free arm lightly rests across my lower stomach.

"Daddy wants you to come. You want to make Daddy happy, right?"

"Yes, Daddy, but…"

"But what?" She continues to stroke.

"I have to pee, Daddy." There is, I hope, just the right amount of whine in my voice.

She laughs, then in a low voice says, "Daddy knows." She flips the vibrator switch on and begins to stroke fast and hard pushing against the front wall of my vaginal canal. "Don't let that butt plug go when you come, girly."

Her thrusts increase in strength, and she turns the vibrator on high. My whole body feels electrified. I know I'm close to coming, and I know when I come I'll piss all over her and lose my tiny butt plug. She knows it too. I moan and move my hips the small amount the ropes allow. I feel her tongue against my swollen clit.

"Daddy, I am going to come," I gasp in between breaths.

Without stopping her skilled tongue strokes on my clit, she pulls the vibrator out of me and moves her face under my cunt. Then pushes just a little on my lower stomach. I come hard and strong. The spasms free the butt plug, and my pee showers over her face, running down her upper body. She laps at the stream of piss and the inside of my wet cunt. When the orgasm subsides, she stands up and cuts the ropes with her knife. I collapse forward into her arms. She picks me up like a virgin bride and carries me to the bed. She allows me to rest a few minutes while she strokes my hair and face before she stands up and sits on the chair a few feet from the bed.

"Daddy's little girl has been very bad today." I half sit up and look at her.

"She doesn't seem to want to keep the toys Daddy gives her. She doesn't seem to have any patience. And," she cocks her eyebrow at me, "she peed herself."

I smile at her.

"Now she's smiling like Daddy's joking." I turn my smile into a pout and she smiles back at me. "Come here."

I get up from the bed and walk over to her. She points to her lap, "Over Daddy's knees, little girl."

I look at her eyes and can see the playfulness in them despite her tone. "But, Daddy," I whine and stomp my foot.

"Come on, now, don't make Daddy any angrier than she already is."

I position myself over her lap so my butt is in the air. She softly rubs her hand over each of my cheeks then lightly pats them as she says, "This will hurt me more than it does you, but Daddy's got to teach you a lesson."

Her hand comes down in a whack, clean and sharp, on my ass. First one cheek then the next. First the plump top then the hypersensitive underside. I can feel the burning and stinging in each cheek as it becomes red; I know I am wet between my legs. After about 20 whacks she stops.

"Are you going to be a good little girl?"

"Yes, Daddy." Even I believe me at this point.

"Are you going to stop being selfish and bratty and be thankful for what Daddy gives you?"

I nod my head yes.

"Daddy cannot hear you."

"Yes, Daddy."

"All right. Daddy has a present for you." I can feel her reaching over to the toy table next to us. Her hand separates my red ass cheeks, and the familiar cool wetness of lube hits my asshole. "Daddy understands that the toy was too small for her queen-size brat. Here's a bigger one for you to play with."

I can feel the head slip into my ass, then a surge of pain and pleasure mixes with the sensation of stretching. "It doesn't want to go in. Be a good girl now and take it all for Daddy."

It feels like it must be at least four inches wide; but these things are impossible to judge when they are being inserted into you. I concentrate on relaxing my muscles and letting her slide it in. She pushes on its base, and it slips forward. I moan as my clit tingles and my asshole burns. It is in.

"Now the wide part, baby girl, let it in."

It isn't in? I gasp, then suck air, but don't say anything. I can feel the light pressure she is applying to the base, and I can feel my body resisting her invasion. I groan, but dare not complain. The balled-out section clears my stretched opening and slides forward as my asshole closes around the thinner base. The pain is unbearable, the pleasure incredible. It feels like my ass is stretched completely open. My clit dances with excitement. *Whack!* Her hand hits my ass again.

"Good girl. Go lay on the bed on your back at the edge the way Daddy likes you." I slide off of her lap onto my knees on the floor. I struggle to rise from my knees. The plug makes each movement a mixture of uncomfortable fullness and exciting pleasure. Walking is difficult and intense. I feel as if I could come again if she just touches my clit with one stroke of her finger or tongue.

I position myself on the bed on my back with my ass at the edge and my feet on the floor. I open my legs. She stands over me and says, "Daddy wants to fist your asshole, little girl, that's what that plug is for. You need to be able to let Daddy in that hole too."

I moan, excited and scared by her words and her desires. She kneels on the floor in front of me, licking both of my inner thighs then running her tongue up from my knee to the top of my inner thigh.

"Daddy is going to give you another present, since you've been such a remorseful little girl."

I feel the cool lube dripping onto my clit then her fingers spreading it around. Three lubed fingers plunge into my wet cunt, working in and out, then a fourth is added. With my asshole so full, four fingers feel immense. I rock my hips in rhythm to her strokes. The butt plug moves a little with the rocking, stimulating and increasing the intensity. I feel as if I am going to explode any second. All of her fingers are inside of me now, and her knuckles are begging to be allowed as well.

"Daddy," I softly say, testing what leeway she'll give me. I am truly afraid I will rip open if she pushes into me and excited about her fisting me with this mammoth plug in place.

"Yes, Daddy's here." Her voice is soft, soothing.

"I don't think...I can't."

"Ssh, little girl, this is what you wanted." She pushes a little with her hand. "You can take it all." She pushes a little more. "Let Daddy into your wet, hot cunt."

She starts to push again, and this time I bear down to meet her. There is extreme pressure, a rush of fear that I will rip, and then her knuckles pop through. We moan together. Her fist is completely inside my cunt. The thin layer of skin between the vaginal canal and the anus is pulled so taunt from my double full-ness, I am sure she can feel the shape of the butt plug with her hand. I take a deep breath. I am consumed by the sensation that my asshole and cunt have merged into one.

She slowly starts to work her fist inside me. I am overcome by the multitude of sensations, the total feeling of fullness, and her taking me so completely. She pumps her fist inside and works my clit with the thumb of her free hand. Stroking and pumping until I come.

My muscles clamp down hard on her hand and the butt plug. A shock wave goes through my whole body. I clench down, my hips thrust forward on their own. My whole body is seized with tension, then with release. When the tremors are gone, she withdraws her fist from my cunt and shifts my weak, shaking body onto the bed. She leaves the butt plug in place and wraps her arms around me, holding me to her chest.

"Now has Daddy's little girl learned patience?"

"Yes, Daddy." I snuggle into her chest. She kisses the top of my head. I listen to her heart beating until it returns to a normal rate. I hear her breathing becoming even and feel her muscles relax. The rhythm of sleep is in her body; her breathing is steady and her muscles twitch randomly.

"Daddy?" I ask, not sure if she is still awake.

"Umm, yes," she says, groggy, almost asleep.

"Again, Daddy, again!" I tug at her, shaking her to wake up.

A SIGN
ALEX BEAL

It was summer in south Florida and my condo complex was empty except for a few year-round tenants. The new tenant was with friends when I first saw her at the beach—they were all signing. I am a hearing child of deaf parents, so her signing caught my attention. She was about my age, I guessed, with shoulder-length brown hair streaked with red, a tattoo around her neck, and a gorgeous body. I learned later that her name is Vanessa.

We became lovers. It started one evening when I let myself into my condo, pulled on a pair of shorts and a tank-top, grabbed a beer and some pretzels, and went to relax on my cool and secluded back balcony. After a few minutes I heard breathy, muffled sounds coming from a balcony below—there was no mistaking it; they were sounds of pleasure. My curiosity piqued, I casually leaned over the rail of the balcony and looked down. One story below and to the right was Vanessa, head thrown back over the railing of her balcony, the tattoo around her neck being tongued by a boyish blond, who was making her way down Vanessa's body, which was covered, as far as I could see, only by a light blue silk shirt with most of the buttons undone. It was pretty clear to me where the blond was headed. Feeling somewhat like a voyeur, I thought for a second that perhaps I should move away, but my clit was telling me to stay. So I did. Vanessa was bracing herself with both hands stretched out behind her on the balcony railing, her fingers gripping the outer edges of the smooth wood, her shirt pulled tight up against her breasts where it was still buttoned. Her right leg was balanced on a patio chair, slightly blocking my view of the blond's destination.

With the blond's head between her legs, Vanessa moaned loudly, her mouth gaping open. She drew in a quick breath, opened her eyes, and saw me watching her. I was surprised and a little worried, but too invested now to move, so I tipped my beer toward her and smiled. She smiled back and, surprisingly, held my gaze. I watched her orgasm, and she watched me watch. As the blond was moving her mouth back up toward Vanessa's, I signed to her, "That was lovely, thank you." She smiled and winked. I left the deck to find my vibrator.

The next evening after work I changed quickly, grabbed a beer, and sat on my balcony hoping for a sign of Vanessa. Just as I was finishing my second beer, I heard a sliding-glass door open below. I went to the railing and looked down to find Vanessa looking up at me. She signed to me "Hi. Did you like what you saw yesterday?" I signed back, "You were gorgeous. I had to leave to get my vibrator!" She grinned, and I could see the laughter in her eyes, but I signed to her anyway, "I hope I haven't offended you, I just couldn't take my eyes off you." "I'm glad you didn't," she replied, "I enjoyed it."

She asked me then, "Want to play again?" I saw no sign of the blond, so I asked, "Are you alone?" She playfully looked over the railing to the balcony below her as if she were expecting someone to be there, then smiled and nodded yes, she was alone. We stood there looking at each other for a few moments until she abruptly signed, "Touch yourself." She didn't have to ask twice, I was already wet thinking about the day before, so I reached down, unzipped my shorts, and found my clit, slippery and hard. Vanessa climbed onto the wide balcony railing and straddled it. She was wearing a skirt, with no underwear. She reached down to the hem of her skirt and pulled it up her thigh until her hand met her crotch. She ran her finger through her wetness and dragged it slowly up to her clit.

She swung her left leg up onto the patio chair, leaned back onto the railing, and I could see she was dripping wet. She sat up then and signed to me, "I'm so wet...do you have a dildo?" I said yes, went inside and quickly chose three, and ran back to show her. She picked the medium-size pink one and asked me to throw it down to her. "What if I miss?" I asked her. I was worried that my dildo would land on Mrs. Simpson's collection of aloe plants. Her eyes lit up and she simply signed, "Don't." I leaned way over the railing and tossed it to her. She caught it with one hand, smiled at me, and rubbed the tip on her crotch. Then she leaned back on the railing and started fucking herself with my dildo. I nearly came right then and there, but I wanted to watch her more, so I moved my hand from my clit and twisted my nipples instead.

I couldn't believe how hot she was; I couldn't believe this was really happening. She was circling her clit with one hand, fucking herself with my dildo with the other, and watching me play with my nipples. I could tell she was getting close to orgasm by the intense look in her eyes as she watched me. I wanted to come with her and I signed so. I slid my hand back down my pants and waited for her to give me a sign. The muscles in her arms and her neck were rippling and when she grabbed the back of the patio chair, closed her eyes, and opened her mouth, I knew she was coming.

Vanessa was still holding the chair and my dildo inside her when I finished. I leaned over the railing, my shorts halfway down my legs, to get a better look at her. She looked up at me and sat up. She eased my dildo out, coyly stood it dripping up on the deck railing between her legs and signed, "Do you want this back now?" I laughed and signed, "Keep it...for another time." She got down off the railing and disappeared for a minute. I stayed where I was. I wanted to ask her out. She came back with a beer, and pants, and I signed, "Will you have dinner with me tonight?" She said yes. Now we share a balcony.

MONKEY BUSINESS
ERICA MORGAN

I don't remember now if it was my late aunt's idea or mine, but opening a gourmet coffeehouse wasn't a good one, that's for sure. And getting the damn thing willed to me after she died was a fate worse than death. Every day customers flooded into the Java Joint, taking a chunk of my self-esteem with them when they left. Name another job where a good tip depends on some fucking rain forest in Central Africa or South America. Simple waitressing, where the server's biggest concern is service, was a huge step up from the expected explanations of why Kenyan coffee was so strong and black or why this week's house blend was more cinnamony than last week's. Shit. Like I care. And beyond that irritation came the taxes. Fuck the IRS in their rosey-red pucker.

"Can I get a chocolate chip muffin and a house blend to go?" the female voice behind me asked. The unexpected sound of another voice—I'd thought I was alone—caused me to turn quickly from the cappuccino machine, spilling a double espresso on the tiled back counter. My cleaning rag gave the mess a quick wipe as I stared up into blue-gray eyes that melted me from heart to clit and back. Some round-trip ticket.

"Coming right up!" I shot back, sticking my 36C tits out as far as I could under my much-stretched T-shirt. I might hate the coffee business, but a little monkey business was something else entirely. "Cream and sugar's over on the coffee bar," I said, gesturing across the room.

"Thanks," she said, grinning. Shooting a quick look at the backside of her jeans as she turned to pour half-and-half into the hot brown liquid started my blood pumping. Pumping, hell. Rocketing through my 28-year-old veins as if I was the space shuttle Challenger was more like it.

Bang! Bang! The sound of construction on the business space next door could be deafening. Nothing positive could possibly come from noise like that. I wanted to grab that construction worker and ram that hammer where only the brave would find it.

"Sounds like a bomb going off," she said, looking out to the street.

"The landlord's crew has been getting that space next door ready for a bagel place going in. Just what I need—another place selling coffee on the block," I said wearily.

"Oh, maybe they won't be selling the same kind. I'm new here, by way of Albuquerque. Barb's the name," she said extending her hand, locking eyes with mine. "Yours?"

"Kelly. Gonna be around for a while?" *Oh, lady, I hope so,* I thought. Maybe my luck was beginning to change.

"Here to stay. I'm starting a business real close to here," she said, momentarily glancing away. "So, any place a lonely gal can meet people around here? Maybe a little women's bar?"

"Yeah, and if you'd like some company, I'd like that too," I added boldly. "You probably think I'm kinda forward, but I could use a night out myself."

Barb smiled warmly. "Well, you just may have a different idea of how to party than I do. I'm gay," she explained, waiting a beat for a reaction. "And believe in being up front about it. Now, does that change your mind any about showing me around?" She didn't have long to wait for my answer, since the question was the opening I'd been hoping for.

"Not at all, sister-friend. Looks like we're kindred spirits. Great place called Lizzy's over on 54th. Drink specials and a dance floor. What else could you ask for?" I quipped.

Barb laughed, glancing down at her coffee mug. "Hey, that's a leading question. We'll talk about that later," she said, her gaze wandering below my waist. "What time does your slave-drivin' boss take off your shackles?"

"I let *myself* off in 30 minutes," I returned, scribbling my address on a piece of torn napkin. "This is my place," I said, handing the paper across the counter. "Just around the corner at the first light," motioning to the right. "Not at all hard to find. How about 7?"

"Sounds good. I'll be there." Barb hugged several notebooks and the muffin sack against her black leather vest, gathering papers from the table. "See ya!"

I watched her walk to the curb, open the driver-side door to a late-model brown Toyota truck, and hop in. Usually I went for femmes, but this butch had captured my interest. I hadn't felt this great in a long friggin' time. *Bang!* That last explosion of sound didn't seem to get to me as bad as the ones before it.

Cleanup flew by as I made short work of all the chores, right down to aiming the black plastic trash bag in the general direction of the dumpster, not staying long enough to make sure its flight landed it inside. I went home to get ready for the evening, straightening my small but homey apartment and wondering what had brought Barb to Phoenix. I hoped she was here to stay.

A few minutes before 7, I felt myself getting nervous. I hadn't felt like this since high school when I caught Miss Langley, the gym teacher, watching me slip out of a lacy bra at my locker, ready to head for the showers. Looking back, I should have jiggled my tits for the lady and got me an A+ instead of the C average I usually took home. That's hindsight for you. No telling where the jiggle would have taken me. Most likely I'd have started doing tongue push-ups with the ladies a hell of a lot sooner.

Barb drove a little faster than the posted 35. She talked about her new job and about her family. "They have a hard time with the idea of me being a lesbian. My brother says I'm a Timex—I take a lickin' and kept on tickin'. He was the only one who could handle it. I think he might be a little closeted himself."

During the short drive I clued her into the name the locals had for Lizzy's—Lizzy's for Lezzies. Liz was notorious for her ability to touch the tip of her tongue to her nose. The regulars joked she could tongue your lungs starting at your barstool. On our way to the bar, we passed women talking, touching, and enjoying one another. I ordered my regular Coke and seven. Barb opted for a margarita, no salt.

Music pounded a driving beat, making the walls appear to breathe. Barb grabbed my hand, leading me onto the crowded dance floor. "Fun place. I like this town already," she said, holding me close against her. My hands held her waist as I imagined what it would be like to hold her like that naked. She moved freely against me, making my breath quicken.

"Yeah, you'll like it a lot more after I show you around," I promised, looking deeply into her soulful eyes. I didn't add that showing her around included a tour of my bed's sheets, but Barb received the message my body telegraphed. Her arms encircled me, one hand dropping down between us to tease my waiting pussy through my jeans. The sudden action caused me to gasp, and she interpreted this as a green light—which it was. Green for "GO!"

The dance floor was jammed; the music pulsated, but we looked like we were slow dancing. I pressed against her fingers, let my lips caress hers softly. "Barb…I…" I couldn't think straight, so why expect something sensible to come out of my mouth? Moist lips engulfed mine, her practiced tongue flicking and darting until I felt I wouldn't be able to hold myself up much longer. I leaned into her. The scent of her leather jacket as I nuzzled against her neck and the strength of her heady cologne set my senses reeling.

The revolving ball above the dance floor shimmered light directly onto the large-gauged piercing through Barb's earlobe, ricocheting into my eyes. Through the pounding music I was able to mumble, "Let's leave…quieter home…know you better."

"Yeah. I want to know you better too, Kelly. A lot better," she whispered, nibbling at my neck. We left the dance floor and moved through the crowd out to the parking lot. Leaning against the brown Toyota, I felt the cool breeze of December float over the beads of perspiration forming on my skin in the Phoenix night. Speed limit signs blurred as we careened through the streets to my apartment. Thank God for doughnut shops! There wasn't a police car anywhere on the streets for miles. As Barb kept the truck on course, I told her how I'd wanted to be with her since the moment she stepped into the Java Joint.

Turning the key in the lock, we entered, leaving a wake of rumpled clothing strewn from the living room foyer to bedroom. Several times we stumbled over each other trying to get to the unmade bed. Silhouetted by the street lamp's light streaming through the window, Barb was everything I thought she'd be. Jesus, she was beautiful. And that butt! Up until now I'd only seen that kind of ass on glossy paper with a couple of staples through the cheeks. Finally, falling over my cat, Ciati (get it? C-A-T). I landed facedown in Barb's magnificent bush, my tongue standing at attention in the militant feminist base of her steaming, fragrant pussy. This babe could squirm! Her dripping cavern was ripe. She wanted me as much as I wanted her. Her hands groped, turning me around on top of her, spreading my lean legs, my love center squarely placed over her luscious full lips, that talented tongue tickling and tantalizing, making me catch my breath and hope to God this wasn't a dream. I pushed my face further into Barb's love tunnel, listening to her moan guttural, throaty sounds rife with meaning yet totally without words. My trembling fingers slipped into her wetness, opening her to my desires and fueling hers further. Her hands found my breasts, working the nipples between her thumb and index finger until they were diamondlike—hard enough to cut glass. Her sticky love juices flowed. And flowed. And flowed. Damn! Did I mention they flowed? This was one delicious bitch. Hey, Baskin-Robbins—are you listening? I got your 32nd flavor.

My fingers teased her virgin asshole as her body humped and bucked, causing my neck to experience something close to whiplash. "Kelly! Oh, God—K-K-Kelly I'm coming!" she wailed into the darkness. "Tongue my clit, baby—there—yeah, there!" she moaned, bumping and thrusting her pelvis skyward. My own orgasm built as my excitement peaked. I shrieked my joy into her pussy, letting the echo bounce between the Alps of her vaginal lips.

Passion spent, we languished in the feelings of the aftershock. This had to have been a 10 on the Richter scale. We lay smoking without ever having lit a cigarette. Finally, as our breathing returned to normal, she spoke, playing with my hair and lips as she did. "Damn, that was good," she whispered, a rasp in her voice.

"Yeah, we'll have to do that again—soon," I said lazily, running my fingers up and down the cleft between her full breasts.

"Oh, yes soon. We'll be seeing a lot of each other," she said, arms clasping me.

My heart danced. She wanted to see me again. Things were looking up.

"And—uh, hope you like bagels," Barb continued, slowly raising up on an elbow. "Great with coffee in the morning. See, I'm the 'bagel business' next door to the Java Joint," she said, grinning sheepishly as she wondered how I was going to take this new information.

Bagel business, hell! She was going to be my monkey business. You can bet on it.

DELIVERANCE
RIVER LIGHT

You want me to touch you. Your skin, flushed and damp, prickles as my breath brushes past—illusion of contact. At this point you are beyond caring how the touch manifests itself. I have starved your skin, tempted it with unfulfilled promises. I have brought you so close to orgasm that your vision blurs, and then I've pulled back, ripping you untimely from the ocean, leaving you gasping for a breath you cannot find. I've tied you in my doorway, where only your wrists and ankles have the relief of any contact—and left you, your juices wet on your thighs, hair disheveled. I've blindfolded you, trapping you in your body. You want me—but you do not want me enough. I look at you, tense muscles, tears, jaw clenched, and I can see that you still care. I will take you when you are beyond caring. I will touch you when your only answer becomes "yes." I will release you when I can walk away and leave you here and you thank me.

You still belong to yourself. You still care if your nose runs. You still care about your own pleasure, about coming. You still believe your release is in orgasm, or in pain.

Yesterday you stamped about in my kitchen in an only partially controlled snit. I had a headache and the sharp disjointed sound of pots and dishes finally moved me from couch to medicine cabinet. I kept my own counsel and ignored the decidedly ungracious manner in which you proceeded to prepare my meal. I didn't have the energy to explain to you what it means to leave the outside world on my doorstep upon entering my home. I am, after all, your Master.

You were supposed to have eaten before arriving, but who knows? You were late, had dressed in a hurry, and you had forgotten the CD that I had instructed you to bring—so certainly arriving with an empty stomach is quite possible. I found myself less and less interested in eating, and considered sending you home with instructions to spend the evening in meditation—but to be truthful I didn't have the heart to see you break down and cry again this evening, only to have you leave my home.

While I contemplated what to do with you, you brought me my salad—kneeling at my feet, naked except for your boxers. Arms raised, head bowed, you offered me the bowl that you carried in your two palms. I had never seen you kneel so completely routinely, so completely on autopilot, and it became the last straw. I discarded the carefully laid plans for the night and instead left you where you knelt. When I returned I had a chain from my bedroom, which I attached to your already locked collar. I took the salad from your hands and brought it with me as I towed you on hands and knees to the guest room. There I locked the other end of the chain to the bed, leaving just enough length for you to lie down, but not enough to climb onto the bed. After I fetched a glass of water, a large jar, and a couple of bananas to go with the salad, I left you there, shutting the door behind me. In the kitchen I finished making myself dinner, smiling as the painkillers finally began to take effect.

Later I heard you crying and had to fight my instinct to go in and comfort you, to hold you. Later still your voice came from the room: "Well, fuck!" you said distinctly. "You can't fucking leave me here all night!" I smiled. Oh, but I can, dear one, I can—but I remained silent. I stayed up late, made popcorn, which I know you love, and watched a movie. You called my name once, but I ignored you. When I climbed into bed I missed your warm body snuggled close to mine, the way you always wrap your feet around my cold toes, the firmness of you. I only get you every two weeks, and there I was alone in a cold bed.

This morning I awoke late and made myself tea before entering the guest room. By the time I stepped through the door you had, much to my pleasure, scrambled out of the nest of blankets you'd made on the hardwood floor and were kneeling, head lowered, arms behind your back. Your eyes were red from a restless night. The jar was empty, meaning you held your pee for almost 14 hours. You lost little of your stubborn pride, then.

I stood, silently drinking my tea and watching you. When I knew that your toes had begun to tingle, and your legs to cramp, I pointed to the jar.

"Empty your bladder, tramp, or you are going to get an infection." You hate peeing in front of someone else, and you went bright pink but silently reached for the jar and positioned it under you. I smiled as I saw you struggle to relax under my gaze enough to pee. Even though I knew you were full to bursting, it took almost five minutes for you to succeed, and by that time there were tears of embarrassment in your eyes. I wanted to squat down behind you and wrap my arms around you, but this lesson is far from over, and I want an assurance that the events of last night are not repeated.

Now, in the doorway, I can see that your defenses are breaking down, slowly being eroded. I take a butt plug, cover it in a condom and lube, and rub it along your ass crack. You arch your back and groan, pushing your butt toward it, straining, opening for me. This time I give you what you think you want, slowly working it into your ass until it is pushed up tight.

I can feel your body shaking through the silicon, and I know it would take only a short time to bring you to climax with just this, but I move away, ignoring your cry of frustrated rage as you yank your body against your bondage. Careful not to touch you, I slip around to your front and lean in, bringing my lips close to yours. You lunge forward to try to capture my mouth with yours, and I slap you as hard as I am able across the face. You cry out in shock and pain. Then, blind, you are caught unawares when I hit you a second and third time.

"I'm sorry, I'm sorry, I'm sorry" you whisper over and over, but I hit you twice more in quick succession, ignoring your cries and struggles. I know that you are frightened of your face being hit, and I rarely do it, but today it is the only punishment that I can think of in which you will not find relief. Even so, I know that it has gone directly to your cunt.

"Stand still, stand very, very still," I order, running my tongue over your slightly parted lips, licking tears form your face, reveling in the feel of your body trembling in shock, with your desire, and with your fight to control all movement. When I pull away, you whimper—but do not follow. I take a dildo and slowly push it deep into your dripping cunt, watching for any sign of transgression, but there is none, and so I strap it in place.

"Now," I whisper, "don't even think of clenching your ass or cunt." I take a pair of clamps strung together with chain and carefully, without giving you even the slight pleasure of my hand accidentally brushing your skin, attach them to your nipples. Next, I roll a pair of earplugs between thumb and forefinger and insert them in your ears, causing the world in which I inhabit to recede from your senses just a little bit more. Finally, I select one of my gags. It is a tacky affair, molded in the shape of a short fat cock. I push it between your teeth and into your mouth, fastening it around your head with a wide leather strap—filling you almost to the point of gagging.

Now I continue with my torture. Careful not to touch your skin, I play with the chain between your breasts, tugging gently on your electric nipples. If you were allowed to clench and unclench your cunt you could come this way, but you know better than to disobey me at this point. Your muscles are no longer tense from frustration, but only in a single-minded attempt to follow my orders, to keep your knees from buckling, to not fall. I let go of the chain and reach for the butt plug and dildo. Slowly I push both of them deeper into you, then release them, then push again. This causes movement but almost no friction, and still you tremble and whimper but do not move. I lick my finger and run it back and fourth along the muscle between cunt and ass, then go back to the chain.

I continue this until I see your body start to sag, your head bow. You are unaware of this movement, and I do not call you on it—for I know your consciousness is slipping from brain to skin, from mind to the soul reality of my presence. Tears run unheeded down your cheeks, but you are not sobbing; these are the silent tears of defeat, the unconscious tears of a woman on the verge of slipping away from the unfulfillable demands of her body. I wait and watch as you finally descend into complete silence and total stillness. The tears have stopped, and I only know that you are still conscious because you continue to stand.

I let you wait, but not too long, for fear the spell will break. Uncuffing ankles and wrists, I recuff your wrists behind your back. Then, holding you from falling, I push you to your knees. Slipping from my clothes, I stand in front of you and slowly rub my wet cunt against your face. After releasing the gag, I continue to rub my swollen lips over your now bare mouth. When my own knees begin to shake, I grab two fistfuls of your hair and push myself against you, stifling your breath and grinding into you. You are perfectly still, not moving even mouth or tongue—not moving even when I know you are dizzy with lack of air, with my smell, with wanting to taste me. Before I give into my own passion, I pull away, yanking your head back so that I can see your face.

"Do you want me to come, tramp?" I ask.

"Please," you breathe, "oh, yes, Master, please." You begin to shake again, and I can see how much you mean your words, can see that this is truly all that you want.

"Can you take my cock?" You nod, your lips forming yes. I quickly strap it on, pushing one end inside me, leaving the other end for you. I spit on my hand and wet it, then rub its tip across your lips, pushing it just inside your mouth.

"Suck it!"

Freed to finally move in at least this one small way, you take my shaft eagerly into your mouth, wetting and stroking it with tongue and lips. Slowly you work your way up, alternately pushing and tugging, sending waves of pleasure through my whole body. Looking down at you—tied, blindfolded, filled, and kneeling at my feet—your beauty and submission fill me with love and awe. And when I push my cock down your throat in one smooth movement, it's like being hit with a shock wave. It's my turn for my knees to almost buckle, and I need to put my hands on your shoulders for support. You go perfectly still again as you struggle not to gag or to panic, but I am too close to coming to stop. The look of you, fighting for control, unable to breathe, intent on my pleasure, is enough to push me over the edge, and I come, one hand pressing down on your shoulder, one tangled cruelly in your hair, holding you to me.

I pull out quickly from your mouth and you gag, gasp for breath, cough, gasp again; but when I rest my hand on your cheek you press against it, smile, tip your head back, searching in your blindness for my face, for my eyes as you see them in your mind. For a moment I give you my lips to suckle on. You curl yourself in my arms, your breathing slow and relaxed, contentment radiating from your being.

Now. Now you are mine. You have completely forgotten the demands of your body. My pleasure, your submission, have been your release. Curled in my lap, your side is pressed against my belly. I take the chain between my teeth and lower my lips to capture yours. At the same time I reach for both the dildo and butt plug, and I begin to fuck you. I can see your eyes go suddenly wide in surprise behind the blindfold. You cry out, the sound muffled by my mouth pressed hard against yours. I have relieved you of your cares and made them wholly my own, the responsibility off your shoulders and into my hands. How much more precious is this gift then, that I can give it back to you? How much more intense the orgasm for your surrender?

Your body stiffens and rocks as wave after wave moves through you. I give you to the ocean and you swim, breath from my lips to yours and back, screaming your pleasure into me.

I seek for you to release your soul into my care, that I may offer it back to you.

HEY, SAILOR!
BARBARA PIZIO

It was a bright sunny day with a pleasant hint of coolness. I was planning on making a quick stop at the store before heading home, when a flash of white caught my eye. Ahh, Fleet Week, I silently remembered as I saw the trim figure dressed in Navy whites walking across the street ahead of me.

As my eyes wandered downward, I noticed the slight sway of feminine hips and detected a delicate white thong beneath those crisp uniform slacks. Mesmerized, I crossed the street and picked up my pace, nearly hypnotized by the tantalizing ass bobbing in front of me. Closing the gap between us gave me a better view of her short, honey-blond hair, shaved short at the nape of her neck, with longer wisps peeking out of the sides of her hat.

She paused at the open door of a bar before taking a deep breath and heading inside. I decided that my errands could wait and followed her in a moment later. Her ass had barely hit the seat when one of the neighborhood guys sidled over and, I presume, offered to buy her a drink. She waved him away with a polite but firm smile. I held back at a safe distance and watched her sitting there, silently drinking her beer. I wasn't quite sure if she was old enough to drink, but I guess the bartender felt her uniform was enough ID for him. After a second suitor wandered off, shaking his head, she seemed about ready for a second drink. *What the hell,* I thought, *worst that can happen is that I'll go grocery shopping.*

I slipped onto the empty stool next to her, "Hey, sailor," I said softly, with a smile. "Can I buy you a drink?" My heart was beating wildly as I whispered my question. Her face instantly flushed pink and her blue eyes slid from right to left, checking out who was sitting nearby. It was fairly early and the crowd was thin. Her lips curled into a smile as she whispered back, "Yes, ma'am. I'd really like that."

The bartender wandered toward us, and I ordered another round. When I turned back, I caught her slyly looking me up and down, her eyes lingering on my braless breasts straining against my tight T-shirt. We introduced ourselves and began chatting jovially over our beers, but honestly, I was having a hard time hearing everything Amy said. Each movement in her seat, each wave of her slim hand caused her uniform to bind and shift in a way that teased me mercilessly, giving subtle hints of the toned female body that was hiding beneath that pristine fabric. She mindlessly flicked at the label on her bottle with her neatly manicured fingertips while she told me all about her hometown. I smiled, feigning appreciation, my mind filled with images of us naked and entwined. As much as I liked seeing her in uniform, I was fervently hoping I could get her out of it.

I was snapped out of my lustful reverie when Amy leaned in a little closer and asked, "So, do you live around here?"

"Yeah, I do," I answered, breathing in deeply. She stared at me, waiting for an invitation. I cocked my head toward the door with a question in my eyes. She silently nodded and we pushed away from the bar, leaving without another word.

We kept a friendly distance on the street, not speaking much. Luckily, I didn't live very far from the bar. The fact that I was actually bringing this cute young sailor home had ignited a fire deep inside me. With each step I felt the moistness in my panties growing, and as my cunt swelled with arousal, the seam of my tight jeans was creating a wonderful friction.

The instant my door clicked shut behind us, we reached for each other with a desperate hunger. I grabbed her hat and tossed it into a corner, before bringing my hand to the back of her head. I ran my fingers through her short hair, momentarily delighting in the texture of her close-cropped locks before pulling her toward me for a kiss.

When our lips touched I relaxed instantly, feeling as though I had just exhaled at the end of a race. I trailed kisses along her jaw and down her neck. Amy tossed her head back and moaned as I covered her throat with kisses and slipped my hands underneath her shirt. My fingers played against her back, feeling the delicate yet toned muscles that rippled beneath her skin. While slipping my tongue into her mouth, I traced her bra strap with my finger.

I pulled back then and took off Amy's uniform shirt and T-shirt, sending her hair into lustful disarray. Her blue eyes opened wide and her lips parted as she breathed heavily. She stood before me wearing only her uniform pants and shoes and a lacy bra so sexy and delicate that I chuckled and asked if it was regulation. "Of course," she said, smiling wryly as I trailed kisses along her collarbone. I stroked my hands along her shoulders and then down her sides to the slight indent of her waist. Her skin was smooth, tasting sweet and clean. I could hardly wait to learn what her pussy tasted like.

She kicked off her shoes before I worked her pants down over her slim hips. Sure enough, there was the matching white thong that had lured me with its siren's call just an hour earlier. I reached around her and unfastened her bra, dropping it to the floor so I could cup her breasts in my hands. They were small mounds of golden flesh, just enough for me to palm every inch of them while teasing her tiny nipples with my thumbs and forefingers. She moaned into my mouth as I squeezed them hard, pressing her hips up against mine.

Hooking my thumbs into the waist of her thong, I sank down to the floor and slowly lowered the tiny garment, kissing my way down her flat stomach. When the material was banded around her thighs, revealing her blond mound, I could already detect the unmistakable scent of arousal. The second it hit me my mouth watered, so I lunged forward, parting her lips with my fingers and French-kissing her clit, making her knees buckle. I swirled my tongue around that little nub of flesh, feeling her juice slowly coating my fingers. Her moans of longing were echoing in my ears, urging me on as I continued to lavish attention on her, despite my limited access to her crotch.

This tease was not enough for either of us. I yanked the thong off so she could spread her legs wider and I could get in deeper. Amy shivered as I ran my tongue along her slit. I teased her swollen labia, nipping at her velvety flesh before continuing to lap at her cunt. As I returned to her sensitive clit, circling it with my tongue tip, I pushed two fingers into her slick tunnel. I began fucking her rhythmically, her thighs quivering around my face as I steadily flicked my tongue at her clit. She was squirming and sighing and moaning. I knew she was having a hard time standing as I toyed with her, but every time she shook and her knees gave in, she dropped herself down onto my thrusting fingers, making her cry out even louder.

Her sweet taste and heady scent enveloped me, overtaking all of my senses. As her wordless exclamations of lust rang out, I was lost in the silky wetness of her cunt, wanting nothing else but to please her. Amy began bucking toward my mouth more furiously, her moans becoming one long scream of joy. It was a difficult task to stay on target, but I kept up the steady motion of my fingers as I continued to manipulate her clit with my lips and tongue. Her fingers dug into my shoulders, and I felt her cunt muscles begin to twitch. She cried out loudly as her whole body shivered and her pussy contracted around my digits, sending a new shower of sticky juice over my hand.

As Amy stood on shaky legs, breathing heavily and struggling to regain her composure, I was keenly aware of the desperate throbbing in my own cunt. Watching me strip, Amy climbed onto the bed and settled back into the pillow. The late afternoon sun streamed through my window, bathing her in the spring light, making her glow like an angel spread against my white sheets.

I climbed onto the bed and kissed her deeply. She held the back of my head and feverishly returned my kiss, loving the taste of herself smeared on my lips. Then, with a suddenness that surprised me, Amy flipped me over onto my back, holding my hands above my head. Her knees pressed against my hips as she straddled me and leaned down for another kiss. Her pink nipples grazed my chest as our lips met. Then, while she slipped her tongue into my mouth, she relaxed, shifting her weight onto me, squashing her firm breasts against mine. We were pressed so closely together it was almost as if I was feeling her deep, panting breaths within my own lungs.

I exhaled and unclenched my fists as her hands held mine pinned over my head. The warmth of her body covered me like a blanket, and I couldn't help but thrust my hips up toward her, longing for contact. She ground her mound against mine, and when I felt the dampness leaking from her slit it made me ache inside.

Amy brought one hand down to my spread legs. I could have easily broken free from her grasp, but I didn't want to. Her fingers played at the entrance to my cunt as I spread my legs even wider to invite her inside. I was so wet that her fingers slipped in easily. My ache of longing was quickly replaced by the luscious warmth of arousal as she worked a second and then a third finger inside me. Amy stared at me passionately as she quickly thrust her fingers in and out of my body. She focused intently on her task, swirling her fingers inside me and making me gasp when she passed her thumb over my clit. That delicate hand, with its neatly trimmed shell-pink nails, was wiggling its fingers inside of me in a way that made me delirious with pleasure.

My eyes fluttered closed as I concentrated on the intense feelings that were building inside of me. Amy's thumb continued to massage and tease my clit as she fucked me hard and fast. I snapped my hips upward, riding her hand furiously, wanting to get every inch of her fingers inside of me. Before long, she had me shaking and crying out loud, locking my thighs around her hand as she gamely continued to fuck me until the last tremors of my orgasm had passed.

When I had relaxed enough to let her go, Amy smiled and lay next to me, her small breasts rising and falling with each breath. I was so thoroughly sated and totally exhausted that I must've dozed off. I was awakened when Amy accidentally dropped a shoe on the floor. Through blurry eyes, I looked up to see her bending over to retrieve it. She smiled at me sheepishly as she laced it up.

"That was great," she said sweetly. "But I gotta go." Before I broke my sleepy fog to utter a reply, she had slipped into her whites and out of my life.

Well, I thought as I lay there smiling to myself, I'm not the first woman who's had a sailor love her and leave her. But I'll tell you one thing, I didn't mind it one bit.

WANT AD
ISABELLE LAZAR

> You: Totally butch. Must be tall, lean, preferably ride a bike. James Dean reincarnate. Me: High femme. No names. No numbers. We meet at Frieda's. You arrive and order water. If I like what I see, I'll come to you and say 3 words: Is it you? Your reply: You'll never know. I'll have a hotel room waiting. If you understand the rules, let's play. Meet me @ 2 on the 12th.

I arrive suitably dressed. Black blazer, slacks, dress shoes. All a deliberate and successful camouflage to the real uniform underneath. I can feel the lace at the top of my stockings ride up high on my thigh. I trace the edge through my linen pants as I walk. It excites me to know what I look like without my street clothes—what my look is meant to inspire in my awaited. I can feel my thong only to the extent of my wetness in anticipation at what I am about to do. Or hope to do. If she's right.

I walk in to Frieda's, give my eyes a moment to adjust to the dim light. I order a double espresso, then find a corner of the room in which to wait. I angle to ensure a direct view of the front door, pick up a newspaper, and glance through the pages. I'm having trouble concentrating, though. My mind keeps floating back to the Drake and the king-size bed that stands there like a lone knight—silent, ready, anticipating.

The cowbell on the door jingles as she bounds into the room. I feel serene, trance-like. Every motion previously choreographed in an alternate universe somewhere. However, in that universe everything moves much faster. There, this luscious dyke crosses the floor in two strides and impales me unceremoniously and unapologetically, in front of God and the world, on her steely forearm. I dangle on it, my feet not touching the ground.

She looks around but doesn't see me. Saunters to the counter and orders bottled water, then looks around without looking around. I flip the page of my newspaper, raising it high enough to obscure my face. I hate the charade. I made my decision in the split second it took her to step through the door.

She sits, throws a nondescript black bag at her feet, and begins to thump a drumbeat on her stool. She nods in rhythm, and I wonder about the music playing in her head. I fold the newspaper, carefully delaying the moment as long as possible. I know the game—and the rules. I know I'm supposed to make her sweat it out, make her wonder if it was a joke, if I wouldn't show, or—worse—if she doesn't fit the bill. But frankly, I'm tired of the game, and I'm changing the rules. My game. My rules.

I walk straight up to her, fists clenched. But when I reach her, the tenderness in her eyes undoes me as she looks up from under her blond shag. I stare into the baby blues and wait patiently as she wades through the seven stages of sex: Confusion, Suspicion, Apprehension, Recognition, Acceptance, Arousal, and Lust. Then I bare my teeth momentarily in a half smile, half snarl (an aggressive maneuver) and say seriously, "Is it you?"

She shrugs and says, "You'll never know."

I chuckle, staring her down, then rasp, "Follow me."

Outside, the daylight does nothing to dissipate my hunger. I look to my car, then at her. She follows my gaze, then nods once to a tricked-out Yamaha Virago XV, which stands awaiting its master. I bow my head to her attention to detail and smile to myself, then follow silently as she leads the way.

We take the LSD to the Drake. The valets don't offer their services. We ride silently up in the lift.

"You do this often, do you?" she ventures.

"What? Ride elevators or place ads?"

Her hungry look is all the banter she is willing to offer. We stop on seven. She doesn't move. I agree to lead the way, exiting the elevator with a purpose and proceeding toward the suite, aware of her silent presence not two steps behind me. If I stop, she's likely to run into me.

I thrust the key in the door and turn the knob. Before I can turn back to her, she slams me against the wall and presses her full body against mine. She's loaded for bear and I can feel her hardness pressing into the back of my thigh. She shifts and slides her dykehood between the crack of my ass. My breathing becomes erratic. I angle to grab for a piece of wall but the sucker's slippery. Like I asked for it out loud, she places my hands on the wall in front of me, holding them there with her weight. She continues to pump the shaft between my cheeks. The teasing is infuriating; I begin to whine for relief. She lets go of my hands and lets hers slip to my waistband. In a millisecond she undoes my loose linen pants and lets them drop to the floor. Then she lets her hands slide down the sides of my body to familiarize herself with the terrain. I can feel her breath hot in my ear. Her lips haven't touched me yet. She withholds this pleasure for the moment but purrs at what her fingers find.

"What a little slut you are. Garters 'n' all." She lets her finger glide inside my thong and inside my folds. She slides in my wetness, and I moan in agony at the delicious humiliation of it all. She teases my clit then slides back to the opening and delves deeply inside. Then back out again, circling my aching, straining clit, then deep inside me again to open me wider, preparing me for what's to come next. In, out, circle, slide, in, out, circle, slide. She pulls my thong down. It gets caught in my garter. She doesn't tear it off but allows me to stand there with my bum exposed like a bad schoolgirl made to stand in a corner. She kicks my legs further apart, as far as the straining thong will allow. It grooves deep welts into my thighs. She uses both hands to open and stroke me now. My clit has become a prisoner in its own home, reduced to constant agitation with no relief.

I hear the sound of a zipper opening behind me and imagine the sound her dick makes as it springs from its confines. I hear a slip as she washes my wetness over her thick shaft. She places both feet inside of mine and opens me again, lifting me nearly to my toes as she positions me. A brief pain as the head pierces my tight cunt—but it doesn't dissipate. It keeps building, the shaft expanding to the width of a fist. I imagine I'm being fucked by the pyramids of Egypt, my body bracing for a relief that doesn't come. It arches out, instinctively angling for a break in the pressure. I am ready to cry out in pain but hold it in like the good little girl that I am.

"Not bad," she murmurs in my ear. My body feels impaled on the sun, the searing hot, wide pain terrible and delicious all at once. Deep inside me she begins to pump even deeper, to make sure I get her meaning with every stroke. She grabs me off the wall and pulls me close, one hand assaulting my clit and the other my straining nipples. She bites my neck and I am entirely, blindingly hers. Impaled now truly on her savage organ, not really sure what she's using and not caring, my body racked with orgasm, I am falling, falling, falling into oblivion and into her.

We slide to the floor, and I collapse completely. She spreads my legs again and slowly, groove by groove, pulls out, leaving me spent and motionless. I feel her raise off me and step around, then the soft swish as she eases into a chair. I try to rise but my arms won't take direction. I venture a look up at her—it's not what I expected. She's not less determined, as after climax, but more. She has a direction, a purpose. No need for words; she telegraphs it silently. She has an agenda and is patiently waiting for me to once again come to my senses. I want to speak but am too tired. I close my eyes and fall into brief but bottomless REM sleep.

"How long have I been asleep?"

"Five minutes, give or take."

"Hmm." I roll over and pull up my thong. It's left a deep red ring above my lace garters, a little red halo with an afterbite.

I stand and dress. Put my breasts back in their sleeves. I'm pretty proud of myself. I want to smoke, then remember I quit three months ago. So I run my hand through my hair and exhale the clean, smokeless, dry air of the room, only slightly punctuated with the scent of sex.

"It's your turn," I say, wondering how she likes it. She just shakes her head.

"C'mon, it's only fair."

"I'm not finished with you yet," she says. "So whenever you're ready…" She nods. I'm intrigued. My own personal fuck bunny. I cock my head. She doesn't bite. I wait a long beat, then shrug.

"What'd you have in mind?" Now she smiles. Or rather her eyes do. She stands and walks toward me. Takes my hand and kisses it softly, then walks me to the couch. She places both my hands on the back of it and instructs me not to move. Stepping deftly around behind me, she kicks my legs open again, the pinching of my thong almost comfortable in its familiarity.

She rips open my shirt and takes out my breasts again. They hang, pouting expectantly, over my bra. She teases each nipple in turn, raising them painfully. I close my eyes to concentrate on compartmentalizing the pain. The sound of a zipper hits my ears and, in a moment, real pain—I cry out loud as she affixes clamps to each of my nipples. I try to stand and turn, and she kicks my feet open farther, cementing my hands to the couch.

"Don't move unless I tell you to move," she growls menacingly. Something in her voice makes me obey. The nipple clamps are attached by a thin metal chain to each other, with one more chain hanging low in the middle. She throws that one over my shoulder and tests it, like reins, from behind, sending searing pain to both my nipples and groin. My knees buckle, but she'll have none of it. She undoes my pants and pulls them down to just below my ass, then does the same with my thong, and bends me slightly over the couch. Her massive hands slide over my ass as she opens it wide, exposing me to the cool room air. I twitch in anticipation, wondering if I should allow her to continue, my curiosity and the rhythmic thump in my cunt urging me on. I suddenly glimpse an image of her drumming a beat on the stool at Frieda's and smile inwardly at the secret revealed.

She strokes my asshole, gently strumming at the opening. It puckers to her touch. My body begins to betray me as it strains towards her Chinese water torture method of foreplay. I hear a rip, then she spits. And before I can imagine what she's up to her second hand begins to caress the crack of my ass with an ease only lube can provide. Suddenly it dawns on me: the size of her shaft that will now burrow its way into my tight flesh.

"No"—I buck. She yanks on the chain and my knees give again. My insides open to her, but I know it's not the opening she's angling for.

"Let's do the other again," I plead.

"Did I say speak? I don't think I did." She makes a sucking sound with her mouth. "Tsk, tsk, tsk. That's not good. Let me see how we can remedy this."

She allows me no time to ponder this thought before stuffing a tight rubber ball into my mouth and securing it at the back of my head with leather straps.

"Now you can make this hard, or you can make this easy," she whispers seductively. "It's up to you, really. Play nice and this is as much restraint as you get. Try to wriggle out and, I assure you, I have thought of everything well in advance. Use your hands, I use the cuffs. Use your feet, I use the leg restraints. Understand?"

I nod my head and wait quiet as a rabbit for what is to come next. She resumes stroking me. I try to relax.

"That's right, baby, relax," she chants. And as she says this, her tool pierces the first ring of muscles in my anus. The ascent is slow, deep, and seemingly without end. This one is not wide. It's long. Very, very long and not attached to her. She wields it with her hand. I can feel the rubbery snake burrowing its way into my abdomen, nudging me from the inside out. When the shaft feels like it's a good two feet inside me, she starts to rock it to and fro. Out it comes, inch by agonizing inch. Back again. She begins to gain speed and momentum.

"Tell me, baby," she whispers in my ear. "Tell me how much you like it. Hmm?" She traces my outstretched lips ever so gently and tests the secureness of the rubber ball in my mouth. "Tell me, baby," she says a bit more forcefully. "Moan for me." She traces my lips again and thrusts the dagger deeper into my rectum. A grunt is all I can muster.

"Oh, c'mon. You can do better than that." I try again, but my moan comes out as a whimper. I begin to count the strokes. On the 40th the pain has become pleasure, the fullness in my ass and belly spreading warmth through me like an opium high. I don't let on, but she senses my pleasure anyway and so begins to ease out of me. I groan in annoyance.

"Tell me…" she beckons in my ear. I try to talk but the ball gag strangles my speech.

"What's that? I can't understand you," she says oh-so-innocently, still pulling at the lengthy shaft. I scream a sea of obscenities at her and shake my head savagely. I stomp my feet and cry out in frustration as the head pops out, leaving a cold emptiness in its wake.

"Oh, poor baby," she murmurs with the concern of a parent. She unbuckles and removes the ball gag, then strokes my hair lovingly, fixing it back into shape.

"Fuck!" I scream in frustration. She leans in close, a look of pain and confusion crisscrossing her face. "Fuck. Fuck! Don't! Don't fucking do this to me."

"Do what, baby?"

"Do what," I laugh acidly, then stare defiantly back at her and say through clenched teeth, "Do. Me."

She knits her eyebrows together as if I'm speaking Chinese. I take a breath and exhale it slowly. "Do me," I say more calmly. Then whisper, "Please."

A snide smile weasels its way into her eyes. She takes a deep breath then grabs a fistful of my hair and whispers savagely in my ear.

"That's right, baby. Beg for me."

I try to pull away, but she only winds her fingers tighter into my hair.

"You'd better fucking beg, 'cause that's the only way you're going to get off from here on out. You hear me? By begging me to get you off."

And with that she whirls me around and into her open and waiting mouth. I try hard to swallow her whole, lapping at her tongue, intoxicated by the softness of her lips. I want the kiss to last forever and whimper when she pulls away, hot angry tears springing to my eyes. She smiles gently.

"What a sweet little mouth my beautiful, precious baby has."

I smile shyly.

"What better way to give the sweetest little blow job to your butch daddy."

She places both hands on my shoulders.

"What? No, I—" is all I'm able to say as she presses me onto the ground, bringing me face to face with her engorged cock. Obediently I open my mouth, my eyes never leaving hers, and wrap it around her wide shaft. I work very hard to do a good job for her, licking the last bit of my juices off, making sure not to miss a spot. I'd never been good at this with guys, never chose to be, but with her, all the rules on cocksucking suddenly sprang to mind: Keep your jaw slack and your throat open, lick the head, the opening. Maintain eye contact.

She throws her head back in ecstasy, pushing herself further down my throat. I stifle a gag reflex, allowing her to make me her tool. I can smell her excitement building, her musky, tough scent making my head spin. Just at the point of climax she grabs me by the hair and drags me to my feet, engulfing my mouth again. Then in one swift motion she lifts me off the ground and enters me roughly. At last, we move in unison like a well-oiled piston, clinging to each other like starving children, like two transients who by accident connected at the intersection of loneliness and salvation, making one last-ditch effort for all fucking womynkind.

IN THE SWIM
JUDITH LAURA

When I first started going to the county pool I concentrated on completing the four-lap goal I had set for myself. Sometimes, I have to admit, after I finished my laps, I ducked under the ropes separating the lanes from the shallow end. Then, checking first to make sure no one was looking, I approached the jets foaming water into the pool. As I cozied up to them, water rushed against my breasts, tickling my nipples into arousal. Checking again to make sure no one was watching, I lay back on the water and opened my legs to the jets' massage, abandoning myself to pleasure for as long as I dared.

After a few weeks I started noticing another woman—a shiny black tank suit clinging to her generous curves, water rolling off her ample thighs as she walked from the pool to the women's locker room. One night after I completed my swim I climbed up the ladder and out of the pool, pulling my tank suit away from my body. I took off my cap and shook out my hair, which of course had gotten wet anyway. When I walked into the locker room, there she was, right in front of the locker where I had put my clothes. Her thick, dark hair hung down past her shoulders as she stood there, a white towel wrapped around her plump waist and tied beneath her heavy breasts.

I caught my breath and tried not to stare at her large brown nipples. She smiled at me. I smiled back, struggling not to seem to excited.

"Hi," she said, not moving to cover her breasts, but stepping slightly to the side so that they swung gently.

"Hi," I said, sounding hoarse. The chlorine maybe. I cleared my throat. "My locker is behind you."

"I'm sorry, I didn't mean to block your way." She moved a few inches more to the side, removed her towel, and reached for her clothes.

I got my things out and turned around. There she stood, in white cotton low-slung boy-short panties and underwire bra that emphasized the beauty of her smooth olive skin and great cleavage.

"My name's Marsha," she said, slipping a peach T-shirt over her head. "I think I've seen you here before."

"I'm Sandra. I swim here two or three times a week."

While my mouth was speaking these social pleasantries, my mind was racing to figure out how to handle the situation. One thing was certain: I had to stop thinking about that deep space between her breasts where my tongue longed to go. I couldn't expose my feelings—not yet, not until I was sure about her intentions.

Yet what could I do? I was standing dripping wet before her. Should I be nonchalant and just strip my tank suit off in a no-nonsense fashion? Or should I hold my towel in front of me while slipping the shoulder straps off and drying my top and then, turning my back, slip on my bra, and then, wrapping the towel around me, dry quickly down there and slip on my underpants?

Marsha zipped herself into her jeans. "I get really hungry swimming," she said. "You eat dinner yet?"

"No, I haven't." I reached for my towel, slipped one strap off, and began drying my shoulder, then my arm.

"I'm going to the steak place across the street. Join me?"

"OK." I slipped the other strap off and tried to keep the suit from falling below my breasts.

"Super," Marsha said. "It's getting kind of hot in here. I'll wait for you outside."

I watched Marsha's rear, its two plump denim cheeks bouncing separately as she walked away, limping slightly. I told myself that at least Marsha wouldn't be watching as I continued to undress and then shower. But, as I put my wet suit and towel into a plastic bag, I realized I actually felt disappointed.

At the restaurant, I ordered chicken and baked potato. Marsha ordered a steak and french fries.

"It's great to have company eating dinner," she said. "I'm so glad you agreed to come, Sandy."

Sandy? No one had called me Sandy since high school. It felt weird. "People call me Sandra," I said. I didn't mean it to sound as chilly as it came out.

"Sandra?" she let the word hang in the air a moment, as though waiting to see if it would fall. "That's so formal. It just doesn't seem right for you. How about Sand?" She started cutting up her steak, then stopped, looked at me across the table and said, "Yes. Sand. You'll flow through my fingers like sand…" Her voice was soft, and she looked at me all dreamy-eyed.

I swallowed hard, even though there wasn't anything in my mouth. Finally I managed, "I guess Sand's OK." I smiled but tried to hide how turned on I was, how much I was liking the idea of having Marsha call me by a name nobody else ever had. I dared to be playful and said, "If you're going to call me Sand, I think I'll call you Marsh."

I guess my words caught her off guard because she laughed so hard she spewed the water she had been sipping onto the white tablecloth, onto her peach T-shirt. "That's wonderful," she said when she caught her breath. "Marsh…moist and squishy."

And then we both laughed, ignoring stares from other diners.

When we calmed down, she said, "I suppose you noticed my limp."

I nodded my head. I had noticed, but hadn't given it much thought.

"It's from a car accident. I guess I'm lucky that's the only thing that hasn't healed," she said. "It was one drunken night long ago. I wasn't driving, but I got pretty bashed up. After I recovered, I got into swimming. Helps build muscle."

"That was my reason too. For stomach muscles after I had my appendix out."

"Even with all the swimming, there was a lot of bone and related muscle loss in that one leg, and the doctor says it could get worse as I age unless I keep exercising a lot. So if you're looking for a perfect body, guess you better look elsewhere," Marsha sighed, then put a forkful of steak into her mouth.

"I think you look fine," I said. "I have an appendectomy scar." It seemed a good opportunity to warn her. "It's faded a lot. But it's still there if you look up close."

"I guess at this stage of our lives we each have plenty of scars, visible and invisible," she said.

After that evening, we timed our swim sessions to coincide at least once a week. We had dinner together after each swim session, and despite our sexy repartee we kept our hands to ourselves. During that time, Marsha told me about the breakup of her marriage to a man, about being an artist but not being able to support herself that way, about getting training and then a job as a beautician, and about her two kids, both away at college on full scholarships.

"No matter how difficult it's been, Sand, that divorce was the best thing that ever happened to me," she said. "It freed me to realize how attracted I am to women."

I told her about my relationships with women without going into much detail. Then Marsha confessed that even before we met in the locker room that day, she had begun timing her swim workouts to the time of day she had seen me at the pool.

In the locker room now we continued undressing in front of each other, Marsha casual about exposing her whole body, until

I became a little more relaxed about being nearly naked in front of her. Yet I still felt a shyness with her that I hadn't felt with other women. Perhaps it was the voluptuousness of her body in contrast to my own, which I considered skinny and bland. Or maybe it was because I so wanted Marsha to like me. Whatever it was, when she went to the open shower area that had no stalls for privacy, I waited until she finished her shower to take mine. This was easy to do, because usually the showers were almost all taken.

But one evening we finished up a little later than usual. As we undressed, the other two women there finished dressing and left. Marsha and I were the only ones in the locker room. My heart began beating wildly.

Looking me straight in the eye, she rolled her black tank suit down over her breasts and her hips, stepped out of it, and smiled. She picked up her towel and, instead of wrapping it around her, held it casually at her side. Sliding her tongue around her lips, she rocked slightly from side to side so her breasts swayed.

I looked at the damp cement floor to try to keep calm as I rolled my suit off. I dropped it into my plastic bag and looked up again.

"Let's hit the showers," Marsha said, laughing. She turned on a shower, and the water skimmed down her body, turning her skin to a gold shimmer. I turned on the shower next to hers and moved into the water, my back to her. When I turned around, Marsha was soaping her breasts slowly, spending an inordinate time on those dark nipples. The white foam made a mosaic of Marsha's tawny skin. She caught my eye and moved the soap down to her exquisite belly. She soaped it in circles, starting at the outside and moving inward. When she reached her navel, she pressed a corner of the soap into it, smiled at me, and then quickly moved the foamy soap down to her dark mound, where she continued the circular motion.

"Let me soap you up, Sand," Marsha said. I took a breath, turned off my shower, and moved under hers. "Let's start with your back."

I turned my back to her. Still nobody in the locker room. She soaped my back gently yet with authority. When she was finished, I slowly turned around, and she began soaping my front from the neck down. By the time she reached my breasts, she had to support my rear with her other hand to keep me from sinking to the sudsy floor of the shower and spinning down the drain. I felt the soap skim over the scar, down my stomach, and onto my mound, where Marsha lathered with the same motion she had used on hers. Then she began again on herself and, as if it were the most natural thing in the world, pressed the soap into the apex of her mound. I reached down to touch myself there, but before I could Marsha pulled me to her. Our bodies pressed together, sharing the soap.

"Marsh," I gasped. But I was drowned out by high-pitched voices vibrating through the steamy locker room, propelling us apart. The soap, now a mere sliver, fell into the sudsy water. We left it there to melt to oblivion. The other women continued their clatter as I scooted over to the next shower, turned it on, and quickly rinsed off. Without looking again at Marsha or the five other women now in the locker room with us, I went back to my locker.

"How about we go back to my place and order out Chinese," Marsha suggested.

"Sounds good to me," I said, slipping on the mid-thigh red silk dress I had worn to work that day. I quickly crammed my bra and panties into my purse.

When I turned to look at Marsha, she was standing there in her tight jeans and scoop-necked white short-sleeved sweater, her large nipples visible through what I imagined to be a very sheer bra. "Ready?" she asked, brazenly running her hand over her luxurious cleavage, then over the sweater, stopping just short of one of those nipples.

We went in her car. When she had to stop for a red light, she reached over and stroked my thigh, going higher at each stoplight, until her finger rested over my clit.

We got to her apartment just in time. As we climbed one flight of stairs, Marsha leading the way, I couldn't resist running my hand over her ass and then between her thighs. When I reached the zipper of her jeans, she groaned.

In her apartment she pulled me to her and we kissed, our tongues entwining until mine began rolling over her teeth.

She stepped back from me, ran her fingers over the red silk that covered my breasts, and said, "I guess I'm forgetting my manners. Do you want a drink?"

I shook my head no and slid her hand down the silk to where it had stopped in the car.

"Neither do I," she said, and we kissed again, her hand staying where I had put it.

Again she pulled back. "Should I phone for Chinese food now?"

I laughed and said, "Not yet, Marsh." I brushed her lips with mine and nibbled my way to her neck and down to her breasts, where my tongue dove again and again into the deep space between them. Her hand moved under my dress, fingers sliding up and down my opening. I moved against her fingers and came quick and strong.

We were on her bed then, her lovely queen-size bed with a flowered spread we didn't take time to remove. I lay on my back, Marsha above me. She took off her white sweater. I reached up for the clasp at the front of her sheer beige bra, savoring the way her breasts looked uplifted, then freeing them to their breathtaking descent. She leaned forward slightly, her dark hair caressing my face, and I took one nipple in my mouth and the other between my fingers.

I reached down and stroked the zipper of her jeans, increasing the pressure with each stroke, wanting so to reach inside. Moaning, she unzipped her jeans and wriggled free of them. Then she lifted my dress off over my head.

While my fingers dipped into her, her mouth and tongue made their way from my breasts to my stomach, stopping to gently kiss my surgery scar.

Then she sat back from me on the bed. "You're so beautiful, Sand," she said. "Please open your legs for me."

I gladly did and she was quickly between them, licking and sucking, and when I came this time it felt like it would go on forever.

She lay down beside me and whispered, "You're salty, Sand, but, oh, so sweet."

On our sides, pressed against each other, we kissed. Her legs clasped me to her, and she moved against me, we moved with each other, lips on lips, nipple to nipple, clit kissing clit. We rode the waves of our coming together, Sand and Marsh.

Later, much later, we ordered out for Chinese. It was a delicious dessert.

WANTED
MARILYN JAYE LEWIS

When was the last time I was really *wanted*? Now, that's a question that goes right to the heart of the matter, doesn't it?

"I don't remember," I tell her more than a little tersely.

"You're not trying hard enough," she says.

I swish the melting ice around in the sweating glass, which I realize I'm now clutching like it's some kind of life-saving device, and I gulp down what's left of my watery cocktail. This mind game is rapidly losing its appeal, and now I'm wishing she would just go. As much as I was wishing she would move closer to me only a handful of seconds ago, so that I could get a whiff of her pretty brown hair, that's how much I'm now wishing she would leave. And by leave, I mean leave me alone. Emphasis on *alone*. Entirely.

Jesus, when did I get so fucking bitter? Arthritis of the heart. If I'm not careful, it'll start creeping in all over my body and I'll be one crippled arthritic mess. And that's when it'll become undeniable, even to me, that I've gotten old.

"Come on," she's going on, like it's her personal mission to fuck with my evening or something. "Just try. When was the last time you felt really wanted?"

But I steadfastly refuse to try. I don't want this young one leading me anywhere, be it hypothetical, theoretical, or rhetorical. Go back to your little dorm, I want to say. Because I'm absolutely certain she's not even out of college yet. Actually, I'm absolutely certain that she is in college. She's not one of those million-miles-an-hour gals who are too preoccupied with real life and with living it to waste precious time on stopping to go to college for four years. This is so obviously a girl who plays it safe straight down the line.

In short, she's not at all like I am. Or I should say, she doesn't take on life the way I do, have always done; in sloppy, careening giant steps, always in such a grand hurry to get somewhere—a place that never fails, when the smoke and mirrors are put away, to be just plain right here.

"Can I have another one of these, please?" I ask the harried bartender as she dashes by me. I hold up my empty glass as proof that she's served me once already and hope that maybe it entitles me to her undivided attention. Right now she's the most sought after woman in the bar. She's the only bartender on duty, it's Friday night, it's nearly summer, we're right off Washington Square, no more than a few crazy blocks from the bulk of NYU undergraduate dorms—need I say more? It's nearing pandemonium in this dyke dive.

"I don't think I've ever been *really* wanted," Chippy's lamenting.

Jesus, why I am doing that? Calling her Chippy in my mean old-bugger brain when she's probably got a perfectly nice name, like Susan or something.

The bartender has splashed together a bourbon and Coke as quickly as possible and now slams it down in front of me. "Five fifty," she blurts.

"Keep it," I say, sliding her seven.

I turn to my new barmate. "What's your name?" I ask.

Right away she looks hopeful. Maybe I shouldn't have asked that question so soon. "Carly," she offers.

I'm thinking, *Carly*? She's got to be kidding. In fact I think I'm actually smirking. Nobody's named Carly except the obvious one who's been on the radio for a million decades and slept with that so vain guy.

"Is that short for Carla, or something? I mean, like a nick-name?"

"No, it's just Carly. Always has been. Is that a problem? It looks like it's bothering you—my name, I mean."

"No, it's not bothering me, it's just making me feel a little old. When I was your age, there was only one woman in the entire universe who was named Carly."

"*My* age?" she challenges me. "And how old is that?"

"Twenty?" I challenge her right back. "Maybe 20 and a half?"

Well, that did it. I think I've finally repelled her. Obviously, I've hit the tender nail right on its perky brunette head.

"And how old are you?" she wants to know, like she's baiting me.

"Oh, old enough…" I trail off vaguely. Then I concentrate on my cocktail. It always tastes best when it's fresh like this—bursting with bubbles and burning bourbon and ice-cold all at once. The bartender even remembered to squeeze the wedge of lemon on top of the still-fizzing Coke. My evening, for this very moment, is perfect. If I hadn't given up smoking and could light up, right here right now; it would be downright sublime.

In truth, that's what I still live for, those moments of sublima-tion. Fleeting moments, but nevertheless worth living for. I have to figure out how to achieve downright sublime again without the aid of nicotine. I'm not convinced that it can be done.

"No, really," Carly insists. "Tell me. I want to know. How old are you?"

"You tell me."

"That's not fair."

"Of course it is. I guessed your age, now you have to guess mine."

"But what if I insult you and guess too high?"

"Live dangerously, Carly. It's Friday night in the big city."

"I don't know." She hesitates. She's obviously giving this a lot of thought. "Thirty-five?"

Carly gets a big kiss right on the mouth. At least in my head, she does. "That's close enough," I say.

"Older?"

"Yes, but I'm not going to say by how much."

"Well, what's your name? Will you at least tell me that, or is that some big secret too?"

"No, it's not a big secret. My name's common knowledge, even the phone book has it."

"Well, then what is it?"

"Roz."

"Roz?"

"You know, short for Rosalind—as in Russell?" Sadly, this reference to a dead movie star will soar over Carly's head, but I'm not going to judge her for it. Or myself either, for that matter. Guilt is not a qualitative part of being too old or too young. Age just is, it's guiltless. You know what you know. I learned that the hard way; the "It's too late, Roz, you mean bitch, don't ever call me again" way. I used to be very judgmental.

"You like old movies?" she asks, surprising me now, throwing me for that proverbial loop.

"I love them," I say, impressed with her knowledge of a movie star who's been dead since long before she was born. "I wish I lived in old movies."

"Really?"

"Sometimes."

"What do you do?" she asks.

"You mean, for a living?"

"Yeah."

Usually right about now, when I'm standing next to a really young, eager one in a bar, I lie about what I do for a living. It's less entangling that way. But for some reason I decide to answer her truthfully. "I work in the movies. Nothing glamorous, though. I'm a line producer. You know what that is?"

She looks at me quizzically, which I take as a no. "It means that I lie about the true size of a producer's budget and then try to get everyone else in the industry to pretend they believe me and cut me their cheapest rates on everything we need to get the picture off the ground and in the can, with a substantial chunk of change still left over for the producer's pocket. In the old days it was called 'jewing them down,' but it's not PC to say that anymore."

"That doesn't sound too fun."

"I'm OK with it." The truth is I make great money and get to travel all over.

Now comes the inevitable question. "So," I ask her, "what do you want to be when you—"

"—grow up?" she cuts in sarcastically.

"Get out of school, I was going to say."

"I used to want to be in forensics, but now I think I should be a bartender. They seem to be pretty wanted, don't you think?"

"What is it with you and this wanted business? Did you just get dumped by a lover or something?"

"No, I discovered that I wasn't even in the running, and right now, probably this very minute, she's fucking somebody who used to be my best friend."

I look back at my cocktail. It's safer that way. I'm starting to think that Carly's a land mine waiting to happen, and I don't want to get any of my extremities blown off. She's too eager; plus she's young, damaged, and very pretty—a potentially deadly combination. If I stop talking to her right now, maybe she'll hone in on some other fool and I'll make it out of this night alive.

"I suppose it's an old story, huh? It happens to everybody, right? Unrequited love and all that. And then the person standing right next to you winds up the lucky winner?"

"Yeah, it happens," I say. So much for not talking to her anymore.

"But it's not the end of the world, right, Roz? Is that what you want to tell me?"

"It doesn't have to be the end of the world, no. But that whole notion of the world going on and on in spite of your heart splintering into pieces doesn't make it hurt any less."

Where the hell did that come from, I wonder? It must be coming from the booze. I'd better slow down. Still, it seems to have caught her off guard. She's quiet now, staring contemplatively into her mug of beer, which is looking rather listless and flat. "You want another beer?" I ask her. "Come on," I try again, when she doesn't answer the first time. "What are you drinking?"

She shrugs. "Bud Light."

"*Bud Light?* Oh, please. I'm appalled. Let's get you onto something with a little more pizzazz. Something foreign, something zesty. Look at all the brands they have on tap here. Heineken—Guinness, for chrissakes. Or maybe go for something kitschy in a bottle. Look, they have St. Pauli Girl; you remember your first girl, don't you? No one forgets her first girl."

Shit. Now I'm actually flirting with her—the walking land mine. Am I losing it?

She smiles. A little wanly, still, it qualifies as a smile. "Do you remember your first girl, Roz?"

"Yes, I do."

"Did you really want her?"

"I really did. Yes, I wanted her." I try to flag down the bartender. Thank God there's a second one on duty now and it's easier to get some attention. I order Carly a bottle of St. Pauli Girl. It's ice-cold and she doesn't want a glass. She wants to suck it right out of the longneck bottle, darting her pink tongue around the green glass rim, licking up every foamy drop. I think twice about ordering a third cocktail for myself, but suddenly I can't resist it. I feel like I have nothing to lose but time.

"How old *were* you?" she ventures quietly—almost too quietly; the din in the bar is growing louder.

I want to say "When I what?" but I know darn well the bone she's gnawing on, that idea of a first girl. "I was 14," I reply. She looks a little stunned. Pretty soon she'll discover that I'm one of those million-miles-an-hour gals. Or at least, I was until the big brick wall of love slammed into me a few years back and slowed me down, indefinitely. "Why? How old were you?"

"I went to school in a small town upstate," she offers as a sort of answer.

"What does that have to do with it? I didn't go to high school in the heart of Manhattan or anything, and I still had a first girl. Haven't you *had* a first girl yet?"

"Of course I have. It's just that, well, I certainly wasn't 14! In my town it was dangerous. There was a lot at stake. You couldn't just go around being queer and get away with it."

"You had to come to New York to do that?"

She pauses oddly. "That's right," she says.

Now I'm wondering what the pause was all about. Had she in fact been too drunk to remember her first girl? Maybe there really wasn't a first girl, per se; maybe it was just a first kiss. Maybe *I* was her first girl and I was the one too drunk to remember? That would be just priceless, wouldn't it? Is it too late to walk away from her? All I did was buy her a beer.

"I was 20," she finally confesses.

"And now you're 20 and a half?" I announce this quietly because it's finally dawning on me that she's too young to be in here drinking.

"Kind of."

My third cocktail is not only placed in front of me now, but in true New York dive bar fashion, it's on the house. Meanwhile, bold red warning flags are popping out all over Carly the Land mine, my newest irresistible bad idea. I want to ask, what does she mean by "kind of 20 and a half"? But I don't really want to hear her answer, because it would mean her explanation of who her first girl had been would not be far behind, and that sounded like nothing but a no-holds-barred drama. And I'm too old for drama. Not that I don't remember it clearly; the exquisite thrill of it, or the searing pain. Then right behind the explanation of who the first girl had been would be that big fat question mark of who the next one would be, now that the unrequited one is out there, this very minute, fucking her ex-best friend.

"Roz, can I ask you a question?"

"Shoot—but I might not answer," I add quickly.

"What did you do with her? At 14, I mean."

I'm not sure how to reply. It's a little personal. "I did enough," I say.

"What's 'enough' mean? How could you possibly be making love with a girl when you were only 14?"

"It was easy. The world was a different place back then. The rules were looser. Teen sex wasn't the PC-fascist compound that it is now, where all the information is locked up tight."

She studied her beer, looking as if my answer were Greek to her. "And this girl, she loved you back?"

"I didn't say that."

"You made love to a girl who didn't love you back? And she was only 14?"

"I didn't say that, either. I was the one who was 14. She was 17, and I was hopelessly in love with her. But she wasn't gay. She wasn't even what you'd call bi. She was just overwhelmed by my persistence and a little curious. Curious enough to let me get what I was after for a few hours one brief shining evening in late fall."

"You do remember it well."

"I sure do."

Carly has the beer bottle poised at her pretty mouth. "Tell me," she asks, before sucking a swig from its long neck again. "Were you still in love with her after she gave up the goods?"

This is a question that necessitates a reflective pause. And I realize that while I'm remembering it, those few brief hours when I'd finally gotten Sara MacDonahue alone, down in her empty basement, when I'd coaxed her out of her jeans, her panties, convinced her that no one would ever find out about what we were doing and persuaded her to spread her legs apart and at least let me see, then let me touch, a finger up inside her, then two. And she was too wet to refuse my mouth then, because no one had ever yet licked her there and it was something she'd been dying to feel nearly as much as I'd been dying to taste...While I was remembering that and wondering if I had in fact still loved Sara when my one allotted evening with her was up, I was staring into Carly's eyes and she was staring into mine. I realized, too late, that I was an open book.

"Wow," Carly practically sighed. "Whatever's going on in that head of yours, it sure looks hot from out here."

If I wasn't on my third cocktail, it would be so much easier to rein myself in, but I'm lost now in that fog of an alcohol-laced swoon. It feels like it's been ages since a girl spread her legs for me and I was that eager to get my face in there. "I don't think I did," I finally say. "Love her, I mean. Not afterward. Or if I was still in love, it only lasted a little while. What's the sense in wanting someone who doesn't really want you?"

"Ouch," Carly says. "My point exactly." Clearly she's thinking of Unrequited and the Ex and it isn't going down easy. "My beer's empty. You want to go someplace? I mean to another bar? Someplace quieter maybe?"

On a Friday night in New York when it's nearly summer, finding a quieter bar doesn't seem likely. Besides, she's too young to be drinking legally, not that it seems to be mattering much so far.

"It's a beautiful night. We could just walk for a while," I suggest. I'm suddenly wanting to work some kind of sex magic on Carly while the alcohol-laced swoon is still in high gear. Why waste it by going to another dingy bar, where she might get carded? It would be more pleasant to push her up against the side of some stone building, down some quaint winding West Village street, kiss her and grope her tits while our tongues are mashed together and then maybe even coax her to let me slide my finger up her hole when we're right out there in the open.

"OK," she agrees. "A little fresh air would probably be good. I need to get myself over this already. Jesus."

I down what's left of my bourbon and Coke, and we squeeze

our way through the throng and make our way out the door.

The rush of fresh, warm night air is thrilling. Somewhere up above the towering buildings that loom around the perimeter of Washington Square, I know for certain there are stars up in that sky. I take it on faith, and the romance of the potential celestial splendor is making me seriously horny. I wonder if Carly is hurting too much to be indiscreet or indiscriminate. I'm hoping like hell she was doing her best to seduce me back there in that bar, because I sure as hell feel like I've been seduced, or at the very least, urged out of my crabby old shell.

I grab hold of her hand and she doesn't pull it away; a good sign. We cross Sixth Avenue and as we make our way through the jam of people coming toward us, I angle her past Cornelia, down Jones Street, where it's always quieter. She comes along willingly. Tonight is going to be a home run, I can just tell. All I have to do is want it. Want her—which I do.

I pull her to a stop in front of what used to be my favorite bookstore 20 years ago. It's long been closed. I don't know what type of business the building houses now, but at this hour it's deserted and dark. I lean her up against the smooth stone wall that's still cold from winter so recently giving way to spring. We kiss. This goes over well with her. I grab the back of her neck to keep her mouth locked tight on mine, and then our tongues go to town.

Sweet moans waft up between us. At first it's just Carly, but then I realize the moans are also coming from me. I'm happy to be out here in the night air, kissing her like this, with no work looming tomorrow. Nothing but night ahead.

I reach for her breast. I fondle the stiff nipple through her shirt and her moans explode into something more intense.

And it all comes back to me; this is the girl who's barely been kissed. This is the girl just waiting to be set on fire. This requires space, privacy, a bed even; a secret, shared experience of lust unleashed at last.

"I live over on Jane Street." My voice comes out hoarsely. "You want to come home with me?"

"Sure," she replies quickly, all eager eyes and slick, wet mouth.

✳

In the elevator in my building I try to keep my hands to myself, make small talk. I know we're on camera, security guards are watching. When I get her in my front door, though, it's hard to be civilized. I want to tear off her clothes, turn her upside down and devour her. Force her legs apart and plant my face between them, right up in there where I know she's already thick with lust, swollen lips all sopping wet, eager to give up the prize, the pink pearl, the little button of her clit. I'll suck that clit until it swells to twice its normal size. Until her thighs ache from being spread so wide and she's too wiped out from a daisy chain of orgasms to come even one more time. I could strap on a thick cock then and ride her hard from behind, keeping at her, working it without mercy, the cock filling her, stretching her hole wider than she thought she could ever take it, until even her anus is bulging open, pushing her level of insatiable desire clear into next week. Her fingers claw at the mess of tangled sheets; she grunts frantically. *Work it, Carly, work it*—until she's past exhaustion. Until that final frontier of ecstasy is reached and the come gushes out of that well-worked hole of hers uncontrollably and she literally squeals for me to stop.

"Can I get you a drink?" I ask, sounding alarmingly calm. How am I managing that, I wonder?

"Well…" She follows me into the kitchen. She gives it some thought, like she's going to come up with a request that's tropical and complex, that might require a bartender's manual or something. "Do you have beer?"

"Yes, Carly, I have beer."

"OK, then I'll have a beer."

I get her 20-and-a-half-year-old self a beer, but I don't bother with any more booze for me. I'm right where I want to be: caution thrown to the wind, my usual cranky reserve now a wide-open field. I'm willing to get reckless, to get down and dirty in the trenches, to unleash pure heaven on the body of a girl who's much too young. For me, anyhow. I've got no business being alone with her like this, even though she's willing and she seems ready. Under the covers of lust and momentary need there's a girl in the throes of unrequited love. But I have no love here. I've got everything but that.

"You want to go into the living room and sit down?" I ask.

"Mm-hmm," she barely answers. She's nursing the beer bottle now, practically suckling it. Her whole body looks tense. She's a veritable filly at the starting gate.

"Don't worry, all the odds are in your favor," I assure her.

"What does that mean?"

We sit down next to each other on my well-worn sofa. A lot of memories are hiding here, down deep in the fabric. Not only the joy and messy orgasms of other women, but tears and miscommunications and apathy as well.

"It means that you can relax, Carly. You look tense."

At this moment, I realize that no matter how many hours I keep her naked in my bed tonight, there aren't going to be any strap-ons. None of the over-the-topness that I'm so famous for; just fingers and tongues. This is a vanilla girl, someone who equates "risk" with "wrong" and the unexpected with anguish. Nevertheless, that trapped libido of hers is going to get a lot of mileage out of just plain vanilla. That much she can count on.

"I'm OK." She tries her hand at assuring me now. "I'm not nervous."

"You want to kiss a little more?"

"I sure do." She moves to set the beer bottle down on the coffee table. I notice she goes right for the coaster—a girl from a good family. That coffee table was expensive in its heyday. "Let's kiss some more," she says.

In a heartbeat, our lips are pressed together again, our tongues exploring. I'm not cautious now. I tug her shirttail up out of her jeans and single-handedly unbutton her shirt.

She seems perfectly content to keep kissing indefinitely while I grope her breasts through her bra. "Come on, Carly," I finally say. "Let's see those titties. Take this thing off."

She slips out of her shirt and then takes off the bra, tossing it who cares where. Her breasts are perfect. Not too large, not too small. They seem shy somehow, quivering a little, the pink nipples rock-hard.

Topless and growing bolder, she reaches for her beer. "Can I see yours?" she asks.

"Absolutely." My own shirt is off in another heartbeat. I'm not wearing a bra.

"Wow," she says, her tongue lingering over the rim of the bottle again, darting in little circles. "Nice." She can't take her eyes off me. "They're kind of big, huh?" The mere sight of my tits seems to have her transfixed. I'm starting to wonder if maybe I'm her first girl, right here, right now. Or at least the first she was able to take any time with.

"Carly? You want to put down that bottle and go for the real thing?"

She's very good at taking cues. She sets the bottle back down, slides over to me, and her mouth sucks my nipple in.

It feels exquisite. My nipples love to be sucked on, and she's applying just the right amount of pressure. In a nanosecond I'm wet, my clit engorged. We're both moaning contentedly on my sofa, topless—the suckler and the sucked-on. I suddenly feel like I could have my nipple sucked on like this for hours and not feel disappointed. I slide my fingers into Carly's hair and gently hold on. I guide her to the other tit. Then I let her take her time with each of them, as she moves back and forth, nipple to nipple. Giving my own pleasure time to swell, as her mouth stays busy.

When she comes up for air I give her a little of her own medicine. I ease her down onto her back and take some serious time with her nipples. Sucking on them, tugging them with my mouth, pulling them with my fingers. Lightly at first, then twisting and tugging them with more pressure, until she's writhing, squirming on the couch and I know that her nipples are aroused enough to withstand some serious torment.

I straddle her. I grasp each nipple firmly and roll the stiff tips like little balls between my fingers—both tits at the same time; I tug on those nipples like I think milk is going to come out. And then I clamp my mouth down on her mouth and shove my tongue in, keeping her searing whimpers jammed down in her throat, as I'm twisting and tugging, her hips writhing underneath me like mad.

This would be a good time to take down her pants, I realize. I slide off her. I undo her jeans. Then she's kicking them down her legs without any help from me. And then she yanks her panties down and off. A thatch of brown hair emerges. She's totally naked, slender and supple. She spreads her legs open, the thick smell of lust gives her away. I want to examine every slick fold of that lust. Right now, I need to have my mouth on her clit, need to slide my fingers up inside her and rub her insides into ecstasy and make her wet herself.

She has one of those hide 'n' seek clits, though. It's maddening. At first, I'm not sure I've found it. But then she lets out an urgent moan and grabs onto my hair. Bingo. My tongue captures it and I wiggle the hell out of its tiny hood. It sounds like I'm making her cry, but from the hold she has on my head, she seems to be enjoying it. Her knees pulled up to her tits, her thighs spread wide; the center of her whole aching world is open for me, and I slide my finger up into it.

Her cry heightens—or rather, the urgency of it. A single finger is a snug fit. Clearly, Carly's a virgin. For now, a single finger will have to do the patient work of two or three. Because right now I don't want to challenge her. All I want to do is make her come, preferably in my face.

With her knees up to her tits like this, my finger finds her spot easily. I rub it, press on it, push against it steadily while my tongue keeps at her clit. But one finger is not going to cut it; I need the pressure of at least two. I leave her clit alone for now. Instead, I suck on her hole. Lick it, stroke it, poke into it with my tongue.

There's a hymen there, all right, but I try sliding two fingers in now and she bears down on them, helping me, wanting the fingers up inside her no matter what.

"God, God," she's repeating in utter delirium. "That feels good, that feels good." She's grabbed onto her thighs now, spreading them impossibly wide. She's bearing down and pushing up. My tongue is back on her clit, my fingers are rubbing hard against her insides. "What's happening, what's happening?" she's chanting. "God, God. It feels good. I'm going to come, I'm going to come."

And true to her word, she showers me with Mount Vesuvius. She comes all over my face. The fluids spurt and splash and keep flowing down my furiously moving fingers, like those fluids have been trapped inside her, trying to come out for 20 and a half years.

"I'm sorry about your couch," she says at last.

"It's OK, it'll dry. You want a towel?"

"I want a lot of things," she admits, a wry smile on her face.

I have no ready answer for that remark. I'd like to be the one to give her those things she wants, whatever they are, but I'm not sure I should say that. I'm not sure how practical that would be. I'm leaving next week for a two-month stretch in Los Angeles. Because of my work, my life is always like that; New York, L.A., Toronto, Vancouver, and sometimes even clear across the world in Sydney, Australia.

She seems to be reading the expression on my face. I must look perplexed, and it's not going over very well.

"We all want a lot of things," I offer in my defense. "Different things at different times."

"Don't worry," she says. "For now, just a towel will be all right."

SLUT
RACHEL ESPLANADE

At the red light on a hill so steep, I need the parking brake, I slip
my hand onto your knee. Then, slowly, I slide my fingers up the
length of your creamy white thighs and under your black mini
dress. As a tease, I reach my hand down so I can flick my pinky
across your panties. "Oh, my," I turn toward you slightly, enough
for you to see my raised eyebrow. No panties. "You little slut." The
light changes, one stroke across your bare pubes before I drag my
pinky away from your pantyless pussy and slip off the parking
brake, turn left, and pass the turnoff home.

"Isn't that where…?"

"Yes, that's where I live." I let it hang there as I take a curve to
the right and maneuver us around the potholes in the snow, then
add, "I never take sluts home."

"Oh," you say it softly, like a sigh. Silence, another red light.

You turn to me. "Where are we going?"

I lean toward you and kiss you deeply, slip my pinky in
between your lips and start flicking your clit up and down with its
tip. The light's green and I keep my finger there. You are soaked.

"Do you really care?"

You squirm in your seat, "Mmm…" and a bitten lip is your only answer.

Then we are driving, driving from English to French Montreal, Canada, along the curve that splits the mountain like the jagged gap of a coffee bean. The trees break for a view of the Oratory, Université de Montréal, and the expanse of Outremont. All under the stars and the cold midnight blue of the cloudless sky. I drive us through the gap between steep cliffs, suddenly slip my pinky deep into your wet cunt, then remove it to turn right and guide us to a spot among the steamed-up cars at the lookout. I put the car into park, turn off the lights, and cut the engine. The only sound in the car is your breathing. I undo my seat belt, then yours. You are still biting your lip.

"So, what were you hoping was going to happen tonight, little slut?" You don't answer, but continue looking out at the Big O with a sneaky grin while wriggling your arms out of your long coat. I turn your face toward me, lean forward, and snog you deeply. I break the kiss to look at you. You look down, blush, then meet my eyes, a naughty look, expectant.

"I think I know what little sluts want." I reach over you and push your seat all the way back, slowly climb over you, not touching, drawing out each moment, teasing, until I am kneeling in front of you. "They want a good fuck." You inhale deeply. I lean toward you, and your lips reach out for me. We start kissing again, rough with plenty of tongue. I spread your knees and pull your ass to the edge of the seat, pulling you right up against me. I bury my face between your tits, biting the soft flesh between them, then stop to ask, "Is that what you want, slut, do you want a good strong fuck?"

"Yes, " you whisper into my hair. I move one of my hands up your thigh, fingertips at the lips of your soaked pussy.

I kiss your neck. "What was that?"

"Yes," you say it clearer and louder this time. I slip two fingers deep into your dripping cunt. My other hand moves to the small of your back. You squirm. I straighten my neck so that I can look into your soft brown eyes.

I ask you calmly, "What was that, slut? Do you want me to fuck you?"

"Yes. Please, please fuck me!" The urgency in your voice inspires me. I start pumping my fingers in and out of your sweet pussy. Your whole body starts to gyrate with the motion of my hand. We kiss again, but you can't concentrate on my lips and keep pulling away, bending your head back to gasp for air. You reach back to hold onto the headrest. A nipple pops out of the top of your dress. No bra either. Nice. I suck hard on your nipple, biting and licking the erect nib. You start to quiver, then thrash. Finally, your body tenses and the muscles in your cunt tighten so hard around my fingers they are almost pushed out. I bite your arched neck as a warm rush of sweet come envelops my fingers. You shake uncontrollably and stifle a scream.

"That's my little slut," I whisper into your neck before kissing you on the cheek. Slowly I remove my hand, wiping it on the inside of your thigh. I wrap my arms around your waist and hold you, keeping you warm as you come down.

"Thanks, baby," you say softly and kiss the top of my head, then return my embrace.

"Do you think that's it?" I smile mischievously up at you. "That was just the beginning. I want to see how much of a little slut you are. Into the back seat, slut." Obediently, you climb over the seat, carefully so as not to hit me with your knee-high leather boots. I catch a glimpse of your bare pussy and sweet ass. Yum. I slap your ass then climb over after you, push you up against the back seat. I flip my seat forward and kneel in the V of your spread legs. Cheekily you lift up the hem of your dress. I slide my hands under your ass, cup and pull it toward me before diving my face into your sweet pussy, licking and sucking until I have had my fill and am completely soaked under my pants.

When I'm finished I sit up next to you on the seat. You are panting slightly and your fists are still clenched. I can see your breath. I bend my head toward yours, your juices still on my face, to kiss you hard on the lips. I pause, then say, "I love fucking my little slut." You smile guiltily. I keep on kissing you, undo my pants until the dildo I've had strapped on the whole time pops out. "Do you want some of this, slut?" You open your eyes, look down, then nod frantically.

"Yes! Oh, please, fuck me."

I pull you on top of me and slide the dildo deep into you, your dripping cunt taking the entire shaft. "Uh-uh, slut, you've got to ride this one." You start riding straight up and down, your hands gripping the seat behind me. I meet your every downstroke with a thrust. Each time we push against each other, the dildo hits my clit. Soon we are both thrusting harder and faster. I grab your ass to hold you still and tight down on my lap while I give you a few strong, deep strokes. You go wild, digging your nails into my shoulders and letting out the sexiest moany scream.

"Take your dress off," I command you between gritted teeth. You pull it up over your head and off in one swift sexy motion, letting it crumple on the seat beside me. I let go of your ass, and you start fucking me again, up and down, up and down, each thrust hitting your G spot and my clit at the same time, your beautiful tits bouncing in my face. I'm in heaven.

All of a sudden, I start quivering uncontrollably. You are still pumping away, but I am only able to thrust my hips into you sporadically. I give into the sensation, feel all of the muscles in my pussy tense and then relax again, over and over until I think I'm going to pass out. I lean my head all the way back, surrendering to the waves of pleasure. You continue to ride, your perfect breasts bouncing in front of me. You are so fucking hot. I love it. Love that you know what you want and how to get it. Love that you are my girl and that you don't always wear panties.

VOYAGE ABOARD THE QUEEN

RONICA BLACK

She stood in front of me, wearing that shirt that could bring me to my knees and make me beg for a taste of her. Tight-fitting and sleeveless, it hugged her apple-size breasts, and an image of their creamy softness and pink, perky centers swirled like delicious strawberry candy. She reached up and scratched the top of her sinewy arm, bronzed from the year-round warmth of the Arizona sun of our home. The wind picked up, carrying a strand of auburn hair across her angled face to tickle her rosy lips.

Catching my leer out of the corner of her eye, she turned to me, tucking the wind-wisped hair nervously behind her ear. "What?" she prompted softly, a shy grin spreading across her face.

She knew *what*.

She knew me like the back of her own hand. And she knew exactly what it was that was written in my gaze. I stood still, unanswering and unwavering. My lust was potent and dripping from me, seeping through every pore and allowing the wind to carry it to her. She stepped closer and pulled the sunglasses away from her hazel eyes. She studied my face, her vision lingering over my lips like a caress. Her pupils widened as she licked her lips with anticipation.

Yes.

She had answered her own question.

I brushed my fingers lightly across her wrist. Her skin came alive with goose bumps; I couldn't wait much longer to awaken the rest of her.

An ominous voice squawked in our ears and pulled us back into our surroundings. The line to board the cruise ship began to move slowly, and I smiled as she walked ahead of me, her ass teasing me in faded blue jeans.

Around me swarmed hundreds of lesbians, buzzing in my ears like bees. Laughter, chatter, and shrieks of excitement warped together in a crooning drone. My focus tunneled, never wavering from the walking sex in front of me. I was uninterested in the bees around me, for I had my sights on the queen.

We walked through the ship's corridors, silently searching for our stateroom, our key already in hand. She felt my eyes on her backside, tickling her with the heat of my desire. When the heat got too much to bear, she'd look over her shoulder at me and toss me a lopsided grin, which carried a penetrating heat of its own.

She stopped ahead of me and stood before a door, waiting for me to come to her before she unlocked it. I moved in behind her with panther-like quickness and leaned in to inhale the scent of her shampoo. My breath was like a sexual stroke on the back of her neck, and her knees quivered as she hastily unlocked the door and flung it open, knowing it granted not only entrance to our room but also entrance to each other.

I swung the door shut with force and she jumped on me, wrapping her long legs around my waist, her mouth on mine, sucking and probing me, tasting me, claiming me. I turned and pressed her back against the wall while I pushed my hips against her; she moaned and clawed at my back. She grabbed a fistful of my hair in one hand and aggressively pulled my bruised lips from hers.

"I want you to fuck me," she whispered hoarsely.

My heart thudded in my chest, and I carried her over to the bed and set her down gently. Kneeling before her, I yanked her shirt from the waist of her Levi's. Wanting and needing to taste her, my desire flooded up from my center, leaving my mouth molten and watering. Her face was flushed with desire, her hands shaking as she grabbed mine to stop me.

"Wait, not yet," she said, reclaiming more of her voice. "Let's wait."

My blood was too busy pounding between my legs for me to comprehend her meaning, and I shook my head in confusion. "For what?" I asked.

"I thought we could wait until after the ball tonight. You know, let the anticipation build?" She leered at me with her dark green eyes flecked mischievously with brown.

I swallowed back my bubbling desire and willed my legs to stand. Her request played in my mind; I agreed to wait. Imagining the impending intensity of the evening helped to ease the pain of patience.

The ball itself was hours away, and I flopped helplessly down on the bed beside her in mock defeat. "I promise it'll be worth the wait," she said impishly as she lightly pinched my nipple through my shirt. I groaned a warning to her, and she jumped off the bed with bounding energy and teasing in her eyes. "In the meantime, we can go swimming..." she said as she began stripping before me and trotting off into the bathroom to change.

✳

My rum and Coke was as warm as the sun. I ran a hand through my short blond hair and squinted into the white afternoon heat. The smell of coconut wafted into my nostrils, carried from the oil-glistening bodies of fellow sunbathers. I watched lazily as my queen exited up the steps out of the pool. Sun-kissed and sinewy, she moved with a catlike gracefulness. Her nipples, erect and wanting freedom, poked at the wet fabric of her bikini, and I licked my lips as I watched her body, slick with oil, effortlessly shed the water off in hundreds of droplets.

"Hi, darlin'. " She greeted me with a grin as she purposely let water drip on my bare abdomen. The leering was now being done on her end, as she looked hungrily at my muscular body. "Where is a piece of ice when I need it?" she asked as her gaze lingered on my breasts. I knew she would tease me as long as she possibly could. Building the anticipation was something she was very good at, and she would play it out until the very end, bringing me to the point of sheer insanity.

"It's almost time," I said with pleasure as she dried herself off before me. I stood, deciding to take one last cool swim before I had to get ready and the evening started.

"I'll see you later." She tilted my chin toward her and planted a soft warm coconut kiss on my lips. She left me with a smile as she went ahead to the stateroom to ready herself for the ball. As previously arranged, she would arrive at the ball ahead of me.

A long swim and two more rum and Cokes later I let myself into the stateroom to get ready. The smell of her perfume hit me like a shock wave of lust, and I tore my bikini off in a newfound hurry. Her presence was strong and powerful, and I jumped in the shower to try to refocus. I only had a short time to get ready before I was due at the ball, where she now awaited me.

Exiting the steamy shower, I felt relaxed and eager to focus on the task at hand. I walked nude and freshly scrubbed into the bedroom, where I unzipped my garment bag and removed a black tuxedo. It had been decided before the cruise that I would be the one to wear the tux to the "ladies and gents" themed ball. I had never dressed in drag before, but the once-crazy prospect now excited me to no end. I suddenly wanted to be the most convincing gent at the ball, and I wanted to sweep my lady off her feet.

I opened up my suitcase and pulled out a bag that contained some men's products. I held up a brand new pair of men's briefs. "Well, here goes," I said to myself as I tried on the tighty-whiteys and laughed. Next, I pulled on a tight-fitting sports bra and squeezed my C cups into it, hoping it would help to flatten them out without turning me purple in the process. It seemed to do the trick.

I then applied some men's deodorant and sprayed on the men's cologne that drove us both wild. I pulled on my white undershirt and stepped into the tuxedo pants. Just before I zipped them up, I carefully placed a small dildo in my underwear, sticking the shaft through the front hole. Feeling its cool base resting just above my clitoris, I became instantly aroused, and I let thoughts of its intended use swim in my brain. Smiling, I zipped up my pants and looked it the mirror, hoping it would look like I had a nice little package.

Satisfied, and feeling strangely powerful, I finished dressing and stepped in front of the bathroom mirror to do my hair. I fingered lots of gel through my thick wet hair and maneuvered it so it looked very modern and masculine—some tussled spikes, but still very debonair. Finally, I placed one small gold hoop in my left ear, and I straightened my bow tie. I almost didn't recognize my own reflection as I examined my classic features, made more prominent by the hairstyle. Feeling confident and very "Sean Connery," I headed out to the ball.

The event itself was held in a large ballroom on the uppermost deck of the ship. The sun had already kissed the Caribbean Sea good night and the sky was purpling with darkness when I stepped into the dimly lit ballroom. The brass band played a soft tune as the last of the gents wandered in, dressed to the nines in various styles of tuxedo. I stood among the others, letting my eyes adjust to the low light, trying to find my queen on the other side of the room, dining and socializing as all the ladies were doing.

The band picked up and began playing a big band tune from the 1940s as I walked slowly through the dance floor to the other side of the ballroom, scanning the crowd, searching faces, looking for the one. Several women said something to me in way of greeting, but I merely smiled and nodded hello, needing to find her, needing to see her.

Not yet able to locate her, I approached the bar and ordered a screwdriver. I was taking my first sip when I caught the faint scent of her perfume. I felt her leaning into my back. "I'll take a slow screw." Her voice purred in my ear and vibrated down to my very core, stoking my fire. I smiled and turned to face her, this creature of my desire. A tight black sequined dress gloved her body and ended a few inches above her knees. My eyes blazed a trail down her legs, noting the dark stockings and wanting to find out how they were held up.

"You look unbelievable," I said as I looked into her eyes and watched them sparkle with wild desire.

"You look absolutely gorgeous yourself." She leaned into me and groped my crotch. "And what have we here?" she asked as she took the tip of my earlobe into her mouth and sucked lightly.

"I brought a friend," I replied with a grin, thinking of all the different positions in which I would like to introduce them. I swallowed hard and felt my pupils enlarge as my eyes took her in. I needed to feel the warmth of her pressed up against me. "Would you like to dance?" I asked, my voice sultry with intent. My lips brushed the top of her hand, my eyes caressing her elegant face. Her auburn hair reflected the soft light from the chandeliers and fell to rest on her tanned shoulders.

Slowly, I led her to the dance floor, where the band had begun to play a slower tune. I pulled her to me, slowly, surely, craving her scent, her very essence. She wrapped her arms around my shoulders and tickled the back of my neck with her fingers, playing me like an erotic violin. More couples moved in next to us, and we lost ourselves among the crowd, lost in each other.

Song after song we danced, our passion slowly escalating. I breathed in deep, letting her scent claim me, and I whispered my desires in her ear and spoke of my dwindling control. Her response was a groan in my ear and a deliberate movement of her hips against my crotch. I eased my hands down her bare back and rested them on the tight globes of her ass, pulling her into me.

My aching mouth suckled her neck, causing a sharp intake of breath on her part.

Clinging to each other ravenously, we stood frozen in time in the middle of the emptying dance floor. The band had stopped playing, and I had failed to even notice, the humming of desire was so alive in my ears. A woman walked onstage and began speaking, but her voice was lost to me before it ever reached my ears. Applause rang out around me as couples focused on the woman onstage. With attention solely on the stage, we took advantage and wound our way through the crowd toward the door. I was being led hastily out of the ballroom and outside to the upper deck.

"Don't you want to see what's going on inside?" I said breathlessly, not really caring. She responded by grabbing my jacket and slamming me up against the wall. Her mouth took mine with a vengeance, causing the fire within me to rage, and I knew now that there would be no stopping us. The anticipation that had been building all day seized my rational thoughts and held them captive.

Hands wrapped tightly around her, I turned and pinned her against the wall, all the while letting my tongue explore her mouth with a fierce hunger. This hunger had been stoked and teased with the crumbs of her teasing throughout the day and it had left me absolutely ravenous for her.

Like a crazed bloodthirsty vampire, I had to feed. I had to feed now. Only it wasn't her blood I craved. As if it had a mind of its own, my hand drifted up her stocking-clad leg to find what my insides craved. I smiled when I felt the warm flesh of her bare thigh flanked by garters, but I nearly choked with surprise when my hand continued upward and felt the hot slickness of her center. My touch to the exposed petals of her center rocked her, and she tore her mouth from mine. "That's my little surprise," she whispered to me, referring to her pantyless crusade, her voice quivering along with her knees.

Adrenaline surged through me like hot liquid lust, and I

grabbed her hand and led her around to the other side of the ship, where we would have more privacy. Once out of immediate sight we kissed again, harder, deeper, letting ourselves go. I reached back up underneath her skirt and stroked her swollen clit with my two fingers. Up and down I milked her for her cries of pleasure. Waves of ecstasy crashed through her again and again at the request of my fingers. Her breath entered hot in my ear and traveled with lightning speed to my own aching center.

I was craving the taste of her on my tongue. I knelt before her and lapped at the hot silk sex until I had her essence running down my chin. My hunger for her still ruling me, I stood and turned her to face the wall. Slowly lifting her skirt, my hands encircled the milky white flesh of her firm ass, and I knelt down like a ravenous animal and bit each cheek in mock dominance. Shrieking with delight, she threw electric words of want over her shoulder, begging for me to take her.

Mouth suddenly dry, ears ringing, I unzipped my pants and maneuvered my dildo carefully into her wet, slick hole. She instantly threw her head back in pleasure and cried my name out into the still, moonlit night, her voice strained in pleasure. My face felt hot with excitement, and blood pounded in my ears—I had never wanted anything more in my life.

With my right hand wound in her hair, I tugged her head back close to my mouth, where I nibbled on her ear and suckled hungrily at her exposed neck. My left hand held her firm around her hips and between her legs, resting on her blood-engorged clit. There, beneath the midnight-blue sky and the soft sounds of the ocean, I fucked her from behind, my own impending orgasm threatening to shake my very foundation.

Breathless and heavenly spent, I rested my head on her chest for a brief moment, until voices from the ball echoed into our private velvet night. People were leaving the ball and staggering with alcohol-laced laughter toward us. With fear of being seen—but mostly with fear of being interrupted—I quickly zipped up my pants and pulled her along behind me and down the stairs to the next level.

She stopped me at the bottom of the stairs and knelt down with deliberation before me, leering up at me as she unzipped my pants. With confident hands she pulled out the dildo, slick with her own juices, and began to slowly suck. The sight of her taking me into her mouth turned me on tremendously, to the point where I could almost imagine feeling her. Then, with her thumbs she found my hungry clit and began to stroke as she sucked my protruding cock. I slammed my head back against the wall and shuddered with pleasure. She laughed wickedly at my obvious enjoyment, then pulled the dildo out of the way and yanked my pants down around my ankles. Her fingers claimed me deep inside, curling snug against my G spot. Her tongue worked its molten magic on my clit, massaging in mesmerizing movements.

The desire she was stirring within me felt purely animalistic, causing me to immediately want her again. The pleasure she was searing into me with her tongue and fingers sent my mind reeling with images of her and what I wanted to do to her to make her mine and mine alone. The flickering projection of my mind's own porn pushed me beyond my rising crest and past the breaking point.

I pulled her head into me as I came, the orgasm smashing through me like thunder rolling through storm clouds. Flashes of lightning from the resciding orgasmic storm lit up her face as she smiled triumphantly up at me. My head spun, my legs buckled with weakness, and the approaching sound of muffled voices pricked my ears.

Hastily yanking up my pants for me, she pulled me, running along after her, to our stateroom. As if it were being replayed from earlier in the day, I swung the door shut with force and she came at me like a cheetah, sultry and graceful, hunting its prey. Chest rising and falling from excitement, arousal, and adrenaline, I stood still and let her undress me. She pulled the sports bra over my head, freeing my bound breasts from their restraint. Taking them in her mouth one at a time, claiming each nipple with the flicking of her tongue, she once again brought me home to the palace of uninhibited pleasure that had been evading me all day. Upon hearing my moans she stepped back and looked at me with intensity as I stood before her completely nude. "You know, you looked good as a man, but I'm so damn glad you're a woman."

"Ditto," I said, my voice faltering, my desire once again escalating as she led me to our bed.

VIRILITY PLUS
LISA E. DAVIS

I sang alto in the church choir at Crestview Baptist mainly because of Barbara, who played the piano at Wednesday night choir practice. She was blond, with a cute pixie frame and round rosy cheeks like an old-fashioned china-headed doll. I couldn't keep my eyes off her big firm breasts, swelling inside her sweater as she pounded away at *"Just as I am, without one plea, but that thy blood was shed for me…"*

The longer I watched Barbara the more I ached right at the crotch of my jeans and almost forgot to sing. Once I saw the choir director looking at me funny, and I knew I'd better straighten up fast.

"You feelin' all right, Lottie?" he asked me after practice was over.

"Oh, sure," I said, "Just a little worn-out tonight. We've been awfully busy at work."

But I was about to perk up. When the rest of the choir filed out of the loft and into the night—"Bye-bye, see you Sunday"—I hung back, heart pounding like that hard knot between my legs.

Barbara was smiling away at the people leaving, still sitting on the piano bench. "Come on over, Lottie, and sit by me," she said, so they could hear. "Thank you for offerin' to help out."

I smiled sweetly and waved goodbye to everybody. "Lottie's

gonna help me with that new piece," Barbara explained to the choir director, "turnin' the pages. She plays a little piano herself."

"That's mighty nice of you, Lottie," he said, "Don't stay too late, though."

Then we were alone. I pressed my knee urgently against Barbara's. She'd asked me to stay, making up excuses. I knew she could've managed the page-turning by herself, and she knew I knew. I guess she'd missed me too. Since she lived with her maiden aunt, we usually got together at my place. Long afternoons on the weekends, and sometimes she stayed over. Any time with Barbara was a real good time. But she'd had relatives visiting, and between one thing and another, I hadn't seen her in a couple of weeks—not since I'd started taking those pills. I wanted her awful bad.

"I guess we better get started," Barbara said, smooth as glass. But she rested one hand on my knee, then gripped it tight like an electric shock running up my thigh. That knot that was my clitoris was exploding inside my jeans, pushing up against the inside seam.

They were working! I almost hollered out. Those damn pills were working!

Suddenly I saw she was leaning down toward the floor, holding on to me, trying to pull the music out of her big purse. She was shorter than me—I'm a tall, rawboned girl—and couldn't quite reach it.

"Lemme do it," I whispered into her backside as I leaned around behind her, snagging the piano music, burying my face in her skirts. She smelled like honey and rose petals, and I sniffed her shamelessly, like an old hound dog.

It was those damn pills; it had to be! I'd never felt anything like it in my life. I screamed out her name as I grabbed her around the waist, hands stealing over her breasts.

"Lottie," she moaned, "Lottie, wait."

But I couldn't wait. I was coming in my jeans and had to feel her close. I slid off the piano bench and pulled her on top of me. Shaking like a leaf, I rubbed myself against her thigh, covering her with kisses. I pressed into her hard, then fell back spent. A warm wetness spread down my leg.

"Oh, Lottie," she moaned again. "What was that?"

I rolled off her, not knowing myself for certain, but pretty sure now that it was those pills!

Her eyes wide, Barbara reached over and touched the bulge at the front of my jeans, then pulled down my zipper. My clitoris poked up at us, rock-hard, just like the ad said; bigger and thicker than anything I'd ever seen that could still call itself a clitoris.

I was scared there for a minute. I'd only taken three pills a day with meals, just like they said. I hadn't exceeded five a day, like they warned. But what if my erection lasted more than four hours? I'd have to seek immediate medical attention, like they suggested.

Then Barbara brought me back with "Don't go, Lottie! Please, don't ever go!" Lying half under the piano bench, she was lifting her skirts and pulling me down on her. My fear evaporated, and I thanked God almighty for those damned pills.

✳

Yes, I told Barbara all about it that night under the piano bench, on the sanctuary floor. I had succumbed to temptation, but hell's bells, they'd made that temptation hard to ignore. For a long time, every time I started up my computer, went to the Internet, what was waiting for me but another half-dozen e-mails about "male enhancement formulas"? Penis enlargement pills, in other words, "100% safe and natural."

Every day another one showed up, announcing "Size *does* matter" and "Please her now." That last one interested me right from the start. But you didn't know until you opened it what they were selling. At first I could just imagine those e-mails going out to everybody in the world—kids, grandmothers, good churchgoing people—who didn't want to read about "spectacular intercourse" and "more frequent, vibrant orgasms."

But then I thought to myself, *What's wrong with that? Wouldn't everybody like to have more frequent and vibrant orgasms?* But most of all I thought of Barbara, and how something a little longer, thicker, and harder between my legs couldn't hurt my chances with her any. She'd never complained about our lovemaking before. But you never knew what women were thinking, and I didn't want her playing around with anybody else in the congregation.

So I pressed that button that said ORDER NOW and made up a name, Lawrence Moon. My credit card read L. E. Moon anyway. They doubled my order for free, and they weren't kidding about prompt delivery. Before you could say "Jack Robinson" that little parcel had arrived on my doorstep in a plain brown wrapper. Inside was my double order with bright red labels that read VIRILITY PLUS and, underneath in smaller black type, NATURAL PENIS ENLARGEMENT.

Well, what's sauce for the goose is sauce for the gander, or vice versa, I thought, and read over the ingredients to see what they put in it, not wanting to damage myself. Cayenne, ginseng, licorice—sounded just like a fancy recipe to me, except for that "extract of bovine testes," and there was just a little bit of that.

I followed the instructions carefully and didn't notice anything the first few days. Then the second week in the shower, when I was washing my private parts, they felt a little more sensitive than usual. In fact, I had to take a minute to calm myself down with a hand job, which I usually don't do in the morning, much less in the shower. But it didn't seem to hurt anything or anybody. I went on to work and forgot all about it.

Until a few days later. Continuing my regular dosage, I was looking through my latest *Playboy*—the gay boy at the pharmacy sets one aside for me and slips it to me when I come in—and I was feeling more than usually taken by the Playmate of the Month. I was always partial to blonds, and she was a doozy— petite, stacked like Barbara, and ripe for the picking. I was exhausted when I finally put that magazine down.

And the first time with Barbara after the pills, I couldn't have asked for anything better. I thought about writing a letter to the company, thanking them and encouraging them to market to girls too. But Barbara said maybe that wasn't smart; they might get the wrong idea and investigate. She wanted to make sure I kept on getting my pills.

*

Then my bubble burst, my heart broke, and I said goodbye to Barbara and Crestview Baptist forever. It was after Sunday services, where the choir had sung a lively version of "Onward, Christian Soldiers," with drums and trumpets from the high school band marching around the sanctuary, and Barbara had played her new piano solo while the collection plate was passed. I was feeling good about everything, looking forward to spending a good part of the afternoon with Barbara checking out the progress of my Virility Plus pills.

But when I handed the choir director my choir robe, he notified me with a blank look, "The Reverend Brumbalow wants to see you in his study for a minute, Lottie."

"Me?" I questioned. "Why would he wanna see me?"

"Lottie, how would I know? You just go along now, don't keep the reverend waitin'."

I knocked on his study door and went on in. Despite his pot belly, the Reverend Brumbalow was down on his knees in front of the nice tapestry sofa. "Amen," I heard him say before he raised his head and looked up at me pitifully.

"Lottie," he cried out, "we're all sinners."

"Yes, reverend."

"And my job, Lottie, is to guide sinners in the straight and narrow that they may come to a safe haven in Christ. *For straight is the gate and narrow is the way that leadeth unto life...*"

I nodded, and he seemed encouraged.

"But lately I've heard things, Lottie, that make me realize I've failed as your pastor."

"I'm sorry, reverend," I replied, feeling uncomfortable.

Still on his knees, not wasting any time, the Reverend Brumbalow pulled a bottle out of his jacket pocket. "Do you know what this is, Lottie?"

"No, sir," I lied. Of course I knew what it was. It said VIRILITY PLUS in big letters on a bright red label. But what was the reverend doing with it?

When I didn't confess, he started acting really strange and tried to pull me down beside him. "Pray with me, Lottie!"

"Uh, I got a bad knee, reverend. Basketball."

He backed off and struggled to his feet. "You must not remember, Lottie, when I preached against crotch medicine?" His voice rose. "All kinds of crotch medicine—Viagra, Cialis, and the rest of it too!"

I put on my best poker face. "I don't know, reverend. Maybe I missed that Sunday."

"Remember the Sabbath to keep it holy," he insisted, not taking no for an answer. "Nobody can be playing around with crotch medicine. It's the devil's own handiwork."

"Yes, reverend."

"Crotch medicine leads you into abominations." He was waving his hands around by now like this was a revival meeting, on the verge of shouting. "Allows fornication to get a hammerlock on you."

When I didn't say anything, he seemed to run out of steam. In a softer voice he said, "Why, I've had grown men in here crying to me, good family men, confessing their sin, repenting and turning in their…" He paused. "Their pills."

So maybe that was where he got them, from those poor sinners who'd yielded to temptation. But the Reverend Brumbalow had a computer just like everybody else, a credit card too, and we were all sinners. He said so. Just like me, he could've gotten a double order free.

"But listen to me, Lottie," he whined, plopping down on the sofa, "I never had any women in here who'd fallen into sin, lookin' to enhance what God gave them for the procreation of the race, the cradlin' of life." He hung his head, the Virility Plus bottle dangling between his knees, and mumbled, "You gotta keep your body the temple of the Holy Spirit."

I sensed his attack of hysterics was passing. But how could he have connected me up with those pills?

"I don't know what you're talkin' about, reverend," I lied again.

"Oh, Lottie, I'm not judging you. *Judge not that ye be not judged.* But I know you do know. I know because…"

He didn't have to finish that sentence. Nobody else knew about my pills, nobody had any reason to know except—and my heart skipped a few beats—Barbara, my Barbara.

"That bitch," I hissed all of a sudden.

The Reverend Brumbalow lowered his eyes, knowing I'd figured something out. "You can't blame anybody else, Lottie," he pleaded now. *"Be sure your sins will find you out.* And that woman asked me for help. She was backsliding into hell."

He stared up at me, begging for understanding. Then a sort of sly grin crept over that pudgy face. "I can help you too, Lottie," he whispered.

Suddenly I felt his fat limp hand on my thigh like he was feeling for something. "Confess everything to me, Lottie, and I'll help make you clean and whole again. *Washed in the blood."* He began to sing as he ran his hand up into my crotch: *"Just as I am and waiting not, to cleanse my soul of one dark blot…"* He was fumbling with the zipper on my best Sunday go-to-meeting pants. "Get down here, Lottie, and pray with me."

I was madder than hell and not about to get down and pray with some jackleg preacher whose mind certainly wasn't on the Lord. I gave him a push that sent him sprawling off the sofa and onto the floor.

"Is this how you helped Barbara?" I hollered at him.

He rolled around until he was sitting up but couldn't answer me because I stomped over to the door and threw it open. On the other side Barbara was waiting, weeping crocodile tears.

"Oh, Lottie, Lottie, I'm so sorry. I had to confess to somebody.

I was afraid I was backsliding, going back to the kind of girl I used to be." She told me things she'd never confessed before, about sleeping around with almost the entire congregation, both sexes, married and unmarried. "I was common as dirt," she whispered.

How could anybody compete with all that guilt? "But did you have to sleep with old Potbelly Brumbalow too?" I asked without mercy. She didn't answer, and I walked out. "I loved you, Barbara," I said to myself, getting into my car.

That night I didn't answer the phone, and the next day I went in and quit my job. The day after, I packed up a few clothes and things I wanted to keep—nothing to remind me of Barbara—and drove off into the sunset that very evening, heading for San Francisco or parts unknown. My Virility Plus pills I stored in the glove compartment for safekeeping.

But I never really needed them again. My clitoral enlargement proved to be permanent, and I've never since lacked for love and companionship. As the good book says, "The Lord loveth a cheerful giver," and thanks to Virility Plus, I've got a lot to give.

NEED
STEFKA

I felt like a caged animal, the tension deep inside me creeping along my spine like fingers, becoming more noticeable with each passing minute. I was wearing down my office floor with my incessant pacing. My hair was wild from my hands running through it, but I couldn't seem to stop myself. Everything—from the way the clothes I wore rubbed along my skin to the fine sheen of sweat gathering across my forehead—was much more vivid to me, more alive, and yet I felt boxed in. I wanted to see her.

I moved to the window as if in a trance and stopped just short of the glass. I saw nothing outside; all I felt was the sun's rays touching my face as it warmed the rest of the city. *Go to her.*

I placed my heated forehead on the cool glass and closed my eyes as my palms settled on either side of my head. The tension built until a simple flicker of movement caused me to shiver. The memory of her touch raked across my skin, and I couldn't hold back a soft gasp as I felt it all over again. The sting of her nails, the pinch of her teeth, and the sweetness of her breath swirled around me as I drowned myself in those memories. *Taste her.*

I ran my tongue over my dry lips and I did taste her. I felt her all over me: the breeze of her hair across my back, the wetness of her lips along my skin, and the breathy gasp of her saying my name in my ear. I felt it all anew and I shuddered once again, my hands clinching into fists against the glass as I shook. *Need her.*

I groaned as I whirled around and began pacing once more. A woman should have no right to have such an effect on me, crowding my head with visions of her skin glistening with sweat, her nipples hard and swollen, her lips bruised from harsh kissing as her hair clung wetly to her forehead. Her intense eyes doing me in with their wide, trusting gaze as her chest rose rapidly up and down with her need. I still could feel it all; I couldn't shut it off even if I tried. I couldn't ignore her voice echoing in my ears; I didn't want to. *Want her.*

I stood in the middle of the room and felt my need for her growing with each quick breath I took. My hands rose on their own, and I could still feel the unique texture of her skin under my fingers, raised welts, and the wetness of her response. I put a finger inside my mouth, and I tasted her all over again. So sweet and tangy on the tip of my tongue, the hard nub throbbing as I lay my lips over it, the way she opened up like a flower as I licked her, her shivers against my ears as her thighs clenched around them. I lowered my hand and raised my head as I wept. *Go to her.*

Do I dare leave this cage and have her set me free all over again? Do I dare show her how much she controls me? God, yes. I opened my eyes and made my decision.

I could hear my need in my voice as I canceled my appointments, but I didn't care; all I wanted was to be at her side. My face was fierce as I walked at a brisk pace to the elevator—people stared as I jabbed at the button again and again. I didn't care what they were thinking; I was focused on my desire.

Everything seemed to slow as I rode the elevator down. The longer it seemed to take, the pricklier my skin became. It hurt. It ached. My need was so strong that my clothes felt like chains. I felt as if I were sitting on spikes yet floating on air. Everything around me smelled like her—the interior of the car, the crisp air outside, everything. Images floated behind my eyelids, and every time I blinked I saw something of her: a flash of a knee, a wisp of hair, the color of her eye, the wetness of her lips. Each image rattled my cage even further, and my chest rumbled with my growls as my fingers clenched and unclenched the steering wheel. Sweat covered me, like her fingers, trailing along and leaving a mark behind.

I ignored all other sounds but the ones that kept playing in my head. Her moans, her laugh, her voice, her commands, all in a voice that held my heart in my throat. It vibrated through me, purred in my ear, caressing me like the rest of her, in soft, sharp tones, leaving its mark all over me.

I shut off the engine, wanting to bolt out of the car, run to her, and never let her go. Instead, I sat there simmering in my world. I wanted to wrap my need around me so she could see without a word what she does to me. I felt hot all over, sensitive and tough, ready for anything and ready for nothing. One touch from her would set me aflame, one word would push me over, one taste would ease me, one look from her and I would die.

Just beyond that door, my need. My breath hurt, my body ached…the animal inside me wanted to burst forth. I could feel its claws below the surface, tearing at me from the inside out. Was she ready? Was I ready? Go and see.

I forced my steps to be slow and purposeful, even though all I wanted was to break into a run and not stop until I saw her. I focused on the sound of my feet as I walked up the sidewalk and onto the porch. My hand shook as I gripped the door and turned the knob. I couldn't hold back a whimper as it opened and I looked beyond it. I sniffed the air and smelled her. She was everywhere. I stepped inside and quietly closed the door. The music hid the sounds I made; the pounding beat banged with the beast's cries, rattling my cage even more. *Find her.*

I bit my lip to keep from calling out to her. I tasted my blood as I walked into the living room. Her presence was so thick in the air, I could taste it. I could feel her all around me, teasing me, tormenting me, and my rumbling chest grew louder. I tore off my suit jacket and tossed it away as I prowled deeper into the house, the cool air sending chills along my wet shirt, making me shiver. I sniffed the air again and followed her scent. She was close, so very close.

I found her in the study. I stopped at the door and took in the sight of her, letting my eyes devour her even though the rest of me needed her more. She wore shorts, close-fitting ones that hugged her ass like my hands had done so many times before. Her feet were bare, the bottoms of them being caressed by the carpet as she unconsciously swayed to the music while she looked at something I couldn't see. Her hair, a dusky brown, was slightly damp and smelled of flowers and soap. My hands tingled with the need to grip the wondrous mane and yank her head back, to bare her throat for my teeth, but I waited. I just wanted to see her, to watch her, to inhale her for a brief moment before I acted. She took my breath away with her simplicity and complexities. *Take her.*

I silently moved toward her, my breathing almost nonexistent. Just as I reached her she started to turn, and I grabbed her from behind and buried my face in her hair, growling a warning as I reached for the opening of her shirt and pulled it apart. The sound of ripping material spurred me on, and I bit into her neck as I pulled her closer. I heard her gasp as I ripped her bra and shoved her shirt aside before grabbing her breasts and squeezing hard.

Her ass pressed against me, and I ground my hips against her as I continued to maul her neck with my mouth, not caring about marks. I couldn't find my voice to warn her, all that came out was my deep rumbling growl as my hands ate her clothes, leaving them in tatters on the floor. The smell of her did me in, and I clutched at her, trying to convey what I needed without words. The cage was open and the beast was out.

I whirled her around and let her look at what she had created, my hand buried deep in her hair as I stood there. Her large eyes widened and then darkened as her tongue moistened her already wet lips. I could feel her tremble. Did she fear this? Did she fear me? I couldn't find the words to ask, so I stared, trying to tell her with every part of me. She continued to look into my eyes as she raised a hand and touched my face. It was a light, almost fleeting, caress, but I felt her need and saw it in her eyes.

My control left me as I grabbed hold of her and literally dragged her toward the bedroom, my grunts vibrating the walls as I pulled her along. She had to know what I was, had to know what she had created, and I prayed that she also knew that it was she who had to control me. I entered the room and tossed her on the bed as I followed her there, covering her body with mine as I took a nipple and chewed. She arched and buried her hands in my hair to press me closer.

Could two people lose control and still be sane after it was all over? There was no gentleness in my touch. When I tasted her lips, it was a cruel kiss, bringing more blood into my mouth as I pressed harder against her.

Her nails clawed and scratched at my back, tearing at the shirt in a frenzy of movement, ripping it as I had hers. I howled against her lips as her nails found their mark and ripped. *Hurt me,* I thought, *make me ache more, make me need more, please.* I begged her with my hands, telling her with my fingers what I needed. I ground my hips harshly into her, looking down at her, seeing my marks all over her, and I growled again as she dug deeper into my soul with her nails. Her eyes were as wild as mine, her breathing as harsh as mine, her need as great as mine—and as I slammed two fingers inside of her and started to push her over, I saw her love as deep as mine as well.

I brought her forth with everything I had, pounding into her like nothing before, and when she screamed and arched I collapsed, breathing like a freight train. She shoved me aside and I rolled off of her, burying my face in the pillow as she got up. I didn't look at her; I still was too raw, too needy to do that. I simply lay there, trying to find some control.

When I felt that first biting sting of the whip across my raw back, I jerked off the bed and stood before her, my eyes blazing. I faced her with every intention of removing that whip and using it on her, but after one look at the fierce beauty standing before me I paused. She took two steps forward and raked her nails down my front, pinching my tender nipples cruelly as she continued to devour me with her gaze. She knew.

I stood before her, defiant, my shirttails still tucked in the waistband of my pants, although the rest was in tatters along my legs. She flicked her wrist, and the whip grazed my chest in a biting caress. I sucked in my breath as I took a step forward. Again it struck me, and I took another step forward, my body humming in a tune only she knew. She pointed to the restraints on the dresser, and I shook my head. The whip came again, tormenting my nipple with its cruel touch, and still I shook my head, a growl bubbling below the surface.

I had forgotten what a fast woman she can be, and I paid the price with a hard smack against my chest as I went flying back onto the bed. Before I could blink, she was straddling me with her firm legs, one of my arms already in a restraint. She bent down and took a nipple between her teeth and chewed, pulling on it and sucking, stealing my breath. I arched under her and closed my eyes, my need bursting forth with her tongue. I heard a click and knew she had achieved her goal.

I arched again and effectively pushed her off me, but she was ready for the move and gripped the chain in between the cuffs. I tumbled half off the bed, and as I struggled to regain my balance she was already on her feet, yanking and pulling on the chain until I got unsteadily to my feet. She never gave me a chance to really fight, her tactics effectively knocking me off balance, her determination etched clearly on her face. Within a few seconds I found myself strung up, and all I could do was watch and growl as she took her time removing my pants. She teased with her fingers, tormented with her lips, as I stood there unable to do a thing. I couldn't speak; she'd taken my breath away. Her touch was infuriatingly gentle, her lips incredibly loving and soft as she tormented the very soul of me with gentle caresses, bringing forth even further the beast that resided so close. God, she knew.

Those gentle caresses were not what I wanted and she knew it, and yet she continued, as if she wanted my frustration to be total, wanted me to be so raw and needy that I would bend to her will. I looked down at her and tried to tell her, but one look into her eyes as she stared up at me and I knew she didn't want to hear it. I was at her mercy, just where I'd wanted to be, and she knew it. I was hers.

Sweat dripped off my skin as she continued to drive me insane with her tongue and fingers, brining me forward only to stop and wait before pursuing it all over again. I bunched my arms and tried everything to get away, but she held on to me like a drowning woman. I hissed in vain as she once more stopped, looking at me as if I were a prize. The torment was as sweet as her lips and as painful as the scratches on my back. My throat hurt from my raspy breath; I desperately needed release. Her own moans told their own story, and I was carried away by them only to be brought back with her painfully soft touches. I was dying, and she knew it. It was time.

When I could no longer hold on she stopped and straightened. My scent was strong on her as she licked her fingers lazily and backed away. I watched in a daze as she exchanged the whip for a flogger. The symphony inside me was ready to crest like nothing I had ever endured, and yet she took her time as she caressed the tails—not bothering to watch me, she seemed fascinated by the leather. I looked on hungrily, whimpering like a wounded child as she slowly swung it, getting a feel for its weight. Her body swayed in a dance all her own as she slowly moved out of my sight, and it was all I could do not to twist around to watch her.

Time stood still as I waited with bated breath. My skin prickled when it felt her gaze on it, burning it with her own desire. I heard a noise, a plea of some sort, and yet I didn't recognize it. I needed what she had to give, wanted it so bad I throbbed from the wait, tears rolled down my face and onto my already wet skin, mingling with the salt already there. And still I waited. Could she feel it? Did she care?

My breath fell away from me as I felt the first hard sting as the hundred tails began their trip all over my back. I sucked it back as she increased it, beating my back with everything she had. Ah, the fire burned so brightly against me, the beast cried out as I shuddered. On and on she marked me as hers, tearing at my back and my soul with her swings. Nothing was left out—my ass hurt, my thighs tingled, and my back sang. It was so delightfully painful that I cried and shuddered, my mind already gone as I simply took everything she dished out. Yes, God, yes, she had learned so well.

No longer aware of time passing, I hung there as her tails continued to eat away at me. Her warm fingers tenderly told me she loved what she was doing before the wicked tails began to kiss me all over again. I hung there as my life's sweat fell at my feet, and I was humming all over. I wasn't aware she had stopped, the echo of each delicious swing still burning in my head, but when I felt her fingers reach back into my soul, I arched as she pounded and licked me right over the edge. Her name echoed all round me as stars began to flicker behind my lids. My body was in motion, a motion I had no control of as it shuddered and shook on the chains. My strength was drained from me as her lips soothed me and I was home. She cared.

I was released in more ways then I hoped, and as I tumbled to the ground I wanted to tell her so, but I had lost all of my voice and most of my will. When she gathered me close, I inhaled her sweetness and drew strength from it. I clutched her like a babe would her mother and let her rocking carry me away. I continued to gather my strength for one last trip, a trip that she would join, a trip that I could rest from. I felt her lips on my damp hair, her fingers gently tracing her marks, and the rumble of her voice, although her words were lost to me. I just lay there, slipping lower until she had no choice but to lay down as well. My fingers, seemingly lazy, traced their way down until I reached her stomach and grinned wolfishly into her skin when her tummy jumped and her gasp echoed in my ear. Her turn.

I rolled over her and immediately planted my lips on her heat and lapped it up greedily as I shoved my fingers once more inside her, as rough as she had been gentle. She moved with me as her own voice grew raspy and joined my own ragged breathing. Her hands raked once more on my torn back, and I howled into her as I pumped harder and harder, until my fingers were clamped in a vice grip as she arched a final time before tumbling back down, my name still echoing in the room around us. My fragile strength deserted me, and I lay in a spot I had thought about all day and rested.

ROCK
TANYA TURNER

The lights go down and the crowd seems to come alive, not as hundreds of separate people, but as one huge, live loud roaring monster. The hipster club, which serves pierogis as well as vodka, is swarming with the dreams of girls who desperately need to hear this music pulsating through them, who need nothing more and nothing less than the screaming guitars and blood-curdling screams of the women on the stage. Well, that and their own fantasies about getting them into bed, about what those fast-moving fingers can do to their cunts once pried away from the guitar strings. The erotic energy tearing through the air moves a million times faster than at any sex party, supercharged, pure and alive with youth and desire and intense lust hidden by practiced looks of boredom and déjà vu that do little to contain the frantically beating hearts and wet panties that lurk all around me.

I'd seen the band the night before in a small club, maybe 200 people, so close I could check out their outfits, hear them singing without the mic, almost reach out and touch them. And while that's the more coveted gig, the intimate feeling of a punk rock lullaby being sung directly into your ear, there's something even more electric about standing in the midst of so many fans, in the dark, alive and eager, the tension of those around me feeding my own. I close my eyes and listen to the roar of the crowd as it seems to rise up into the air. I shiver as I feel the waves of sound as guitars take over the room and every available space is invaded by the blazing howl of the band's opening number. The songs are from an album that will soon be released, and they surge with the newness of their sound, the shrieking possibility of it all. The specific words don't matter at this moment, only the spirit of the chords as they shake the room and seem to travel through my body, pulsing inside me, vibrating the room with a force rivaling that of dozens of Magic Wands.

It feels like we've been transported far outside of the city—away from the scenesters and critics, record stores vying for the most obscure posters to put up on the wall, the need to impress strangers on a train with your musical allegiances—almost to another planet, where the only thing that matters is the music, its desperate urgency having the power to distill the world into a single song. And it's almost true; we are physically here, but this space feels like nothing else on earth. I close my eyes and can almost believe we are moving, spinning, all of us collectively launching ourselves into another dimension, one ruled by fierce guitars and a rising power that could take over the earth, and I have to shake myself occasionally to remember where I am, floating on a combination of vodka, rock, and utter sensuality that nothing else can replicate.

I finally open my eyes to see the women tear up the stage, a blur of movement as heads, arms, entire bodies move to the beat while coaxing forth music that feels like the only thing that matters, to us and to them. They were supposed to go on two hours ago, but now, in typical fashion, at midnight, they are just starting. Which is fine with me, as I waited through the average opening bands and warmed myself with several cocktails, making small talk with friends scattered amid the crowd. It makes sense to close my eyes, focus on only one of my senses—my hearing—

though this music shakes me to my very bones. But there's another sense at play too; as I tilt my head back and let myself float on the alcohol running through my body, I feel a hand reach forward and stroke the skin of my stomach, bared underneath my tiny shirt. I know it's Amber by the gentle way she rubs against me, lightly, almost tickling; she's been playful like that with me before, but never in a darkened room filled with hundreds of people. We've been standing as close together as we can without touching all night, the tension palpable, but I didn't want to be the one to make the first move. We've flirted before but always let it go right before things got interesting, then forgotten about each other until the next chance encounter brings our hormones colliding once again. I let her pull me toward her and rest my head back against her shoulder, losing myself in her touch and the pulsing noise that blazes all around us. I've never done it, but I can now see why people crowd surf at shows, how easy it is to get carried away, literally, by the music. I let the fierce, unfamiliar sounds pound through my body, not bothering to try to crane above everyone to see the stage.

Amber's hand strokes my belly, scraping her nails over the sensitive, almost ticklish flesh, kneading it like she would my nipple, sending waves of heat straight to my cunt. Nobody around us cares what we're doing; they're too engrossed in their own sensual responses. I reach behind me and pull her closer, my eyes still closed. My hands stroke her back, her ass, anything I can grab onto as long as it's hers. Then I feel someone in front of me move closer to us. I open my eyes; it's not someone I know, but she's cute, in a black velvet tank top and hip-hugging black pants, long silky black hair gleaming down her back. Her ass and back are now firmly pressed against mine. I wriggle and feel the two bodies surrounding me.

This isn't something I'd normally do, but this isn't a normal night. The stranger's hand sneaks behind her and slowly reaches under my shirt. She rests her hand on my belly, next to Amber's, subtle as can be; to anyone glancing our way, she looks like she's just enjoying the show, leaning against a friend, foot tapping, head bobbing, lost in her own musical world. I lean my head onto Amber's shoulder and feel her plump breasts push against me, then her tongue snaking out to lick my neck. The tickle jumps its way from my neck through my belly, and she does it again, making me jerk slightly. My body is on sensory overload, and I'm loving every minute of it.

Amber's tongue and teeth continue to attack my skin, licking from one shoulder to the next, pausing at the most sensitive spot at the back of my neck. I want to grab her, stop her, because it's almost too much, but I don't. I let her mouth work its magic as her teeth sink into my skin and I bend my head back, my tongue curled around my teeth lest I'm tempted to scream. The stranger has now turned around and is facing me, her dark eyes and blood-red lipsticked mouth intent as they focus on me. I don't know why she's chosen to touch me, to seemingly ignore what's happening on stage, but she has. Amber reaches around the front of me and brings the girl's hand along my leg, from my knee upward until she's under my skirt, while Amber moves up to cup my breast. As her fingers pinch my nipple, hard, the way I like it, as they keep twirling and twisting and working one nipple and then the other, the other girl's hand quickly finds out that I'm not wearing panties. This is a decision I'm starting to regret as I feel streams of wetness start to make their way down my legs, but I'm too far gone to care.

Her fingers slide through my wetness, stroking along my slit, teasing me as they seem about to enter me and then don't. She's a tease, this one, and she knows it, but they've got me pretty much trapped. I could try to push her hand farther, could grab her by the hair and pull her up for a kiss, but I like letting them run the show, and I'm not ready to give this up. Instead I clench my pussy tightly, trying to urge her inside. Amber's tweaking of my nipples is sending waves of fire into my cunt, a heat so fierce I feel like I could collapse right here and now. I close my eyes, then open them, shake my head back and forth, anything to make the agonizing arousal bearable. I bite my lip and squeeze my eyes tight, the way I do on roller coasters and plane rides, almost prayerful, then open them to see the girl's face staring up at mine. Her kohl-rimmed eyes are beaming into mine as she now slides her fingers into place, pushing one, then two, then three into my needy wetness. Her eyes stay fixed on me as she pushes, not shoving but firmly working her fingers around as I press down against her. Tears spring to my eyes out of nowhere, and I blink to push them away. Amber's fingers have made my nipples hard, heavy, twisted points of heat that are almost beyond feeling. She pushes and pulls, twists and torments them, wringing out the last shreds of pain and pleasure before they become almost numb. I don't know if they are trying to work in concert but their hands have combined to send my body into overdrive, bringing me closer and closer to what I need. The music is a faint background noise, as my whole body buzzes with the rush of their fingers frantically flicking at me. Mystery Girl slides yet another finger into me, her wrist swiveling as she moves her fingers all around me.

I've almost forgotten where we are, my eyes closed or focused only on my most immediate surroundings. I don't dare to look at the people around us, hoping they're ignoring us, or getting off at a distance. But now the blistering sounds of the band's latest anthem shake the stage and the room. People are bouncing up and down around us, shaking the floor, moving us ever so slightly as the auditorium seems to lift itself up with the combined energy of so many screaming, ecstatic kids. As it does, I feel myself release, a tremor rushing all through me, racing to my cunt as the girl pushes even more urgently. I come fast and fierce, and even though I knew it was going to happen, it still takes me by surprise. Amber's hands lay still on my breasts, and the stranger slowly eases out of me, her hand resting on my inner thigh. I pull the girl to me with one hand and reach for Amber behind me with the other, tears now streaking my face as the last few lines of the final song reach us.

We stay like that through the chanting and stomping as the

crowd demands, and receives, an encore, and I watch the drummer thrashing around, her entire body moving as she supports the songs with her pedals and drumsticks. All the women onstage seem to be flying, moving in their own special universe, a place the rest of us can only hope to access. They can't give it all to us, only part of it, the part that we hear as they put their entire beings into these last few songs, leaving us with ringing ears and soaring hearts. I'm not moving, simply standing, but I can feel the music as it courses through me, touching me as surely as these girls just touched me, strong and fierce and demanding. I savor the last few minutes of the show, pressed between my girls, shaking slightly. As with any show worth its ticket price, I don't want it to end.

MINDING THE GAP
LYNN COLE

The train rocked with an unsteady cadence. Every time I found my balance among the crowded car we would turn a corner or hit a rise and I would be thrown slightly off balance. The man behind me chuckled softly to himself, whether from my annoyed sigh or because the train had delivered my ass directly against his crotch, I didn't know.

We slowed, and the doors parted at the tube station for South Kensington. People brushed by me, mostly younger 20-somethings headed for the clubs. I stayed standing, waiting.

Waiting.

I found the rhythm of the train as the stops became a blur. The train emptied out gradually, people shuffling off and a few more shuffling on as we drifted through the night. I checked my watch. Almost 11 already. Time was running out. Soon. It had to be soon.

London trains are not at all like New York trains. They're cleaner, safer, better lit. Here in the last car, I waited. Waited for the people to leave, waited with a sense of urgency that pulsed through my veins like the roar of the train through the tunnel.

She had been watching me since the first loop of the yellow

line. I met her stare and smirked, shifting on my heels to allevi-
ate some of the calf pain. She sat at the opposite end of the car,
watching me watch her. I spread my legs a bit to accommodate
the rocking of the car and my coat fell open, revealing my short
skirt and sheer blouse. Her gaze shifted to between my legs, my
skirt drawn tight over my thighs.

There was only one other person in the car—a girl, maybe 20,
no more than 22. A college student, I thought, headed home after
a night of studying in the library. She sat a few seats away from
the other woman, a messenger bag on the seat beside her, a
paperback book folded backward in her hand, breaking the spine.
She seemed oblivious to her surroundings, dark-rimmed glasses
slipping down her nose. She read intently, her fingers turning the
pages with quick, hummingbirdlike motions. I bit my lip, wondering when we would reach her stop.

The older woman nodded toward me, a sharp tilt of her head
that made her chin drop down into the dark red blouse she wore.
Her coat was tossed over the briefcase in the seat beside her. I
shifted as we slowed to a stop, and the doors opened on Sloane
Square station. No one boarded and no one got off. I sighed, the
noise lost in the sounds of the train.

This time, as the train gathered speed, the woman gestured
toward me. I knew she wanted me to go to her, but I hesitated,
sliding a questioning look toward the girl. She never looked up
from her book. The woman shook her head and motioned me
toward her.

Damn. I wanted to follow those beckoning fingers. Wanted it
so bad I could feel my thighs tighten, my cunt clench. I bit my lip
again and shook my head.

"Now," she mouthed, a frown twisting her attractive face into
something angry and urgent under the harsh lights.

I swallowed hard. As if feeling the weight of my gaze, the girl
looked up. Her eyes didn't seem to focus at first, as if she was still
lost in the words of her book. Then she saw me, really saw me. She
looked me over slowly, studying me as she'd studied her book. Then

she looked to the other woman. I wondered what she saw, what she thought. I wondered when she would get the hell off my train.

The girl went back to her book, and I screwed up my courage and crossed the car to stand in front of the woman. I held on to the bar above me, my camel-colored coat falling open, my breasts straining against the white blouse, nipples hard and outlined through the thin, almost translucent, fabric.

I spread my legs for balance, barely registering the fact that the train had stopped once more and started up again. I had them memorized by now, of course, but it took me a moment to remember where we were in the route. It didn't matter. We could make endless trips until the tube closed for the night. Which was sooner than I wanted.

The woman scooted forward in her seat until her knees were between my spread legs. I felt the warmth of her through her tailored trousers, the fabric soft as silk against my calves. I shivered, but it wasn't from cold; the train was warm, almost unbearably so, but I hadn't taken my coat off because of the nearly indecent blouse I wore.

I wanted to look over to see if the girl was watching us, but I didn't dare. I was afraid I'd lose my nerve. And as the woman's hand slid up the inside of my bare thigh, the last thing I wanted was to move.

I held my breath as her hand inched higher, mentally urging her on. I didn't speak; I could barely breathe. Her hand crept up my inner thigh, warm against my bare skin, almost more than I could stand. I watched her as she followed the movement of her hand, higher still. The fabric of my skirt got in her way and she impatiently tugged it up, leaving me exposed to her gaze.

"I knew you wouldn't be wearing panties," she murmured, so softly I almost didn't hear her in the din of the train.

Her fingers inched higher, moving closer to that sweet, wet spot between my thighs. The train rocked and my sweat-slick palm on the bar above my head barely kept me from tumbling into her lap. She chuckled, then thrust a finger inside my cunt. I gasped, thighs clenching tight around her.

"Open for me," she said firmly.

I slowly shifted my weight, spreading myself as wide as I could, my skirt hiked up to my hips. I had better balance this way, but I was open—so open I was vulnerable, and afraid. Almost too afraid… and yet I wanted this.

I dared to look at the girl, hopeful she was so engrossed in her book she hadn't noticed our perverse display. Her book was clutched in her hand as before, yellowed pages reflected under bad fluorescent lights. But now her gaze was on us, on me, her jaw slack, making her appear almost comical as she watched the finger gliding in and out of my wet cunt. I wanted to laugh, wanted to ask her if this was better than reading a book, but just then another finger slipped into me. Two fingers, rocking into me, thrusting up and forward, rubbing insistently against my G spot. I lost the power of speech, lost the ability to be embarrassed as I fucked those fingers. The girl's fingers were white-knuckled from where she clutched her book, and I stared at her pale knuckles until pure sensation took over and my vision swam.

I was going to come. I could feel it building as the train accelerated from a stop, the hum of energy inside matching the rhythm of the fingers fucking me. I looked down and saw the woman's forearm as it angled up, seemingly disappearing into my body. I felt the cuff of her blouse scrape against my thigh, the stiff fabric feeling almost painful on my sensitive skin. Delicious ripples coursed through me, every muscle strained to near breaking. My fingertips barely skimmed the bar now as I braced on the balls of my feet like an acrobat caught in mid motion, balancing only by some strange gravitational luck. On the verge of coming while the train rode its familiar course.

Suddenly, she stopped. She withdrew her glistening fingers and held them up. "Wet. So wet."

I bit back a groan of frustration, my grip tightening on the bar over my head. "Please," I begged. "God, please."

"On your knees."

I did as she said, immediately and automatically. I was at once glad to be off my sore feet and disappointed that I wouldn't be getting the release I needed. Not now, anyway.

I looked at her expectantly, waiting for the words that would follow. She didn't speak at all, she simply nodded.

I reached for the zipper of her trousers, tugging it down with the impatience of a puppy seeking out a new toy. She wore white cotton underwear. I hooked a finger in the crotch and pulled it to the side. I wouldn't want to be bare-assed on a train seat and I didn't figure she would, either. Her cunt was covered in soft, red hair; her engorged clit glistened under the bad lighting. I groaned softly.

I heard an echoing whimper and knew it was the girl. I was beyond caring that she was watching us, too far gone to worry. I glanced at her from under lowered lashes and smiled wickedly. Let her watch. Let her see what I could do.

I lowered my mouth to the woman's cunt, licking the tip of her clit with the broad flat of my tongue. I tilted my head back so I could watch her as I licked. My licks were slow, deliberate, and, judging by the expression on her face, excruciating. I enjoyed my moment of power, knowing that before too long she would take control once more.

My knees began to ache from the hard train floor, and I lowered myself to ease my weight. I tugged her pants lower until they were around her ankles, which allowed her to spread her legs a little wider. Her cunt seemed to blossom under my mouth, and I sucked her clit between my lips, my senses filled with the taste and smell of her skin.

She gathered my long hair in her hand and tugged, forcing me to resist her if I wanted to keep my tongue on her clit. The corresponding pain spread across my scalp and with a taunting chuckle, I sucked her clit hard. Her thighs quivered beneath my hands, as if all the pent-up energy of the train was humming beneath her skin. I sucked her faster, then released her clit and slid my tongue into her cunt, drawing up more of her juice and lapping her gently. She made a sound like a feral cat and relaxed her grip on my hair as I licked her harder.

She took my right hand from her thigh, lacing my fingers with hers. "She's watching," she gasped as I slid a finger, then two, into her cunt.

I paused long enough to meet the gaze of the girl, who had overcome her shock and now sat next to the woman, their hips almost touching. Her mouth turned down at the corners as if she disapproved, but there was heat in her eyes. It was my turn to be shocked.

"Go on then," she said, her voice as firm and demanding as the woman's. "Lick her."

I idly wondered if they knew each other, but it didn't really matter. I hesitated only until the girl reached out and pushed my head between the woman's thighs. The woman slumped in her seat, her knees falling open, her feet still pinned close together by her trousers. Like the train, I settled into an unsteady rhythm, guided by the girl's hand in my hair. Mouth on the woman's clit, fingers buried in the wetness of her cunt, I forgot about the ache in my knees, about the time, about everything. My world shrunk until it contained only the three of us, in a state of perpetual motion with me at the center, the pendulum in the metronome as the girl stroked my hair and the woman rode my fingers.

She jerked her hips up against my hand, gripping my wrist as if fearing I would stop. "God, yes, faster!"

I obliged, my attention shifting, my tongue swirling around the tip of her clit while I fucked her hard. She thrust against my fingers and mouth once more, then she came. Wetness tickled my chin as I buried my face into her crotch, intent on devouring her. She throbbed around my fingers, her cunt gripping me as if she would never let me go. Finally, when she quieted, I went to raise my head, but I was held down by my hair.

"Not yet," she said softly, and I heard the girl giggle. "Not quite yet."

I tongued her clit gently as it retreated under its hood, hearing the sighs of the girl and wondering if she was touching herself while she watched me. I reached out blindly and found her stocking-covered thigh. She tensed for a moment and then pulled my hand higher, under her skirt and between her thighs. She had a hand down her panties and was rubbing her cunt fiercely. I rested my head on the woman's thigh as we both watched the girl. I covered her hand with my own, feeling her fingers through the satin of her underwear as she fucked herself. She leaned her head back against the train window and moaned softly, her thighs quivering as she came.

After a moment the girl opened her eyes and looked at me a little self-consciously. I licked my lips, still tasting the woman. They were both looking at me now, eyes languid and half-closed.

"Come up here." The woman punctuated her command by tugging my hair.

I straddled her lap, feeling the bite of her zipper against my tender thighs. I wanted, needed, to be fucked. My breathing came in soft pants as she pulled my face down and kissed me. The taste of herself in my mouth seemed to arouse her; her hand tightened in my hair, tugging painfully as she slid two fingers into my slick cunt.

I gasped against her mouth as she fucked me like that, awkwardly straddling her lap, my body straining for release.

She pulled me back by my hair so that my head and neck were arched away from her. She leaned forward to suck my nipples through the thin fabric of my blouse, biting them hard as I whimpered and twisted on her lap. Her fingers fucked into me, hard and insistent, driving me upward with each thrust and forcing me to cling to her shoulders so I didn't tumble from her lap.

"You want it," she growled. "Come on now, show me what you need."

Her words, her fingers in my cunt, the taste of her lingering in my mouth, all my senses were filled with her. I came then, digging my nails into her shoulders as I arched my back and went rigid against her. She kept fucking me as the walls of my spasming cunt clutched at her fingers, as if trying to coax more from me. I collapsed against her chest then, spent and exhausted both physically and emotionally.

Her fingers slowed to a gentle massage and her hand loosened in my hair. I would have a headache and bruises to show for my adventure. The thought made me smile.

"When did you get back into town?" she asked, lips brushing my forehead.

It took great effort to make my mouth form words. "Just this morning. I wanted to surprise you."

"And so you did, love. So you did."

We stayed like that for several minutes. I came to my senses and raised my head when the train slowed. The girl was gone. I looked up into Jane's warm brown eyes, having trouble speaking past the sudden fatigue that had overtaken me. "Where did she go?"

"She snuck out when you started coming." She grinned. "I think you scared her away."

I slid from her lap to the seat beside her and watched as she pulled up her pants. Once she was presentable, we laced our fingers together again. I had been away too long.

"Friend of yours?" Her fingers tightened on my hand as if she didn't want to know the answer.

I shook my head and laughed as the train chugged into our station. "I was going to ask you the same thing."

SEX AND CHOCOLATE
SPRING OPARA

Akina stood erect, poised, arms outstretched and nude before The Designer and The Groomer. The high, stiff leather collar made her neck look regal, like the ancient queens of Africa. The warm Majorcan breeze air-dried her freshly shaved and showered body. She had been bathed in milk, vanilla, and honeysuckle, and all her body hair had been removed for the evening's event. The Groomer knelt before her, trimming the remaining stubborn hair from her pubis. His nimble fingers worked quickly. Akina was beautiful; she was her Master's favorite.

Akina was the eldest of nine girls and had grown up in a small, backward town in the Midwest. By the time she was 19, she had been molested by her dentist, gang-raped by her boyfriend and three of his friends, and had won a language scholarship to Berkeley—she spoke three fluently.

She thought of herself as a hard shell with a soft center—detached, realistic, yet compassionate. She had learned a lot in her life. The Ph.D. in public policy she had scratched out from the clutches of a system that denied her most things was sweet vindication. She never thought of her failed marriages, and she hadn't heard from her kids in four years.

She swallowed the tears hard. *No crying now, you'll ruin your makeup,* she chided herself. Her children were spread to the four winds. Antonio was a professor of theology at Tennessee State University; Dallas was touring with Missy Elliott as her hairstylist and makeup artist. Ashley was a pediatrician at Children's Hospital in Oakland, and Alexander was in the Air Force. The last she heard, he'd been in basic training. She had taught them well. *Be independent. Live your lives as you see fit. Have no regrets when you die. And above all, acknowledge and respect your Higher Power.*

She was more spiritual than religious, growing up a religion mongrel—her mother had practiced Baptist, Southern Baptist, Jehovah's Witness, African Methodist Episcopal, Seventh-day Adventist, and Catholicism. She had experienced it all in her mother's attempt to find solace for a life she believed not worthy of the air her God provided. If religion was truly the opiate of the masses, as Akina had heard, then her mother was an addict and overdosing on it. She had carted Akina and her sisters around to every tent revival she could find. "Looking for peace, some inner peace."

Akina had opted for the older religions; Ifa had set her free, and Religious Science had quenched her intellectual understanding of Spirit. She'd have none of that hell and damnation just for being born.

This, this was about her Healing. The choosing to be submissive, especially in satiating her libido. Before, she had no choice in the sex and the beatings. Life with Khane had taught her a lot about the many facets of pain and endurance. This time all were on her terms, and she was being well compensated. Her philosophy was one of strength and power through submission. Akina felt that those who needed to control were themselves weak and scared. Only the truly strong could relinquish the need to be in control.

It wasn't about money either. She had worked as a VP of business development for a major investment firm, so this was *not* about money. It was nice—she chuckled deep within—but this was definitely not about money. This was about power and choice. This time things had been negotiated and contracts signed. Taureans love order and consistency. In her mind she had achieved both.

Her fetish had developed from a dark desire that perceived deviant behavior as sexually appealing. It had started with small things. The drive down Highway 80 from Oakland to Berkeley, Flanagan's dildo jammed up her cunt while she sat on her lap to drive. Both hands engulfing Akina's breasts, tweaking her nipples between her thumbs and index fingers. Her musky, warm breath invading the fields of hair on Akina's nape, followed by showers of little kisses, all the while whispering that she'd better not wreck her Jag.

Then came the time she first finger-fucked her bi friend Kitty in front of a small crowd. It wasn't her fault the video was arousing, she'd rationalized. It started out innocently enough, and it wasn't like the crowd was watching them exclusively. The video was playing, and the girl-on-girl action was good; her hand slipped down the front of Kitty's blouse and touched her nipple. Kitty moaned. Akina tried it again, and again her friend had moaned.

Kitty braced herself against the wall for support, slightly moving up and down in anticipation. Her delight fueled Akina's desire to please her, to make her come. Kitty pulled up her blouse to give Akina better access to her small, round nipples, and she sucked and teased them until Kitty's hips began to fuck the air, gyrating with little forward thrusts accompanied by grunts, letting Akina know she wanted to be taken. Akina had buried her face in Kitty's cleavage, wrapped her arms around Kitty's small waist, and she was moving to match the rhythm of her hips.

She moved her right hand from her back and began to massage her way down Kitty's torso until she reached her zipper. She slid her hand down her pants without unzipping them. Her fingers met a shaved cunt with a throbbing clit and soaking panties. Akina rubbed Kitty's clit gently, using her juices as lube. Kitty's thighs began to shake and tighten as she thrust her hips up, trying to maneuver Akina's fingers into her cunt.

"Beg," Akina had whispered. "Beg me for it. Now!" Kitty melted in her arms. Akina teased her until her cunt lips engulfed her fingers. She used her pinky to gently part her labia. With her middle finger she circled her clit a few times to get some moisture and then inserted her finger. Kitty bit her lip; her chest caved in as she exhaled that first sensation of penetration, almost doubling her.

Akina's fingers found fleshy warmth. Kitty's walls pulsated, squeezed, and then released their grip on her fingers. She moved her fingers excitedly in her; as Kitty began to come her walls became tight and unyielding. The pulsating became rapid and then dropped to intermittent jerks. Kitty's head was thrown back, her throat exposed and her mouth opened wide toward the heavens. Only a low growl escaped on a gasp of hushed ecstasy.

Akina reached around with her left hand and placed it over Kitty's mouth to muffle her cry. Cunt juice trickled from the tips of her fingers down her hand like drops of sap escaping a tree. If this had been her lover she would have licked the nectar.

Because Kitty was her friend, however, what happened there stayed there. It excited them both to test the waters and to have sex in public.

But all of those antics were just the prelude for this. Akina had come to understand her desire for domination was insatiable. It took on a life of its own. After a few failed str8 lesbian affairs she stepped into the more "dark" side of female domination. She placed the following ad:

```
AFRICAN BEAUTY SUB...


Greetings. I am an attractive, edu-
cated, African-American femme sub in
need of training. I am very good at
pleasing and seek to serve. I require
firm training and a gentle touch. I
am quite the Sacred Whore, and I
```

learn very quickly. Trust, safety,
and honesty are very important qualities to me. In order to unleash the
true submissive in me, I require a
very strong foundation consisting of
the three qualities mentioned along
with a few others. Please
be emotionally and financially
stable and available for this
venture. Additionally, a positive
disposition, a sense of humor and
adventure, a grounded spiritual foundation, and a willingness to go the
distance are my assets. Until we
chat, peace.

✳

It was Mistress who replied. They had talked for seven months. Attorneys were retained, medical tests exchanged, backgrounds checked, contracts drawn, and trust accounts activated. Everything was legally and properly ironed out.

Akina had requested that her identity remain anonymous and that only the attorneys would meet face to face. Mistress was leery, but agreed. They had also agreed that they would write to each other to learn more and would talk for two hours, once a month, by phone. It was a strict schedule; if you missed the call, no extra time was added. This was Akina's sense of control. It fed her fantasy, she'd justified.

A tug on her collar's lead ring brought her back to the present.

She was usually adorned in leather strappings with an elaborately plumed dildo resting snugly in her firm ass. But today would be different. Today was her Mistress's birthday, and she had instructed that Akina be shaved, cleaned, and dipped fullbody into a vat of chocolate and served as dessert to her party guests. Mistress's birthday parties were infamous. Everything, except for the elaborate orgies and a few intimate details, was reported in the society pages.

The Designer had concocted a smooth blend of java mocha chocolate, Bavarian white chocolate, and milk chocolate, along with a secret binding ingredient to ensure that the chocolate stayed on Akina's body and that it wouldn't melt before the guests ate her.

She secured Akina's hands in the harness and lowered her into the vat of warm chocolate, then removed her briefly to allow the chocolate to harden. This was repeated several times to achieve the desired thickness. The chocolate was warm and made Akina horny as it crept into her private parts.

As it reached the outer lips of her cunt the tingly feeling she was experiencing changed into a throb, as the heat and rising smoothness of the chocolate further aroused her. She thought of her Mistress and the many guests who would be using her as a party favor and her cunt became wet—even more stimulated. She would have to control that. She wanted her cunt to be like those chocolate Easter eggs with the creamy centers. She wanted it to be a surprise for the first guest who explored her. She wanted her juices to flow out white and creamy just like those eggs. Hard shell with a soft center.

Once she had been properly dipped she was laid on a bed of white chocolate and walnuts four feet thick and wide enough for two people to lie on. The Designer added a muted semi-sweet milk chocolate blend to build Akina's breasts. Her nipples were accented with strawberries. A combination of sweet milk chocolate, dark semisweet chocolate, and butter white choco-late was used to create Akina's pubic area. She built the labia out of mocha chocolate and grated almonds, a cherry made the clit, and butter white chocolate represented the come escaping Akina's cunt. The Designer then took a cake-decorating tool and, using frostings and various food colorings, created an enchanted garden scene of exotic orchids, rare flowers, fairies, and cherubs on Akina's body. All fucking, even the flowers.

The party came to an excited lull as everyone watched as Akina was rolled in on her bed of chocolate. Her legs were spread wide, revealing little fairies hungrily eating at the chocolate and whipped cream adorning her cunt. First one clap, then another and another until the entire room resonated with adoration for the feast set before them. The Mistress had exceeded even herself with this, as one guest exclaimed.

The Mistress was a striking woman with firm breasts, long strong legs, and a small round ass. She was very feminine in appearance but as strong as any man. She had the complexion of a porcelain doll. Ruby lips and piercing sea blue eyes made the fact that she was of Asian descent elude many voyeurs. Her hair was the color of midnight, groomed into a polished pageboy. Sharp, long bangs cut her face in half, and she wore little makeup.

Mistress was born into a wealthy family and lived most of her life abroad. Spain was her favorite country. She had attended Ivy League schools and received debutante training from the best ladies of high society. Her IQ was 203 and she was fluent in several languages.

A consummate clarinetist, her social obligations required that she travel five months of the year. The rest was spent practicing and indulging her isolation. She loved music, and her library consisted of tracks by Nina Simone, Chet Baker, Melissa Etheridge, and Prince.

This was an interest she shared with Akina. Charlie Pride and the Buena Vista Social Club were a few of Akina's favorites, she had learned. They had spent one of their two-hour sessions talking about nothing but music.

Her family indulged the idea of her bisexuality as an unspoken taboo—a fad. To them it was like a Rolex, commonplace. It was considered a sign that one was bored and needed a pleasant distraction. The intrigue of an actual homosexual lover, however—though it pleased the elite's gossiping grapevine—save her family reason to worry. Thus, her decision to buy the villa in Majorca was approved without a fuss. Her stepsister had approved of the idea, declaring that it was too stressful for her to explain to her unborn child that auntie was a bull dyke or whatever. Spain was too hot for her, so the chance of an impromptu encounter would be minimal.

"Besides, I didn't know pretty girls were lesbians. You can get a man!" her sister exclaimed as she slammed the dining room door behind her.

Her family knew that she hated pretentiousness, so they knew her lesbianism was no fad. Pretty or not, she had been queer since before the time her mother caught her in the pool house intertwined and nude with the French governess's niece, who had been visiting for the holidays.

Mistress had learned about the "secret society" in college. She dabbled at first, only partaking in humiliating grimy old rich men and stoic professors who promised better grades if only she'd let them eat her untainted, young cunt. "I'll beat you, mistreat you, and make you lick my boots," she was heard whispering to a Texas oilman who had disrespected her at a casino night fund-raiser by groping her breasts. Two days later her first million as a dom was deposited into her bank account. She didn't look back.

When news of this new "fad" reached her family, her mother feigned a heart attack to dissuade her new course. "Ladies don't do such things," her mother's trembling voice pleaded. "You a pretty girl. You marry nice man, give me babies." Her mother's weak English annoyed her—with all their money and social status, it was obvious she had chosen it only to enhance the guilt trip. Mistress responded in their native tongue, signaling to her mother that the conversation was closed. Her mother's hand fell to the side of the bed in anguish. She rang for the doctor as she exited her mother's room, leaving her to her private pity party. That was five years ago.

It was the Texan who had introduced her to Master. It was amazing how the extraneous activities of the rich were so deviant in nature. Another tidbit she shared with Akina.

Master was 10 years older than Mistress. He pissed her off initially by assuming that because she was so beautiful, she was submissive and not his equal. It took him two years to win an audience and another three to give her a contract she would sign.

He learned early on that she had a penchant for women. It did-n't bother him at first. All his previous Mistresses were too insecure to have another woman around and had opted to indulge his bisex-uality. He relished the thought of two women sharing his bed. Not until she donned her own strap-on during one of their scenes did he realize how truly equal she considered herself. When she had finished fucking him and the woman he'd chosen for that night, he realized how much better a man she was then he. Especially when he found he wanted her to fuck him that way again.

When Akina was to be purchased he had to complete the transaction. Mistress had not been in the society long enough, and she was too young. Thus, officially, Akina was purchased as a house slave. When she arrived that first day she felt the tension, the lust, and the fear. There was something else too, but she couldn't call it.

Master began to salivate and quickly looked at Mistress to see her reaction. She was stunned by Akina's beauty. Putting a face to the letters and sultry voice made her heart flutter, and a look Master had never seen, but one that worried him, came to her face. Master had moved quickly that day. "Look at those legs. They're made for running and prancing. And that ass is definite-ly a dancer's ass," he smacked it as he took inventory. "Yep, this one is for the races," he declared definitively. Master decided then and there that Akina was to be a pony, and everyone knew Master's ponies had only one sexual partner. Strict training and synchronicity required it.

Pony training also required an overseer, thus Mistress was tasked to watch Master take Akina, ensuring he did nothing to damage the "house property"—but she herself could never touch her. This was his way of disciplining Mistress; there was nothing she could do, and initially this was OK. She hadn't put much stock into the letters and had kept the conversations strictly within Master-slave guidelines. She had refused to think of Akina as anything more than a slave; after all, it never crossed her mind that she would not be able to partake of her.

But now, after seeing her and only being allowed to interact with her in general household ways, a yearning to know this slave on a more intimate level consumed her. They found ways of interacting—virtual sex could be just as exciting. The thought of being denied intrigued them both; secret acts of defiance were deployed, but no public or obvious disrespect was ever displayed toward their Master.

Those seven months of preparation for Akina's addition into their household had piqued various curiosities, and Mistress often found herself in the library during Akina's personal time. Akina was a writer and had a mesmerizing voice, like a phone sex operator. She could often be found in a pristine retreat reading aloud. Mistress began leaving books or excerpts of material she wanted to hear glide up Akina's beautiful throat, the words sailing through those luscious, pouty lips to resonate the hidden codes of lust and desire to her ears. On a few occasions she found herself in a secluded foyer masturbating to the readings, jerking the dildo determinedly in and out of her cunt. It was frustrating. She wanted those reciting lips to talk directly to her yearning pussy.

Akina simply sat, not missing a beat in reading as she too let her throbbing cunt release its own orgasm, sticky, warm juice greasing the upper part of her inner thigh. Knowing glances and slight touches were exchanged in passing. Mistress would often stand in silence as Akina was being washed or whipped; after all, she was the overseer. Denial was a more powerful stimulant than either had realized.

But now, after three years of wishing in secret anguish to meld with this slave she had grown to love, through elaborate, clandestine meetings, she would finally have her. Tonight Akina's ownership would be transferred to her while their Master sulked in a corner of the room over a lost wager.

The guests watched in an enthused hush as Mistress's strong fingers began to stroke Akina's chocolate-covered clit. Akina couldn't respond to her Mistress's touch; she had to remain still in order not to break the chocolate. This was another reason she was chosen for this task—her endurance was infamous.

In a whipping contest, she had been paddled for 45 minutes nonstop. She didn't shed a tear nor cry out from the pain. She won her Master a quarter of a million dollars that day—10% of which went into her trust account. Yeah, Akina had endurance, all right, especially when it paid well. But sitting still now was harder than any endurance training she had experienced, especially with her Mistress playing with her clit.

Her Mistress bent over and began to lick the whip cream and fairies from between Akina's legs. The large dildo hanging from her leather strap-on was a birthday gift from her lover, who stood salivating among the guests. She mused at how thoughtfully the Designer had used all of her favorite chocolates and nuts. She would be sure to thank her properly later. She licked and bit until the chocolate melted away.

Once she reached Akina's fleshy clit she began to make figure eight motions with her tongue. She reached up with her middle finger and began to massage her hood. The teasing was deadly, and Akina was wrecked with lust, but she remained still, her eyes fixed on her Mistress, taking in every moment of the experience.

A fist found its way into her cunt. In a matter of minutes, chocolate pieces pelted the floor as her Mistress's fist disappeared and reappeared from Akina's inviting cunt. "Moan, bitch," her Mistress whispered. "Moan, I dare you." Akina felt her firm fingers tickling her cunt walls. She couldn't respond on the outside but she could show her Mistress gratitude by responding with a very wet cunt—and so she did.

Her Mistress, stripped down to nothing but her strap-on, climbed on top of the chocolate bed and pushed Akina's legs further apart to break the chocolate. She positioned the dildo at the entrance of her cunt without the use of her hands, tickling it, making it even wetter. She leaned forward and pushed a little, met with some resistance, and then with one powerful thrust she was in the center of Akina's chocolate Easter egg. She drew her tongue down Akina's cleavage and then began to draw that wonderful figure eight again, encircling both nipples, devouring the strawberries that were adorning Akina's breasts.

The ache, the yearning to pull her Mistress's head hard to her bosom was extinguished by remembering her status in all of this. Akina relaxed and enjoyed it.

Her Mistress reached under and grabbed her ass and dug her nails in for what seemed like dear life. Her primordial chant took Akina back to passionate nights in Paris with her first Mistress. She remembered the libidinous acts in the glow of the fire's ambers, and it made all of this feel so right.

Whispers were let loose throughout the party that it was now time for the others to have her. Akina withdrew her gaze as her Mistress slapped her appreciatively, popping the cherry into her mouth as she sauntered off toward the music. The guests now began to surround the table, fueled with their own ideas about how to truly enjoy sex and chocolate.

MERRY FUCKING CHRISTMAS
HEATHER TOWNE

I showed up for my first night of elf duty just as the chain holding back the screaming horde of kids from Santa's Winter Wonderland was lifted. The mob of SC-worshippers quickly trampled the plastic Rudolphs and Styrofoam Frosties in their headlong rush to throw themselves onto the plush velvet lap of Mr. Claus. And my somewhat tardy arrival didn't go over well with less-than-jolly old Saint Nick.

"Where the hell—heck—have you been?!" Father Christmas yelled at me as another elf escorted a hyperactive 3-year-old out of his mother's arms and up and onto the promised land. "You should be here at least 15 minutes before we open for business!"

"Sorry," I soothed the throned demigod as I scratched my elfin headgear with my middle finger. "I guess you've never tried to spoon yourself into a costume three sizes too small."

He gave my stretched-tight holiday attire an appraising glance, his twinkling eyes lingering an inappropriately long time on my bountiful breasts, until the sucrose-charged kid with the inch-thick want list pulled his beard like it was Mommy's chain. "You are a big girl, all right," Santa said to me, ignoring the excited whisker-tugger, his voice hitting depths Barry White used to call home.

I one-finger adjusted my green, felt cap and red feather for a second time, then turned my back on his hearty leer. The last thing I needed to go along with a polar Green Giant job was a randy Claus. After getting laid off from my regular job, breaking up with my girlfriend, and putting my cat, Señor Whiskas, to sleep, I'd only just recently begun to rebuild my shattered life by snagging a couple of part-time jobs and picking up Señor Whiskas Jr. from a neighbor whose cat had littered. Christmas was only two weeks away, and I was determined to make it a white, as opposed to blue, Christmas.

The gushing stream of babbling boys and girls dwindled down to a sticky trickle as the evening wore on, providing me an opportunity to get better acquainted with my fellow merrymakers. My elf-mate, Brandi Gilky, was a teenaged chain-smoker with a set of horse teeth wrapped up in the kind of braces I thought they'd outlawed with the iron mask. Her job was to lead the little lambs from parent to Pere Noel, but even that simple task proved difficult for the high school equivalency grad, as she was more often than not chatting up the packs of aimless boys who circled the decorated mall like hammerhead sharks around a school of tuna. Or she was running off to the bathroom to do God knows what— or who—leaving me pulling double duty as greeter and retriever, steering the chattering tykes in and out with a minimum of free candy and tears. Still, the girl had a cute butt and a pair of nipples that dimpled her vest in a most appealing manner, so she wasn't all bad.

Santa, on the other hand, wasn't all good. He was a short little guy with a deep voice, blue eyes, and roving hands. He was sporting enough padding to fill a living room set, and when he wasn't two-fisting coffee, he was patting my costumed epidermis like he worked airport security. The dolly-jolly old coot was also constantly caressing my hand or arm, or squeezing my elbow, whenever I came to collect his toy-seeking cargo. I figured that either Mrs. Claus was an icicle, or Santa wasn't shy about stuffing his stocking whenever and wherever he could, because the sawed-off Christmas icon was as horny as a Salvation Army brass band.

I didn't mind his light-fingered, white-fingered pawing so much, but when the crowds really started to thin out, in prelude to mall-closing, he started blatantly groping me—patting my hip, rubbing my thigh, goosing me. Now, that was too much. "You and me are gonna have a little talk at 10 o'clock," I told the lecherous pole-dweller.

"Just a talk?" he rumbled, his eyes gleaming as he fondled the oversized belt buckle that no doubt compensated for an under-sized Yule log.

I handed him a glare that would've frosted most men's chest-nuts and finished out my shift in chilly silence. And when the candy-cane clock finally struck 10, and buttalicious Brandi with the braces rechained the entrance to kiddy nirvana, I grabbed the crimson-clad lothario by the arm, pulled him onto his booties, and shoved him inside Santa's snow-painted workshop.

"OK, bub," I said, shaking the chunky little ho-meister like a suspicious Christmas present, "let's get a few things straight. First of all, if you ever touch—"

I shut up when he kissed me full on the lips.

I gawked at the festive cherub like Daddy must've gawked when he caught Santa French-kissing Mommy. The guy was maybe 5-foot-3, 110 pounds, while I'm almost six foot and 175 pounds. It wasn't going to be a fair fight, but that was fine with me; he hadn't treated me fair all night. "OK, you asked for it," I snarled, pulling back my fist.

He held up his hands, started laughing. "Wait a minute, Joy! Don't you recognize me?"

"Yeah," I responded, nodding, my big fist quivering like a bow-flexed arrow. "I know your type."

He chortled some more, then said in a voice gone from gong to bell, "It's me, Joy! Sandra!" She pulled off her wig and beard.

My arm dropped to my side and my eyes widened. I unscruffed her collar and gasped, "Sandra?!"

"Yes, it's me, you big lunk." She peeled off her gloves and coat and then quickly stripped away her boots, pants, and padding and stood in front of me in nothing more than a black bra and panties.

Wow! She had unwrapped one hell of a Christmas present! My incredulous eyes flew up and down her hot body, landing briefly on her pussy and tits, while memories stirred in my head like a mouse on the night before Christmas. Sandra and I had gone out a number of times two years previous, before she'd moved to another city, and during those dates I had discovered depths of desire, heights of passion, and intensities of orgasm that I'd never known existed. And with those sugar-plum sweet visions dancing in my dizzy head, I eyed the sexy blond babe and licked my dry lips with a wooden tongue. "You're back in town?" I whispered.

"What does it look like?" she replied, blushing under my heated stare. She plucked out some hair pins and ran her slender fingers through her long, silky tresses. "Things weren't working out, so I quit my job and moved back here about a month ago. I just took this Santa gig to earn some extra money." She grinned. "I'm quite the actress, don't you think?" she said, in the bottom-of-the-monkey-barrel voice that had fooled all the kids—and yours truly.

"I don't wanna think," I muttered, then grabbed the tiny honey in my arms and crushed my lips against hers.

"Yes, Joy, yes," she breathed into my mouth, her erect nipples pressing urgently into my soft breasts.

We kissed long and hard and hungrily in the cramped, shadowed confines of Santa's sweatshop, and then I parted her full-bodied lips with my slippery pink spear. It had been much too long for both of us, and we savagely took up where we'd left off a couple of years ago, swirling our tongues together in a ferociously erotic ballet.

She broke away from my mouth and said, "Shouldn't we, uh…shouldn't we find a more, um, comfortable spot for our reunion?"

"What better place to be naughty?" I responded with a wicked smile, knowing that my overpowering desire demanded to be quelled right then and there. I tore off my elfish duds like they were blazing with chimney fire, and then more slowly and sensuously slid my panties over my big, round butt and popped open my bulging bra. My snow-white breasts spilled out into the open in an avalanche of flesh, and my ultrapink nipples peaked at full one-inch hardness in the humid, superheated air. My pussy was moist and raw, aching for fingers and tongue.

"You put the hour in hourglass figure, baby," Sandra said, staring admiringly at my overripe body and reaching up to stroke my short, black hair. She then cast aside her own undergarments, along with her inhibitions, and we passionately embraced again, our nude, lewd, flaming bodies and need threatening to reduce the faux-gingerbread house to a smoking lump of coal.

We Frenched some more, then I captured Sandra's darting tongue between my teeth and began sucking it. She stuck her slimy pleasure tool as far out of her mouth as she could, and I urgently sucked up and down its wet, rigid length like someone might suck a swollen candy cane. She caressed and fondled my tits as I did so. Then the petite cutie broke away from my mouth and really went to work on my chest. She clutched my breasts, squeezed them together, and teased my sensitive buds with her playful tongue—spanking first one distended nip and then the other, swirling her tongue around my huge aureoles. Then she swallowed a nipple in her mouth and tugged on it.

"Yeah, Sandra! Suck my tits!" I shrieked, my lust-addled voice booming out joy to the world.

The faint whir of floor-buffing machines could be heard after my scream-echoes had died down, as the mall cleaning staff worked away just outside the thin walls of our sugar shack, but at that moment—and the sexually charged moments that followed—I couldn't have cared less if the real Claus himself had stormed down the chimney demanding milk and nookie. Sandra was working miracles on my tingling tits, sucking hard on one engorged nipple and then the other, bobbing her blond head back and forth between my boobs, cheeks billowing, breath steaming out of her flared nostrils as she greedily fed on my tits.

"God, that feels good," I groaned, as she kneaded and tongued my Christmas mams.

She looked up at me, her eyes wild, her hands and mouth full of titty, and she asked, "Can you still handle the vertical 69, baby?"

I stroked her golden hair with trembling fingers, closed my eyes while she painted my glistening nipples with her hot saliva. "For you, sweetie, I think I can summon the strength," I murmured.

And with that assurance, she jumped into my arms and wrapped her legs around my waist. I opened my eyes and set myself, then carefully maneuvered the gorgeous, light-as-a-feather hottie around until I was facing her delightfully drenched blond pussy. I held her easily, shouldering her smooth, supple legs as she coiled them about my neck. She wasted no time in spreading my pussy lips and plunging two fingers inside my burning snatch.

"Fuck, yeah!" I yelped, my knees buckling as the anxious girl frantically finger-fucked me, as she probed my clit with her warm, wet tongue. I gripped her taut little ass cheeks, breathed in her moist, musky scent for a couple of ticks, and then drove my tongue into her pussy.

"Yes, Joy! Eat me!" she squealed, hammering her fingers in and out of my soaking wet pussy, buffing my swollen clitty with her tongue.

I felt a wave of incredible heat rise like a fiery tide up my quivering body, and I knew that devastating orgasm was not far away. I lapped at her smoldering twat, tongue-stroking her from clit to butt hole in long, sensuous strokes. She squirmed in my arms, but I held on tight, never wanting to let go, ever again. Then I latched onto the girl's pink, protruding nub with my lips and sucked for all I was worth.

"I'm coming!" she screamed, even as she desperately plowed

my pussy with her fingers, polished my electrified clit with her thumb.

She let out a high-pitched, almost inaudible moan and spasmed uncontrollably as an orgasm exploded inside of her. She was jolted again and again with ecstasy, as orgasm after orgasm thundered through her, shattering body and soul.

I quickly joined her in our rediscovered sexual utopia. "Merry fucking Christmas!" I bellowed, as a searing orgasm churned through my quaking body, rapidly followed by another, and another. I blindly struggled to tongue up Sandra's scalding girl juices as she came over and over, as she sent my own senses skyrocketing into the blissful clouds of ecstasy with her unrelenting fingers.

Finally, when the roof had settled back down on our fantasy-land fuckhouse, I weakly turned Sandra around and put her back on her feet. We kissed and licked each other's sugar-coated lips, tasting our own cumdrops as we fiercely hugged each other. And it wasn't the 12 days of Christmas I was looking forward to now, but rather the 12 nights.

HEALING
SACCHI GREEN

Sunlight filtered through the hemlock branches. An hour ago it had blazed onto the water-smoothed granite, and radiant heat still penetrated into places I'd thought would never feel warm again. My body adjusted to the stone's contours and felt, briefly, at peace.

A sudden rustling among the trees on the bank above made me tense. Somebody stood there, watching. *Move on, damn it,* I thought, hating the new sense of vulnerability, the suppressed jerk of my hand toward a gun that wasn't there. I kept my eyes closed, trying to block out everything but the ripple of water and the scent of balsam. Far below, where the stream leapt downward in the series of falls and slides known as Diana's Baths, there were swarms of vacationers, but they didn't often climb up this far. I'd hoped, foolishly, for solitude.

Maybe I was only hallucinating being watched. Maybe the lieutenant was right. Maybe I really wasn't ready to get back into uniform. After seven years, it wasn't as though I had anything left to prove about a woman being as good a cop as any man. Did I still have something to prove to myself, though?

I sat up abruptly. A hemlock branch twitched, and through its feathery needles a pair of bright eyes met my challenge. A child, I thought at first, glimpsing tousled russet curls and a face like a mischievous kitten. Then she moved into clearer view, and I got a good look at a body that could have held its own on one of those TV beach shows—the bikini helped.

She looked me over just as frankly. "Hi there," she said throatily. "I'm afraid I've got myself lost."

Eye candy or not, I resented the intrusion. "Well, there's upstream, and there's downstream. Take your pick."

"They both sound so good, I can't decide!" Her glance moved deliberately from my face over my body and down to the long, semihealed scar running from mid-thigh up under my cutoff jeans. The scar didn't seem to startle her a bit. I began to suspect a plot.

It's not that unusual for women to come on to me when I'm in uniform, and I've taken advantage of their fantasies a time or two; but I was in skivvies, and this was way over the top. She was so blatantly acting out a scene that I was more amused than anything else. Well, maybe not *anything* else. It had been a long time. A definite tingle was building where it counted most, and my nipples threatened to assert themselves through my gray tank top. I pulled on the sweatshirt I'd been using as a pillow. The New Hampshire State Police logo on the front didn't seem to surprise her either.

I looked downhill. "Hey, Dunbar," I called to the head poking around a mossy boulder, "who's your little friend?"

"How's it going, Josie?" Jimmy Dunbar emerged from concealment. "I'd have introduced you, but you cruised right on by without so much as a nod for an old friend."

"Sorry," I said. "Been a bit preoccupied lately."

"So I heard. You OK?" He looked toward my injured leg and then met my eyes with genuine concern. Aside from his taste in practical jokes, Jimmy's not a bad sort, and we'd been friends since our teens, when we cleared trails and packed supplies up to the Appalachian Mountain Club huts.

"Can't complain," I said shortly. "A couple of weeks of enforced R&R and then I'll be back on the job. What are you up to these days?" I should've known better than to come where I'd be recognized. The newspapers had made the hostage case into a big deal.

"He's building sets at the playhouse," the sex kitten chimed in, clearly tired of being ignored by everything but the mosquitoes. In that outfit, she was damned lucky black fly season was over. "We open with *Oklahoma!* tomorrow night. I could get you a ticket if you'd like." She picked her way carefully down the bank, gripping bushes and gnarled, exposed tree roots. Any bits of previously covered anatomy were revealed as she bent and stretched; I was willing to bet her breasts owed nothing to silicone. I admit, it might have been more than just gallantry that prompted me to help her down the last, steepest bit, but when she tried to cling I spun her around and set her on her feet at a safe distance.

"This is Katzi Burns," Jimmy said. "She plays the Girl Who Can't Say No." Instead of grabbing the line and running with it, as I expected, she shot him a ferocious look.

"I should've had the lead! But at least I can have a little fun with this role. I'm so sick of doing 'wholesome' I could puke!"

"That's what you get," Jimmy said unfeelingly, "for starting your career playing Daddy Warbucks's little orphan Annie."

She yowled and took a swipe at him, and, while I figured he deserved a good clawing, my peace-keeper instincts kicked in. "So, Katzi," I said, with a hand on her elbow, "what kind of parts would you rather play?" Then it hit me. "Holy shit! *Annie*? How long ago?"

She turned that feral kitten snarl on me. The anger in her amber eyes was a lot more attractive than the bimbo act. "Long enough! I'm legal! You wanna see my driver's license?"

I grinned and looked at her scanty outfit appreciatively. "You bet, if you've got it on you somewhere."

Her scowl cleared. "You could search me," she teased.

I just patted her cute round butt and turned to Jimmy. "I hope you two have some clothes stashed somewhere. As soon as the sun gets a little lower the mosquitoes will be fierce. I don't much care what they do to your scaly hide, but it would be a shame to let Katzi get sucked dry just before opening night. The bites would be kind of a challenge for the makeup department."

"What time is it, anyway?" Katzi asked, with a stricken look.

"Close to 5," I told her.

"Oh, damn! I'm screwed!" She slid and lurched down the hill toward where they'd left their clothes and towels. Jimmy and I followed, ready to pick up the pieces if her fashionable sandals skidded on the loose layers of leaves and needles.

"So what the hell is that all about?" I asked Jimmy. "I may be on the injured list, but I can still manage to do my own hunting."

"Hey, little Katzi takes hunting to a whole new level. She's only hanging out with me because she wants to meet you, and I said I'd heard you were back in the valley. She clipped your picture out of the paper. Lord only knows what she does with it!"

And Lord only knows what you've told her about me, I thought, and swatted him on general principles. Maybe I should just go back to communing with nature. Then I watched Katzi's sleek legs keeping up with our longer ones and reflected that nature's blessings are many and wondrous, surely not limited to rocks and trees. Being back in the mountains had always healed my spirit, but surging hormones might well spur the healing process of the flesh.

At the road, without saying a word, I held open the passenger door on my truck. Katzi scrambled right in. Amazingly, she had the sense to keep quiet during the short drive into North Conway, while I considered my next move. If I was going to make one.

She darted a glance or two at me, almost shyly, then looked off toward Cathedral and White Horse ledges looming to the west. It occurred to me that her vamp act might require an audience, even if it was only Jimmy.

We crossed the Saco River, easing our way through the sunburned kayakers and rafters reclaiming their cars at the bridge. I let the tension build until we were waiting at the traffic light just before the turnoff into the Eastern Slope Playhouse.

"Do they give you any time off for dinner?" I asked.

"Just an hour," she said hopefully. "Seven to 8, and then we do the final run-through."

"Want me to bring a picnic?"

Her face lit with pleasure. "That would be great! I can't eat too much just before two straight hours of dancing and singing, but if I don't eat anything at all, I'll keel over by the second act."

When she'd disappeared into the theater I considered my options, then drove north to Jackson Village, where the men are golfers, the women are skiers, and every view is above average. "Fine dining" isn't something I think much about, but I have contacts at a four-star inn there. When I was a kid I used to forage wild mushrooms for the chef, who built a good part of his reputation on his creative use of them, especially the golden, earthy chanterelles. My half-French, half-Abenaki grandmother had taught me where to find them along trails and stream banks back when I could barely walk.

My welcome at the inn was so warm as to be embarrassing. They even had one of the damned newspaper articles posted in the kitchen. I was a few minutes late getting back to the theater, and Katzi was outside, managing to be outrageously provocative even in a demure calico dress for the benefit of the photographer taking publicity shots.

Publicity! I nearly turned the truck around. Then Katzi saw me and came running, a look of unstaged happiness replacing the vamping she'd been doing for the camera. I got out to open her door.

The photographer followed, of course. I recognized him from high school. "Hey, Jo Benoit!" he called. "How about a shot with Katzi?"

"Hey, Ted. Sorry, no time." I gave Katzi a brief hug to let her know being seen with her wasn't the problem. She'd already resumed her knock-'em-dead stage smile, but she was perceptive enough to feel the tension in my body.

"That's right," she said quickly. "I'm starving. We'd better get going." She waved to the photographer, who got a shot of the truck anyway as we pulled away.

"I'd planned to drive up the Cathedral Ledge road," I told her. "Great views, but I'm not sure there's time."

"Way up there?" She looked uneasily at the domed cliff looming above the valley. "Well…I think I'd rather look at it from down here anyway."

"Does that mean I can't talk you into going rock climbing?" I teased. It was probably just as well that we didn't have much in common. I wasn't looking for a soul mate.

"There isn't much you couldn't talk me into, but that would be a hard sell." Her little grin managed just the right touch of seductive charm. I hadn't noticed before quite how deliciously shaped her mouth was. "They mentioned in the paper that you were a rock climber."

"Can't we just give all that a rest?" I said, maybe a little harshly. If she was going to press for juicy details, it was all over, right now.

"Sure," she said quickly. "But if there's any other way I could dangle from ropes, completely at your mercy…"

"Not and still have time for dinner," I said, relaxing. The usual tell-me-about-yourself-before-I-explore-your-underwear routine seemed refreshingly unnecessary. Although I was, in fact, beginning to feel some real interest in getting to know her.

We parked in the pine woods at the foot of the cliff, where we ate duck salad with mango, asparagus-chanterelle tarts, and French rolls still warm from the oven.

"Wow!" she said, when the food was gone. "That was incredible!" She glanced at me sidelong with a mischievous quirk of her lips. "But I'll bet you hear that from girls all the time." That impish mouth demanded a kiss, which I provided, in full view of the last climbers of the day trudging back with their cables and hardware.

There'd have been more to see than kissing if I hadn't guaran-

teed to get her back by 8. It was hard to pull away from the insistent sweetness of her mouth. Her arms around my neck and her
breasts pressed against me didn't make it any easier. I peeled her
off and started the engine. "Better save some adrenaline for the
play," I admonished as I pulled onto the road.

"You'd be amazed how fast I can get recharged," she said hopefully.

"Behave yourself now, and I might let you amaze me later," I
told her sternly.

"Yes, sir!" She subsided against the backrest, letting one hand
rest not-quite-accidentally on my thigh, carefully avoiding the
dull red scar. When a pleasant tingle spread to the injured flesh,
it became a throb that under other circumstances might have
been pain. She felt me tense.

"Does it still hurt?" She took her hand away. I reached out and
pulled it back.

"Once in a while." There was a deeper pain I needed to con-
front, but at the moment I couldn't imagine any finer medicine
than Katzi's exuberant sensuality.

"I could kiss it and make it feel better," she suggested wickedly.

Oh, yeah. Much, much better. "Right, and I could get pulled
over by the local guys for erratic driving. Tabloid heaven."

"What made you decide to be a cop, anyway?"

"Well, I got as far as a semester into law school and realized I
belonged on the front lines instead of in an office. Plus I couldn't
afford it. I'm still paying off student loans."

"I don't suppose all that many girls fantasize about lawyers,
anyway," she teased.

It had never bothered me before to be the subject of fantasy,
but this time, oddly enough, it stung. "Look, I'd better warn you
that I don't have my uniform with me, and even if I did, it does-
n't get used as a prop for a scene." I may not keep my gear as trim
as I should, but I have respect for what it represents. "And
besides..."—something I hadn't realized myself until just then,
but had better get out in the open—"there are some kinds of

games I'm just not going to feel like playing for a while yet." A stab of pain shot through my leg into my guts. I could see my best uniform pants, sliced open from knee to crotch, soaked with more blood than could ever be washed out.

"That's OK," she said quickly. "It's what's underneath that turns me on." She slid a finger under the edge of my cutoffs, revealing a more dramatic section of my wound. "Oh, jeez! Did you ever think about getting hurt?"

"You don't let yourself think about it," I said brusquely, and changed the subject. "Look, there's a full moon rising. I'll take you for a moonlight ride when rehearsal's over, if you'd like." We pulled up in front of the playhouse.

"Will you throw in sunrise too?"

I leaned in for a quick taste. "Can't stop the earth from turning," I said against her soft cheek, then nibbled from her earlobe down to her tender throat. It was just as well that her calico costume had such a high, modest neckline.

When she'd gone I sat there for a minute, hardly noticing the people strolling along the village sidewalk. Then I headed north, up through Pinkham Notch, needing to center myself in the mountains.

The peaks loomed dark against a backdrop of moon-gilded clouds: Madison, Adams, Jefferson, and, crowning the range, Mount Washington. I'd never needed more intensely to be up there, on the rocky slopes above tree line, looking down on a world made tranquil by distance. Or, even better, looking down on clouds filling the valleys with a pale, ghostly sea, while the stars above seemed closer and more real than the shrouded earth. Best of all would be watching the dawn in the cold, still air, when nothing exists except stone, and space, and the coming of light over the edge of the world.

My gaze followed the contours of the mountains, my hands almost feeling their harsh ridges and swooping ravines. Then the thought of Katzi's softer curves and sweet valleys beckoned me with increasing urgency. I didn't want solitude, after all. *At least not right now,* I thought as I drove back down the winding high-way. *Just a quick fling,* I warned myself, *a little summer diversion. She'll head back to New York or wherever soon enough. That's all you want. That's all she wants. Nobody gets hurt.*

Katzi smelled of sweat, excitement, and greasepaint, although she'd scrubbed most of that off. She was close to exhaustion but tried to hide it. I got out and helped her into the truck, patting her tight jeans where they were molded to her heart-shaped ass. I've never understood how some girls wear them so tight, especially in the crotch—you'd think they'd get sore if they had any pussy lips worth mentioning. I said so as I drove, and Katzi laughed and perked up.

"You wanna check 'em out?"

"A fine idea." I swung into the official "scenic overlook" just north of town. The moon and mountains would have been breathtaking if I hadn't had more intimate scenery on my mind.

Katzi raised her hips while I unzipped her pants and worked them down just far enough to get my hand where it wanted to go. Her pussy lips were full and moist and clinging. "Just fine," I said against her mouth, working my thumb toward her clit. That was just fine too, and getting finer. "Nice preview."

"God, Jo, don't stop there!" She hauled her shirt up, and then her satin bra. I held my breath, waiting for the moment when her breasts surged free of confinement, setting off a surge of heat deep and low inside me. Her nipples were hard and rosy even in the white moonlight.

"You guarantee you're rechargeable?"

"Yes, damn it!" She wriggled and thrust against my hand.

"You sure?" My other hand stroked across her breasts, flicking one nipple and then the other. "The night is young yet."

"So...ah!...so am I!" she gasped, and stuck her tongue out at me. I wanted to grab that impudent bit of flesh in my teeth, wanted to yank her jeans the rest of the way off and chew every part of her impudent, tender body, but my leg wasn't up to the calisthenics necessary to accomplish all that in the cramped space of the truck cab. I rolled one of her nipples in the angle between my index and middle fingers and worked her pussy harder, meeting her accelerating thrusts, until the truck rocked and she yelled so loud it would have echoed from the cliffs across the valley if the windows hadn't been closed. Which, of course, meant steamed-up windows to clear before I could drive on.

By the time we reached my cabin Katzi seemed to be asleep, head nestled against my shoulder. We were far up a dirt road along a branch of the Saco River, entirely surrounded by national forest. There must have been a story behind how my grandmother managed to keep title to the land, but I'd never thought to ask until it was too late. I rent a place farther south too, where I'm stationed, but the cabin has always been the center of my world. I grinned inwardly, thinking that I'd come back here to lick my wounds but found something much more worth licking.

When the truck stopped, Katzi raised her head. "Just a minute, kitten," I said and got out to open the padlock on the chain across the driveway. The building was still hidden in the trees.

"Rowr," she said, in a distinctly feline tone, when I climbed back in. "Can't you see my fur sparking?" She ran her fingers through her short curls.

"Does that mean you're recharging?" I asked.

"Stick a finger in my socket and see!"

So, of course, I did, once I'd lit an oil lamp in the cabin so I could see as well as taste her delectable flesh. The gleam of lamplight on her full breasts and tender belly was almost worth lifting my head occasionally to see, especially when I'd sucked her nipples to wet, hard engorgement and left faint tracks of tooth marks from her navel to her smooth, shaven pussy.

And that was only the beginning. Katzi wanted to go places she'd hadn't been yet, feel places she hadn't felt. "I don't need lube!" she said when I grabbed the tube. "Just feel how incredibly wet I am!"

"You're gushing like a river at spring thaw," I agreed, flexing my gloved fist, "but we do it my way this time."

"Yes, sir!" She spread her legs. I stroked her, and she arched her hips, showing me glimpses of pink as tender and lovely as the lady's slippers that bloom along the river trail in spring. I bent to touch my tongue to her glistening sweetness. But tenderness wasn't what Katzi wanted just then.

"Fuck me hard, Jo, please!" she begged. "I want it all!"

"You'll get as much as I want you to have," I said. "You'll just have to trust me."

Two fingers into her tight, clinging cunt, I knew it was going to be a gradual process, and it was, compounded by her amazing capacity for multiple orgasms. "I'm sorry," she panted, after the first spasms gripped my hand. "But I really…in just a minute…I need more!"

"Don't apologize," I murmured against the luscious flesh of her belly. "Take everything you can get." My own cunt was throbbing; I wanted desperately to grind against her thigh, but my wound threatened to flare into serious pain. I didn't want any distraction from the joys of fucking Katzi.

Fifteen minutes and four orgasms later her moans were fierce and low, and my whole fist was twisting gently in her depths. Hard pumping could wait for another session. Half an hour later, as she slept in exhaustion, I watched the rise and fall of her breasts for a long time before drifting off with my face pressed against her warmth.

We didn't manage to catch sunrise, but the morning light was still pure and clear when I went down to the river and waded into the deepest part. The cold water rushing down from the mountains could always sweep away sweat, doubt, confusion. Then I sat in the sun on my favorite boulder and tried to clear my mind of everything but the intense blue of the sky.

"You look like one of those paintings," Katzi said, coming to stand below me. "You know, the ones with girls sitting on rocks with mountains and waterfalls and stuff."

"Maxfield Parrish?" I asked, without turning.

"That's the guy. You look like what I wish he would have paint-ed, instead of all those cute fluffy girls."

"You'd have fit right in," I said. "But I always wondered how they got up onto those jagged mountains with bare feet." I wrig-gled my own river sandals, which were all I was wearing.

She looked at my feet, then my legs. I steeled myself not to clamp my naked thighs together, and let her look.

"Oh, Jo," she cried, aghast at the full extent of my wound. "Did he cut you that way on purpose?"

I couldn't bottle up the anger, the guilt, forever. "Yeah. Probably. His wife had been going to leave him for a woman, but luckily the papers didn't get hold of that tidbit. We could've charged him with a hate crime, I suppose, from the names he called me, if he'd lived."

Her hand was on my thigh, and she could feel me shaking. "You had to do it, Jo, it was self-defense, and who knows what else he'd have done to them?"

I remembered the woman's screams and the child's terrified cries. I remembered climbing the back of the building, finding foot- and fingerholds on ledges and chinks in the bricks, while my partner watched the front. Then came the shatter of glass as I plunged through the window, and the flash of the knife as I wres-tled with him. I hadn't been able to climb with my gun drawn, and then it was too late. My most searing memory was the crum-pling of his larynx under my hand.

"There had to be another way," I muttered. "If...maybe if I had been different, gentler, softer somehow, I could've talked him around. That poor little kid had been through enough, without having to see all that."

"But the mother lived, didn't she? My God, Jo, how can you kick yourself? I know it must have been awful, but..." She stood on tiptoe and nestled her head against my side, and I bent to hide my face in her soft curls. Then she worked her lips gently down-ward toward the scar. "Let me, please..."

I began to tremble in a different way. I wasn't sure I could bear to be touched. She looked up at me so pleadingly, hungrily, that suddenly I couldn't bear not to be touched, by her hands, her mouth, her indefinable flame of life that warmed something in me deeper than the flesh.

I leaned back with my arms braced against the rock and let my thighs spread farther apart, let Katzi's mouth move up, and up toward where I needed it most. She reached her arms around my waist and pressed her lips and tongue against me so softly, gently, that I felt no pain, only a tantalizing stimulation I thought would drive me crazy. I tried to pull her head closer, harder—maybe I was healed enough!—but she resisted. "Trust me," she murmured against my flesh, and I had to, even had to let her hear me whimper and moan. She kept on and on, driving me closer and closer to the brink, until I begged and swore and her wet tongue and fingers pressed harder and faster, sending me hurtling toward the headwall of the ravine—and then I plunged over in an avalanche of fierce joy.

Much later in the day I kissed her, told her when I'd pick her up, and watched her hurry into the playhouse. I really was healed enough, I realized, to go back on duty. Why rush it, though? I could still taste her, still feel her body against mine, still smell her scent clinging to me. I couldn't handle thinking about the future yet, but I was going to savor every moment of the present, and the healing force of nature that was Katzi.

BIKER BARBIE
RAKELLE VALENCIA

The plate said BARBIE. I had to laugh. Biker Barbie. If I'd only had a doll like *that* when I was a kid. Maybe it would have changed things. Maybe it would have changed me. But I don't think so. I probably still would have dragged her about the Town House by her blond locks or those extra-petite ankles with a stolen G.I. Joe from my brother.

Biker Barbie. So I stared. I know it's not polite. Whatever. The outfit she was wearing invited me to gawk, and I slid my hand from my knee upward along my inner thigh. I'm not quite sure how to describe her suit—"futuristic," maybe, and painted-on. There was no doubt as to her shape beneath that serious ensemble. My sweating palm came to rest in the crook between my leg and pussy as I half-sat and half-leaned against my ride.

She was Barbie brought to life. You've seen the doll. She was all that: legs to her armpits and an unbelievably thin waist expanding into deadly pointy, full tits. The small parking lot all of a sudden seemed too vast, even for discretion. I wasn't getting *busy*, but I was thinking on it. My mind conjured images of me on my knees, rubbing my face up one of those leather-clad legs, just for the feel of it, and the smell.

I watched, propped sideways on the seat of my Harley, as she unfolded herself from one of those crotch rockets. It might have been a Suzuki, maybe a Katana, I'd have guessed at first glance. No doubt the bike was fast and hot. But I found my sense of heavy metal worship blinded by the legs that had unwrapped themselves from the machine. I'd have hauled my balls over broken glass, so to speak, to be the purring metal owned by her, to have her legs hugging *me*. That inseam had to have been 35 inches or more, because those long legs had been folded like an accordion, making the seams of her leather scream.

And I recognized the leather: Teknic Venom. I recognized that as my straight, lecherous brother would have recognized any matching pair of bra and panties from Victoria's Secret. OK, so we both had too much time on our hands back in our youth, and I had once rivaled him in memorization of skimpy women's lingerie, naming the models too. But that was neither here nor there, because I wasn't a kid any longer, and femme wasn't my thing at present. Not to say this bitch was butch.

She wore the anatomically precurved, supple goatskin as one piece, jacket and pants connected via zipper in the back. Barbie had opened her jacket. Burgeoning bosom ballooned free, before she removed her helmet; head protection by Shoei. I was familiar with the snake graphics swallowing the full-faced headgear. I had perused that very same helmet before buying what looked like a chamber pot, which I thought brought out the Harley attitude I was sure to have acquired with the purchase of my bike. Rough and tough, that was me.

So this Barbie—who rode in on some serious CC's—flipped her lengthy blond hair loose from her helmet and shrugged out of the top half of her second skin. And I did stroke my crotch at that moment, moving my large coffee in front to cover the action.

Well, her jacket hung behind her as if it had fainted. Somehow I had the urge to offer it aid, a little mouth to mouth. But the jacket's plight was soon lost on me for the bigger picture. Shit!

She had no more than a straining wife beater covering breasts too large to go without the help of some kind of support, not that they needed it. I wanted to raise my hand and volunteer like a good Girl Scout, you know, to help out, to give support. Jesus, I was going to come from the thought of it. An embarrassing wetness marked my blue jeans. I jerked my hand out of my crotch and drummed fingers on the black and chrome chamber pot resting on the gas tank instead, forcing myself to drop my gaze.

I needed to calm down. Guzzling the last mouthfuls of coffee, I figured I could hit the road and let the vibes get me off. But I wasn't on a crotch rocket, which so easily puts your body forward to rub and hump in a wonderfully discreet fashion. My bike placed me upright, and if I wanted to look cool, I could even lean back a little and slump my spine. Some anal action was all I'd get. Maybe I could ride one-handed to play with my stiffened clit through its denim prison. I was almost, in those fleeting seconds, considering trading my hog for a similar megavibrator when I got home.

A blush grew from my neck to cherry-coat my face, as colorful as the Dunkin' Donuts sign I had parked under. I toyed with the empty Styrofoam cup in feigned interest. Then I looked up again.

She was at the door, half-undressed, her attached jacket obediently following behind like a puppy on a string. It took her only one look—well, that and a nod. I'm not that easy. OK, in that very second I was desperate. She flipped her blond mane, summoning me to follow her, and like that compliant jacket, I did.

Trotting across the parking area didn't get me there fast enough. She was gone. I was looking through the glass entryway, searching while hauling the door open, but no Barbie. Then from around the corner, off to the side, a crooked finger showed me the path.

I knocked on the door to the ladies room. I had already visited and knew it was a spacious, tiled one-seater. A hand reached out around the door and hauled me in by my black leather lapel.

Twirling in a whirlwind, I was shoved against the back of the door, heard the stainless steel lock click.

She ripped my biker jacket open to jerk it halfway down my back, securing my arms. And no kidding, she sucked face like she was starving, one of her hands gripping under my jaw, the other unbuttoning my already dampened jeans.

Desperation made me lose my leather to the floor and kick it aside. Her skinny waist barely filled my hands when I got them onto her. The white tank was in the way of the real mother lode I sought. I wrenched and tugged, but she was pressed against me. With a smile that I felt more than saw, and only our tongues still greeting, Barbie arched away, allowing the ribbed tank top to be thrust over her tits, shelved above.

As soon as my palms filled with her flesh, she clamped each of my wrists and flexed them over my head, securing me to the door with enough pressure to make my fingertips tingle. I bit her, just her lip, and not enough to draw blood.

In response, she pulled away. It was taking long seconds to formulate the thought that I might have made the worst mistake of my life, when Barbie stuck a pointy-tipped orb into my gaping mouth. I suckled to her moans, flicking the taut nipple with my tongue and over the crooked fence of my teeth.

From there it only took one of her hands to hold onto my wrists, such a willing slave I'd become. She ripped the Velcro adjustable waistband of her armored Venom pants until her fly was hanging open.

It didn't take much on her part to shove me onto my knees. That was where I had wanted to be. Barbie had a strip with an arrow shaved down from a full muff. The short, golden ringlets pointed to the beginning of her slick slit, where I sunk my tongue. The live doll thrust at my face in an ever-increasing rhythm as her fingers entwined in my hair, pushing me hard against her, then pulling my hair to pluck me away. I fought this insane play with tears leaking from the corners of my eyes as I struggled to keep my tongue buried in her slit.

She pumped little circles against the tip of my nose, and I sucked onto an outer lip to remain with her. A cool breeze from under the door made me very aware how wet the crotch of my jeans had gotten. I groped into my sopping boxer briefs; the touch of my own familiar fingers was like a raw invasion. And I couldn't hold back.

The scream of my orgasm was muffled as she held my head jammed into her slit, my crammed mouth humming and buzzing, her clit clasped between clenched teeth. Barbie came before I was finished. She surprised me by bathing my face as she squirted, her slick juices sopping the front of my cotton T-shirt.

She dismounted and left me sprawled on the tile floor to crawl after my discarded leather, racked with aftershocks. When I was capable of pulling myself up, I washed my hands and splashed my face. I tucked, zipped, and left the women's bathroom, half-expecting looks, but really wanting cheers.

In the warm sun I searched for that hot, yellow Suzuki Katana. She was gone. She had been built for speed. And the doll was more like Hit-and-Run Barbie than Biker Barbie.

I smiled as another aftershock rumbled through my body when I threw a leg over the seat of my Harley. Revving the throttle, I left the doughnut palace with a catchy tune in my head, "Dunkin' Donuts, it's worth the trip."

NEXT FLIGHT OUT
KAI BAYLEY

The meeting had not gone as planned.

Standing on the moving sidewalk in Boston's Logan Airport, Cole reviewed the events of the day. Thoughts raced through her head like so many people crowding the sidewalk eager to reach their destination. Given the slight tilt to her head and the intense look in her unsettlingly golden brown eyes, it was no wonder the few people who bumped into her were quick to apologize and step away. Her ex would tell you that was just her "thinking expression," but anyone who didn't know her would think themselves in serious jeopardy.

Once again blunt hands pushed their way through her cropped salt-and-pepper hair in a practiced gesture of exasperation. Her business partner, Marty, had assured her that the deal was all but in the bag. Just one more eager company desperate to keep up in the burgeoning world of technology. The price was right, the service came with impeccable references, why the sudden change of heart?

She was startled from her reverie by the squeaky voice of an acne-riddled boy who couldn't be more than 20.

"Step over here, please, sir."

The unattractive uniform that hung on his gangly body identified him as some sort of airport security. They must be getting desperate to find people without some type of police record if they are hiring kids like this, she thought to herself.

"In an effort to ensure our continued security, we conduct random passenger searches." he continued with what seemed a well-rehearsed spiel. "We appreciate your cooperation and will make every effort to keep your delay as brief as possible. If you would, please spread your legs shoulder-width apart and raise both arms parallel to the floor."

"I believe it is customary practice to allow female security personnel to search your female passengers," she pointed out dryly, anticipating his embarrassed reaction.

A flush raced up his neck and set fire to his ears as he stammered, "Uh, yes, uh, ma'am, uh, sorry, ma'am. Umm, wait right here for one second." His eyes never left the geometric pattern of the rust-colored carpet as he raced off to retrieve another guard. She had briefly considered letting him off the hook, but after the loss of a multimillion dollar deal, his squirming brightened her day just a little bit.

The small smile faded, taking with it the laugh lines that had just started peering around the corners of her mouth. Her job often led her in and out of high-security areas, and she'd spent hours of painstaking work creating a harness for her cock that wouldn't set off a metal detector. The simple lines of the leather and rubber fittings disguised the effort put into the planning and construction of the harness—all of which will be wasted the minute she is searched.

"You are a woman who loves women," her ex would say, "where does a penis fit in with that?" Obviously it didn't fit in well with *her* at all. That woman didn't know a cock when she saw one.

The only thing to do was brazen her way through the situation. When "Matronly Marge" the security guard figured out what was up, she would just tell it like it is. Hopefully the horror of discovery would keep Marge's jaw on the floor, offering an avenue of escape.

Squeaky-voice pushed the wrong way through a crowd of commuters, leaving a wake of angry people for his fellow guard to travel in. Studying the carpet like a road map, he led poor unsuspecting "Marge" straight to her and passed by without so much as a nervous glance. As he passed, Cole forced herself to stifle the low whistle threatening to push between her lips.

Chestnut waves threatened to burst the ties holding her hair severely in place. Retro tortoiseshell rims framed clear green eyes sporting lashes that seemed long enough to grab you and pull you in. The severe uniform that hung so poorly on the boy clung flatteringly to the curves of her breasts and hips. A dash of red lipstick outlined full lips, a rebellion against the attempt at making the employees sexless.

Oh, man, Cole thought, *it's a good thing that the source of my problem isn't real or we'd have a different reason for embarrassment.* The thought of those sexy lips leaving a faint trace of red along the length of her dick had the blood tumbling in eagerness straight to the base of her cock. It looked like plan A was going to be a bust. There was no way to be nonchalant when every nerve in Cole's body was crackling, anticipating the moment when this woman's hand could grasp the bulge barely concealed by her black dress pants.

Darla, as her badge identified her, repeated the boy's instructions word for word confirming Cole's notion that a script must be included in the orientation packet for new employees. Those green eyes never wavered from Cole's gaze as she complied with the request. Not a good sign, Cole mused: Intimidation is not an option in this scenario.

The guard moved behind her and began swiftly running her hands down the length of her arms. Cole flinched slightly as the stranger's hands passed along the undersides of her small breasts. Hands shifted to her back, and she allowed herself the brief thought of those hands dragging nails that matched the lipstick, making furrows in her skin. Momentarily lost in that thought, she almost missed the woman moving to kneel in front of her.

Grasping the left calf just above the hidden boot tops, the guard explored the first leg and then moved to the right. Her red-tipped fingers traveled first the calf, then the thigh, inching closer and closer to the moment of truth. Was everything moving in slow motion? The bustle of travelers seemed the same as before, and yet the search moved at an agonizing pace. A hot, prickly sensation started between Cole's shoulder blades and traveled the path created moments before by Darla's hands. A sheen of sweat crawled from her hairline to settle on her upper lip.

Relief from the agony of dread finally came as hands hesitated then settled on her cock. Cole released the breath she hadn't even realized she had been holding, eyes daring to seek the guard's expression. Almost imperceptibly she leaned closer before raising her eyes to meet Cole's tight stare.

Those luscious lips were so close to her dick, Cole could imagine that she could feel every breath teasing her in those tense seconds. There was a flicker of something inscrutable behind the eyes that met hers and held the moment. Abruptly she pushed herself up and away from Cole using her thigh as leverage; her lips had tightened until they seemed like no more than a paper cut where her mouth should be.

"I'm going to need you to come with me."

Cole paused at the double entendre, shaking the thought away with an unconscious movement of her head. The guard raised one delicate brow at the gesture of defiance, causing Cole to start with concern.

"I didn't mean, um, I mean…uh, sure. Of course." Wasn't that just great. Who was the bumbling punk now? She hadn't acted like such a blithering idiot since that time with Katie Kolazch senior year of high school, when too many feet in one bathroom stall had gotten them caught by the music teacher.

She was led to a small room spartanly decorated with a lone picture on the white walls and a narrow table taking sentry duty in the middle of the room. Cole recognized the picture as the same pastel floral number gracing the walls of the rundown hotel outside her hometown in rural Illinois. She had spent the longest five minutes of her life staring at that picture while she lost her virginity the night of her junior prom.

"You may place your bag on the table."

Cole reluctantly traded the nightmare of memory lane for the unpleasant moment at hand and followed the guard's suggestion.

"I'm afraid I'm going to have to perform a more thorough search for possible weapons. Would you please remove your shirt and pants and raise your arms parallel to the floor?"

A minute later Cole stood defiantly in her undershirt and boxer briefs, acutely aware of how the cotton cloth of the briefs molded and outlined the shape of her cock. Determined not to show her discomfort, she affixed her gaze to that horrible painting on the wall and prepared to stoically accept whatever came next.

She was surprised when, instead of moving behind her like before, the guard stepped up until she was only inches away from her.

Darla couldn't believe what she was doing.

Tilting her head upward slightly, she studied the pulse hurling itself against the column of Cole's neck. The time to change her mind had come and gone, so once again she raised her hands, mimicking the searching gestures of before. But gone were the efficient motions of the guard: This was the touch of the woman roaming the body of a lover.

In her nearly 30 years she had never done anything as bold as this. Momma always said, "Say it with authority and they will never question you," but Darla was certain her mother never intended her to apply that advice to a situation quite like this one. She wasn't sure what she would've done if the handsome butch had questioned the fact that she was being strip-searched by a solitary member of the security personnel. Of course Darla was breaking at least a dozen rules and possibly a few laws, but that was the last thing on her mind. Right now she was concentrating on the play of the muscles beneath her fingertips.

Judging by the tenseness of those muscles, this butch still hadn't figured out what was going on. Some people just need to be hit over the head with the brick before they know it's a brick, Darla determined.

Rolling her hips forward, she pressed her eager heat against the hardness she craved resting on the butch's thigh.

Cole's eyes snapped from the horrid picture to the wide eyes in front of her. The nearness of the woman had already been nearly enough to drive her mad. The lavender scent of her shampoo and the barest hint of perfume that emanated from her skin were torturing her senses.

Snapping the slim elastic band holding the guard's hair hostage was easy, and soon Cole was burying her hands in that gorgeous hair. Pulling Darla to her, she firmly coaxed her lips apart, exploring her mouth. A hint of cinnamon and the faint taste of lipstick registered as tongues met and tangled together.

"My turn." Cole broke through the current of the whirlpool, dragging her deeper into the kiss. Her eyes glinted with mischief as she continued: "Spread your legs shoulder-width apart and raise your arms parallel to the floor."

Concern marched across Darla's face, leaving footprints of uncertainty in her features. Seeing her hesitation, Cole moved toward her, dipping her head to the hollow where Darla's neck and collarbone met. Exhaling softly but never quite touching the skin, she made her way up to the ear. Teasing the sensitive skin sent shudders through Darla's body and she leaned forward, desperately wanting those lips to touch her.

"Please…" At that husky request Darla found her arms moving up, her body making decisions for her.

This search was anything but professional. Cole's hands and eyes languidly investigated the guard's generous curves. She liked there to be something to hold onto during sex; she certainly didn't like not knowing which skinny body part was which without looking. Cole was impatient to see what was under that drab uniform that made it look so sexy.

"I'm afraid I'm going to have to perform a more thorough search," Cole continued. "I'll need you to remove your pants and shirt, please."

The heavy belt was the first to go, baton and pepper spray echoing loudly against the gray tile. The radio skidded to a halt against the wall and burst open, but neither of them noticed. Slacks chased blouse to the floor. Soon Darla stood in only her sheer violet bra and panties. A flush had crept into the spaces between the freckles on her chest.

Cole moved behind her and could feel her breath coming shallow and fast against her chest. Her hands continued their torturously slow exploration, lingering to draw lazy patterns against sensitive skin. A rhythmic undulation of her hips against Darla's ass received an answering sway. The tempo of the silent song increased as Darla tried to push more of herself against the hard cock.

Darla's swollen breasts were set free in a quick flick of Cole's right hand. Blunt hands brushed the distended nipples in a light circular motion. Gentle ministrations gave way to rougher treatment as she rolled the pink crests between her thumb and forefinger. The answering whimper was all the encouragement she needed. Deftly she pushed the guard's panties to pool at her ankles, smirking at the darkness of the fabric at the crotch showing her how wet the woman already was.

She moved in front of the guard and captured her lips again for a punishing clash of teeth and tongues. Driving with her mouth, she steered Darla's body with her own until the edge of the table bit into the sensitive flesh of her thighs. She was going to pay for every second of fear and uncertainty she had caused.

Darla bit Cole's bottom lip in approval, daring her to respond to the taunt. She answered by hooking her feet around the table legs where they met the floor and pressing the guard down onto the table. The cold tabletop was a jolt to Darla's hot skin, and she arched her back retreating from the shock of it. Cole seized the blood-darkened nipples between her teeth and began flicking her tongue across it, exhaling warmth on the peak.

Darla's head was cushioned against Cole's worn carry-on. She turned her head to inhale the scent of leather. It carried with it an undertone of aromas: the musky smell of Cole's body and cologne, the tang of metal snaps and clasps, saddle soap from a cleaning an indeterminable time ago. The unique smell of leather had always turned her on, and coupled with Cole's mouth clamped on her tit, it was making her head spin. Hands on her body pushing against her skin were pulling reactions from her body she didn't know were possible. When Cole's arms grazed the fine hairs on her arms, the brief touch was so light it was painful. She needed hard contact, but she didn't have to ask for it.

Cole's mouth wandered from point to point like a tourist with time to kill. She nipped and sucked every pulse point and sensitive area from her fingertips to her navel, her hands following closely behind her mouth. She paused, contemplating which direction to take when she reached the Y intersection of the guard's legs. Darla tried to push Cole's head toward her aching cunt, but Cole just grinned slyly and chose the right fork.

Tending to the outside of the leg on the way down, and the inside on the way up, she stopped to reward the arch of Darla's foot when she discovered toenails painted the same fuck-me shade of red as her fingernails. When she returned to the top of the first leg she was faced with a neatly trimmed pussy just a shade darker than Darla's chestnut hair. Unable to resist, her thumbs stroked the outer lips, pulling them aside. Cole fixed her eyes like a bird mesmerized by the treasure glistening in the light. One long, slow stroke with her tongue, then another, before she abandoned the prize for her previous task. Darla growled her disapproval, but it got her nowhere.

Fueled by her premature taste of victory, Cole's patience had returned tenfold. The guard's frustration had only increased, and she wiggled her hips, trying to relieve her swollen clit on Cole's shoulder. When the second leg had been attended to, instead of returning to her cunt as desired, Cole leaned in for another kiss. Salt and cinnamon combined to make the sexiest flavor she'd ever tasted.

With her mouth locked on Darla's, Cole's hand probed and found the right spot, massaging it with her knuckles. She slid two fingers inside her wet hole and moved them around, feeling Darla's pulse from the inside and making room for one more to move in. It was the third finger that made the guard gasp, breaking the seal between them.

"Are you gonna fuck me yet or what?" Darla demanded. Gone were the clipped, proper sentences of the guard in charge.

"No." Was the reply she received as Cole replaced her drenched hand with her mouth, eager to clean up the mess she was making.

Her tongue made several slow passes from bottom to top, increasing the pressure each time and resting between laps to nibble on her clit. Her hands weren't idle; they dug into Darla's thighs, spreading her further and further apart. They moved up to tease her nipples as she sucked Darla's clit into her mouth. Holding it with her tongue against the roof of her mouth, she alternated between gently sucking and stroking, careful to maintain a steady pace. A dam within Darla burst, and suddenly she was flooding Cole's mouth with come while she beat the table with her palms.

"Fuck you," Darla whispered as she kissed away her come from Cole's chin. "Why couldn't you just give me what I wanted?"

Cole gave her a look of mock surprise and said, "You don't think you're done, do you? I just wanted to make sure you were good and wet."

She lightly stroked Darla's come-covered clit as her mouth perused the flesh behind her ear and down her neck. Nipples that had faded after climax darkened again as the skin puckered around them.

Cole fumbled blindly through a zippered compartment of her

carry-on, unwilling to stop playing with her favorite new toy for even a minute. She successfully retrieved a strand of foil-sealed pouches and a tube of thick, creamy petroleum hand lotion without her mouth breaking contact with Darla's skin. Now free to roam, she found herself back at her pussy in no time.

Showing mercy to the tender skin, she traced light wet circles against the flesh in a wide arc. Darla grabbed fistfuls of Cole's short hair and pulled her mouth so hard against her that Cole's chin was grinding her pubic bone. Pulling away briefly to gasp for breath, Cole soon dove back in, her tongue probing the delicate folds of her asshole. Crushing her hips against the table, Darla tried to move away from this sensual assault, but her unbroken guttural moan told the true story. Patience won out, and soon Darla's hands crept back to curl into Cole's hair, insisting on a quicker pace.

After applying a generous amount of the lotion to her hand, Cole replaced her mouth with her right hand and coaxed the muscles to relax for her. Following a few solid smacks of her palm on Darla's ass, she opened up like church doors on a Sunday morning, eager to let the worshippers in. Giving her a few minutes to adjust to the sensation, Cole pulled out a little and pushed back in, building the pressure.

Reaching behind her, Cole felt around on the floor until she found the guard's baton. Tearing at a foil packet with her teeth, she unrolled a condom over the shaft with her left hand. Soon she was substituting the baton for her right hand. Bit by bit Darla's eager asshole gobbled up several inches of the weapon. She was thrashing around on the table, knuckles pale from gripping the edges of it. Her moans had turned to a continuous string of grunts.

One more condom appeared; this one was stretched tightly over Cole's cock. Leaving the baton buried in Darla's ass, she positioned it loosely between her legs, the handle hooked behind her knee. The knob of her dick was poised at the entrance of Darla's cunt.

"Now I'm going to fuck you," she announced as calmly as she would ask for a glass of water in a restaurant.

It was Darla's turn to beg, "Please, oh, yes, please!"

Grasping the woman's shoulders, Cole slid easily into her wet hole. Setting a slow rhythm, she pulled most of the way out, then eased back in. Soon Darla's cunt had stretched to accommodate her, and Cole was thrusting in all the way to the base of her cock. It wasn't difficult to imagine slight contractions gripping and releasing her smooth rod, each different texture she had felt inside caressing the length of it.

The tabletop had become slick with sweat and Darla's wetness. Cole put the guard's ankles on her shoulders and wrapped each arm around a leg, sliding her just a little off the edge of the table. The backs of Darla's thighs slapped wetly against the front of Cole's thighs. Her grunts of pleasure and exertion mingled with Cole's until it seemed that there was only one voice of ecstasy and its echo inside the room.

Cole knew it was only a matter of time before she would be lost inside that hot cave, and she moved her thumbs to work over Darla's clit. Grasping the butch's forearms, Darla used them as leverage to impale herself on her cock.

"Oh, shit, don't stop. Don't stop, don't stop, don't stop, don't ahhhh...*God!*" she screamed, her eyes clenched shut and her head moving from side to side. Her whole body arched tightly and collapsed into convulsions, her hips still swiveling of their own accord.

Cole was close behind, groaning as she pumped her cock to a head-splitting orgasm. She toppled over, resting her head on Darla's heaving chest. When the heartbeat beneath her ear slowed and hers began to match it, she pulled away and began cleaning up. Wiping her hands on her undershirt and throwing it into the case, she turned and pulled on her pants and shirt. Bending over, she placed a hard, quick kiss on Darla's swollen lips.

"Thanks," she said as she slipped the case off the table and made her way to the door.

Smiling, Darla stretched, uncurling her body and her hands. Nestled in her damp palm was the handwritten tag previously attached to the leather case, declaring the name and address of its owner. It couldn't hurt anything to call, could it?

Ignoring the knowing looks from travelers who were checking the flight schedule posted on the wall outside the tiny room, Cole slung her carry-on over her shoulder and whistled her way to the moving sidewalk. Cheerfully she retrieved a credit card from her wallet and gave it to the man at the ticket counter.

"Champaign, Illinois, please. One way."

She was going home; there was a picture hanging in a certain hotel there that would look great in her bedroom.

PASSING FANCY

BETH GREENWOOD

Dusky skin the color of deepening night. A kind of skin so black as to haze contours and specifics. Willa watched her coolly stroll down the crosswalk—regal and oblivious to the world around her—head bopping slightly this way and that to music, tinny and sharp, leaking from her headphones. So black that it took a long second, a stretched moment, for Willa to see exactly where her cheekbones gently rose, where her delicate hands met her supple wrists. She was striking: an elegant beauty walking coolly across the street. In another moment, a beat of Willa's heart, she was naked and shining with reflections—a gleam of sweat in Willa's imagination that would show her full, glorious curves, breasts heavy and full, nipples dark delights, gentle rise of belly, curly thicket between strong thighs—as daylight never could.

Then fear dropped through Willa—a body terror that paused her in the middle of the crosswalk, froze her in mid stride. Heat built up, an anxiety and panic fire that covered her body in a patina of cold sweat.

It wasn't really thoughts that came to her mind, because she didn't think in words—it was more the bellows of mental breaths: hot and fast surges of fear, hysteria.

257

A discordant blast jarred her, forced Willa from her terror to her situation: standing, hunched over, in the middle of the street. Traffic blurred by, and the driver of the red Miata leaned, again, on his horn, startling her. Finally a gap opened in the stream of cars and she was able to sprint to the safety of the sidewalk.

This time she had thoughts, an unconscious stream of English tripping through her terror—and it had nothing to do with standing in the middle of a very busy street: *I don't like that, I don't, I don't like that, I don't understand: What's happening to me?—I don't like black women...*

*

She hadn't—didn't—ever. Yes, she saw the skin. Yes, she even admired the beauty. But it wasn't anything special, wasn't something that would take her eyes, turn them from the view of the street. It wasn't racism—she wasn't guilty of self-loathing. No, it was something else, something she couldn't understand.

Her eyes left the sidewalk, and she saw another, had to look, had to see—even though her mind pleaded with her eyes and the subsequent surge of imagination not to:

Elegant form, a sweeping urban gazelle, striding purposely down the street. Skin...yes, skin the color of chocolate—a deep, imported kind of chocolate that seemed at any moment on the verge of melting into a warm and delicious puddle, especially between a pair of equally tasty labia. Her stride was more hesitant than the other girl's—as if she was suddenly trapped, wild and passionate, in this strange city of fast-moving, gleaming machines.

Willa didn't want it, but the fantasy came anyway—as if some other person's desire, some other person's passion: She saw the girl, naked, as if stepping from the shower, innocent and caught unawares. It was a sight a lover might have, after a long morning of fucking in dawning light: her body, long and lean, gleaming with a subtle kind of dampness, wrapping her in reflections. She didn't want to, but Willa did imagine her nipples, darker than her deep black skin, like licorice bouncing at the tips of small but deliciously tight breasts.

The panic came again, a tension that wanted out in the form of a scream—but it didn't come, because that frightened reflex had clamped down on Willa's ability to breathe. Finally it slipped down to her legs and, without a thought of where she was going, Willa ran.

It had happened quickly—so quickly it was obvious that it wasn't just a new fondness blooming inside her. No, it had rolled up through her, shocking in its complexity, its immediacy: One moment Willa had been happy cruising the blonds and redheads walking by as she went about her business, and the next—the next she was captured, taken hostage by a wandering eye that was, simply, not her own.

The worst part was that she could feel it, like an invisible presence, lurking over her shoulder, taking her head—and thus, her eyes—and turning it, hard, to stare and drool over women she hadn't even been attracted to before its visitation.

Finally, her breath scraping in and out of her twitching lungs, she couldn't run anymore. Panting, waves of nausea breaking over her stomach, making her retch nothing onto the sidewalk, she stopped. She didn't know where she was, but she wasn't worrying about that.

It didn't feel like it had only been a few days. Willa, an accountant in what had been her comfortable, normal life, always had a good sense of time. She'd always been good about the feel of minutes and hours. It didn't feel like just three days...this had the oppressive weight of decades.

Worse was the confusion—her accountant's mind again tried to move the figures, to make it all balance, but she couldn't: Three days before a black woman was a black woman, just and nothing but—someone to be looked at, yes, but not someone to make the head twisted and the fantasies start. Then, with the slow crawl of hours, then a day, the presence within her had built—till she was obsessed, forced against her will to watch, to look, and to dream of sweaty, glorious dark skin.

Is this insanity? she thought, mentally holding herself tight against the feelings that controlled her. *I don't understand—*

Fear and exhaustion dropped her to her knees. Again, she didn't care where she was, what was on the street her knees rested on— all Willa wanted was to be away from where she was, to be free of the haunting desire.

She felt like…well, she didn't feel like herself.

Her run, her panic had brought her somewhere dark—the only lights those of streaking cars. Breathing heavy, alone, and thus alone from the visiting passion, she worked herself up till she was unsteadily standing. One of those streaks flashed around the corner and splashed her with hard brilliance.

Behind her, her reflection was crystal clear in shop glass—her own dark skin visible in the headlight glare. For a single slamming beat of her heart, Willa saw herself and again felt the alien desire burst through her: She saw herself naked and passionate, large black breasts heaving from an athletic fucking, lifting and rising with sensual weight, nipples dark and tightly erect. The dim veld of her cunt open and freely flowing with moisture.

Then the car was gone, and with it the view of her own dark body. Again she was alone in the safety of the quiet street.

The knowledge was slow in coming, as it had to work its way through the hammering fear that made her heart beat, beat, beat. No, she didn't feel like herself. But she knew, absolutely and positively, someone who did feel the way she did now, someone who saw black skin as a delight, as a sensual playground. She felt like Fancy.

※

The relationship was hot—but fast. When Willa thought of it, her time with Fancy, it was in firework terms: brilliance, an earth-shuddering crack of thunder, then stillness.

Willa smiled when she thought of it—but she didn't smile with delight. The brilliance had been because of Fancy's passion, not her own, the thunder had been the fight...and the quiet? That had been the calm after the storm.

The night was just beginning, so people were out and about. White, Asian, and yes, the glorious charcoal (no!) of delicious (No!) dusky female skin (NO!). The visiting passion was hot and heavy in Willa, and getting from downtown to the Haight was difficult. More than once she thought about screaming, letting the hysteria go—once and for all—in a madwoman dance. Somehow she put one foot in front of the other and made it from the cold steel of downtown, the Financial District, to the gentle—and mostly quiet—painted ladies of Haight Ashbury.

Willa stopped outside of 112 Page St. and looked at the one lit window.

I don't believe this, she thought after a while. *I don't.* But the memory came, again without words—or, at least, her own words.

"I love you," Fancy had said, smiling her little girl smile and looking up at Willa with her dolly eyes. The adoration had burned her, had been an unwelcome caustic swallow for Willa. She remembered the pain of it, the way it had caught her in the gut. She didn't want this girl's love, hadn't wanted her infatuation.

The sex had been good, the attention had felt comfortable—a warm blanket around her. But as they spent more and more time together, Fancy had started to irritate her. At first it was just the feelings—looking over and seeing her large brown eyes staring, just drinking her in. The way she always seemed to want to be with her, as if Willa was the only thing that was important to her. Attention was one thing, but someone wanting her so much was just...uncomfortable.

Other things too—like the way Fancy wanted Willa to be part of her life. Some things Willa actually enjoyed—like the time Fancy took her to the opera and then to dinner afterward. But other times, like when Fancy's mother was hospitalized and the girl had just wanted to cry—that had just been too much.

Then those words. Willa didn't ask for them, didn't want them. Yeah, the attention was sweet. Yeah, the gifts and the sex…they were nice. But Willa didn't want the rest of it.

"Well, I don't feel the same way about you," she'd said back to those words, feeling the power and the righteous anger in saying it. "I didn't ask for that, Fancy. I don't want you. Yeah, you're fun and all, and maybe I like you, but I don't want to be that way with you. Look, why don't you get your head together, and maybe I'll call you in a few days."

The tears had started again, and Willa's anger right along with it. "It's not me, anyway—is it? Face it, bitch, you want the black lovin' right? Fuck you—I've seen you. I know it's all that you want. Stupid bitch. You're racist—that's what you are: nothing but a fuckin' racist. You want me for my fucking skin. If I were white, you wouldn't be saying this shit to me, right? Well, find some other stupid black bitch to fuck."

Then she'd left, slamming the book on Fancy's screaming tears, her earnest pleas. Anger had flushed Willa's face, hammering in her ears—anger at being shown Fancy's disgusting soft underbelly, the secrets and the pain that she'd never asked to see. She'd wanted out—then and now, so she said what she knew would do the job and walked right out.

But now she was back. Fancy was more than a haunting memory—Fancy was haunting her.

✳

It was the ghost of Fancy's passion—the passion that Willa had struck down with cold words. Killed it dead. After a few months of wandering the cold, mean streets of San Francisco, it had found its murderer, taken up residence in Willa's soul.

The house was somewhat the same—a dark Victorian, heavy-lidded bay windows, simple stone steps to an elaborate front door—but Willa suspected her senses. It *appeared* as she'd left it—anger making her face flush, her breath quick and sharp. She suspected her eyes, because the theory of a haunting desire made too much sense; the house on 112 Page only *seemed* similar. She remembered the chimes above the door making sickly sweet music when she'd walked those same steps only months ago. She remembered the god's eye, full of disgusting candy colors, in the hall. She remembered the door chime, a saccharine handful of optimistic notes. She remembered the tiny plant and the sadness that it had always brought Fancy as it died, one pathetic leaf at a time.

The night was a cold cushion around her senses—but even so, she could see, hear the differences. The wind chime was gone, leaving only an ugly black hook above the door. The god's eye was gone, showing nothing in the casement but dirty brown carpet. The plant was gone as well, its only ghost a black ring of crusty soil.

And the doorbell…was store-bought. Its tune, when she rang it, was artificial and as cool as the night air.

Slowly, a pale shape descended the stairs. It paused at the bottom, and Willa felt herself examined through the peephole. "Oh, it's you," a calm—too calm—voice said through the door. "What do you want?"

The night wasn't the only thing chilled on that doorstep. "I-I have to talk to you."

"Haven't you said enough, Will? What's left to say?"

The last was final, and Willa could feel her presence retreat from the door, move up the stairs.

The terror washed through her again, the fear of walking the streets carrying something that didn't belong to her, being at the mercy of someone else's passion. "Fuck you, stop a minute!" she yelled, feeling her words bounce off the thick door. "Let me in…damn you."

"No, Willa. I won't. You didn't want me then, you must not want me now. Go away."

Fucking bitch—the heat rose to Willa's face, matching her fear. But through it all, a small crystal point of clarity. Saying the words, she felt the panic ebb, the sweat start to vanish: "I have something of yours."

"What, Will? You took everything."

"That's the problem—" Willa's voice was suddenly low and quavering, and her eyes started to burn...like she wanted to cry or something. Ridiculous.... "Just let me in, Fancy—I have something of yours I shouldn't have."

✳

It was a different house. It was easier that way. To categorize the differences between the rooms she walked through, the halls, the pictures, the debris of life that filled the place and the warm, brilliant—maybe too brilliant—house on 112 Page St. would have taken too long, too much attention. It was easier for Willa to just consider the place new—it was that unfamiliar.

It had a color, an image. It had a smell, a sound, a feel—and she was sure it would have had a taste if Fancy had offered her something. But the possibility of that was remote, as remote as where the house and the woman Willa remembered had gone...

The room felt as cold as the night outside—so much so that Willa automatically put her arms around herself for warmth. It was gray, a kind of oppressive, uncaring color: a color that comes from not caring about color at all. The color of abandonment. The only sound in the room was the gentle howl of the wind outside, like a cry from an injury that won't heal. It smelled of dust.

"So, what do you have? Give it up and get out, Will." Fancy's voice was low, not so much a growl as something perching on the edge of tears.

"Believe me, I want to get rid of it. But I don't know how."

Fancy sat down in an overstuffed chair Willa didn't remember. Willa stood in front of her, on a scattering of newspapers—crackles echoing through the room. "I don't want you here, Will. It hurts too much. Give it to me, whatever it is, and leave me alone."

"Christ's sake, Fancy—we broke up. Shit like this happens. Get the fuck over it."

Fancy was looking at the floor. "It hurt a lot, when you left, but it doesn't hurt anymore. Now I don't feel anything."

"I was mean, OK? Does that make you feel any better?"

"No, Will, it doesn't. It doesn't make me feel anything. I just wish you'd leave."

"I will, damn it. I will—but you've got to...take this fucking thing back. It's driving me *crazy*. I can't get rid of it."

"So give it to me, then, and get out, Will. I don't care about you anymore, but having you here—maybe I'll start thinking about you again, and that would be bad."

"I don't know how," Willa replied, each word a spike of frustration. "I don't know how to get rid of it. I just know it's not fucking mine—it's yours."

"I don't understand you, Will," Fancy said, her voice as cool as the room. "Give it to me and get out. Stop bothering me. Can't you see you hurt me?"

There—right there. Maybe the light in the room was so dim that she could see it, or maybe Willa had done it so many times, to Fancy and others, that she'd started to understand its effects—whatever the cause, Willa did see something: she saw the tightness in Fancy's body, the glaze of tears on her cheeks, the profound uncaring, passionless nature of the room. She saw it. She saw it for the first time.

She'd been standing, looking down at Fancy's tiny form, so she lowered herself down, down, down till she was sitting on the floor, looking up at her moon-white face. "I said it before—look, I said I was...no, that's not right—"

"Fancy," she started again, after a rasping breath, "I'm sorry. I know you loved me. It's just that...you scared me. You scared me bad. I thought you were crazy, stupid—clinging on me, forcing me down. I wanted you to get away from me...and saying that, saying those things, was the only way I could get you away from me.

"I thought I knew why I wanted you gone—I thought it was because you pushed so hard, hung all over me. But that's wrong. I think I know...no, I do know why I wanted you to go, wanted to hurt you. I look at myself, Fancy, and I don't see anything desirable. I didn't hate you for loving me, Fancy—I hurt you because I didn't think I deserved loving, didn't deserve you.

"If I let you love me, then I might love you—no, I *would* love you—and that would be too damned scary. So I hurt you before you could hurt me."

Willa's face was wet. Still, she kept talking, trying to get the truth out through the tears: "I loved you too, Fancy. I know I did. Your passion, all the beautiful stuff inside you. I know I killed that, I know I tore it out of you—that's what I have. That's what I have to give back to you. You are a good person, Fancy—a woman worth loving, and worth being loved by."

Fancy looked up finally. Her cheeks were wet as well. Willa saw her lip quiver, saw a gentle smile light her face—then she leaned slowly, carefully forward and touched her own lips to Fancy's. The touch was sweet, tender, salty, and almost innocent. Almost, because as it lingered, a slow surge of warmth spread up through them—Willa knew it had to have been both because she had never generated such heat herself. The heat grew into a sweaty fever. Then their tongue tips touched. Then Fancy's hand was on Willa's shoulder. Then Willa's hand was on Fancy's breast.

Fancy moaned, slow and deep, and her hand left Willa's shoulder and eagerly wrapped around the other woman's hand, guiding it, asking Willa, without words, to squeeze harder.

Willa did, and Fancy's moan grew slower and deeper, her nipple under her blouse and between Willa's tight fingers growing more and more erect.

"Off," Willa said, fingers to buttons.

"You too," Fancy said, eyes half closed, mouth slightly open. Heat, yes, but crackling ice below as well.

Willa heard it, mixed in with those two words. Hesitation, doubt—fear. "I'd love to," the black woman said, standing up.

Fancy looked like she was going to say something but didn't. Willa instantly knew what it would have been. But just as instantly she knew she didn't want her to say it, so she prevented Fancy's "You don't have to." Because she wanted to. It was as simple as that.

Not a strip tease, that was commercial and performed. Willa, instead, undressed for her lover. As she did, each item falling to the floor, she saw herself reflected in Fancy's desire.

Desire…yes, that was it (bra and panties a cotton pile at her feet). That was it. Naked, Willa stood there, hot and wet and ready. She felt the desire—in Fancy, back where it belonged.

Its departure didn't diminish Willa—it didn't leave a gap behind. As she descended to the floor and wrapped her arms around her lover, something else began to occupy her. Where it had been, no one but the ghost of Willa's compassion could say, but all that really mattered to Willa was that it was back where it belonged.

As her lips went to Fancy's nipple, a kiss then a suck; as her fingers went between the white girl's thighs, a stroke then one steady finger within; as Willa spread gleaming lips and gave Fancy another kiss, another suck, it rose inside her. As they touched, caressed, sighed, and then cried together, Willa felt it filling her: a new possession, a new spirit that would live in her—a new feeling, a unique feeling.

One that brought tears to Willa's eyes as she held Fancy, both of them shining with pleasure and happiness, and said "I love you."

IN THE PINK
KRISTINA WRIGHT

"I fucking hate taffeta." My assertion was met by stares and silence from the other three bridesmaids who were crowded into the country club powder room with me. I don't know what I was expecting. These girls were career bridesmaids, whereas I was just the token dyke in the wedding party. My new sister-in-law, Ginny, was a wonderful girl, but it was an hour into this little shindig and I was ready to kick her ass for forcing me into a pink taffeta gown and matching underwear (a gift from the giddy bride). Then again, what did I know? If it wasn't jeans and a T-shirt, I hated it. And I hated the fucking pink taffeta dress so much, I was getting hives.

"But you look so pretty," cooed Melanie, one of the Stepford bridesmaids. She was dolled up in the exact same dress I was, but she somehow managed to look like she *belonged* in taffeta.

"I don't want to look pretty," I snarled, tugging at the neckline of the dress, which barely covered the peekaboo lace of the matching pink bra I was wearing. "I want to get the hell out of this dress and into something that will let me breathe."

A collective gasp went up from the bridesmaids.

"Oh, no, the reception has just started. You have to wear the dress for the reception pictures," scolded Victoria, the militant maid of honor. "And stop messing with your hair, you'll pull out the curls."

Me, with curls piled on top of my head. Me, in lace underwear. Me, in taffeta. "Shoot me now," I muttered. For the sake of my big brother's future happiness, I left the curls, the itchy lace underwear, and the hideous dress alone.

The girls powdered their noses, and we moseyed en masse back out to the reception room of the Crystal River Country Club. Camera flashes blinded me as everyone but the waiters took my picture. I tried to be a good sport: I danced with the father of the bride, who said I looked lovely; I danced with my own father, who said he'd lost a $50 bet with my brother that I would actually keep the dress on through the reception; and I smiled pretty for the endless amateur photographers who wanted just one more picture.

Finally, I'd had enough. I grabbed an open bottle of champagne from one of the tables, hiked up the miserable taffeta dress with my free hand, and stalked outside before another wedding guest told me how pretty I was or another drunk guy asked for my phone number.

"Hey, babe, where you running off to?"

The voice came from the shadows cast by the palatial white columns of the country club's entrance. I saw the flicker of a cigarette, but little else. At first I thought it was one more guy attempting to score at a wedding. "Some place where taffeta gowns and lace underwear don't exist," I muttered, stalking past my interrogator.

"Too bad. I was working up the nerve to ask you to dance."

The voice was deep, but not that deep. I paused mid stride and turned. "What makes you think I'd want to dance with you?"

She stepped out of the shadows and leered at me, her tanned face bare of anything more than a glisten of perspiration from the steamy Florida heat. "Because I hear I'm you're type."

Her hair looked like she spent a lot of time running her hands through it. It was short, red, and tousled like she'd just climbed out of bed. My gut reaction was instant and surprising: I was turned on by her just-fucked hair. The rest of her wasn't so bad either. She was tall and lean and dressed all in black—black shirt, black pants, black jacket, black shoes. The red hair above the unrelenting black was striking. It was also unmistakably a family trait, because Ginny, the taffeta-happy bride, had the same color hair, albeit longer and more fashionably styled.

"I'm Jae, Ginny's sister." I'd heard about Jae, the nature photographer who was currently living somewhere in the wilds of Australia. Heard of her, but in the two years my brother had been with Ginny, never met her. She was at least 10 years older than me and sexy as hell in a confident, quiet way.

It figured I would be wearing taffeta when I met the dyke of my dreams.

"I just got in this afternoon, so I missed the rehearsal dinner," she went on, taking a drag off her cigarette before flicking it away. "I've been waiting all night for Ginny to introduce me to her hot new sister-in-law, but she's been a little preoccupied."

"I guess you know I'm Beth."

"Uh-huh."

The silence was awkward. I was actually nervous. Picking up chicks at weddings while wearing a gown is kind of outside my area of expertise.

Voices drifted toward us from just inside the country club doors. Jae grabbed my arm and pulled me behind one of the columns. I was so startled, I nearly dropped the champagne.

She put her fingertips over my mouth. "Shh. They'll be looking for you to take more pictures."

With that, my mouth slammed shut—I nearly took her finger off at the knuckle. Sure enough, I heard someone call my name. One of the bridesmaids, it sounded like. I snuggled up against Jae and waited for the person to go away.

"Thanks," I murmured, suddenly aware of how close we were.

She kissed me, hard. Her breath tasted of wine and cigarettes.

She slid her hands around the back of my dress as she hauled me up tight against her. She was several inches taller than me, but my heels took away some of that advantage, bringing us hip to hip. I pulled back slightly, laughing. Even through layers of taffeta, I could tell she was packing.

She gave a little tug that sent my curls tumbling in black ringlets down my back. "Let's get out of here."

I didn't attempt to play coy. She knew I wanted her as soon as she kissed me. Hard to argue otherwise when I'd just had her tongue down my throat. She grabbed my hand, and I hung on to her as tightly as I was hanging on to the champagne bottle. We took off around the side of the country club, running full out for the golf course. I couldn't keep up with Jae while wearing heels, so I kicked them off and groaned as the blood rushed back into my toes. Jae just laughed and pulled me along, stumbling on the hem of my dress as we ran.

The rolling hills of the golf course were dark and silent and blissfully free of people with cameras. When we were a safe distance from the country club, we slowed to a walk. Somewhere around the ninth hole, we flopped down on the green, the pink taffeta billowing out around me like a puddle of Pepto-Bismol. I took a long drink from the champagne bottle and passed it to Jae.

"Whatcha got on under that dress?" she asked, leaning toward me on one elbow, her bottom lip glistening from the champagne. She looked predatory, like she wanted to eat me. I kind of hoped she did.

"Itchy lace underwear your sister made me wear."

"Poor little baby dyke." She made a tsk-tsk as she took another hit from the bottle and put it down beside us.

"Who you calling a baby?"

She was quick. She rolled me over onto my back in one swift move and pinned my arms above my head. "You, baby."

"OK," I whispered, my voice sounding as shaky as I felt.

She kissed me again, sucking my bottom lip between her teeth and nipping it until I moaned. The rustle of my dress was the only noise for the next several minutes as she kissed me breathless. When we finally came up for air, we were both laughing. A bird sent up a startled cry of response from a stand of trees nearby, and I giggled again, lightheaded from the champagne and lust.

Jae licked her bottom lip as if still tasting my mouth. "I've been wanting to do that all night."

I hadn't even known the legendary Jae was in town, but she'd been watching me all night. It made me grin like a fool. "If I'd known I had that to look forward to, I might have actually smiled for some of the wedding pictures."

"Well, if that makes you smile…" she said, letting the words trail off as she found the hem of my dress and slid her hand up the inside of my thigh.

I spread my legs for her, but she took her sweet time getting where I wanted her to be. She stroked my thighs softly while she kissed and sucked on my neck. I fumbled under her jacket and found her nipples through the thin fabric of her shirt. She was slim and small-breasted, but her nipples pebbled like diamonds under my fingers. I tugged them through her shirt, and she bit down hard on my neck.

The dress was cut low, and it didn't take much wiggling on my part for the neckline to slip even lower, baring my lace-covered breasts. She buried her face between my tits, nuzzling them through the itchy fabric until I reached up and tugged the cups of the bra away from me. She moaned softly as she licked my skin, sucking on the sensitive undersides of my breasts. She toyed with the lace waistband of my panties while she licked and nibbled her way across my chest.

"I'm going to die here if you don't touch me," I gasped when I couldn't stand her teasing any longer.

Her laughter was muffled against my chest. She stroked down my stomach and then lower, running her fingers over my panty-covered mound. When she found the crotch of my panties wet and clinging to me, she whisked them away and tossed them on the grass beside the champagne bottle. By now, my dress was up around my waist, and the cool grass was tickling me intimately, but I wasn't complaining.

Jae pulled away from me, and I made a little whimper of protest, but she didn't go far. She knelt between my legs and stripped off her jacket, then rolled up the sleeves of her shirt as if she intended to go to work on me. I shivered as she used her thumbs to hold me open. She looked at my cunt like she was starving for a good meal.

"Baby, you're almost as pink as that damned dress."

I couldn't have given her a smart-assed retort if I'd wanted to, because at that moment she leaned forward and sucked my clit into her mouth just as hard as she'd sucked my bottom lip a few moments before. I let out a whimper, clamping my thighs around her head and burrowing my fingers in her short, silky hair.

She nursed on my clit, alternately lapping and nibbling at it until I was writhing beneath her. But then I felt her shift, felt her hands sliding away from my hips. I raised myself up on my elbows and watched her fumble with her pants. She dragged them down her thighs until I could see what she was packing. The dildo was tucked inside a pouch, and she pulled it free.

"Want my dick, baby dyke?" she whispered, stretching out on top of me, one hand braced against the ground, the other guiding the dildo between my spread thighs.

"I want whatever you'll give me."

She drove it into me, deep and hard, and I screamed with the suddenness of it. Keeping up that hard, fast rhythm, she pressed her wet cunt against my thigh and moved with me. I clutched at her back, moaning as she fucked me, sending a couple more birds into frenzied flight.

"Keep your voice down or the police will be out here."

I yanked at her shirt until a button popped. I pulled it away from her body and bit down on her shoulder to keep from screaming again. I could feel her muscles tense and flex as she rode my thigh and fucked me with the dildo. She slid higher on my body, until her tits were in my face. I pulled one of her hard, rubbery nipples into my mouth and sucked it, feeling her grind even harder against my thigh.

"Oh, God, you're driving me crazy," I gasped as she dragged the dildo out of my cunt and thrust it back in. "You're gonna make me come on your big dick."

"That's the idea, baby."

I was incoherent after that. She fucked me hard and steady, and we were sliding across the grass, propelled by the slippery taffeta of my dress. I had visions of us splashing into a water hazard, but she drove that thought from my mind as she pummeled my throbbing cunt.

I sucked hard on her nipples until she was humping my thigh so hard I knew I would have a bruise in the morning. Despite her warning me to be quiet, her own moans wafted across the still golf course.

"Fuck me," I begged, every inch of my body straining for release. "Please."

She angled the dildo up high and hard and that was all it took. My body convulsed around the thickness of the dick inside me, and I wrapped my arms and legs around her as if I would never let her go. She fucked me steadily, riding out my orgasm while I clung to her and panted her name.

I managed to roll her over as my orgasm faded to a gentle pulse. I was so weak I couldn't do much more for a few minutes than lie on top of her and kiss her. She was still moving against my thigh, leaving a trail of wetness on my skin.

I finished unbuttoning her shirt and kissed my way down her chest and across her stomach. Her cunt smelled like heaven, musky and sweet with arousal. I gave a quick swipe up the length of her slit and felt her jump. Sluggish from coming so hard, I settled between her legs, my dress still hiked up to my waist and the humid night air blowing a tepid breeze across my fevered cunt.

I nuzzled her damp thighs, wanting to take my time with her

and knowing once I started I wouldn't be able to slow myself down.

"Eat me, baby," she growled, her hands reaching for my decimated curls. She gave a sharp tug, which was all the encouragement I needed. I buried my face between her thighs and feasted on her like an overripe fruit, reveling in the feel of her wetness on my cheeks and chin.

I sucked her clit between my lips and was rewarded with a soft, plaintive cry. I slid two fingers into her wet, clutching cunt and continued to suck her clit as it pulsed like a wild thing against my lips. She was so hot and ready, it didn't take long. A few more hard licks and she was coming in my mouth. I kept the flat of my tongue on her clit, feeling every ripple of her body as she alternately clutched at my hair and pressed at my shoulders.

Finally, I let her push me away. She pulled me up her body, and I heard the distinct sound of fabric rending as my knee caught in the taffeta.

"Oh, shit," she muttered against my neck. I was draped across her body, too exhausted to move. "I think I ripped your dress."

"That's OK. It should go nicely with the grass stains."

"Sorry." She sounded like she was trying not to laugh.

"Please. I don't care if we torch the dress, just let me get out of it first," I said, groaning for an entirely different reason than the soreness in my well-used cunt. "On second thought, I might want to keep it as a souvenir."

"I'll take that as a compliment."

I suddenly had a thought. "You're the sister of the bride. So how the hell did you get spared the torture of being in the wedding party?"

Jae gave a little tug on my hair, which was now spread across her bare tits like a shawl. "Don't ask."

"I'm serious. I want to know."

She chuckled softly, twirling a curl around her finger. "It's simple, baby dyke. I fucking hate taffeta."

AT LIBERTY
TOBY RIDER

Icy spider-fingers of salt spray rasped the nape of Vic's neck. She could have turned her collar up against the wind, but her hands were full, pressing Tory's body so hard against her own that the pleasure verged on pain. Even discomfort was joy, though, proof of reality, after so many dreams had dissolved into yet another desert morning, and unending war, and her own fist hot and wet between her thighs.

Tory reached up to tweak the wool collar, rubbing herself against Vic, her nipples hard as the buttons on her opened shirt. "We could get out of the wind," she murmured against Vic's cheek. Her own cheek was damp and salty, even though Vic's taller form sheltered her from the worst of the spray. Tears? Not that she would ever admit to it.

The boat had turned so that they were no longer on its lee side. Everyone else had drifted toward the bow, watching Liberty Island loom closer through the mist. At least they had some real privacy where they were; the National Park Service people had become, after introductions and sincere handshakes, genially oblivious, but years of "don't tell" had wired Vic for caution verging on paranoia.

"What, I'm not keeping you warm enough?" Vic teased, trying for a light tone. She eased back and began to button Tory's shirt. They would dock in a matter of minutes, and there were still some limits to be observed, after all, in the respect due a national monument.

Tory blocked Vic's sun-browned fingers with her own, but only briefly. "We're almost there," she admitted, turning to nestle her butt into her lover's crotch; then she gasped as Vic reached around under her jacket to fondle her through her shirt.

"Almost there?" Vic murmured into Tory's froth of russet curls. "How close?" She scraped her nails across sensitized nipples, keeping on until Tory's breath came swift and ragged.

"Vic...ah!...yes...oh...damn it, if I don't get sucked one way or another pretty fucking soon, I'll scream!"

"You'll scream even louder if you do." Beneath Vic's cocky tone she was blessing Tory for not asking, "Why? Why now? When you wouldn't touch me last night? Or this morning?"

Last night, exhaustion after the flight from the Mideast had been excuse enough. Not that Vic had slept soundly; time after time her dozing had given way to a panicky wakefulness. Where? Who? New York...Tory's bed...Tory's body beside her, warm curves as smooth and graceful as wind-carved dunes, but so sweet and tender...Impossible! And her dreams, filled for months with images of Tory so sensual and raw they'd inflamed her to the point of combustion, now roiled with violent images she needed desperately to leave behind. All she'd seen, done, *had* to do...all those she couldn't save...

Deep sleep must have come at last, until sunlight filtered through the February-bare branches outside Tory's window. When Vic stirred, Tory came to kneel naked above her, bending to nibble lightly at the tender skin exposed in the gap between T-shirt and boxer shorts. Vic sighed, stretching, letting the gap widen. Tory pursued this opening with enthusiasm, nudging the shirt upward with her nose, tugging the shorts downward inch by inch, exploring with lips and tongue and teeth; and every little kiss pressed into Vic's vulnerable belly sent tongues of fire darting toward her cunt.

She needed to arch upward toward that teasing mouth, ached just as hungrily to pull Tory down, roll on top of her, and fuck her supple, wriggling body until she lay limp and sated. But her own body wouldn't obey her impulses. A ponderous gravity weighted her limbs, as in dreams of fleeing from unseen, pursuing terrors.

Somewhere a truck backfired. Vic stiffened. A tremor began deep in her chest, threatening to ripple outward, and suddenly she heaved herself over to lie with her face buried in the pillow. Damn, damn, damn, why now, when she had stood firm for so long against anything war could hurl at her?

"It's OK, babe," Tory said. "It's kinda soon. You're just not really all here yet." She leaned back and patted Vic's butt, more in camaraderie than seduction. Then she ran a finger along Vic's thigh and tugged the hem of her shorts upward. "Sure didn't get those tanned legs in a New York winter, but your ass could still pass. No nude sunbathing in a war zone, I guess."

One deeply probing caress beneath the shorts, and then she was off the bed and turning on the burner under the coffee. Another grope like that and Vic sure as hell *would* be all there, she thought; but she wasn't sure enough to say so.

Over breakfast, Tory chatted casually about her work as an urban park ranger and her plans for the day. "I wrote you about the bald eagles, right? It's been so cold upstate this winter they've been riding ice floes down the Hudson to fish in open water. I'm recording sightings, seen some myself from over on the Palisades, and one flying over Grant's Tomb." She reached across to rumple Vic's short, dark hair. Those glints of silver radiating from a small, jagged scar above her left ear hadn't been there a year ago. "A couple more decades or one more war and you'll be looking like one very fierce, sexy eagle yourself."

That called for a kiss. Vic tensed to deliver, but Tory went on in a rush, "Anyway, some National Park Service guys from Ellis and Liberty reported one flying way down off Battery Park, so we got together, and that's how I managed to fix up this trip today."

Vic wondered if she'd missed something. Tory glanced at her a bit nervously. "So we're going to Liberty Island. Unless you'd rather not. But I thought you might want to see the Statue."

Vic couldn't say no to those hopeful hazel eyes. "Yeah, sure," she said. "Sure, I do," and she wondered whether it might even be true.

They'd met in the rubble of Ground Zero, where Vic's Reserve unit had been posted for search and security duty. Even dust-covered and drawn with strain and weariness, Tory had caught her eye like a beacon. It hardly seemed like the right time to make a pass, though, until the evening Tory came up behind her on the ferry dock as she gazed out over the harbor.

"You ever been out there?" Tory asked casually. "To the Statue? Or Ellis?"

"Not yet," Vic said gruffly, glad to have her grim thoughts interrupted. In the gray distance the Lady rose from the harbor, ageless and erect—but how could she bear it? How had she felt, when terror struck, and the towers fell, and she couldn't even turn to face them, only stand and look steadily outward?

She shook off such craziness. "My ancestors didn't come through Ellis, anyway. Half of them were French fur traders, and the other half were cousins of the guys who sold this real estate cheap to the Dutch. Always figured the whole deal about 'Miss Liberty' was pretty ironic, in fact, but looking at her now…Damn, that's some woman!" Tragedy and politics aside, there was something powerfully sensual in all that steadfast, nurturing serenity; or maybe it was just that Tory's closeness put sensuality powerfully on Vic's mind.

She didn't realize she was flexing her fingers until Tory laid her own across them. "She has a 10-foot fist," she said wickedly, "and a 40- or 50-foot arm."

"Kind of makes me feel humble," Vic responded. Tory laughed, and gripped her hand, and two hours later they were showering off the dust and soot and anguish together in Tory's tiny studio apartment.

The boat emerged into sunshine just before it nudged against the dock. At the far end of the island the Lady stood, solitary, monumental; along the wide pathways a surprising number of tourists strolled and snapped pictures, drawn here even though the statue itself was still off-limits after two and a half years.

Vic felt drawn too, but oddly reluctant to go closer. "This is great," she murmured to Tory, "but I can't wait to get you back home." Maybe the sea breeze had blown away the last of the desert, or maybe sheltering Tory from the wind had restored her confidence. Whichever, she was sure whatever had blocked her had melted away. Almost sure.

But Tory tugged her along the dock to where a 40ish, wiry woman in a Park Service uniform waited.

"Maddie, this is Vic," she said, a bit breathlessly. "Vic, meet Madlyn."

Vic put out her hand and felt it gripped with a force just short of challenge. Madlyn looked steadily into her face for a long moment. "OK," she said abruptly. "We can go up."

She strode off toward the monument, with Vic and Tory following. "Up inside the Statue? All the way?" Vic asked, and Tory nodded.

"She wouldn't promise until she'd seen you."

Vic wasn't sure this wasn't some new dream, but when they rounded the huge pedestal and she had to tilt her head back to look up, and up, into the Lady's face, it didn't matter. Whatever name or role men had given her, she rose beyond it, the archetype of the strong woman, powerful without swagger, stern and compassionate, nurturing and commanding. Vic wanted to reach out, to touch something more of her than the copper shell of her robes, smooth away the tension between her brows, stroke her full, beautiful lips gently until they curved into a smile.

A sidelong glance at Madlyn showed her watching with something close to a smile herself. The ranger led them toward an entrance, stopped to speak to two security guards, and then they were inside, riding the elevator to the top of the 10-story pedestal; and then, under the cavernous shelter of Lady Liberty's robes, Vic was jogging up the spiraling staircase well ahead of the others.

She mounted higher and higher, through the massive, complex network of girders forming the statue's bones. The thud of her boots on the metal steps was like a giant pulse accelerating along with her own heartbeat.

In spite of the exertion, the farther she got the faster she needed to go. At last, in the tiny room at the top, where a row of windows looked out from the Statue's crown, Vic braced her hands against the inside of her copper brow and gazed out with her across island and sea and sky. Harbor lights were flickering on as afternoon flowed toward twilight, tiny sparks echoing the blaze of her great lamp.

Vic's whole body seemed to be growing, stretching. She ached to stand eye to eye with her, breast to breast, heart to pounding heart; to comfort her, share the endless standing guard, the grief at the chaos human hatred could inflict. Vic understood all that. And suddenly she wanted to share something else she understood, something filling her to bursting: She wanted to show her the piercing joy of a woman's body.

Vic's breath came even faster now than when she'd been climbing. She was still alone in the room. Then Madlyn's head emerged above the stairwell. "Are you OK?" she asked.

"Just meditating," Vic grated. Madlyn gave her a keen glance and then nodded and stepped back down, gesturing for Tory to wait.

Vic didn't give a damn. She was inside the great body, swelling to fill it, her head brushing the copper ripples on the reverse side of her hair. She clenched her fist low against the side of an arching support and leaned her hips into it, pressing her crotch against her flexing thumb; a desperate comfort she had sought before, in rare moments of solitude, leaning on walls, trees, once, even, an armored tank. This time, though, she felt far from solitary. Another presence filled her, surrounded her, intensified the heat Tory had already ignited in her. The pounding tension in her clit and cunt swelled, and rose, higher and harder, until joy burst forth like rays of light from her crown.

But a whole lot noisier than light. Vic could feel her shout of triumph reverberating through the Lady's copper body as though it had become her own voice.

When the cry had died away and Vic's gasps subsided, Madlyn reemerged. "Meditating, huh? How about teaching me that mantra?"

Tory pushed past her and rushed at Vic, who turned to meet her. They leaned against each other, both shaking, until Tory slid to her knees and buried her face in Vic's damp, musky crotch, then raised her head. "There'd better be more where that came from!"

Vic had no more doubts. Wherever that had come from, the way was clear now. "All you can handle," she said, and she drew Tory's head close again for a moment before pulling her up, and toward the stairs, and home.

On the return ride they stood pressed together, Tory's back warm against Vic's front, and watched the city skyline with its aching gap grow closer. "Vic, I..." Tory had to pause to clear her throat. When she began again she managed a lighter tone. "I can't believe you fucked the Statue of Liberty! But don't go thinking you did it all by yourself. I was rubbing that railing so hard my hand aches, and Maddy—well, she was crouched over muttering something I'm pretty damned sure wasn't the rosary."

Vic wriggled her crotch against Tory's round ass. Too bad she wasn't packing—but, she reflected, inside the immense Statue that might have felt, well, inadequate.

She didn't feel inadequate at all, though, when she had Tory all to herself in the tiny shower...and up against the refrigerator...and over the back of the sofa...and in bed. There was one brief moment, as Tory's guttural moans took on a tinge of pain, when Vic hesitated; until Tory squeezed her thigh savagely with a hand as strong as her own. "Don't stop!" she commanded. "You can't hurt me, damn it! More! Harder!"

The last subconscious shadow of war vanished. Vic was all there, in every urgent moment, feeling, breathing, tasting the intensity, knowing without question where she was, who she was; free to take her long-unused gear for a wild, slippery ride, free to let Tory drive her to her limits, hold her there for long, cruel, delirious minutes, then thrust her over the edge into the sweet, howling maelstrom. And, at last, into sleep and peace.

EL BAILE
TATIANA DE LA TIERRA

She has huge tits, and I wonder if they're soft like mine or duras como el mango verde. I'm thinking about tasting them.

"¿Quieres bailar?" I have to get into her face to ask her to dance 'cause the music's so loud. She shakes her head, won't budge. Sips something or other. Keeps her eye on the dance floor while I keep an eye on her. Es una noche de salsa y merengue, with some '70s and techno thrown in. A Saturday night in Miami.

I have all night to get her.

Meanwhile, my lover takes me by the hand, drags me practically, a bailar. I'm sorta pissed off at her 'cause she was rude earlier, and I wanna make sure that she knows it, so I dance, playing aloof. Ella marca el ritmo con su cadera, presses into me, and I let my body respond in sync, but I refuse to make eye contact. I focus on las otras mujeres bailando, glance at the ceiling, watch the bartender. I'm spinning and doing ese un-dos-tres, digging Guayacán, snarling and being a bitch all the while. My lover, she knows what's happening, y le importa un carajo. That's what I like about her.

And then I catch that woman watching us intently; she's shifted her stool around to face us. Sits with her legs open and smokes a cigarette. Does nothing but watch. Turns me on.

I face my lover and go full force con el Grupo Niche, let my pelvis loose, let her lead me into her and away and around and back again. Es la salsa, I think, it's so powerful. Y es mi amante, she's such a galán. Pero también es the audience, esa mujer watching us con sus ojos claros.

"I found someone," finally I tell my lover. We're dancing slow and close to one of those old-time boleros. She has a firm grip on me, and I'm fluttering into her like silk sheets strung out on a line to dry. My eyes are closed, and somehow my feet are still going with hers, and for a moment there I think that, yes, it's unexplainable, but I *am* in love.

"¿Con quién quieres?" my lover asks. I point the woman out with a glance as we go back to our seats. She's not smoking anymore and her legs are crossed.

My lover goes to the bar to get our drinks, and I wipe the sweat off my face and strategize. It's been a while since we had someone else in bed with us, and this woman, whoever she may be, is the one. It's really not about her tetas, although they are appealing. Or her big Viking body. Or the golden hair that shimmers or the eyes that seem like clear quartz crystals.

She's different from the usual in Miami. No painted nails, no high heels, no makeup, no perfume, cheap or otherwise. Just casual slacks and an oversize shirt that shows her cleavage. Sandals and a big woven bag. And just like that, plain as she could be, she's alluring. Me intriga, that's it. I want to crack her code and give her a show of my own sexual dance. I want her to watch my lover break me open. I want my lover to do her like she does me.

Rum and Coke in hand, I go over to her once more and leave my lover to watch. "¿Quieres bailar?" This time she smiles, gives me her hand, and goes with me. Es un merengue and I lead. She's sorta stiff at first, but she loosens up soon enough. I guide her side to side, turn her out and then back in. I keep a respectable distance. In the midst of our dance, her tits brush against mine. They're hard. Like green mangos, I think. I want to taste them, just like I wanted to when I first saw her.

The song ends and another begins. I get close to her face and cup my hands around my mouth. Tito Nieves sings "I like it like that" with a techno-Latin thump thump, and I ask her, loudly, so that she can hear me above the music, "¿Te quieres acostar con nosotras?"

"All you had to do was ask."

Her name is Mía and she's from Buenos Aires. She's catching a flight to Paris tomorrow afternoon for a queer youth conference, donde va a presentar some sort of manifesto. She looks like she's in her 30s but she's only 22 years old. She has a raspy voice and is totally unpretentious. We'll never see her again. Perfect.

We take her home.

Upstairs we go, into the bedroom. "Me quiero duchar," she says, and I show her to the bathroom, hand her a clean towel. She looks me in the eye, starts undressing right away, as if testing me. "Is this what you want?" Off with the shirt, bra, pants, así nomás. Before me is a fat woman from a Botero painting, big-breasted, big-bellied, big everything. Beautiful. La quiero chupar ahí mismo, but I don't dare, not yet. I nod. *Yes, this is what I want.* I turn toward the door. "Venga conmigo," she says, and suddenly I am scared. I can only do what my lover allows; she has to direct me. Those are the rules. But she's downstairs fixing us drinks.

Mía extends a hand. I don't move. She takes a step toward me, stands at my back, and unzips my dress. Pulls the fabric off my arms, down my legs. Unhooks my bra, pulls my panties and hose down with two hands. Nudges my right foot in the air, flicks my pump off, repeats the procedure with my left foot. I am naked before her, and terrified. "Qué linda," she says in approval, and I'm embarrassed. This was all my idea, but somehow she has the upper hand. "Ven," she says, and this time I give her my hand and step into the shower with her.

My nipples respond immediately to the cold blast of water. I let the water drench my head, run down my body full force. Mía is behind me, pressing her warm panocha into my cold ass, wrapping her arms around my stomach, biting into my back. She takes my ear into her mouth and cruises the ridges with her tongue. Blows hot little breaths that give me instant goose bumps. Cups her hand so I can hear her whisper above the sound of the shower. "Esto es lo que querías, Linda?" *Sí, es ésto, y más.*

She tickles my armpit with strands of her long wet hair. Slides her hand up to my tetas and fondles me, making me spin like a record on the turntable. That's it. Estoy caliente. I extend my back, push my ass into her, reach for her with my hands behind me until I've got her nalgas at the tips of my fingers. Already, I want to fuck. And then her body tenses up behind me, and the water stops abruptly.

"I see you have everything under control," says my lover. She dries her hand on a towel, lights a cigarette, sips from a tall glass she brought up, puts the top down on the toilet, and sits.

"She wanted to…She made me…"

"And you just couldn't defend yourself, could you?"

"I didn't know…I…Te quería dar la sorpresa…"

"Put your clothes back on."

Mía watches, open-mouthed. I step out of the shower, dry off, and dress while she and my lover watch. *Qué comemierda,* I'm thinking, but I don't say a word.

"Dry her off," orders my lover. Mía asks me questions with her eyes when I face her. *No hay problema,* I want to say. *This is part of the game.* But all I do is smile politely while I dry her body, patting the cloth on her thick arms and legs, swiping it down her back, sliding it into her crack, drying her wet pubic hair carefully, drop by drop. It takes all of my will power not to drop on my knees and eat her.

When I'm done drying her off, Mía steps out of the bathroom and I hear her plunk down on the bed in the next room. "Ya está," I say to my lover, handing her the wet towel, as if her watching wasn't proof enough. It's my way of saying, *I'll be a good girl now, I promise.* It's my way of saying, *I'm yours, I'll do as you say.* She knows all of this, and she could give a shit. These are all givens, anyway, not novelties.

Mi amante no dice nada. Instead, she smokes her nasty cigarette, knowing that it makes her mouth taste like toxic waste, knowing that it makes me nauseous. She pulls me to her with one finger placed behind my knee. She makes me sit on top of her on the toilet, my legs spread completely open, my dress riding up so that my crotch is right there, vulnerable to her whims. She drags on the cigarette one more time, sucking it as if it were the last smoke she was allowed before facing a firing squad. She forces her mouth on mine, slides her poisonous tongue in, insisting that I respond. And I do, of course, and it's not only 'cause I have to. It's just that all the while, she's milking a tit with one hand, and letting the cigarette burn near my crotch with the other. Lighting my fire, you could say, coqueteando con mi concha. I grimace when I smell the stink of my pubic hair burning. I jump when she grinds the cigarette out on the delicate skin of my inner thigh. I gag as she continues to shove her tongue into my mouth. And then she pulls her mouth and hands away and orders me to breathe.

In the bedroom, Mía is naked, eating a green mango, one of the huge ones they sell at the beach, hard and sour, with salt sprinkled on top. There is a small pocketknife on the night table. She is sitting on the edge of the bed, the contents of her big purse spilled out around her. Scraps of paper, a Pentax, passport, cigarette case, Chiclets y pintalabios. Ella nos ofrece a wedge of her mango, and I wish I could go get the salt and suck on a piece myself but my lover says no, thank you, for both of us. She takes the pocketknife and Mía says, "Ay, estas mujeres estan locas," exasperated, as if she were talking about other crazy bitches who weren't right in the same room with her. But even so, she sits up on the bed, as if preparing herself for a private show, which is exactly what this is.

My lover takes me by the hair and pushes me onto the floor. I have not yet been properly punished for acting without her approval. Me preparo para lo que sea. The terrazzo floor is cold on my back, and I hear the central air conditioning kicking in; I'm bracing myself.

"I am the only one who can take your clothes off. ¿No lo sabías?" She has me by the throat. I nod obediently. Yes, I know. She slaps my face. I close my eyes, turn away. She grabs my hair, slaps me again. I wince and swallow my cries as she slaps my body with her open palm. Face, tits, hips, legs. And then I moan, make the wrong noise. This is punishment; I should be thrashing about in pain, and nothing else. She rams my crotch with her knee. "Hay algo más que no sabes?"

I whisper a very long no, and then I realize that my sounds are all too prolonged, but I'm in no position to measure them. She throws my body this way and that, unzipping my dress in a fury, pulling it off, ripping the bra, jabbing my ribs, hurting me, repeating, in a supercontrolled tone that always terrifies me, "I am the only one who can take your clothes off. ¿No lo sabías? ¿Es que no lo sabías?"

She stops to take a breath, and I don't give a fuck if I am being punished. I hump my papaya into her leg, squeeze, thrust hard, moan long, prop myself up on my elbow, and suck on my own damn teta. Fuck her and the visitor too. I'm still only half naked but I'm 100% caliente, ready to kill them both if they don't fucking fuck me, and soon, hijueputas de mierda.

My lover laughs. She knows I'm ready to kill her. Takes away the leg that I am riding. Pulls my hands and mouth off my body.

"Deja eso," she says. "That's my property."

Motherfucker. *Well, then, do something with your goddamn property,* I want to scream. Instead, I pant, pucker my lips, get ready to cry like a little girl who must have that cloud of pink cotton candy. Must have.

Knife in one hand, she grabs the crotch of my underwear with the other. Mía and I catch our breaths in unison. My lover pulls out the fabric, pierces it with the blade, rips a hole through the pantyhose and underwear, teases my exposed labia with the tip of the knife. I become as still as humanly possible, afraid of making the wrong move.

"Yo hago de ti lo que me da la gana," she says, and I recite my motto for her: *Do with me what you will.* She smiles and kisses me on the forehead, flings the knife across the floor, rips the fabric completely open with her hands. Spreads my legs out wide, looks me in the eye as if to say, *Aquí estoy mi amor, aquí siempre estaré.*

Finally, finally, she fucks me. And I'm moaning now, all I want, singing the I'm-getting-fucked-please-don't-ever-make-me-wait-so-long-and-don't-you-motherfucking-stop-fucking-me-ay-mi-amor song. But you know, you gotta pause sometimes even with all that fucking and moaning 'cause you just might pass out then and miss out on getting fucked even more. It was during one of those pauses that I heard another woman moaning, just above me. Mía.

"You have a guest to attend to," says my lover, pulling her hand out without finishing me off.

I am one horny fucking bitch as I get up from the floor, take off whatever clothing is still clinging to me, and eye Mía sprawled out on the bed. She's all there, ready for me, legs open, stroking herself.

"Te estoy esperando," she says in her low raspy voice. She needs me as much as I need her. I'm on my knees, finally sucking on her tetas, and they really are hard like I thought they would be. I watch her melt beneath my tongue, doing her woman swooning, her little woman whimperings. Finally get the sassy bitch under my control. She has 22-year-old flesh, deliciosa. I brush her hand away from her panocha. Lick her fingertips and take in her aroma. She's been working herself, pumping her juices while I was getting fucked on the floor.

For the third time in one night I ask her, "¿Quieres bailar?" Except now she has no choice 'cause I'm pressing my palm on her mound of Venus, on the verge of discovering her fat pussy, her plump lips, her enormous pepa.

"Let me have the pleasure of leading you in this dance," I say, and she closes her eyes and opens her legs wider in response. She takes my hand, squeezes it while I caress her papaya with my other hand. We could be girls holding hands in the playground, but we're hot dykes fucking for our lives. I make her clit hard like a pebble. Ella me aprieta la mano, digs her fingernails into my palm, moves her body from one side to the next, dancing for me.

"Ay mujer," she says. "Fóllame, fóllame, fóllame…"

Inside I go. Two, three, four fingers. Slowly. Deeply. Lovingly. She wants it hard and rough, though. I can tell by how she milks my hand, as if I just couldn't fuck her hard enough. I can tell by the way she's breathing in hot fast spurts. I can tell by the way she's dilating inside, making room for more, harder, bigger fucking. I lean into her, chupándole las tetas along the way to her neck. Bite her earlobe. Whisper, "¿Quieres que te coja completamente adentro?"

She nods, stills her pelvic dance. I keep fucking her slowly, side to side, opening her further. Tuck my thumb into my palm and carefully curl my fingers into a fist and continue fucking her, completely filling her inside. We are doing a slow and cautious fist-fuck dance, the two of us. We are embracing like lesbians in love do. "Ay, qué linda que eres," I tell her. "Bellisima."

It's too intense, though, for both of us. Too much vulnerability, too thick a love haze. I uncurl my fingers, pull out, take her clit in my mouth. But she moves fast and furious, and so once again I go inside, fucking her hard like she always wanted. Fuck her to Paris and back. She's so damn close to coming.

And then, I can't help it, I have to stop. My lover is ramming into my panocha from behind, and all I can do is drop my hands down on the bed and raise my ass and let her fuck me and fuck me. Mía is moving on the bed, pero no me doy cuenta porque I am just a whore in heat and I'm getting fucked and nothing in the world can distract me. There's a mouth on my breasts, a finger in my asshole, a hand slapping my ass, a polla in my panocha, panting all around me, a tongue on my pepa and that's it, that's it…"Ahí me tienen, hijueputas, ahí…" Me estoy corriendo and I'm still getting fucked and then I just drop right on top of Mía, pobrecita, she's still toda caliente, and I lose all my decorum and fall on her, her cunt in my mouth. Bury my face between her legs and cry, long and soft. My lover strokes my back, and Mía gives my panocha little kisses. I drift away, I don't know for how long.

When I awake from my orgasmic daze I am still in bed with two women, the one who owns me, and our foreign playgirl. My lover is leisurely licking the visitor's tetas. My lover is excitada as hell, I know, because soon she is grinding her extremely wet papaya on my ass, humping me with precision, making sounds as if she may finally break, stone butch that she is. I brace my arms firmly on the bed while my lover is getting off at my back and focus on our guest's papaya. It is gleaming, beckoning, pleading, urging that I attend to her. Entonces me la como. Suck each lip luxuriously, dip my tongue inside, make circles around her pepa until it grows huge and hard again. I spy the mango pit on the night table. Big, hard. I take it in my hand, plunge it inside her, fuck her with the seed, lick her. At my back my lover is grinding with that final rhythmic rush she gets before coming. She stiffens and sings, "Mariconas, que mariconas que son, sacándome la leche, grandisimas putas." Se está viniendo with a violence that I just fucking love. Fast and furious I eat our visitor's bulging clit. She screams once, twice. The playgirl slices her nails into my back while her papaya contracts in delicious waves. My lover falls on top of us both.

We are all silent except for our heavy breathing. The mango pit is still inside the playgirl's cunt. I take a bite.

CONTRIBUTORS

Kai Bayley is an ordinary Midwestern butch who has inexplicably fit the country's terrorist profile for years and who says, "Here's to you, Boston. Just don't ask me to take off my boots."

Originally from New Jersey, **Alex Beal** came to Washington, D.C., for college 15 years ago and hasn't left. A data analyst by day, she has been writing lesbian erotica ever since she first read the steamy sex scenes in a Karin Kallmaker book.

Ronica Black devotes her time to dreaming up short stories, working on a lesbian detective novel entitled *In Too Deep,* and raising a family. Many of her stories can be found on the Web. She shares her home in Phoenix with her partner and their wild kingdom of children and animals.

Rachel Kramer Bussel (www.rachelkramerbussel.com) is senior editor at *Penthouse Variations.* Her books include *The Lesbian Sex Book (2nd Edition); Up All Night: Adventures in Lesbian Sex; Glamour Girls: Femme/Femme Erotica;* and *Naughty Spanking Stories From A to Z.* Her erotica has appeared in more than 40 anthologies—including *Best American Erotica 2004* and *Best Lesbian Erotica 2001* and *2004*—and she contributes to *Bust, On Our Backs, Velvetpark, The Village Voice,* and other publications.

M. Christian has authored the critically acclaimed and best-selling collections *Dirty Words, Speaking Parts, The Bachelor Machine* and the upcoming *Filthy;* edited the books *The Burning Pen, Guilty Pleasures,* the *Best S/M Erotica* series, and, with Maxim Jakubowski, *The Mammoth Book of Future Cops* and *The Mammoth Book of Tales From the Road;* and has had short fiction published in more than 200 publications, including *Best American Erotica, Best Gay Erotica, Best Lesbian Erotica, Best Transgender Erotica, Best Fetish Erotica, Best Bondage Erotica* and…well, you get the idea.

Lynn Cole is a freelance writer and graduate student. Her eclectic interests include kickboxing, cooking for friends, belly dancing, and playing guitar in her band, Bubba Chryst. Originally from Florida, Lynn currently shares a cheery flat in London with her girlfriend, Rose.

Jess Davis is the pen name of a deviant bear from the wilds of western Massachusetts, well known for the causing of ruckuses, the jamming of gender, and the expanding of other people's horizons.

Lisa E. Davis has lived in Greenwich Village for many years, but she was born and raised in the deep, deep South. There, she attended church services every day and three times on Sunday for 18 years, from whence cometh the inspiration for this story. She is the author of *Under the Mink,* a novel about lesbian and gay entertainers in the Mafia-owned Village nightclubs of the 1940s, and she's hard at work on a nonfiction book from the same period about a lesbian FBI informant.

Urszula Dawkins lives in Melbourne, Australia. Her stories appear in anthologies in Australia and the United Kingdom, and she has performed her work in Melbourne, Sydney, Newcastle, and Adelaide, Australia, and in San Francisco. "The Butch Doesn't Eat Strange Fruit" was written during a stay at the Norcroft writing retreat for women in Lutsen, Minn.

A Colombiana eternally in search of home in gringolandia, **tatiana de la tierra** is author of *For the Hard Ones: A Lesbian Phenomenology/Para las Duras: Una Fenomenología Lesbiana* and the chapbook *Porcupine Love and Other Tales From My Papaya.*

Kate Dominic is the author of *Any 2 People, Kissing,* a 2004 finalist for *Foreword Magazine's* Book of the Year Award in the Fiction: Short Stories category. She has written more than 300 erotic short stories, under a variety of pen names. Her work has appeared in Alyson's *Lip Service, Early Embraces III,* and *My Lover, My Friend* as well as *Tough Girls, Wicked Words,* and several volumes of *Best Women's Erotica* and *Best Lesbian Erotica.*

Born in Galway on the windswept west coast of Ireland, **Rachel Esplanade** is named after an intersection in Montreal's bohemian Plateau district. The brainchild of a sexually frustrated software engineer, Rachel's stories slowly developed in a cold, televisionless flat during hot phone calls to a long-distance lover.

A white girl and confirmed femme-bottom who lives life like a spontaneously choreographed performance, **Amie M. Evans** is the founder of the Boston-based performance troupe PoP/DoD, PussyWhipped Productions, and Philogyny: Girls Who Kiss and Tell. She is a published literary erotica writer, experienced workshop provider, and a burlesque and high-femme drag performer who graduated magna cum laude form the University of Pittsburgh with a BA in literature and is currently working on her MLA at Harvard.

Sacchi Green has published work in five volumes of *Best Lesbian Erotica,* four volumes of *Best Women's Erotica, The Mammoth Book of Best New Erotica 3, Electric 2, Penthouse,* and a knee-high stack of other anthologies with inspirational covers. Her first co-editorial venture, *Rode Hard, Put Away Wet: Lesbian Cowboy Erotica,* is scheduled for release in 2005.

Beth Greenwood's stories have appeared in *Skin Deep 2, The*

Big Book of Erotic Ghost Stories, Faster Pussycats, Of the Flesh, and *My Lover, My Friend.*

Bianca James is a 24-year-old lady vagabond living in Kyoto, Japan. Her favorite things include fried food, fuzzy and/or shiny pink things, and sex toys that have faces. She recently finished her first novel, *Stars of Persia: A Post-Queer Love Story.*

Karin Kallmaker is best known for more than a dozen lesbian romance novels, from *In Every Port* to *All the Wrong Places.* In addition, she has a half-dozen science fiction, fantasy, and supernatural lesbian novels under the pen name Laura Adams. Karin and her partner will celebrate their 28th anniversary in 2005, and they are Mom and Moogie to two children.

Judith Laura's lesbian fiction has appeared in *Hot & Bothered 3* and is forthcoming in *Harrington Lesbian Fiction Quarterly.* She is author of the novel *Three Part Invention,* and two Goddess books: *She Lives!* and *Goddess Spirituality for the 21st Century.* She lives near Washington, D.C.

Isabelle Lazar is a Latina-Russian hot tamale who has left women from New York to Los Angeles panting. Details of her electric encounters have appeared in *The Mammoth Book of Lesbian Erotica, Early Embraces 2, Skin Deep: Real Life Lesbian Sex Stories, Set in Stone: Butch-on-Butch Erotica, Wet: True Lesbian Sex Stories, Philogyny: Girls Who Kiss & Tell, Unlimited Desires: An International Anthology of Bisexual Erotica, Harrington Lesbian Fiction Quarterly,* and *Lesbian News.*

Marilyn Jaye Lewis is the founder of the Erotic Authors Association, the first American organization to honor literary excellence in the erotic genre. Her short stories and novellas have been widely anthologized in the United States and Europe, and her erotic romance novels have been critically acclaimed. Upcoming books include *Lust: Bisexual Erotica;* the novels *Twilight of the Immortal* and *Greetings From the Dream Factory,; Freak Parade,* a memoir; and a short story anthology she edited, *That's Amore!*

River Light is a poly-dyke switch from Vancouver, Canada, who has been involved in the BDSM community for 13 years. Her work has appeared, among other places, in *Diversity Magazine, Hot & Bothered 2* and *3, Best Lesbian Erotica 2000, Fusion,* and *Wild Child.*

Erica Morgan lives in the forest of Prescott, Ariz. Besides writing lesbian erotica, Erica writes grants for nonprofit organizations and is currently establishing her own nonprofits for adult literacy and children with progeria. E-mail her at ericamorgan2005@yahoo.com.

A graduate of the University of California, Berkeley, and a lesbian mother of four, **Spring Opara** currently resides in Oakland, Calif. She has been writing for three years and has had poetry published in the National Library of Poetry's anthology *Last Good-Byes.*

Barbara Pizio is an editor and writer living in New York City. Her work has appeared in *Penthouse Variations, Penthouse Forum,* and *Naughty Spanking Stories From A to Z.*

Toby Rider keeps to the hills of western Massachusetts and the mountains of New Hampshire, with occasional forays into the real world. When she's in New York City she always tips her hat to the lady in the harbor.

Lori Selke has loved fairy tales and playing with knives for a very long time. She is the editor of *Tough Girls: Down and Dirty Dyke Erotica* and the 'zine *Problem Child.* Her fiction appears in *Blowing Kisses, Bottoms Up,* and other diverse publications.

A part-time fiction writer and poet and full-time flirt, **Aurora Spark** seeks out adventure wherever she can and enjoys shaking things up. "A Little Help From My Friends" is her first published erotic story.

Stefka lives in Washington State with her partner, Rebekah, and their six cats, the queen being a black female named Butch. Without them her inspiration would be sorely lacking. Her work has also appeared in Alyson's *Up All Night* and in *Bad Attitude* magazine. Without desire and need, there would be no passion. Contact her at slkmiecik@hotmail.com.

Caelin Taylor lives in Seattle with her partner of nine years. She is a visual artist, Web designer, and writer currently working on her second full-length novel. A Washington native, Caelin enjoys travel, film, the arts, drinking bad beer with good friends, and, yes, the rain.

Heather Towne's writing credits include *ssspread, Options, Hustler Fantasies, Leg Sex, Penthouse Variations, Penthouse Forum, 18Eighteen, Abby's Realm,* and stories in the anthologies *Skin Deep 2, Mammoth Book of Women's Sexual Fantasies,* and *Wicked Words 9.*

Tanya Turner's erotica also appears in the anthologies *slave* and *Naughty Spanking Stories From A to Z.* She lives in New York City, where she is a frequent concertgoer.

Rakelle Valencia has had short stories printed in the anthologies *Best Lesbian Erotica 2004* and *Ride 'Em Cowboy* and in *On Our Backs* magazine. Suspect Thoughts Press has commissioned her and coeditor Sacchi Green to produce *Rode Hard, Put Away Wet,* a collection of lesbian cowboy erotica, for 2005.

Elizabeth Wray is a freelance writer who lives in San Francisco. Her poetry, essays, and columns have appeared in such journals as *Partisan Review, Performing Arts Journal, New Letters, Sierra,*

Health, House Beautiful, and *Body & Soul.* Her plays have been published in *Theatre of Wonders* and *West Coast Plays* and have been produced in San Francisco, Los Angeles, New York, and points in between.

Kristina Wright lives in Virginia with her indulgent husband and a menagerie of pets. Her erotic fiction has appeared in numerous anthologies, including *Best Women's Erotica 2000, Best Lesbian Erotica 2002* and *2004, Ripe Fruit: Well-Seasoned Erotica,* and *Bedroom Eyes: Stories of Lesbians in the Boudoir.* Visit her Web site at www.kristinawright.com.